THE LITTLE BUREAUCRAT

P.M. MATTHEWS

PUBLISHED BY CAVU II, LLC.

THE LITTLE BUREAUCRAT. Copyright © 2012 by P.M. Matthews.
All rights reserved. Printed in the United States of America.

This is a work of fiction. All of the characters, organizations,
and events portrayed in this novel are either products of the
author's imagination or are used fictitiously.

Library of Congress Catalog Number:
2012945335

ISBN 978-0-9859086-0-7

To my loving wife
Samme,
who has always
encouraged me to
be what I am, and
forgives me for
what I'm not.

ELKO, NEVADA
October

The air was thick with the smell of dust and sage, and the sounds of pounding hooves and breaking branches. The grey gelding was at a near gallop, undaunted as he crashed through the high sagebrush on his way toward the cliff edge. Conner drew a quick breath as he and the grey flew in to the void of the steep arroyo. He stood in the stirrups and squeezed hard with his legs. The gelding's head pitched downward and Conner leaned back till his shoulder blades nearly touched the croup.

Everything seemed to move in slow motion as they fell through the open space between the canyon walls.

Conner exhaled through clenched teeth as he felt the jolt of hooves return to earth. The horse's hocks slid through the dirt and his front feet searched for traction as they plummeted downward. A choking dust billowed up around them and rocks tumbled in front of them down the nearly vertical wall. Conner remained full in the stirrups with his back tight to the cantle as his horse slid and pitched downward. Sweat stung his right eye and he wiped it with the back of a dirty hand. It continued to burn as he squinted to see the ground in front of them and concentrated on keeping his saddle.

The gelding was oblivious to the danger, obsessed with keeping up with the horse in front of him.

The bottom of the ravine finally came and Conner grinned wildly through a mixture of thrill and relief. Courage renewed, he jabbed hard with his spurs.

"Com' on grey, let's go!"

Bud was thirty yards in front, rowels pressed firmly against the flanks of his bay. A hundred yards ahead of him was the herd, racing up the worn trail at the bottom of the dry gulch. The mares and yearlings were at a hard gallop but the stallion was well in front, no longer in sight of the riders.

Conner leaned forward in the saddle, holding his reins in his left hand as he hit his horse over and under with the extra line in his right. The narrow trail coursed through high sage and boulders, making it unfit to pass the horse in front but Conner wasn't about to let his friend pull away.

Conner cussed out loud when again they ran out of flat ground and started up the other side of the wash. Badger's gallop slowed to a lope and then to lunging as he tried to get up the steep grade. There was no trail, only loose dirt and rock covering a rocky rim. Sweat ran from under Conner's hatband, making streams of mud on his dust-covered face. His shirt stuck to his back and his jeans were pulled high on his boot tops from the pounding of the last ten miles. Conner urged his horse on as he looked up the slope to see Bud jump from his saddle and run to the front of his horse. Reins in hand, Bud pulled the bay up the last few feet as it scrambled on its belly to make the final grade.

Conner's right foot hung in the stirrup as he swung from his horse. He shook it free but not in time to keep his balance. Conner hit hard on his side but managed to hold on to the reins and pull himself to his feet. As he brought his right foot forward, his toe caught his left spur and pitched him face first into the rocky soil. The struggle continued toward the top as the horse lunged ahead of him, mercifully pulling him toward the summit but often jerking him off balance and once slamming his knee in to the rough, igneous rock. In his final lunge to clear the rim, the big gelding stood upright above Conner and seemed to teeter backward. Conner froze, sucked a deep breath and jumped to the side before he finished the last few feet on hands and knees, still clutching the reins in his bloody right hand.

Bud stood on the rim, grinning madly as he looked down on his friend, white teeth gleaming through dust and mud.

"Murph, you are such a pussy. I thought I'd have to wait all day. Come on we'll run 'em to the stock pond." He turned and swung in to the saddle and spurred his horse to a gallop. Conner followed as they raced only feet apart on the worn desert trail.

The sun was hot, but the riding was easier on the flat of the plateau. The wind felt good in his face and cool through his sweaty shirt. His knuckles were bloody and his right knee throbbed, but Conner Murphy was on top of the world. They raced at a full gallop, oblivious to the consequences of badger holes and washouts, emulating the immortal kids they used to be.

That portion of the Owyhee Plateau is a flat plain broken only by ravines and gullies. Sage as tall as a man, purple mountains that loom on the horizon and always seem a hundred miles away and a sky so intensely blue it seems surreal. Conner had always been drawn to the expanse and desolation of the desert country. As a boy, he'd spent every chance he could in its vastness; horses, fishing, hunting, always enamored with the wildness of it. God it was beautiful today.

They flew down the trail, making slight bends like slalom skiers through the sage. Their horses were tired but more than willing to keep up the chase; to catch the horses ahead was as much their sport as the riders'.

The whole run had been great, but Conner was enjoying this last part the best. He loved going fast on a horse; on a horse that that had a purpose and desire to run. He loved being with Bud and being in this country again.

The herd had put more distance between them and their pursuers during the climb out of the ravine, but the two riders had reclaimed half that ground as they neared the stock pond. The wild horses started to stop for a drink as Bud yelled, "Come on Murph, screw 'em, that's my cows' water" and the riders continued to gallop hard toward them as they picked their heads up and filed off again.

Finally, Bud reined in as they neared the pond and both men walked their horses in to the cool, clear water. The horses drank for only a moment before the riders pulled up their heads and turned them out of the pond, forcing them to rest before drinking more.

Saddles and blankets were pulled to let the horses cool out faster. Dust and sweat had covered them in a thin layer of mud except where their tack had been. Necks and chests were white with lather.

"That's a hell of a way to treat my best headin' horse, Murph." Bud smiled and shrugged his shoulders.

"He is a nice one; athletic as hell. The kind of horse that makes a man brave."

Bud pulled two bottles of water from his saddle bags and tossed one to Conner, "How 'bout something to eat."

"Sure, what you got?"

"Apples and Snickers bars."

"You know me, Bud. I'm Mister Atkins, no carbs. Gotta be an apple."

Bud threw Murph an apple, "Mr. Atkins? I always thought it was Mr. Ass...."

"Atkins, boy, Atkins."

The two men didn't talk much while they ate and drank several bottles of warm water. Once they watered off their horses they tacked up and started back.

"Take a look at that, Murph." Bud was turned in his saddle.

The herd stallion stood on a mound three hundred yards out, his mares behind him, watching the riders and waiting to come back to water.

"Come on back, caballos, there's enough water here for everyone."

Conner spoke after a bit. "Damn, Bud, I can't believe we did this today."

"Murph, you wouldn't believe it if I told you the last time I ran horses. It's been forever. Obviously the BLM boys frown on us doing it, especially on the permit." Bud thought a minute and then added, "But that's not really it, seems I'm just too busy for such nonsense anymore."

"Bud, you'll be glad to hear that I only busted my nuts on the horn twice today. Man that was some hard riding."

"It was hard. I'll tell you Murph, you're about a fit old bastard. Hell, when's the last time you rode."

"It's been a little while, about a year, probably."

Bud pulled a can of Copenhagen from his shirt pocket and stuck a dip behind his bottom lip, "You still team ropin' any?"

"Naw. Not for about two years. Ever since I sold the place in Ocala and moved to the Gulf. How far you figure we rode today?"

"I don't know, probably a mile or so before we saw the herd. I'll bet we chased them for at least ten miles, though. Yea, that's pretty close. I know we've got a fair ride back to our little set up."

The two were quiet again. Enjoying each other's company like old friends can do in silence. Bud Ingles was a tall thin man in his late fifties. About six foot three inches tall but only weighed 185 pounds; sinew and muscle. Conner had often said that about half Bud's weight was in his hands and forearms.

He was a handsome sort that had aged well, his face weathered from an outdoor life, but as yet he only looked mature and masculine. His hair was the color brown that never grays and there was that legendary smile. Bud hadn't really filled out much over the last 35 years but a life time of hard work had made his big hands even bigger and stronger, and added a few scars.

Bud was a fourth generation rancher in Elko County. By the time he was college age, the Ingles ranch consisted of the main place, another ranch 15 miles south, another near Midas, and one south of Battle Mountain as well as considerable BLM permits. They ran mostly commercial cows and a small purebred Hereford herd.

Bud, Steven P. Ingles III, was thrown in to it early when his father crashed his plane in the Ruby Mountains while scouting bighorn sheep for the upcoming season. No one knew what had happened, everyone assumed a mechanical failure, but it was never proven. Bud was only out of college two years and, between him and his mother, they had the reins of a small empire. He married his college sweetheart, Maggie, two years later and his mother died from an aneurism in her kitchen the following year.

Bud never looked back. His father had been a shrewd businessman as well as cattleman and had forged a big enterprise that was nearly debt free. This let Bud survive through tough times. He'd been unable to build on what he'd been left, but he'd managed to hang on to all of it. No small feat for the cow business.

Two hours after leaving the stock pond they heard Bud's two German wirehairs barking, signaling their return to camp. They dropped off the plateau into the river bottom. The Owyhee, like most desert rivers and streams, has few trees along the bank, only scattered willows and the occasional cottonwood. The river was running shallow, as it always did in October.

The riders turned their horses on to a dirt road that led down to the river crossing where it widened and shallowed to only a few inches. A pick-up and stock trailer were parked only a short distance from the lone cottonwood. Two dogs, tied to pickets in the shade of the tree, jumped and barked as the riders approached. Bud yelled at them to stop their barking and on the third time it worked.

Conner dragged his saddle and blanket off Badger.

"What's the plan for the horses, Bud? Water "em off and then picket them?"

Bud pulled his Copenhagen from his shirt pocket to freshen his dip, "No, they won't go anywhere tonight, they're wiped out. You can just turn the grey loose. I'll hobble this bay horse and they'll be fine."

Conner held Badger while Bud hobbled the bay, once loose both horses headed straight for the middle of the creek and a long drink. Bud went to the dogs and untied them as he lovingly cursed them for bouncing all over him. They too headed for the creek and plopped down on their bellies, soaking up the coolness of the water as they looked back at Bud, heads cocked in anticipation, or hope, of some command that would entail fun. Conner respected what superb chukar dogs they were but was always amused at their comical expressions. He remembered when Bud bought his first German wirehair, thinking it was one of the ugliest dogs he'd ever seen. He teased his friend relentlessly until they took her chukar hunting that first time.

Bud nodded toward the sun noting it was near the western horizon, "What do you say we have a toddy before we worry about dinner. I'll tell you what, you grab the scotch and I'll figure out what the hell we're eatin' tonight."

"You got it. The ice in that cooler by the tree?"

Bud gave an affirmative nod as he dug around in a big ice chest by the truck. "Grab those good glasses; they're by the scotch in that grub box."

Conner flipped the lid back on the weathered box and grabbed the bottle of 18-year-old McCallan. Next to it were two glasses wrapped in paper towels. As he unwrapped them, Bud said "Don't you dare tell Maggie I brought those out here."

"Wouldn't dare. But I like your style."

"Nothing but the best for you, my man."

As Conner dropped ice in the glasses and covered them with the smooth brown liquid, he suggested to Bud, "Let's say we strip these nasty clothes and sit in the bathing hole while we drink these."

"Sure, we oughta have enough light to do that and get some dinner going after. Sounds great."

Drinks and towels in hand they made their way down the bank dressed in boxer shorts and boots to where a little waterfall had made a deeper pool. Several large flat rocks created a ledge around the edge forming a natural spa.

Bud was first to kick his boots off and shed his shorts, stepping gingerly in to the water. The barely submerged rocks were slick with algae, something Bud remembered all too well from previous trips

7

and he took care not to relive another back jarring fall; nor give Murph a laugh at his expense.

Just as Conner was starting to kick his boots off he blurted, "Hey did you bring any soap over here?"

"Naw, shit I forgot. It's in the same duffel where I grabbed the towels. I think Maggie threw in a bottle of liquid stuff or somethin'".

Conner returned with the soap and kicked off his boots, "How's that water feel, you look comfortable."

"It's a little cool, but it feels great."

Conner stepped in up to his knees, "A little cool my ass! I've been swimming in the gulf all summer; in 90-degree water. Jesus! How about holding my nuts while I sit down in this ice water?"

"Yea, you bet." Bud shaped his big right hand into a claw.

Once both men were seated on a flat rock leaning back against the bank, drink in hand, Conner admitted, "You know this water feels pretty damn good. It makes my aching ass and legs feel better."

"How's that knee of yours, looks like you gave it a pretty good smack."

"It's really not that bad and fixin' to get better after a couple of these scotches. I'm afraid tomorrow will be a different story though. You drinking mostly McCallan now?"

"No, not really. Balvenie, Bunnahabain, Dalwhinnie, I like a lot of "em. I have gotten away from some of those more smoky ones, like Talisker, though."

The conversation stayed with single malts for a while then drifted to wine and on to cigars as they sipped their drinks and relaxed in the cool, flowing water. The dogs returned from an exploration of their own, laid on the bank, and watched the men intently as if either one at any minute might do something to induce some grand excitement. The horses, finally rehydrated, had made their way to a grassy area downstream, anxious to fill their bellies.

The late afternoon brought a chill to the air and the sky was again cloudless except for a couple of puffs on the western horizon;

peaceful and quiet, only occasionally disturbed by the call of a nearby chukar.

"Just stay close boys and you'll be ready for the frying pan tomorrow."

"God I hope so", replied Conner. "The only thing more fun than shooting chukar is eating them, and it's been a few years for me."

Bud took the last sip from his glass; "You know we ought to get a pretty sunset with a lot of color as damn humid as it's been today."

Conner spit out his last sip of scotch in a sudden blurt of laughter. "God damn, Bud, you know how goofy you desert rats sound talking about humidity. What is it about six percent, up from its usual four? It's so dry my nose is bleeding and my lips are cracked for Chris' sake. Don't tell a Florida boy about humidity."

"Alright I'll tell you about cooking dinner instead. You weren't always a cracker you know; you used to be one of us."

Bud grabbed the soap bottle and lathered up his hair and scrubbed the rest of his body before squatting in the deep pool and dunking his head to rinse. Conner waited till Bud was out to have enough room to perform the same ritual

"Man it's starting to cool off now, huh." Conner remarked as he rinsed off the last of the soap.

As Bud walked back to the camp under the cottonwood he called out to remind Conner to bring the glasses. The dogs left their post by the bank to follow Bud. He slapped them both on the sides and briskly rubbed their heads as he reassured them it was time to eat. Bud grabbed their bowls and dipped them full from a Purina bag in the bed of the truck. Gretta, the smaller blue merle, curled her lip and growled at her companion as Bud set the first bowl on the ground. The bigger brown bitch demurely backed away and waited for the second bowl.

Bud only shook his head at the dog, "I don't know why you don't just snatch her head off, Hilga, you've got twenty pounds on her."

Conner lit the lanterns as darkness enveloped their little camp.

"Another drink, Bud?"

"Does a one legged duck swim in circles, Murph? How's this menu sound; salmon filets, some potatoes au gratin ala Maggie that we just need to heat up, and some fresh asparagus fried up in olive oil."

"I'm hungry enough to eat a dirt sandwich, but that sounds a whole lot better." Conner made two more drinks and grabbed the camp chairs from the back of the truck as Bud unfolded his cooking table and put the gas stove together.

"I want you to sit back Murph, and enjoy the sunset. I've got the cooking handled. Be sure to face down river, unless you find an intensely pink sky too overwhelming. Cracker boy."

A hard day and the beautiful setting made a good dinner even better.

"You know you were the one that got me started putting mayonnaise on asparagus, Murph. I'm thinking it's the only good advice you ever gave me."

"I think Molly was the one that got me doing that. I don't remember doing it as a kid."

Bud sipped his scotch between bites, "Molly, now she was a star. How long has it been Murph."

"She died the end of October, nearly four years ago now."

"I know we've talked about it before, but you still haven't had any thoughts about getting remarried?"

Conner Murphy finished chewing his last bite of salmon and grabbed his scotch glass as he leaned back in his chair. "No, Bud I really haven't yet. I might be getting fairly close with Jan, I don't know. It just seems to be a hard step for some reason."

"Well I know Molly set the bar awfully high, man."

"She sure did, Bud, awfully high. But it's more than that. I don't think I spend any energy comparing other women to Molly; that won't get me anywhere. I'm just not ready to share my life again. Sound weird to you?"

"I don't know, probably not. I guess I did think that you and Jan were pretty serious, though. You're still going to see her in couple of days, right?"

"Yea, I am. And you're right; I think the world of Jan. We'll see, I guess."

Bud changed the subject, "How's Sean and his brood doing?"

"Great, actually. They're still down in Tampa and by all signs doing great and loving life. Let me see, Karen is six now and Jeremy is eight. Mo has been able to quit her job with the bank and is a stay at home mom. She loves it and I'm real happy for that."

"So are they paying Sean more money or did they just decide to make due? That seems like a fairly bold move in these shitty economic times."

Conner got up and walked to his duffle to grab cigars. "No," he responded, "the magazine is paying him the same, but he's starting to kick ass on his blog site. It's been very well received and he has quite a following. Subscriptions just keep going up and up. It's been great."

Conner punched a cigar for Bud and handed it to him along with the lighter. Bud took both and struck the lighter as he held the end of the cigar over the flame.

"How's the magazine look at him doing the Internet stuff on the side?" Bud began dragging on his cigar, puffing great wafts of smoke in to the still night air.

"Sean's always been right up front with them from the beginning; telling them he wanted to start it and what the content would be, etc. They've been great about it. Sean thinks they like the added exposure it brings to one of their top columnists. Anyway, so far so good."

"Well good for him and good for Mo, too."

"Yea, I'm really happy for her. She's a great mom, and now she's got even more time to concentrate on her family. You know, just before I left to come out her she was having some problems with some nasty headaches. And just the fact she's not working allows her to rest some and take better care of herself."

11

Conner took a minute to light his cigar while Bud got up and stirred the campfire. Both dogs were curled up near Bud's chair. Occasionally, the horses could be heard clomping around down by the river; the only sound in the night air.

"I sure hope all this humidity doesn't fog things up in the morning and screw up our shoot," Conner said under his breath.

"Go to hell, Murph."

"What is the plan for tomorrow, anyway?"

"Well, we'll hunt tight here in the morning. Up and down the river, we've got a good chance of catching chukar coming down to water." Bud stopped to draw a couple puffs on his cigar, "We'll come back here for lunch, if we can find our way in the fog, smart ass, and then load up and head over to the sheep permit. There's a draw over there where they always seem to covey up in pretty good bunches. It's a steep, nasty hike, but I've never been skunked in that draw. Besides, it'll be a way to torture your sea-level ass."

"Has it been a good year for the birds? Plenty of them?"

"From what I'm hearing it's been a great year. The winter wasn't too severe, and the spring had a good amount of moisture but not too, much, so it was just right for the hatch. And lucky for us, it's been dry lately, so there isn't a bunch of standing water or puddles to keep "em spread out too thin."

Conner asked Bud, "You still hooked up with that Chukar Unlimited or whatever that group is called?"

"It's the Nevada Chukar Foundation, and yea, I am. I've done it for over ten years and really enjoy it."

They sat for a minute in silence sipping their scotch.

"Hey, by the way, what's with the Bic lighter, Murph? You used to always carry some fancy butane thing that you could weld two bumpers together with."

"Oh, hell, I just lose them. I've spent more money on butane lighters over the years than you can imagine."

"Sounds like me with sunglasses."

The fire started to burn low and Conner stood and handed Bud his drink glass. "You do the honors while I fix this fire."

Bud returned with fresh drinks just as a breeze started to blow, causing him to move his chair several feet to avoid the smoke. The dogs looked up, quite annoyed; the smoke wasn't bothering them. As Bud got settled in his new position, both dogs made the obligatory move to his chair. Hilga expressed her annoyance with a deep sigh.

"Bud, you got any tomato juice for red beers in the morning?"

"No drinking and shooting guns, you silly bastard. Besides, what part of your ass I didn't ride off today, I'm hiking off tomorrow."

"Simmer down you stodgy old prick. I was only kidding. But I was just thinking about all the goofy shit we used to do when we were kids. Always had to have red beers in the morning on those fishing trips. Drink red beer till noon, then drink it 'raw' till dinner, then switch to the hard stuff around the fire."

"You know Murph, we've said it a hundred times, but it still amazes me that we lived through all those times. We should have been dead time and again." Bud started laughing as memories came in to view. "But damn we had some fun."

"We crammed a whole lot in to four years of college, I'll say that." Conner started laughing as he thought about an incident in a bar in Austin, Nevada. "Remember one of the sage hen trips we took out to that country between Austin and Ely?"

"Yea, the Diamond Valley. Great hunting."

"It was you and I, Roger and Don Munroe and Tony Shaker. We played blackjack in that little bar that night; remember? They only had one table in the place and we took all the house's money."

"I remember that," Bud blurted out as he leaned forward in his chair laughing. "The dealer had to get the owner, who went behind the bar, picked up a floor board and pulled out a sack of money. He gave the dealer a stack of chips and cash and we kept playing. Unbelievable."

"Yea and we kept winning." Conner was still laughing. "That dealer couldn't get a hand to save his life. Remember, they finally just shut us off before they went broke."

13

"Yea, damn it, that was funny. It was like a scene back around 1900. Where else besides Austin, Nevada would you have seen 'em dragging money out of the floorboards to keep a black jack table open. Their only table!" Bud threw his head back in laughter.

"But Bud the best part of that night was when that big asshole started picking on Shaker; remember that."

Tony Shaker was a quiet sort, who minded his own business. He was a pilot in the air force, home on leave. A local mechanic drinking beer at the bar saw something about Tony he didn't like and was pressing to make it evident. The mechanic was missing one front tooth, had a bushy mustache, and a three-day beard. He stood a head taller than Tony and enjoyed the advantage, using the brim of his greasy red cap to tap the pilot on the forehead with each degrading expletive he grunted. Tony backed up and set his beer glass on the bar, prepared to throw the first punch rather than listen to any more insults from this drunken gorilla.

Roger Munroe glanced over in time to intervene. He covered the distance to the bar doing an absurd little dance step, graceful and comical at the same time; a prancing move that belied his bulk.

As he completed his little shuffling dance he stepped between the two men and nudged his friend Tony to the side. He looked straight into the mechanic's eyes and smiled with a broad toothy grin when he spoke.

"Don't pick on Shaker for cryin' out loud. He couldn't whip a kitten. Whatever he said to you I promise I'll slap the shit out him later. Right now let me buy you a drink and we'll forget about him."

Bud chimed in, "Yea now I remember that. I had just come out of the bathroom when he was trying to appease that big jerk."

"You should have seen Roger's little dance over to the bar. He looked like Belushi in Animal House when they were sneaking in to the Dean's office. Eyes wide open and flashing back and forth, looking about half-ass feminine, it was a stitch."

The mechanic didn't want any part of forgiveness. If he couldn't knock Shaker's teeth out he'd just as soon do it to his 'dumpy little faggot friend'. As the big guy turned his abuse toward Roger he started to thump him in the chest with his index finger. Roger kept his signature toothy grin, part comical, and part sinister. He looked toward his friends out of the sides of his eyes, bouncing his eyebrows like Groucho Marks.

Conner and Bud were laughing aloud as they had a clear vision of that night in their heads. Conner said, "Don looks over at me with a big smile and says 'I think big boys crowdin' his luck.'"

Roger Munroe wasn't accustomed to losing fights; it didn't matter how big nor how many. All eyes were on him as the big mechanic was building his insults and pokes to a crescendo. Roger finally cocked his head to the side and said loudly enough so the big man could hear him over his own rant.

"Please stop poking me, it kind of hurts."

The plea only made the larger man lean in further and poke harder as Roger glanced toward his group of friends with a look of mock exasperation and rolled his eyes. Then, in a single motion, he stepped back and grabbed the big man's index finger in the tight grasp of his right hand. He spun the man's entire arm by his finger; spinning it in large circles as if he was starting the motor on a World War II airplane. The speed and ferocity with which he spun the man's arm startled everyone. After five rapid revolutions the big man dropped to his knees with a loud thud. The sound that emanated from the kneeling man's lips was more of a whimper than a scream as Roger looked down at him and said in a loud effeminate voice, 'Even us dumpy little faggots know not to poke people.'

Bud wiped the tears from his eyes; "I think that's the only time I saw a guy leave a bar under his own power after fucking with Roger Munroe. But I'll tell you this; his finger still looks like a corkscrew."

The two men went from story to story as they piled wood on the fire and continued to drain the scotch bottle. Recounting their college days often happened when they got together, but this night they seemed to relish it more and laughed until the tears flowed.

"We were like most kids in their twenties, then and now,

15

invincible and immortal. But I'll say this Bud; it was a great time to be young. The world was safer and better. We were tough young guys, but we never really hurt anybody. We brawled, and it was the culture then, at least in Nevada."

"Yeah, and nobody sued anybody back then."

"Now we're just old guys."

"Oh, I don't know. How about 'tough old guys'." Bud winked at his friend and walked to the table to fill his glass with water from a jug. "Come on girls, leave that sappy puss to himself, we're going to bed." The dogs rose from their stations around his chair and went over to Bud's cot. As he crawled in to his sleeping bag they found places to lie underneath.

"Thanks for a great day, Bud. Running those horses was exciting as hell. I'll bet I haven't done that for twenty years."

"Enjoyed it, 'night."

CHICAGO, ILLINOIS
October

"Nick we need to talk."

"Sure Mr. Costello, whatever you want."

The 43rd floor on Michigan Avenue provided a gorgeous view of the lake. It was windy and cool and there wasn't a cloud. In the distance, the blue of Lake Michigan fused with that of the sky. It reminded Costello of the famous view of the Mediterranean from the terrace of the Villa Cimbrone in Ravello, 'the view of infinity'.

Nick hated that he always felt intimidated in that office. Walls and ceiling of mahogany, dark heavy furniture, expensive oil paintings on the walls; everything designed to create a theme of power and strength. It oozed from the walls, but a different strength than Nick's physical power; much more potent.

"Sit down, Nick, this is a serious discussion and I want to be sure that you understand me completely." Costello continued to stare out the window, his back to the room.

"Sure, Mr. Costello." Nick attempted to sound respectful, but also relaxed. He took a seat in one of the high backed leather chairs across from the large wooden desk. He sat with his back straight, trying to appear attentive as he licked his thick lips and looked straight ahead with his small, steely blue eyes. Nick made the oversized chair look small.

His employer, a slight man in his sixties, turned from the window and sat in his chair behind the desk. Dressed in a hand tailored suit with his tie flawlessly knotted and silver hair perfectly quaffed, he provided a strong contrast to his visitor.

"Nicky, it has come to my attention that you've been moonlighting. As you know, as I've told you emphatically, moonlighting is absolutely forbidden with our new arrangement."

"But Mr. Cos...."

"Shut up Nick!" The older man screamed as he slammed his open hand to the desk. "You listen to me and keep your goddamned mouth shut till I'm done. Ya' follow me?"

"Yes, sir."

"It came to me from a very good source, someone I trust completely, that you created a little incident over at Arlington about a week ago. You went over to the backside, found a trainer that owed Johnny Laruso some money and you roughed him up. Hell, you broke both his arms and burned his face with some kind of water heater or some shit. Then you dumped him in a stall with one of his horses."

Nick squirmed in protest, but knew better than to open his mouth. Just to be certain he did, the older man stopped talking and glared at him over a pointed index finger.

Costello continued, "The security guard on the back side of the race track recognized you going in, put two and two together and called one of my people. The guard was savvy enough not to say anything to the cops, or anybody else for the matter, and was nicely rewarded for that lack of effort. But the bottom line is this. You came within a hair of being exposed in this deal. And don't give me any shit about the trainer wouldn't talk, and that you'd get away with it...none of that's the point. The point is that I need you totally off the radar from now on. We spent a lot of money and did a lot of favors to get your records lost; your sheet is squeaky clean right now and..." Costello raised his voice as he finished his sentence, "that is how it better stay! Ya' follow me?"

"Yes, sir."

"You're making more money than you've ever made, Nicky. And you're working less than you've ever had to in order to make it. You've got the good life." Costello paused, then started to raise his voice with each word, "If that ain't good enough, if you need to pick up extra shit money from Laruso or anybody else, then fuck you Nicky, you and I are through. Ya' follow me?"

"Yes sir, Mr. Costello. Can I say somethin' though?"

"Yea, go ahead."

"I didn't do that for any money. I'm not lookin' for more money. You pay me good, like you said. Laruso and I go way back. I was just doing him a favor."

The old man stood up and turned his back on Nick Kowalski. He stood there a moment, staring at the lake before turning back around, "Nicky, you big stupid Polack. Tell me you realize that being paid is not the issue here."

"Yea, er, yes, sir. I get it. I just wanted to make it clear that I'm real happy with what you pay me and I wasn't looking for any money."

"Well, that's good. I hope that's true." He leaned across the desk, "I don't even want you to get a speeding ticket. I don't want you in a bar fight. I don't want you slapping around or cutting up some whore, like you're so fond of doing. I want you to be a quiet, Chicago citizen. No trouble, no recognition. Just waiting for the occasional instructions. I've invested a lot of time and energy in to you and I don't want you screwing it up. Ya' follow me?"

"You bet I do, Mr. Costello."

With that the older man turned back around to look at his lake. "You can go now, Nicky. Stuart will have something for you in a few days."

Nick Kowalski was sweating through the armpits of his shirt and was grateful to be leaving. As he headed to the door, Costello continued to stare across the blue expanse, "Johnny Laruso is in that lake. Way out there. On the bottom. You made him in to a loose end, Nicky. Think about that."

ELKO, NEVADA
October

When Conner woke it was still dark. He lay there as thoughts of Molly ran through his head. It happened most when he'd had a good day, memories coming back of sharing his day with her and melancholic thoughts of how much he missed that. It was part of the answer to Bud's question. He hadn't found that in another woman, someone genuinely interested in sharing his adventures, his thoughts and dreams. Molly genuinely enjoyed hearing his excitement and witnessing his theatrics when he shared his experiences. It reinforced his soul, gave him strength. God, he missed that about her.

Conner's father had always preached to him that life isn't fair. 'No good comes of complaining about how unfair life can be', he'd say. There was no better proof than losing his Molly.

Light from a lantern and the rattling of a coffee pot crowded out his melancholy and he smiled when he heard Bud whisper to his dogs to be quiet. Conner laid there, sizing up which body parts hurt the most. His hands were sore, feeling it most as he opened and closed his fists. His right knee certainly hurt, but his butt, right over his pubic bone won the contest, a result of losing a stirrup as Badger lunged off a ledge.

The utilitarian nature of the cot became too much and he wrestled his way to the top of the sleeping bag and unzipped it enough to swing his feet out. Conner stood on the grass beside his cot, rubbing his head and thinking about yesterday's events. He felt pride in the fact that he could still physically do anything he wanted.

Bud yelled over to him, "You look like you need some coffee, mister. It's ready. I even remembered your half and half, because I know what a puss you are."

Conner dug around in his duffle for a pair of flip flops to walk to the fire. "It's a little chilly this morning."

"Jesus Christ. It's October, it's 5:30 in the morning and you're in skivs and a T-shirt, dumb ass. Have a cup. Oh yea, and you're a fuckin' cracker to boot."

"I see we still got two hounds, we still got two horses?"

"I think so. I think I hear 'em down by the water. Remind me to hobble Badger too when we go hunt. I don't think he'll leave Pudge but I'll feel better."

After breakfast, Bud tended to the horses and Conner took care of the dishes. The sun was just rising as they were getting their hunting gear together.

As Conner pulled the guns from the back seat of the truck he said, "It still surprises me to see you driving this Ford. I thought I'd never see you give up on those Dodge trucks."

Bud finished with the dogs and walked to the other side of the truck to help his friend with the guns. "You know I switched after 2009. When our illustrious president spent countless billions bailing those sorry bastards out and gave all that stock to the unions and fucked the primary lenders. I refuse to buy any product that the government makes....shit, it just drives me crazy."

"Sorry I brought it up." Conner unzipped two guns from their cases and smiled at Bud. "Sean wrote some great stuff back then about what an awful precedent that was setting."

"I remember that. The word is prescient, I believe. Sean was prescient."

"He was. It's only gotten worse. The dogs are ready." Conner nodded toward Hilga and Gretta, shaking with anticipation upon seeing the guns.

Bud set his Browning Citori on the table and picked up Conner's Benelli. He threw it up to his shoulder before setting it on the table next to his.

"Man those synthetic stocks really make these guns light don't they?"

"Yea they do. That little automatic has really been a great gun; and man it's taken a beating over the years."

Bud strapped shock collars on the dogs as Conner stuffed water bottles in the main pouch of his vest.

"You don't need those much for these two do you?" Conner asked.

"Oh Gretta might need it. Hilga never does. I don't even turn hers on."

Bud pulled his vest on, grabbed his water and a hung a whistle around his neck. Conner threw him a box of shells.

"Lead the way."

Fifty yards down the river Bud stopped and held his hand up; turning toward his friend he grinned, "Hear 'em?"

Conner nodded his head as he looked around for the dogs. They were working back and forth on hillside above them; they'd heard the chuks but still didn't have any fresh scent.

Gretta was a little too far up the hillside for Bud's liking. He blew his whistle, "Here to me, Gretta, here to me." She didn't respond and Bud blew his whistle again. She looked back and started down the hill.

Thirty more yards down river Gretta began to wag her tail rapidly and sniff the ground frenetically as she crept through some low sage.

"Murph, Gretta's getting birdy up there. Let's go."

23

Conner looked back up the hill at the blue merle as she stopped and went into a point. Hilga saw her now too and made her way up the hill.

Bud urged Gretta to hold, "Easy Gretta, easy. Hold there you little bitch, hold there."

Hilga was ten feet from her, creeping toward the same clump of sage.

"Easy Hilga, easy".

Conner and Bud were fifteen feet apart and still ten yards from the dogs, struggling with the steep grade as they tried to move quietly. Conner had the grip in his left hand and the forestock in his other, muzzle to the sky and Bud in his peripheral vision. Both men watched the ground in front of the dogs for any movement.

Gretta took a couple of steps forward, head still extended and motionless, tail straight out behind her.

"Easy Gretta, damn it, easy."

Hilga was in point and motionless. The two hunters made it to within a few feet of the dogs. There was no movement on the ground in front of them.

"You good, Murph?"

"Yea, I'm good."

"Let's go", said Bud as he started to walk briskly toward the dogs. Bud pushed his safety off with his thumb and Conner did the same with his index finger, ten feet to his friend's right.

Bud spoke to his dogs, "Come on, let's go."

The dogs started forward as Conner saw a chukar run from a sage in front of them. Hilga saw the same bird and ran the few steps toward it. Both dogs bolted forward as the air exploded with a loud rush of wings. Conner snatched his gun to his shoulder and instantly assessed the covey. Five birds were in flight, headed up hill. Two veered left, flying downhill toward the river, as the other three peeled off to the right to head sideways across the hill. Both men shot at the same time. Bud, on the left, took the two headed downhill. Boom! Boom! Two shots from Bud's gun brought down both birds. Conner fired three times; his first shot missed but his second and third were deadly, and two of his three folded their wings and fell hard to the earth.

"Hell of a deal," blurted Conner. He reached in his right pocket for more shells as he heard Bud close his chamber on his double barrel.

"Murph, look at Hilga. This bunch may not be done."

The brown dog was on point fifteen yards further up the hill. Both men hurried toward her as two more birds jumped into the air. One flipped, flying a few yards and landing to run up the hill. The other turned direction and flew down over top of the hunters as both shot and brought it down.

Gretta brought a bird back to Bud and dropped it at his feet. She turned and started sniffing the ground for the others.

"Good job girls! Dead bird, Hilga; dead, dead now," Bud spoke in cadence.

The dogs found all five birds in short order, stacking them at Bud's feet one at a time.

"Damn, Bud, that's a hell of a start. Your dogs are spot on, amigo."

"They really are doing great for the first outing of the season. They held those birds perfect. Let's go back down the hill and work the river downstream."

They made their way downstream and heard more chuking, but it seemed to come from the other side of the water. The dogs worked constantly but didn't pick up fresh scent and after an hour since shooting the first covey Bud finally stopped. "Let's take a break and then we'll cross over the river here and hunt that other side going back. There's that bench you can see a short ways up the slope, which we can follow back toward camp. We might catch some birds going back up now."

"Sounds good," Conner pulled a water bottle from his game pouch.

25

Bud blew his whistle and the dogs came in. They quickly realized that it was break time and headed to the river. Hilga thirstily lapped up the water as Gretta plopped down in a shallow spot to cool herself.

Conner sat on a patch of grass, propped up against a boulder, and drank from his water bottle. Bud had sucked down half of his and was busy digging in his Copenhagen can for a dip. He replaced the can to his shirt pocket and leaned forward to spit some loose flakes of tobacco from the tip of his tongue.

"So, you still see a lot of Bubba?"

Conner responded, "Bubba Striker?"

Bud started to chuckle and then choked and coughed. As he cleared his throat a final time, he hung his head and shook it from side to side.

"I don't care if you grew up out here or not, man, you are a genuine cracker now. Do you know how many people a Nevada boy knows named 'Bubba'. Well let me give you a clue. I'm probably the only one in three hundred square miles, and I guaran-fuckin-ty ya' I don't know more than one! Bubba Striker? Bubba Striker?"

Conner laughed. "Well I do know more than one. And I also know a Dude, a Major, and a Jasper. You're just a parochial S.O.B., buckaroo."

Hilga had given up on her soak and walked over toward Bud. He watched her with a wary eye, fearful that she'd come close to shake herself dry all over him. She stopped out of range to do her shaking before coming to her thankful master and lie next to him. Bud reached over and scratched her behind both ears with thick fingers.

"Yea, I see your Bubba a lot actually. He's about quit shoeing horses and spends most of his time raising a few thoroughbreds and fishing in the gulf. You give him the slightest excuse to take the boat out and he'll go."

"Why's he shoe at all anymore? He's got to be in his mid-sixty's by now isn't he? Does he need the money?"

Conner smiled as he looked at Gretta, still lying in the water, staring up at them with her perpetually silly expression.

"Oh, I'm sure the money doesn't hurt, but he just works for old clients that became good friends over the years. They bend to his schedule and, you know, they just think he invented the horse's foot and that no one else can do what he can. To be honest, he is a master and I don't blame them."

Gretta came out of the water and shook off on the bank before coming up to where the men sat.

Bud continued, "He fishes for reds out there mostly, right?"

"Yeah. He'll get in to the trout a fair amount, but he loves those redfish. You know, I've got such a soft spot in my heart for that guy. We've been friends for over thirty years, and he was so instrumental for me getting over Molly's death, him and his wife. Not only does he have a good heart, but he's very spiritual and he helped me a lot."

"I remember that," Bud shared ear scratches with both dogs. "He's not a Christian though, right."

"No, he's not. As Bubba puts it, he prays to the God that was here before all the religions. He's actually adopted a lot of his beliefs from the Native Americans, and other beliefs, and Christ too, I guess."

"Well I remember him as being one of the best guys I'd ever met, so you be sure and say hey to him for me. And tell him I expect to get out on that air boat again when I'm down there and catch the hell out of the fish."

"Like I said he will use any excuse. He'd love to take you, I'm positive of that. You rested up enough, old man."

Bud got to his feet. "Let's do it. Come on girls."

They crossed the river at a shallow part, trying but not succeeding to keep their feet dry as they jumped from rock to rock. Up the steep slope, they reached the bench running parallel to the river, and followed it back toward camp. The only birds they saw on the way back were far above them and running up the hill. Bud knew that game, and they didn't engage in the futility. Back at camp Bud tossed the five bird carcasses in one of the coolers and turned to his friend. "What say you dig the sandwich stuff out of that cooler there while I check on the caballos."

"You got it", answered Conner. "We taking a little siesta after lunch, amigo?"

Bud looked back over his shoulder as he walked toward the sound of the horses. "I needn't remind you about the one legged duck, do I?"

Conner lay on his cot after lunch; content, sleepy. He had moved it in to the shade of the cottonwood to escape the hot sun. Bud stayed in the sun, reading his book while both dogs vied for the shade his cot provided. Conner thought he'd fall asleep right away but thoughts of Molly had driven sleep from his grasp. He heard Bud toss his book to the ground and whisper something to the dogs. It wasn't long and Conner could hear the heavy breathing of his sleeping friend.

Conner's thoughts weren't of how Molly had died anymore. There had been years when those nightmarish memories blocked out everything else. Now he was able to mostly think of the good times; the laughter, the special moments, the love making; so many good times. He could see her in his mind very easily, her beautiful face with her kind, sweet smile. God he missed her so. Nothing had been the same since she left him.

"Time to do battle, Rip Van Winkle", Bud shouted. "The dogs aren't going to put up with your laziness much longer."

"I'm ready, I'm ready. Hilga, Gretta, tell your steer shit buddy to hang on."

They loaded the dogs in the back of the truck and put their vests, guns and shells in the back seat. They drove two miles to the ravine that Bud had described earlier. He pulled off the road at the base of a steep hill.

"That's where we're headed. That hill flattens out a little at the top and then spills into a narrow gulch heading back off the other side to a little creek. It should still be running a little water this time of the year and the gulch seems to hold birds in it all day. Plenty of cover and feed for them in there."

They climbed the steep slope and just as they broke out on top they saw both dogs at point just feet apart in front of a clump of sage. The men positioned themselves behind the dogs, safeties off, watching the ground in front for any movement. As Bud was about to give the command to go in, Hilga broke off. She wagged her tail, circled the big clump of sage and moved on. A few seconds later Gretta broke her point as well.

"Nothin' here. They must have been here pretty recently to fool them both."

"Hilga might have 'em", Conner said as he nodded toward her at point about twenty yards ahead. Gretta had moved off to the right and was hard at work but hadn't noticed Hilga. The two men walked quickly but quietly toward the motionless brown dog. Just as the men approached Bud saw two birds run out of the brush in front of the dog.

"Get 'em girl, get 'em." Bud called to his dog. She lunged several feet forward and six birds took flight as the air filled with the sound of beating wings. They flew fast and straight away from the hunters. The report of both shotguns reverberated off the hillside. Five shots fired within a few seconds and three birds fell. The other two flew over the crest of the hill and set their wings to sail down to the bottom of the draw. Gretta came at full tilt to the action and together the dogs were sniffing and moving rapidly over the ground in search of the fallen birds.

"Dead birds, dead,"

As Hilga brought Bud the first of the three, Conner headed to the spot he thought his bird had gone down.

"Bud, do you ever miss? You've fired five times and shot five birds."

Conner couldn't find his bird.

"Sure. I miss plenty." He grabbed a bird from Gretta.

Conner called to Hilga, "Hilga, here girl, dead bird, dead bird."

Hilga came and began to sniff and search the area where Conner stood but it was Gretta that went immediately to the bird, not two feet from Conner's boot.

"Jesus Christ, I swear you'd lose most of your birds without dogs. They are so damned hard to see in this brush it's amazing."

"Well, you wouldn't have to worry about it because you wouldn't shoot many without them either. We're going to drop off the same direction those two birds went. I'll be shocked if we don't find more in this draw."

On the way down the hill toward the stream the dogs never picked up another fresh scent. Bud pointed out the two birds that had escaped earlier as they got up again a hundred yards in front to fly to the other side of the ravine.

The descent got steeper as they got closer to the stream. Conner could feel it in his legs, especially his knees and quadriceps as he braced for each step. He took his time, knowing there were plenty of ways to tumble off that steep grade between the clumps of cheat grass and loose rocks.

Conner's big toe on his right foot hurt with each step as it slammed in to the front of his boot. The pain made him wince, but it mostly annoyed him. Years ago he had spent two days hunting with Bud while wearing boots that were too loose. The toenails of both his big toes had turned purple by the end of that hunt causing him to hobble around for days. Never again would he be ill prepared, he'd said. Shit, this pissed him off.

Conner looked at Bud, now ten yards further down the hill, descending effortlessly. Conner was always impressed how capable his friend was; it didn't matter what he was doing. Hunting, riding, roping, operating equipment, negotiating a business deal; hell it didn't matter. 'I'll bet his toes don't hurt, either, the bastard.' Conner smiled and shook his head.

Once at the bottom the men set their guns down and found a place to sit with their backs against the steep hillside. It was warm

30

and the sun was still high enough that there was no shade from the opposite hillside to the west. The men drank their bottled water and talked while they rested. The dogs had found the water long before the men had made it down to the stream and were cooling off as best they could.

After a while Hilga came up to lie next to Bud for more ear scratching, but the younger Gretta went off exploring. Bud was in mid-sentence talking about his mining lease when Gretta's bark distracted him. He fell silent and turned his head.

"Shit!" Bud jumped to his feet and grabbed his gun in one motion.

Conner was startled. He leaned over to grab his gun when Bud yelled back over his shoulder.

"Grab Hilga and keep her there."

Hilga woke and was getting her bearings; ears perked and looking toward Bud as Gretta's bark registered. She bolted up. Conner lunged and grabbed her collar in time.

"Stay Hilga, stay there", Bud disappeared behind the rock ledge.

Bud could see Gretta now. She was barking wildly; leaping forward and backing up; repetitively, frantically. Bud traversed the steep slope at a run, twice slipping on to his side, cussing as he regained his feet. He knew he had to hurry. In two more steps he could hear it and see it. The rattlesnake was coiled and rattling, waiting for Gretta to come within range.

"Come here damn it, come here Gretta! Gretta! Gretta, goddamn you, come here!"

Bud never stopped running as he shouted at the dog. Her focus was on the snake, oblivious to anything else. Bud thought about shocking her with the collar but changed his mind; worried he might make her jump forward involuntarily. The snake was coiled against the rock face of the cliff, rattling, menacing, with its large head elevated well above its body. Bud couldn't take a chance of shooting from that side and spraying himself and the dog with the ricochet. He continued running.

31

Gretta was three feet from the snake, maniacal, oblivious to her master. Bud's mind was made and he headed straight for the dog. He planted his left foot in to the dirt of the steep slope and kicked with his right as hard as the precarious footing allowed. His right foot landed squarely in Gretta's rib cage and she grunted as she flew in to the air. Bud's forward momentum took him the same distance. He turned his body and stuck his gun into his shoulder as he hit the ground. The shot took the snake's head off and reverberated off the rocky surfaces of the narrow ravine.

Gretta wasn't hurt, but knew she was in big trouble as she stood next to Bud with her tail tucked, head down and ears back.

"You silly bitch. I oughta kick your ass." Bud's voice cracked. "Come on."

Conner was still holding Hilga's collar when Bud returned.

"Snake, I'm assuming."

Bud nodded his head, "Yup. It's still hot enough for those treacherous little bastards to be out sunning themselves." His hand shook as he set his gun against a rock.

"Everything OK?"

"Yeah, fine. As good as this little bitch is at finding birds she can lose her fuckin' mind at stuff like that. Damn it."

Conner didn't have to ask anything else; he knew today was only part of it. A rattler had bitten one of Bud's dogs several years ago; struck on the face when she stuck her nose under a sage. When Bud heard the painful yelp he'd known instantly what had happened. The dog whined in agony as Bud rushed to pick her up, dropping his gun and shedding his vest as he scooped the dog in to his arms. He hurried the two miles back to the truck with his sixty-pound dog in his arms. Up hills and down, running when he could. The dog whimpered the entire way but became weaker and more limp in his arms. He could feel her life slipping away as he struggled to maintain his pace. She was dead by the time he reached the truck. When Riley Smith finally caught up, he found his friend stroking her lifeless body with tears streaming down his face.

"Hell, Gretta was probably going to be fine. She obviously knew where the snake was and, hell; she probably knew to stay her distance. I mighta got too excited for nothing'"

"Seems like you did the right thing to me, buddy. Not worth taking any chances."

"Yeah. Yeah. I guess." Bud nodded toward his friend and attempted a smile. "Let's head out. We're going downstream just a bit and back up the next draw to the right."

"Sounds good to me. Let's do it." Conner pulled his vest back on.

They bagged three more birds that afternoon, shooting a covey almost back at the truck. Bud never missed all day. Conner had joked about why the hell they ever left the truck and hiked their asses off when most of the birds just hang around the truck anyway. When they reached camp the sun was low and the heat was breaking.

"Hey, weren't we supposed to put some of this salt out back there?" Conner asked as he nodded to the blocks stacked at the front of the truck bed.

"Well, I was, as a matter of fact. But we're short on time and, well hell, there's always manana; siempre hay manana. As a matter of fact, we need to hustle a bit. You mind cleaning the birds while I get the horses and start packing up. Sorry to give you the shit duty but I can probably pack faster."

"No sweat, I get it."

"Thanks. I told Maggie we'd try to make it back by seven for dinner. A few folks are coming over. I'm not sure you know them all, but I know you'll enjoy 'em."

At 5:30 they left the dirt road and hit the pavement as the radio speaker under the dash spewed static. A woman's voice followed, "Bud can you hear me. Come in Bud."

Bud leaned forward and pulled the radio handset from the holder. "I got ya' babe. What's up?"

"Just making sure you guys are all right and wondering how you're running," replied Maggie at the other end.

"Everything's good. We oughta be good on time, maybe a touch early even."

"Great. Looking forward to seeing you hon. Hey to Murph. Love to both you guys."

"See you in a bit." Bud hung the handset back up and pushed a CD in to the player.

It was 6:45 when they drove under the log overhead into the Ingles' headquarters. First stop was the horse barn, to drop the horses and tack. Sergio was still at the barn and was, as usual, eager to help. Conner shook his hand warmly, having established a rapport with the fellow horseman over the years. They unloaded horses and saddles and Bud dropped the trailer next to the barn. The dogs were still in the truck bed, too tired to bark or even show interest in familiar sights and people.

The hunters drove the truck across the yard to the main house; a large home built for entertaining and lodging guests. More than half the year the Ingles' had at least one overnight guest and usually several at a time. Often a collection of family or old friends like Conner, but just as frequently there were business associates and new friends. The Ingles' generous and congenial manner was always evident, representing a piece of Old Western Americana not easily found anymore. They were well known and well liked in many circles, generous with their time and their money, and they enjoyed people from all walks of life from their Peruvian shepherds to the governor of Nevada. Their house reflected all of this history and warmth.

It was a gorgeous home of mixed architecture. A fact Maggie laughed at, saying she certainly wasn't a purist and just 'liked what she liked'. It had the flavor of a southwest hacienda but the heavy timbers throughout created the look of a western lodge. In front was a large covered porch well suited for the rocking chairs that resided there. Off the back of the house was a beautiful covered deck for warm weather cooking and dining. Everything about the house impressed, from first climbing the stairs onto the spacious front porch to entering through the heavy antique mission doors.

No one passed through those doors for the first time that didn't stop to admire what they saw; a twenty foot ceiling with massive exposed trusses constructed of huge timbers and heavy iron; walls of heavy plaster and textured finish providing an old world look; hard wood floors salvaged from an abandon stamp mill, the planking revealing its past life through the scars, old nail holes, and burn marks scattered throughout. Numerous original paintings of different mediums adorned the walls; bronze sculptures throughout the room; all original and most with a western motif.

The furnishings provided a wonderful compliment to the architecture; a mixture of heavy dark woods and leather or tanned hides. There were three different seating arrangements around the large room. In the center were several couches and chairs arranged to accommodate a large group for conversation. Near the massive stone fireplace and hearth was a couch and two oversized chairs. Across the room, closer to the kitchen and dining room, was an area with a large round table and chairs for playing games, which in the Ingles home was usually a card game of some sort.

Several game heads adorned the walls; all had been Nevada records at one time and one still was. Elk, mule deer, antelope, but the mount that always drew comments from new guests was above the fireplace. From the massive stone chimney, a large flat rock protruded in to the room and on it crouched a large mountain lion as if she intended to pounce on the person below.

Conner never tired of entering that magnificent great room and took a minute to soak it in; as he stood there, he felt warm and welcome, and always a little awed. He thought about the first time Bubba Striker had come to that house. He had spoken of the energy it had, that it had a spiritual aura; the old wood and timbers had stories of their own to tell.

Conner dumped his gear at the foot of the stairs and made his way to the kitchen. Maggie had just returned from visiting her sister in Reno.

"Hey, baby, how are ya?" Conner's grin was wide.

Maggie turned from the stove, her eyes smiled brightly as she opened her arms for a hug. "You luscious thing; how was the hunt?"

They hugged and gave each other a peck on the lips as they pulled apart. "It was great, hon. What about you, everything good? You know for two days your old man was telling nothing but great things about you, so, you're either still beatin' the shit out of him or you've changed your ways."

"He's a coward, you know that,"

Conner laughed, enjoying her beautiful smile and feeling the warmth of being there.

"You've got your hands full down here and I need to get cleaned up so I'll run upstairs."

"Sounds great, we've got all night to catch up, hon. I'm so glad you're here, not only for me but Bud lights up so much when you visit."

"That's awfully nice. Thanks, Maggie. See you in a sec."

Conner climbed to the top of the stairs going to the first bedroom he came to. It was always reserved for him, even if the governor was staying. There were four bedrooms along this upstairs hallway. Each room was a suite with a king sized bed, sitting area, and its own bath. Conner dropped his hunting gear next to his other suitcase. He'd been thinking about a shower for the last several hours and couldn't undress fast enough in anticipation of standing under the hot water.

Several men were assembled around the hors doeuvre counter with a glass of wine when Conner finally came down; all raving about Maggie's creations. Bud was opening a second bottle of wine as he looked at his friend.

"Murph, you better dig in while they're hot. I know you love these."

"You better dig in while there still are any," said Mitch Jeffers as he stuck his hand out to shake Conner's. "Long time, no see old friend. I was tickled when Bud said you'd be here tonight."

Conner shook his hand heartily, "Great to see you, Mitch. You look great."

"We're all having some white to start with, that suit you, Murph?" Bud said as he handed Conner a small plate with several hors d'oeurves on it.

"Sounds great, Bud. Thanks."

"Introduce yourself to these two gentlemen while I get you a glass."

Conner realized that he had met Chet at the ranch years before. They were bankers from the agricultural branch of the bank Bud did most of his business with, and had for years. The older man was retiring within the year and had brought his replacement for an introduction. Chet had handpicked him, and was hoping that everything would go well. Even a bank as large as theirs realized the value of clients like the Ingles. The bankers were staying the night and would be going on a site visit of all of the ranches with Bud the following day.

Maggie finally shooed them from the kitchen area and asked Bud to open some wine for dinner. The men made their way to the dining room and waited for Maggie.

"It's such a small group, let's not make a fuss about where to sit. Please gentlemen, sit where you like," said Maggie.

Bud Poured wine at each setting. "I've got a pretty fancy California cab here, is that OK for everyone?" He glanced at everyone as he continued to pour the 2003 Caymus. Everyone nodded their approval.

Mitch said, "That's more than a little fancy, Bud old boy."

"Well I mean no offense to the rest of you fellas, but it isn't every day we get Murph back in our midst. It's always reason to celebrate."

Bud took his customary place at the head of the table and the others sat in a fashion as to incorporate Maggie in the middle of the group.

"Tessa, you can bring the meat now, honey. That'd be great." Maggie spoke to the Mexican woman that had helped her prepare dinner.

Tessa returned with a large platter of thickly sliced cuts of bone-in prime rib. Maggie turned to the younger banker and motioned to him with her hand, "Tessa, would you please start with this gentleman. You'll have to forgive me Bill; I don't know your preference. The rest of these boys like their meat fairly rare. I like an end cut. There are two end cuts and the one next to them is more medium than the rest. Please take what you like."

"I'll take the other end cut then please."

"Take the larger one, then, please, Bill." Maggie added, "That platter is a two hand job for Tessa, please take what you want."

"Oh, of course. I'm sorry." Bill was embarrassed that he had waited for Tessa to serve him. .

"That's quite all right," Maggie said. "By the way, you are all ordered to save room for fresh apple pie alamode for dessert."

As the food made its way around the table, Conner raised his glass and said, "A toast to old friends and new, as well as the best hostess the West has ever known."

Mitch Jeffers was a geologist and a frequent visitor to the Ingles Ranch; he related several fascinating statistics about the amount of dirt moved and processed to harvest a single ounce of gold in today's mining operations. All of the conversation was light, punctuated with old stories and laughter until Chet began talking about a dear friend of his that had just passed away, succumbing to cancer. He was angry at the fact that the new Public Health Agency had denied her treatment, because they deemed her too old to receive it. Bud glanced at Maggie as Chet talked and saw her eyes fill with tears as she looked down at the table.

"Excuse me, Chet, I'm sorry." Bud interrupted the banker.

"Maggie, hon, how about that pie and some coffee before it gets too late."

Maggie sniffed and brought her napkin to her face dabbing below her eyes. "Certainly, great idea. I'm insisting on the pie, fellas, but does everyone want coffee? Perfect, why don't you follow Bud in to the living room and Tessa and I will bring it out there."

Maggie got up from the table and went toward the kitchen carrying several dishes with her.

Over the sound of chairs being pushed back from the table, Bud said, "Chet I'm sorry to interrupt you. But..."

Chet said, "It's no problem, I saw Maggie's reaction. I'm sorry."

"Well, she just lost a very dear friend to cancer herself. The poor girl had breast cancer. You know with this goddamned PHA they won't allow women to get mammograms any more until they're fifty years and older. Apparently there's a shortage of the equipment now, or shortage of the people that can read them, or some such crap."

Chet said, "I actually think it's worse than that. It's another cost saving measure because the damn system is so broke. Stupid bastards."

"Well whatever the reason, its bullshit. But this was a case where Judy was forty-eight years old and apparently had a tumor that she couldn't detect with self-exams. She was pretty well endowed and apparently this thing was right in the middle of her breast and against her rib. Anyway by the time she detected it, it had metastasized to her liver and bone in several areas. So the bastards say it's too advanced and denied her treatment. No cancer therapy, only stuff for pain. She died ugly. Man it was bad."

"Again, I'm sorry', Chet said sadly.

"Hey, not your fault. But let's not talk any more about our lovely government health care tonight if you guys don't mind."

They all nodded in agreement as they rose to follow Bud in to the living room. Maggie returned with a tray of cups and cream and sugar, Tessa followed with the coffee.

"I made decaf since it's so late. I hope that's OK."

In spite of remarks made of being 'so full' or 'nearly foundering', there wasn't a forkful of pie left on any plate. After dessert and a round of coffee, the group didn't last much longer. Maggie excused herself and they all decided that was a wise move.

Everyone was up early for breakfast. Bud would have the bankers in tow all day, giving Bill as good an overview as could be had in a day. Mitch had a meeting with one of his clients in Elko later that morning. Conner was leaving also, heading north to Jackson, Wyoming to spend a few days with another good friend.

"I made you a thermos of coffee for the road, Bud. Do you want anything else?" Maggie asked as she cleared Bud's empty plate from the counter.

"That's great."

"Tony and Maria are expecting you for lunch at the Midas place, is that still on?" Maggie was now busy clearing all of their plates.

"I think that works great. Well, Chet, Bill, you guys ready," Bud glanced at Conner, "Or is it 'y'all ready', Murph, my ole' cracker buddy?"

"You are a mess, my friend."

Bud and Conner stood to shake hands, "You stay away too long and don't stay long enough when you come."

Maggie had her hands on her hips and a mock look of anger on her face, "Never truer words spoken, Murph."

"Hell, I've been underfoot for nearly a week. Matter of fact, it's a week today."

Maggie's tone was sharp. "Conner Murphy, you have never been 'underfoot' in this house and you know it!"

Bud was grinning again, "Don't rile her Murph, you know better."

Bud turned to the two bankers, "You guys grab a jacket? It dropped quite a bit last night, first real chilly night of the fall."

"We did, we're ready when you are", responded Chet.

Bud looked over to Bill. "Bill, you got all your pencils and a calculator?"

Bill smiled and turned to Maggie, "Thank you very much for a great dinner and breakfast, Maggie. Chet had spoken of what a great hostess you are and you even surpassed his lofty praise."

"Well thank you, Bill. Now remember that good food when you are figuring your interest rates and we'll all be all right." Maggie turned toward Conner, "Never let up on a banker." She turned back to wink at Bill.

The two bankers shook hands with Mitch and Conner and Maggie and followed Bud out through the side door leading to the mud porch. Soon after, Mitch stood and said his goodbyes, stating that he needed to watch his time. Maggie and Conner were alone, her standing at the counter and him sitting behind it, finishing a last cup of coffee.

"I'm sorry about Judy, Maggie. I know it was tough. I'm sure it still is."

Tears came to Maggie's eyes as she thought about her friend. She sniffed and blinked and then shook her head in a vain attempt to fight off the tears.

"She was so damn young, Murph. So damn young."

"All her kids out of the house yet?"

Maggie shook her head; "Her youngest had just started college when she was diagnosed. He goes to the community college here in Elko. Was still living at home."

Conner remembered Judy's husband's name, "How's Doyle doing?"

"Bad." Maggie came around the counter to sit on a stool facing Conner, "He's very sad and very angry. He's angry at God and angry at our god damned government. That stupid regulation of not allowing mammograms for women under fifty. Aaaagh!"

Maggie gathered herself and continued as Conner reached over and put a hand on her knee. "You know in years past, she would probably be alive. Mastectomy, chemo, radiation, yea, but alive. You know, she suffered miserably and she died young. But Murph, you know the very worst part of it all?"

Tears ran down Maggie's face now, "Judy was a fighter. She was like you and Bud and me, and a million others. She wanted to live. She would have endured anything just have had a chance. But that fucking PHA and those fucking bureaucrats denied her the chance to fight. It all makes me so sick. What has happened to our country, Murph?"

"I don't know, Maggie, I don't know."

Conner handed Maggie a napkin from the counter. She wiped her face and stood up with arms open, inviting a hug. They embraced, squeezing each other hard to vanquish the sadness Maggie felt.

"I love you, Murph. Thanks for coming and thanks for asking about Judy, too."

"I love you guys, and I'm sorry for your loss, Maggie."

MIAMI, FLORIDA
October

Stanley sat behind his desk, staring at the door that had just closed. To the left of the door was a solid row of file cabinets with papers and files stacked on them in such disarray they looked as if the slightest bump would send them toppling to the floor. Against another wall was a long low table, similarly burdened. Stuffed under the table were file boxes adorned with letters of the alphabet written in black marker. Above the table hung two pictures: one of the President of the United States and the other of the current director of the Public Health Agency. The wall to Stanley's right had a window that looked down three stories to the parking lot. He loved his window, it served as a reminder of how far he had come.

The desk was large, made from metal and fiberboard covered in a wood-grain paper, offering a poor disguise. There were no pictures on the desk only a telephone, a computer monitor, a pewter cup holding pens and markers, a ceramic coffee cup, and yet another chaotic stack of files and papers.

Stanley was dressed in black shoes and pants with a white shirt. The short-sleeved shirt was a cotton and polyester blend, button down, and as usual, not pressed. He wore a tie of alternating stripes, with a small stain near the tip. His new secretary had just left his office after asking if he needed any help "organizing his papers".

"Why did God have to make so many spics? And then why the hell did he have to drop them all in Miami?" Stanley was incredulous that they had sent him another Latino. The fact her English was perfect and she was raised in Homestead didn't matter to Stanley; a spic was a spic and he was sick of them. He could remember when real Americans outnumbered them; Christ, has that ever changed. He leaned back in his chair and closed his eyes, thinking about how many white people he worked with anymore. Two; two damned white people and all the rest...Christ.

His lament was disturbed by the telephone.

"Yea Yolanda, what is it?"

"It's Mrs. Robertson, again. She's still hoping to get an appointment with you before next week."

"Standard answer, Yolanda."

"Sir?"

"Oh God damn it, tell her there are absolutely no breaks in my schedule for at least two weeks. End of story. Calling back over and over isn't going change that." Stanley slammed the receiver down.

"Christ, spics and nig...." Stanley Mesh stopped himself and leaned forward to grab his coffee. He leaned back and turned his chair to put one foot on the desk. The unspoken racial slur sparked a memory of his boss and mentor.

"Stanley, someday you're going to figure it out. Think of it as if you were a radio or TV broadcaster" Sid had told him. "See, you couldn't afford to cuss and swear with abandon in your personal life because you'd eventually screw up while on the air and potentially ruin your career. I understand that once in a while, when you're with people you trust, it's cathartic to let loose and call the lower life forms by the appropriate names. But you can only afford to do it once in a while, Stanley, once in a while, God damn it." Stanley chuckled to himself, enjoying how Sid referred to niggers and Jews as 'lower life forms'. This made Stanley feel like an insider.

Stanley continued to lean back in his chair and think about the first night he had met Sid.

He had stumbled in to Sid Leach's life by accident. Stanley taught health and driver's education for five years at a Miami high school and realized that he couldn't last much longer. He had thought he'd chosen an easy path with a lot of time off and few demands. But what Stanley had never bargained for was how much he would hate the kids. Each year became progressively worse and after five years he was at the end of his rope, no longer able to put up with their insolent remarks and their rude, intimidating behavior.

Stanley liked education because he knew how to play the system, but he had to find a way out of the classroom. Some sort of position in administration seemed to be the key, but to qualify he needed either an advanced degree or more years of teaching under his belt, neither seemed doable.

Then a seemingly incidental decision changed his life. Another teacher at the school asked him to go to a small political rally for a woman running for the school board. At first Stanley was reluctant but his colleague talked him in to it by pointing out that if Loyola Struthers won, she could potentially be helpful to Stanley in his aspirations for an administrative job. It was all the incentive Stanley needed; only later did he find out how right his friend had been. By the time the rally began, Stanley had convinced himself to be very proactive in showing support for Ms. Struthers. He concentrated on meeting her face to face that night to shower her with praise and assure her he was willing to do anything to help her get elected. He also made certain she would remember his name by repeating it to her and her staff several times during the evening. At one point, while fawning over Ms. Struthers, he was introduced to Sidney Leach. Stanley remembered thinking how out of place Leach appeared at this neighborhood rally. The man had the appearance and manner of someone too important to be at this small event, a man of patently more stature than anyone else there. Leach was smartly dressed in a very expensive suit while most everyone else was very casual. His charming, charismatic manner was made more evident by how many people recognized him and were obviously gratified by his recognition of them. Although Stanley remembers being impressed, at the time he couldn't fathom why a man like Sid Leach was there and felt the introduction would be the last he would ever see of him.

Before leaving the rally that night, Stanley revisited the volunteer desk and found out what he could do to be one of "Struthers's Soldiers". He signed up for several evenings on the phone bank and picked up a handful of yard signs to put up in his neighborhood. He ended the evening by shaking the candidate's hand one more time and again pledging his support.

Stanley left there that night feeling empowered. He was euphoric. He couldn't put in to words exactly what he'd found but he knew he had just found the path way to where he wanted to be.

Stanley had impressed himself with how forward and talkative he'd been; able to smile and shake hands and act so interested. It was even more surprising considering Ms. Struthers was black as were many of her volunteers. Talking to them in such an easy, friendly tone wasn't something that came easy to Stanley Mesh. But that evening he'd had an epiphany; the road to getting what he wanted was through those kinds of activities and interactions.

His performance as a teacher was dismal, he acknowledged that fact and he didn't care; knowing from the start of his teaching career there was no future for him in meritocracy. Even at that early stage he had understood the value of the union for people like him but he had never taken it further than that. What Stanley needed were avenues provided by connections; Christ, how did it take him this long to figure this out! He could glad hand and back slap with niggers if he had to. Hell, he'd even kiss the fat bitches on the cheek if he had to. Christ, he was on his way!

Stanley was in quite a state as he headed home that night, feeling better than he'd felt in years. All was coming together in his world. Everybody could just go to hell. Stanley Mesh had had an epiphany that was going to change his life!

He turned down Palmetto Avenue in to his neighborhood; rows of small cinderblock houses with flat roofs, typical of 1960's Miami. The single car driveways and little road frontage meant cars were parked in most of the yards. Stanley's house was no different than many others, bare of landscaping and in need of paint.

It was 10:30 when he got home from the rally. Sheri's car was in the driveway so he jumped the battered curb and parked on the lawn. Stanley knew his wife would be in bed by now, but hoped she was still awake. He was in a mood; more revved up than he'd been in a long time and it was making him horny.

It was still hot and muggy when he walked from the car to the house. The mixed odors of mildew and cigarette smoke weren't enough to disguise the smell of the Chinese food Sherri had brought home for dinner. He walked through the living room to the kitchen, intent on something cold to drink. On the small kitchen table were several red and white boxes of unfinished food. He peered in to each one before taking a breaded shrimp and dipping it in the sweet and sour sauce. He opened the refrigerator door and grabbed an open carton of chocolate milk. It was that or beer, and Stanley didn't drink. He drained the carton and ate one more shrimp before venturing down the hallway to the bedroom.

Sherri was in bed, propped up on pillows, smoking a cigarette and watching an old Survivor episode on TV. Stanley walked in to the room just as she exhaled a large waft of smoke through both nostrils.

"If you're gonna fuck around and make a racket, turn it up so I don't miss nuthin'." Sherri leaned toward the nightstand and dropped her cigarette butt into an empty beer bottle. She grabbed a different Budweiser bottle, leaned back against her pillows and stared back at the TV.

Sherri was seven years Stanley's senior, but looked older. Her ears poked through her coal black hair that laid flat to her head. Gray roots at her part indicated the need for another dying. Her face was thin and taught, with deep lines at the corners of her eyes and mouth and a pale, ashen complexion accentuated by her black hair. Sheri Mesh had all the appearance of a heavy smoker and an accomplished alcoholic.

"Things went well tonight, Sherri," Stanley turned to walk out of the bedroom toward the bathroom down the hall as he pulled his still buttoned shirt over his head.

"That's fucking wonderful Stanley, how 'bout you wait for a commercial", Sherri slurred.

In a few minutes Stanley returned to the bedroom and glanced at the TV, confirming it was a commercial he'd heard. He was clad in a pair of thin black socks and white jockey shorts when he approached her side of the bed. Sherri turned her head only slightly and looked at him from the corner of her eyes. She took a deep drag on her cigarette.

"How about if we do something besides talk during the commercials, honey," Stanley hoped he sounded seductive.

"Honey, how 'bout you fuck off, 'honey'. Can't you see Little Richard lying there? I've already had my fun." She nodded her head toward the nightstand as she spoke. "Survivors on for Christ sake, you fuckin' moron."

Stanley saw what he hadn't noticed earlier behind the empty beer bottles. A vibrator shaped like a penis was now obvious to him on the table. Sherri turned back toward the TV and exhaled a cloud of smoke from her nostrils.

Stanley's face flushed as he turned away and walked out of the room. He slapped his feet to the ground as he walked, daring to be as noisy as he could.

"That Goddamned bitch" he muttered as he went back toward the kitchen. "She's so Goddamned stingy with that pussy it's unbelievable. The worst invention ever is a goddamned vibrating dick. How can I complete with that, Christ."

Stanley finished the last of the shrimp as he slumped in a kitchen chair feeling sorry for himself. It wasn't long till he rekindled the euphoria of earlier, certain that what he had learned this evening would be life changing for him. He decided to go out to his bunker and give all of it some more thought. Stopping at the refrigerator again to grab more chocolate milk, he found another open carton in the door and brought it with him. The faint sound of a commercial ditty on the television reached his ears as he walked through the living room toward the glass slider in the far corner. The door only slid partially open and stopped. No amount of pushing helped as he squirmed and forced his belly through the opening.

He fought the slider closed and walked to the door of a small cinder block shed that stood only several feet from the back of the house. He used a key from under the mat to open the padlock on the hasp screwed in to the metal door. There was no knob, he pushed the door open and reached around for the light switch.

A sigh left his lips. Here he could think about all he learned tonight, away from all of the assholes that populated the world.

Yolanda's voice came over the intercom.

"Mr. Mesh, I'm going to lunch now," said Yolanda.

"Sure. OK," responded her boss.

"I'm going to the Derby Deli across the street for a salad. Can I bring you anything back?"

"Naa, I'm fine. I might take off in a bit."

Stanley remembered his 2:00 o'clock conference call and realized he couldn't leave early today. He tried Yolanda on the intercom, but she'd left her desk. He hurried to his feet and ran through the outer office in to the hallway.

"Hey, Yolanda. Hold it."

Stanley had caught her in front of the elevators. He pulled some cash out of his pocket, "Get me one of those Philly cheese sandwiches they do. And some chips and a Pepsi. Not diet." He handed her a twenty.

"Sure sir, no problem. I'll have them make it when I'm about to leave so it'll be warm when I get back."

"Yea, good. Bring me the change." He had already turned to walk back to his office.

Stanley returned to his desk and opened the folder labeled 'Pending Cases' to prepare for his conference call. Bored, his mind wandered back to Sid Leach.

Loyola Struthers was elected to the school board that fall. Stanley had followed through on all of his promises during the campaign. Nine months after the election, Stanley applied for the vice-principal position at Marsha Davis Middle School in Pembroke Pines and was called for an interview at the school several weeks later. The interview took place in the principal's office at Marsha Davis.

Sam Johnson, the principal, stood in his office and greeted Stanley as he walked in. He offered Stanley a chair and walked toward the door.

"It's great meeting you, Stanley," said Principal Johnson. "I know we'll work well together and I look forward to it. Now I'll leave you two to your business. I'll want to show Mr. Mesh his office before he leaves, Loyola. Thank you."

Mr. Johnson had left the room before Stanley realized he hadn't even spoken. Was he sure he'd even heard correctly? Wasn't he here for an interview? He looked at Loyola Struthers and was about to speak when she held up her hand.

"This is how it works, Stanley. You're in." Loyola smiled as she spoke. *"You've been doing all the right stuff and there's more for you to do. That is if you want to keep moving up."*

"Well, yea. I mean sure. Sorry. I'm a little flustered. I thought this was just an interview today, a chance for the job."

"Officially, it is your interview." Loyola continued, *"The other candidates have been interviewed and you were the last. Most of the others had stronger resumes, but you were so very impressive today that Mr. Johnson and myself had absolutely no doubt you were the perfect person for the job."*

Loyola stood up to take a seat behind the principal's desk. She leaned forward and put her elbows on the desk, *"You remember Mr. Leach, Sidney Leach."*

"Yeah, I do. I remember him from a rally you had. I remember him because, I don't know, he seemed out of place there, or something. I also remember being impressed by him." It was all Stanley could do to focus on the conversation. *Vice-principal! Unbelievable!*

"Well Sid was there that night, as you remember, and actually several other nights, because I'm one of his 'soldiers', as he puts it. I know that I've gotten where I am because of him. I also know that if I toe the line for him, the sky is the limit for me."

"Wow. I had no idea."

"Yeah, well, there's more to it." Loyola leaned back in her chair and smiled at Stanley. *"It seems that Sid has taken an interest in you, for which I get more than a little credit, by the way. Anyway, he thinks you may fit well in to his 'army' and he wants to see how well it may work for both of you. This may just be the start for you Stanley, good luck."*

Mesh remembered starting at Marsha Davis within the month and thought he had gone to heaven. In his new position he had virtually no contact with the students, a work schedule that barely filled the mornings and a seventy-five percent pay raise.

His next meeting with Sid Leach was firmly ingrained in his memory. Sid had called the school and made an appointment to see Stanley that following Tuesday, prompting him to miss a planned sick day. Sid Leach was the same as Stanley had remembered, smartly dressed and perfectly quaffed.

He stood in front of his desk to greet his visitor as he entered the office. They *shook hands and Stanley offered him one of the two guest chairs as he made his way to sit behind his desk.*

As Sid took his seat he said," Why don't you sit on this side Stanley, I don't like talking to people across their desk." Any sense of a subordinate position didn't suit Sid Leach.

"I'm sorry, Mr. Leach. That was stupid. I'm sorry."

Sid raised his hand and smiled, "You like your new job, Mr. Vice-principal?"

"I certainly do. It's been great. I know I need to thank you for what you've done, Mr. Leach."

"Please, call me Sid. What I've done? Whatever have I done, Stanley?"

"Well, I guess I don't really know. But I'm getting the idea that many things seem to happen because of you."

"You flatter me Stanley. But you're not too far off." A faint bell sounded and Sid pulled a phone from his pocket and glanced at it before going on. "Let's talk about what could happen next. You are already a member of the union and have been since you started teaching I believe."

"Yes, sir, I am…that's correct."

"How would you like to advance within that organization to the point that you could escape this school environment all together and just work within the union's organization? Better pay, no rude little bastards, no obnoxious, so-called concerned parents; none of that. Would that interest you, Stanley?"

"More than you can imagine Mr. Leach, er, Sid."

"Frankly, I didn't perceive having such a conversation with you this quickly after your last promotion, but some things just move swiftly at times. Let me explain how you can help me."

Sid explained how Stanley and one other 'soldier' had been 'selected' to be watchdogs for the upcoming union election results for their district. The duty was simple really. In fact Stanley didn't have to do anything; simply certify the election results as being honest and accurate. Sid explained that it was imperative for the good of the union that the "pesky Jew boy' didn't win. His heart might be in the right place, but the "stupid fuckin' Hebe" just really didn't get it. Besides it would just be healthier for him if he lost.

Stanley was thinking how fast things had moved for him through his association with Sid Leach. Within a year, he was in the regional comptroller's office of the union. Stanley Mesh didn't know a credit from a debit, but all he had to do was watch out for Sid's interests. Stanley knew they weren't only Leach's interests, but he never had any contact with anyone else in Sid's circle. That suited Stanley; he had no desire to know too much.

Years later, when the Public Health Agency of the United States was fully operational, Sid moved Stanley to that organization. Stanley knew his loyalty and discretion were his only qualifications. Powerful people continued to manage his ascendance if he continued to 'toe the line' as Loyola Struthers had so aptly put it.

He had been promoted twice since joining the PHA. He was making more money than he had ever imagined; benefits, pension all beyond his dreams. As Regional Director of Arbitration he was the final decision on who received medical treatment from the Public Health Agency for well over twenty million Floridians. In spite of millions of citizens under his wing, his day to day was relatively simple due to the layers of bureaucracy below him. Most of the cases were resolved before they ever reached his desk. Of those that did, a high percentage of them were the result of a call from Sid's office. In those instances, the case might be anywhere in the system and in reality; those phone calls left no question for Stanley as to what his decision was to be.

Stanley leaned back with a foot on the desk and continued to revel in the past that had resulted in the present. No medical training, no training in psychology or social work, no degrees in business administration, just loyalty, discretion, and the ability to play the system.

"Sir I have your lunch. Do you want me to bring it in?"

"Yea, of course."

Stanley looked annoyed as Yolanda put his things on the desk. She held out her hand with his change. "Reminding you about your 2:00 o'clock conference call, sir."

"Yea, I got it."

IDAHO FALLS, IDAHO
October

Conner exited Nevada through the border town of Jackpot, with its billboards and flashing signs all testifying to the most liberal slots and the cheapest rooms, making it senseless to drive further; 'sorry boys', Conner thought. He gassed up at a convenience store, grabbed a large coffee and some peanut butter crackers, and drove in to Idaho, deciding to push on to Idaho Falls for lunch. He set his cruise on seventy-five and shoved in an Ottmar Liebert CD; perfect scenery for some Spanish guitar.

At two o'clock Conner took the Broadway Street exit into Idaho Falls and headed west in to town. A small Mexican restaurant caught his eye. If there had been a lunch crowd, they'd since left, as there was only one other couple in the restaurant. Conner nodded at the old man dressed in coveralls and a t-shirt as he walked to a table. He didn't take much time with the menu, settling on a taco salad with some extra salsa.

He glanced at his phone, noted the cell reception was good and decided to call Jan. He was curious about the weather her way. Bud had been right; the temperature had dropped last night and had continued to get colder all day. The phone rang several times and then clicked before it rang again.

"You've reached Jan Thomas of Teton Gallery. Please leave a message and I will return the call as soon as I can. Have a great day."

"Hey, Jan, Conner. I'm having a bite in Idaho Falls and then headed your way. Call me if you get a chance. Thanks."

The waitress brought chips and salsa and Conner didn't hesitate; the aromas from the kitchen made him realize how hungry he was. The old couple got up to leave and Conner gave a wave of his hand to acknowledge the man's nod. They stopped at the hat stand near the register where the old man helped his wife into her coat. He pulled on his own worn denim jacket as the waitress came from the kitchen carrying Conner's food. She smiled and said goodbye to the couple as they thanked her in return and the old woman touched the girl's arm as her husband smiled on. They were outside before he put his hat on, pulling it low against the wind.

Conner poured a bowel of salsa over his taco salad and dug in. Within two bites he knew his instincts had been good to stop here. The salad was big, or maybe he'd eaten too fast, but he couldn't finish it. He checked his watch as he waited for his check and decided to have a coffee and call his son.

It rang several times and went to voice mail. He hesitated but decided not to leave a message, not trusting the cell signal on the road ahead. He sat there, disappointed, thinking how nice it would be to speak with Sean. Hell with it, he'd get his coffee to go and get back on the road. He pushed his chair back as the waitress arrived with a large mug of coffee.

"I'm sorry took so long. I brew you a fresh pot. The other too old."

"That's quite alright. No me gusta el café viejo. Gracias," Conner smiled as he said it.

He looked at his phone again and hit 'Sean's house' and it began to ring. After just two rings a man answered the phone.

"Hey, Dad, how're you doing?"

"I'm great buddy. I thought I was going to get Mo. I had tried you a little bit ago on your cell but didn't leave a message. You're home early aren't you?"

Sean's voice was flat, "A little I guess. Mo and I just got back from the clinic. We're still trying to get something done about these headaches. She's really suffering, Dad."

Conner didn't respond at first. "I'm glad she's getting it checked out. It must be miserable...I mean for her to go to the doctor."

"Doctor? I wish we'd seen a doctor. It's obviously been a while since you've been, Dad. This PHA has devolved to the point that you can hardly see a doctor. You have to go through so much red tape it is unbelievable. We spent all afternoon there almost three weeks ago and not only didn't see a doctor; we didn't even get scheduled to see a doctor! Which, by the way, also means we have no diagnostics scheduled. After four hours of waiting, all they did was take her history and give her a cursory exam. It was bullshit. They prescribed some pain meds but unfortunately they barely touch it. So we went back today to tell them just that; that she's no better. Shit this has been going on since August, now."

The frustration in Sean's voice unnerved Conner. "I'm sorry buddy. It sounds frus..."

"Oh, hell Dad, I'm sorry. I don't mean to hit you with this while you're away and trying to have some fun."

"Please. Don't be silly. I want to know what's going on. The headaches are bad, huh?"

"Yeah, they're bad. You know how tough she is and this thing's really kicking her ass. But how about you? Where are you now?"

"Idaho Falls. I'm hopefully going to get to Jan's tonight, in Jackson. I'll call you tomorrow once I'm there. Good luck with... everything, Give Mo my love."

"Thanks, Dad. Sorry to vent; we'll be fine. Love ya."

"Love you too, buddy."

Conner's coffee had cooled off so he got another one to go. His phone started ringing as he pulled his keys from his pocket. He set the coffee on the roof of his car, retrieved the phone from his shirt pocket, and glanced at the number.

"Jan, how are ya?" Conner put his cup in a holder before he climbed in his seat.

"I'm good sweetie, how are you? It's great to hear your voice. You on the road yet?"

"Just getting back in the car. I plan to take 26 out of here and pick up 22 over Pine Creek Pass and through Victor. That's the fastest, right?" Conner pulled a cigar and lighter from a side pocket of his old leather brief case on the passenger seat. "So what is it, about three more hours?"

"Oh, no, probably less than two. But you could hit a little weather, as you get closer to here, so maybe a little more. Listen, though, you need to watch for High Way 31 coming off of 26 to Victor. 31 turns in to 22 after you get in to Wyoming."

"That's right thanks for reminding me. Listen, it's about 3:30 now, so I'm guessing about 5:30?"

"Yup, sounds right and that works great. I'm going to leave the gallery at 5:00, so we should be getting to my place about the same time."

They said goodbye as Conner pulled out of the parking lot and headed north on 26. He took a swallow of coffee and cracked the window before lighting his cigar; glad to be headed out of town and away from the traffic.

It was near dark and the air was filled with a heavy mist when Conner spotted the sign for Hwy 31 toward Victor. A battered old sedan was on the side of the road just past the intersection. The car was well off the road, with both front doors, the right rear door, and the trunk all standing open. Conner turned on to 31 and slowed his Toyota, his attention drawn to a little girl, alone, standing behind the sedan. He checked his mirror and slowed to a stop. The little girl was motionless and continued to stare in to the trunk of the car. Conner pulled off the road and stopped. His brow furrowed as he peered in to the woods. He saw no one else. Conner rolled his windows down. No sounds of anyone. The girl never moved. She wore a short dress and a nylon windbreaker and never moved. He looked in to the woods once more.

Conner felt for his pocketknife as he opened the door to his car, never taking his eyes off the Ford as he opened his rear door and grabbed a coat. The air was filled with a chilling mist, made colder by gusts of wind. Conner pulled his cap down further and turned the collar up on his jacket as he approached the sedan.

He moved his knife to his jacket pocket as he looked again in to the woods. The girl never moved.

"Hey, honey, are you OK? My name is Conner. Are your parents around?" Conner walked toward the girl, smiling as he talked to her. Without turning, the girl bolted to the far side of the car. She stood by the passenger door, silent, looking at the ground, her face wet from the mist and red from the cold.

Conner changed his approach, circling wider around the back of the car to visualize the other side while he kept his distance. He glanced toward the woods again and then behind him. It was then he heard a voice.

"Sheila. Sheila. Stand back away from me. Stop you're crowdin' me girl."

Conner realized there were a pair of thick legs and a large butt sticking out from the passenger door of the car. Sheila had wrapped an arm around one of those big thighs.

"Hello. Are y'all OK?" Conner called, slowly approaching the car, keeping the woods in his peripheral vision.

"Huh? What the hell?" The muffled voice came from inside the car. A large form started to back out of the car, laboring, grunting. The little girl backed up with it, now both arms wrapped around a thigh. "Sheila! Girl, you've got to back outta my way!"

Conner had come as far as the back bumper when the woman finally waddled free of the car and stood to face him; a disheveled form of medium height and nearly as wide. An unlit cigarette hung from her mouth. Her head was covered in a tousle of bleached hair, as she looked at Conner through narrow slits, a face squashed between heavy cheeks and chins. She wore a coffee stained grey sweatshirt that was stretched to its limits and didn't extend far enough to meet her equally challenged black sweat pants. Laceless tennis shoes bulged open to expose thick ankles, shining bright pink from the cold.

"Hi there sugar, did you come to rescue us?" A toothy grin sported a solid gold upper tooth as she stuck a pudgy hand out toward Conner, "I'm Linda. This here's Sheila." Sheila made her way behind the big thigh to disappear from sight.

They shook hands and the cigarette bobbed up and down as she continued, "and this here is Lawrence."

Letting go of Conner's hand, she made her way back in to the hole from which she had just emerged, like a fat, greedy badger squeezing in to a gopher hole. Rewarded for her effort, she extricated herself holding a diaper-clad infant that matched his sister.

Sheila's head appeared from behind her mother's leg to look at Conner. Neither child had a dark complexion, but both had the hair and features of an African American.

"I was about to fix this flat when Lawrence here started fussin' so much I had to just quit and get him changed. He's got some lungs on him now; I'm here to tell ya. His sister never could holler like this boy. I don't know what it means, but it might mean somethin'. Got to, don't it? I mean loud, now. You can't hardly think when he's goin' at it. But you see, with a clean diaper he's as good as can be. Somethin', huh?"

"I'm Conner. Y'all are..."

"Well, hi Conner. Sure pleased to meet you." Linda stuck her hand out again.

Conner shook her hand and tried again. "Are y'all alone out here? You're husband?"

Linda turned her head from right to left in an exaggerated fashion to make a joke. "Honey, he not only ain't here, I ain't sure where he is. And I'm even more sure I don't care."

Conner stepped past the open passenger door to view the right front tire, "All right, so you've got a spare, I guess?"

"In the trunk there. Got a jack and a lug wrench too. If you get as many flats as me, you don't bother putting much else in your trunk."

"OK. Well you get some clothes on that little boy while I get your tire changed and we can all get on the road."

It was dark and the mist had changed to snow when Conner finished with the tire and closed the trunk. The flakes melted as they hit the ground but Conner was anxious to get on the road before that changed. The flat tire had been totally without tread and the spare was worn unevenly with wire exposed. Conner inspected the other three tires and found them not to be much better.

"We're good to go, I guess. How far do you plan on going tonight?"

Linda had finally lit her cigarette.

"Oh, not far. Got a place just before Victor. My Dad's place really. I'm stayin' with him now. Works out good, really. The checks I get help him a little, and I do the cookin'. You know. Anyway, Mr. Conner, I sure appreciate you bein' a good Smaartin, or whatever."

"No problem Linda. Listen; do me a favor. Drive slow and carefully. I'm worried about these tires. I'll follow you in case you have another flat, and I'll just take you home if that happens."

Linda tilted her head slightly, "You are awful nice. Come on kids."

Linda put Lawrence in the car seat behind her and Sheila got in the front seat next to her mother. "Buckle up now, honey. Did you thank Mr. Conner?"

Sheila turned and made a little wave at Conner through the window. He waved back and headed to his Toyota. He followed them up the two lane road, thinking about their lives; how Linda had never had a chance to be anything other than who she was; and now neither did her kids. 'So few people break out of that family paradigm,' he thought. He was glad he came along when he did today, although he was certain Linda had handled that situation all by herself many times before.

Fifteen minutes later Linda put her right blinker on. Conner slowed behind her, hoping it wasn't another flat. He saw her hand come out the window and wave at the same time he heard the honk of her horn. Her car bounced down the two track as Conner looked for lights in the trees. A dim yellow bulb burned above the front door of a single wide. He honked his horn and headed to Jackson.

CHICAGO, ILLINOIS

October

The voice on the on the other end of the phone always made Nick Kowalski's blood pressure rise. The man said to meet him at 2:00 the following afternoon at the Fielding Museum. He told him, in a surly tone, to be on time and to be at the Lions of Tsavo exhibit. Nick's agitation could be heard in his voice when he told the man not to worry, he'd be there. 'Oh, I'm not', was the man's response.

Nick purposely arrived a few minutes early. He looked at the mounts of the lions and read the display boards about how these two behemoths had managed to kill 140 railroad workers around the turn of the last century. He started to read about the scientific enigma of why male lions in that area of Africa are maneless, and then decided he didn't give a shit. They killed a bunch of people and that was amazing, but who really cared about their hair coat for Christ sake.

Stuart appeared beside him, "Let's walk around a bit."

The two men proceeded down a corridor of continuous display cases, all designed to resemble the natural habitat of the animals they encased.

Stuart continued the conversation. "In this book you'll find an envelope. In it are your plane tickets, car rental information and some extra cash. You'll also find the home address of a man living in Denver. He is to be disposed of. It is to look like a home invasion or robbery. He is the only one we care about, but we want no potential witnesses. Anyone that happens to be in that house needs to go. Do you understand?"

Stuart was no Mr. Costello. Nick not only didn't like him, he certainly wasn't afraid of him. "I got it Stu baby. No problem."

"Good, I'll be sure to relay the fact that you've wrapped your massive intellect around this project. Your flight leaves at 11:50 tomorrow morning from Midway. You're on Southwest. No first class, chum."

Stuart handed Nick the book, pulled his ball cap down a little further over his eyes and disappeared around the corner.

JACKSON, WYOMING

October

At Victor the snow fell harder but the wind had stopped, allowing the big flakes to fall softly and stick. Conner crossed the Wyoming line; glad he hadn't much farther to go. The traffic was light and the snow turned out to be short lived, turning to rain as he descended Pine Creek Pass toward Jackson. Even the rain stopped as he turned on to 191, south of Jackson, only a few miles from Jan's.

It was 6:30 when Conner pulled his bags from the back of the SUV. The well-lit porch and smell of wood smoke were welcome sensations on a cold dark night. He dropped a bag to ring the bell when the door swung open.

"Well howdy stranger. Come on in out of the cold."

"Don't bother to ask twice, this Florida boy is about to freeze." Conner dropped his things on the floor and shut the door behind him. They hugged and Conner gave Jan a little kiss on the lips.

"Who you kiddin' with that," She reached up and held his face in her hands and kissed him hard on the mouth. "There's more to heat you up around here then that old fireplace, mister."

"That's good, because I had intended to do more than chop

wood. Damn, you're as gorgeous as ever."

"Well, thank you, sweetheart. It took you a little longer than I thought, was the pass bad?"

"No, I stopped to help a little gal with a flat tire. The driving wasn't bad."

Jan turned toward the kitchen, "Leave your bags for a minute and come finish opening the wine while I get a few things to snack on before dinner."

Jan took the wine from the refrigerator and placed the bottle on the island behind her. "Dinner won't be ready for a bit. How 'bout a glass of wine and a snack and then I'll give you a chance to get cleaned up before we eat?"

"That sounds about perfect, actually."

Jan bent over with her backside to Conner as she gathered the items from her refrigerator. He smiled at the vision in the faded jeans.

"I see you're still running and working out."

"What's that honey," Jan said, setting several things out on the island.

"Nothing, come over here."

Conner was looking at the outline of her breasts in the satin blouse as she walked toward him. They kissed again, several times, holding each other tightly.

When they separated Conner pulled off his jacket and hung it over a chair at the table. As he opened the wine he commented, "Looks like this is more of your Sonoma County stash from your trip last year. If I remember right this was a great cab."

"Good memory. Some cheese, a little dry salami, olives; want anything else."

"How about more of those sweet kisses," Conner said as he walked around the other side of the island and took her in his arms, kissing her on the mouth and then her face and gently nibbling her ear before kissing her neck. She sighed and cooed softly as he gently bit her neck.

"Oh, I'm so glad you're here, Conner, so glad."

"If I don't stop now we'll never get to the hors d'ouevres." Conner was becoming aroused and felt warm and good all over. When he pulled away from Jan he noticed that her nipples were hard and very evident against the thin satin of her blouse.

Jan took two glasses from the cupboard and Conner poured the wine as she fed him an olive. They picked up their glasses and clinked them together, nothing said, looking in to each other's eyes as they took a drink.

"It's as good as I remembered. Thanks for breaking it out."

"You're worth it. I remembered how much you liked it. As a matter of fact, I've saved it for you."

Jan pulled out one of the stools from the other side of the island and sat down. "Tell me about Elko and catch me up on the Ingleses. All's fine with them?"

The wine went down easily as they talked and ate. Conner became energized and animated as he related the story of his trip. Jan's eyes were bright as she looked intently at Conner, smiling and then laughing aloud when he described the wild horse chase and the terror he experienced baling off the steep sided ravine, cussing Bud all the way to the bottom. Jan knew horses and she knew the Elko terrain, all of which allowed for a clear vision of Conner's adventure. They laughed and talked through all of the food and into their second glass of wine before Jan mentioned dinner again.

"I need to turn the oven off and get the rest of dinner ready. Why don't you get your stuff put away and get cleaned up if you like, while I do that?"

"Sounds perfect. What is for dinner?"

"I made mandarin chicken. You've had it before and liked it; if you don't remember."

"Yea, I do. It's very good. You make it with wild rice I think."

"Yuppers. Same thing tonight, but with some fresh broccoli. OK?"

"Perfect."

Jan stood and headed toward the oven but Conner put his hand on her belly as she passed him and turned him in to her. They kissed for several minutes before Jan said, "Enough of that for now unless you want rubber chicken."

Conner took his glass of wine and retrieved his things from the living room on his way to the master bath. The bathroom reflected Jan's creative style; a combination of tile and marble, spacious but with a warm, comfortable feel to it. He undressed to a pleasant mental image of her soaking in the old-fashioned pedestal tub as she looked out the window toward the mountains.

Conner stood on the marble floor of the big open shower, the heat and pressure of the water on his back and neck put him in a trance, making it difficult to get out. Finally he stepped out of the shower and drained his wine glass as he toweled off. He hung the towel on the hook and decided to shave before getting dressed. With lathered face he was wiping the steam off the mirror when Jan entered with another open bottle of wine.

"That is one good looking naked man I have in my bathroom. I may get my camera to capture the memory." Jan poured more wine in to Conner's glass.

"Don't mock your guests, it's not polite," responded Conner, turning his head but keeping his body facing the sink and mirror.

"Don't give me that modest shit. You look half your age and you know it." Jan set the wine bottle on the counter next to Conner's glass and reached over to put a hand on his waist. She pushed against his hip, turning him toward her. Jan gave him a big smile, almost laughing, thinking it funny that his face was lathered white, as he stood there naked in front of her. The expression on her face changed as her gaze moved slowly downward. The smile disappeared and she pursed her lips as she took in his broad chest and flat, muscled stomach. A faint moan of appreciation left her lips as she looked at his penis and she cocked her head slightly to the side, reaching out with one hand to cup his balls in her hand.

"I might be the luckiest woman in Wyoming tonight."

"You're sweet, baby, but I'm the lucky one," Conner placed his hands on her arms, just below her shoulders.

"Shhhh." Jan said as she held the finger of her other hand to her lips. She then squatted down on the ground in front of him and took him in to her mouth. She played with her tongue and sucked while one hand held her balance against his thigh and the other hand still cupped his balls. Conner's penis began to grow and get harder in her warm mouth until it was firm and large but not yet erect.

Suddenly Jan stood upright and said "Dinner's ready. You are such a bad boy." She was walking out of the bathroom as she said, "Clothes are optional at the dinner table tonight."

"Tease!" Conner threw a hand towel at her exiting behind.

He turned back to the sink and leaned forward toward the mirror to start shaving. Now fully aroused, his erection bumped the counter in front of him. "Damn, that's a little cold."

Dinner was delicious. The conversation was nonstop, punctuated with smiles, laughter, and touching. It became obvious that the dishes would have to wait till morning. Conner stood and took Jan's hand, urging her to her feet.

"It's time for me to be forward, now." Still holding her hand he led her toward the bedroom. "But luckily for you, I'm not a tease."

They made their way to the side of the bed and Conner sat on the edge, facing Jan. He started unbuttoning her blouse slowly, not wishing to rush any aspect of what was about to occur. She just looked down at him, holding his head in her hands and gently stroking the sides of his face. He pulled her unbuttoned blouse back as she slid her arms to her side. Her breasts exposed, he looked at them, drinking in the beautiful, sexy vision before cupping them in his hands. He began to kiss her left breast, using his tongue and his lips all around her breast before sucking her nipple. He played with and teased her breast until she raised her forearms close to her sides, goose bumps covering them, as she cooed softly. Then he went to her right breast, repeating the same motions with his lips and tongue until finally sucking and nibbling the nipple. As he increased the intensity her knees buckled slightly and she threw her head back, moaning as she did so.

Conner unbuttoned her jeans as he continued to enjoy her breasts. He pulled his head away just long enough to work her jeans down over her hips. Jan helped by wriggling her body as he gently tugged at her jeans, finally kicking them off behind her several feet. Conner took his hands and put them on her hips and suddenly, firmly spun her around, facing her away from him. The quickness of the movement brought a little laugh from her lips.

"Now what are you up to?" she said gently, not with the slightest objection.

"I missed this ass. And it is so gorgeous, baby." Conner pulled her panties off and let them drop to the floor. He slid off the bed so that he was nearly sitting on the floor, still holding her ass in both hands, admiring it, letting himself become even more aroused by it. He then kissed her on one cheek and gently bit her on the other. She let out a little yelp and he spun her around again, quickly and firmly. He let his butt sink to the carpet and reached behind her, pulling her into him while holding the cheeks of her ass in both of his hands. She almost fell against him as she bent her legs forward bringing her knees against the side of the bed. His face was between her legs, the perfect level for what he wanted to do.

Conner began licking and kissing her very gently at first. As she became more aroused he began licking more, and harder, and with a more intense rhythm. He held her ass and helped her little thrusts in to his face as he continued to lick her. He pressed his lip covered upper teeth hard in to her, just above her clitoris as he continued to lick below, strongly, intensifying the rhythm even more. She started to quiver and her legs became noticeably weak. He had almost her entire body weight in his hands as she rocked forward in an intense orgasm. He didn't stop the licking or the pressure from his mouth as she screamed out and had to grab the his shoulders to keep from falling over. Finally, her entire body shivered and she involuntarily pulled her pelvis back, away from his mouth; too sensitive to take any more.

"Damn, you are unbelievable Conner," she whispered finally.

"Me? Get up here you sexy thing."

Conner had slid on to the bed and was pulling her after him by the hand. They lay back on the bed and kissed and fondled for a while. When Conner had decided she wasn't too sensitive any more, he propped her head on the pillows and went back between her legs. He teased her for a while before intensifying the rhythm and incorporating his fingers along with his mouth; the result was another orgasm more intense than the first. After her climax, he simply held her trembling body in his arms. Conner could finally wait no more, he had to have her; he wanted to be inside of her. He knew Jan loved being on top of him and he gently guided her up and himself in. The fit was perfect for both of them and as he thrust, she rocked; slowly, taking their time and savoring. When Jan started to get closer to another orgasm and her rocking became more intense, Conner leaned forward and pulled her in to him. He began sucking on a nipple as Jan moaned wildly. His thrusts were becoming quicker and involuntary as her rocking did the same. They exploded in ecstasy; noisily, sweating, culminating in involuntary, jerking movements and finally sighs. She lay forward on top of him; both of them were spent and breathing hard. She laid there for several minutes before sliding off of him and pulling the covers over them both. Conner stayed on his back and Jan on her side, tucked in his arm with her head on his shoulder. They fell asleep almost immediately.

Conner woke first and lay there thinking about whether to

get up or not. Jan had moved away from him during the night and was on her side, facing the other way. He turned on his side to face her, but could barely make out her form in the dark room. He listened to the comforting sound of her slow, rhythmic breathing as he thought how much she had come to mean to him, how much he enjoyed being with her. If the geography of their lives were different, he knew he wouldn't hesitate to marry her. He needed someone in his life again; someone to combat the loneliness he felt. It was time to talk frankly about these things; it was time to make some changes so that he could have another woman in his life. The thought of addressing this today made him feel good, relaxed. He fell back to sleep.

He awoke to find Jan's face only inches from his, staring at him. He saw she was smiling as his eyes focused.

"You're an incredible lover, Mr. Murphy. I haven't felt that good nor slept that good in...Well let's see, since you were here last."

Conner smiled back, "that was fabulous. You have an extraordinary body, baby."

"Well, thank you, sir. There are a couple surgeons that would say thank you as well."

"You get most of the credit and you know it." Conner brought his face to hers and kissed her on the lips. "Are we ever getting up today, lazy bones?"

"I don't know why we should. What time is it?"

There was just enough light in the room for Conner to see his watch without the light, "7:00, lazy bones."

"All right, I've had enough of your insults," Jan punched Conner in the arm and swung her legs over the side of the bed. Looking back at him, "Well, you don't seem to be moving, you lazy old thing."

"You think I'm going to miss the opportunity to watch you walk across the room naked? I'll just lie here while you get your robe," Conner bounced his eyebrows in Groucho Marks' fashion as he spoke.

THE LITTLE BUREAUCRAT

"I'd tell you that you're a cad, but I like the compliment too much." Jan leaned in and kissed him on the cheek before getting up. She walked around the bed to the bathroom, looking back before she disappeared to smile at her lover and bounce her eyebrows in return.

Conner was thinking how lucky he was as he pulled on the lounging pants from the night before and headed to the kitchen. After putting the coffee on he stood at the sink and looked out toward the Tetons, absorbing the beauty of the morning. Everything was covered in a thin blanket of snow and the early morning sun gave it a subtle pink hue. As Conner stood there a familiar thought returned to him; how fortunate he had been to see so many beautiful places. Conner was still standing there when Jan came in.

"You want any breakfast, or just coffee?"

"I'll get dressed and then you can tell me the plan for the day over breakfast." Conner took his coffee with him to the bathroom.

The plan was simple in that there was little they had to do. A gallery client had recently purchased a painting that Jan needed to deliver to their home. The client lived in Driggs, Idaho, about an hour to the northwest, an area Conner had mentioned as wanting to see.

"So you see, this is perfect timing," Jan said. "And I know a great spot for lunch where the food is good and the view is spectacular."

After dropping the painting they explored the country on the northern side of the Tetons. Fall was well established and the air was crisp and the scenery beautiful. They both enjoyed the drive and Conner felt a sense of contentment. He acknowledged it, smiling, as he held Jan's hand. Hunger finally persuaded them to head toward the restaurant.

The hostess led them to a table by the large picture window. The last patches of snow, fading in to islands of melting ice, glistened brightly in the sunlight. The rocky crowns of the majestic peaks stuck boldly through the cover of snow and seemed to literally reach in to the heavens. Conner winked at Jan in acknowledgment of her perfect choice for lunch. He then ordered a bottle of sauvignon blanc and explained to the waitress that they wanted to enjoy their wine for a while before ordering.

"Well, at least some people have some money left. That was a gorgeous house your Mrs. Sutter has."

"Yea, I guess. But you know it's amazing, things are not the same anymore. The people that I used to call 'bullet proof', those that I thought had more money than God, even they seem to be slowly drying up."

Conner sipped his wine.

"How's the gallery doing. It seems tough to be in any high end business anymore; so many have gone under it seems. Hell, there are entire industries that hardly exist anymore; private jet manufacturers, yacht builders. It's unbelievable."

A couple was walking by the table and Jan smiled, vaguely knowing them. "You know Conner, I'm very lucky. When Roger died the insurance benefit set me up quite well. I really don't have to work. The gallery makes a little money and I think it's important for me to stay engaged. I've always enjoyed it and I've got a great staff that lets me leave when I want and, within reason, for as long as I want."

The waitress brought a basket of fresh warm bread and butter and politely acknowledged that they weren't ready to order.

Jan continued, "As to the state of business; yeah it's off. Compared to the old days, it's off horribly. The artists charge only half of what they used to and then on top of that, we only sell about half of what we used to. The math doesn't work very well. I guess, for once, our economy never will recover."

Conner handed Jan a slice of buttered bread. "Well, even this optimist might agree. You can't squash free enterprise, build huge government with massive debt and entitlements, and expect to recover."

THE LITTLE BUREAUCRAT

"Whatever happened to 'It's the economy, stupid'? It is amazing that these people stay in power."

"Well, according to Sean, and I think he's right, they focused on power while the citizens have worried about the economy. Give him two hours and he'll have you convinced. Remember back to ASPON, now there is Citizens First and others, federally funded supposed public service organizations that are used to corrupt the electoral process beyond comprehension. You add to that, the massive number of people that have been added to the public dole, the huge increases in government employee union memberships, and it becomes impossible to get these people out of power."

"And at the expense of our freedoms," Jan said.

"Sean tells frightening tales of how corrupt the system has become, the coercion with organized crime..."

Jan reached across and took Conner's hand.

"I'm going to the ladies room. I don't want to spoil the mood. No more politics when I get back." When she rose she leaned over and kissed him on the cheek.

Conner was glad she ended the discussion. He had wanted to talk about them today, not politics, for Christ's sake. He sipped his wine and looked out across the meadows toward the mountains, relaxing again. He smiled at himself as he acknowledged feeling anxious talking about their relationship. He reasoned his nervousness was testimony to how much he cared for her.

Jan had been widowed one month after Conner had, four years ago. She had been married to Roger Thomas for twenty-two years before he died of a massive heart attack playing summer league softball. Conner had met Jan that next summer in Steamboat Springs at an art gallery opening. A mutual friend owned the new gallery and Jan had come in to help with the event. They had gotten along from the minute they met and a romance began to flourish with Jan making several trips to Florida and Conner to Wyoming. On one of his visits they had driven to Elko and spent a week at the Ingles's ranch, where Conner's friends embraced her whole-heartedly. But the logistics of a long distance relationship had prevented Conner from taking the next step.

Jan sat back at the table, "Isn't this a marvelous view."

"Yes it is." He looked back toward Jan. "Listen, Bud asked me one day last week if I had a woman in my life yet." Conner took Jan's hand in his. He had her full attention. "I told him that I didn't have anyone in my life that I felt a strong connection of sharing with. Someone that truly wants to share my life; the little things, the big things; a genuine interest in me. Someone that appreciates me. And someone that I feel the same way about. What I realized after I spoke was...well, that it isn't true. I have found that in you."

Conner laughed at his next thought, "You know, Bubba says the only thing men truly want from women is sex and to be appreciated." He squeezed her hand. "Bubba's pretty basic."

They both laughed and looked in to each other's eyes for several seconds before Jan spoke.

"I don't know how many times Bubba may have told you that, but I was there one of those times. We were out on his patio watching the sun set that evening, talking. Do you remember what he said about women that night?"

"Maybe. Well at least I might remember it if you remind me."

Jan squeezed Conner's hand a little as she continued, "He said all women really want is to feel that they are the most important woman in that man's life and that he will protect her. Conner, I know you will protect me and if you tell me that I am the most important woman in your life, I will believe you."

"You truly are, honey. I love you and I want to figure out how we can be together all the time."

Jan now reached across the table with her other hand to hold both of his. "I love you, too. I'd like that very much. And by the way, I love the sex, too. I'm not sure that's just a man thing."

Conner laughed and squeezed her hands as the waitress

approached. They pulled away from each other and both grabbed their menus, realizing they hadn't even looked at them.

"Give us a minute, please, we haven't done our homework yet."

"Take your time," the waitress said as she poured more wine.

Jan said as she looked over the top of her menu at Conner, "There's no reason at all we can't make this work you know."

Jan and Conner had returned late from Driggs and made a light supper. Conner sat with a cup of coffee and called his son as Jan headed for a bath.

"Hey, Sean, how's it going?"

"Hey, Dad, how are you? How's Jan doing?"

"Actually great, both of us. It was a gorgeous day up here today. Cold, I guess, but really beautiful. We went over to Driggs, Idaho and had lunch and drove around that country a little. It was tremendous day, really. How was your appointment yesterday?"

Sean's response was muffled, "I'm gonna change phones, Dad. Hang on a second." A minute passed, "You there? I'm sorry. I didn't want to rehash yesterday where Mo could hear me."

"That bad?" Conner was concerned.

"That frustrating. This public health system is unbelievable, Dad, just un-fucking-believable. We were there from 1:00 until nearly 4:30 before we even saw anyone. Then, just as before, no doctor. At least we saw a physician's assistant; I guess that's a step up from a nurse. Naturally we had to go through all the same history again, same bullshit exam. I mean what the fuck are they going to tell you about headaches by repeating the same little chicken shit physical? Sorry, but I'm getting all worked up just thinking about it again."

"Hey, son, you don't have to apologize to me."

"I know. Thanks. Well the day finally ends up with some progress in that we got an appointment scheduled with a neurologist. And through him the physician's assistant was able

to prescribe some other pain meds that seem to be helping a little bit. Unfortunately, they also kick her ass; you know, make her groggy."

"Well hopefully the neurologist will have some answers or at least know where to go next. You know; diagnostics and such."

"Yea, but Dad, listen to this shit. Six weeks. Six fucking weeks. She is miserable, I'm telling you six weeks is ridiculous."

"There has to be something that can be done about that, this sounds like more of an emergency then to just be put on a list."

"Well, I've started making some calls. I can't believe that I can't find someone to budge this, at least a little."

Conner sighed. "Sean, I don't even know who to call. All of my MD buddies have retired, most of them prematurely because of this stupid PHA, they just couldn't deal with the bureaucracy. Hell, I don't even have a personal physician anymore. Not even a urologist, which is really stupid for someone my age."

"Dad, I hate to tell you, but you really are out of the loop. No one has their own doctor anymore. There is absolutely only one way to have your own doctor; get elected to congress." Conner was quiet; he felt sad; worse, he felt impotent. He'd had many conversations about the public health care system, but they were just that, conversations. None of it had been personal, until now.

"Damn, Sean, I'm so sorry you are dealing with this. I'm sorry for Mo and how bad she feels. Is there anything I can do?"

"No, not really, Dad. It will be OK in the long run. It's just a bitch dealing with the frustration of so much bureaucracy. But listen, I won't be coming to Colorado next week to hunt. I just can't leave Mo right now."

"Of course not, I understand. We haven't missed a year in a long time; we were probably due. I'm headed down there Friday, going to drive through in one day from here. Call me here or at the cabin if anything changes, OK? You've got Jan's number, right? Well, hell, my cell works here just fine; it's at the cabin that it's so bad." He paused, "I'm rambling,' sorry. Take care. I love you. Kiss my grandbabies for me and tell Mo I love her, OK?"

"I can do all that. Take care and have fun. Don't let this put a damper on your good time. You going to hunt anyway?"

"Yea. Hell I don't know. I'll see how I feel when I get there."

"Good night, Dad, I love you."

"Good night, buddy."

Jan came in to the room as he was hanging up. "How's Sean and Mo, doing?" She looked in to his eyes. "Everyone all right?"

Conner stuck his hand out and guided Jan on to his lap. Jan rubbed his shoulder as he talked. Concern and frustration was evident on his face and in his voice. When he finished she held his face to her chest, thinking of a friend of hers that has been on a waiting list for eleven months for a hip replacement. She said nothing; another tale of woe was not what Conner needed.

"So anyway, Sean won't be meeting me at the cabin this week with all of this going on."

"Are you going anyway? You could stay here the extra time."

"No, I need to go. I have to winterize the place because I won't be going back until the spring. And, I don't know, I may hunt."

Jan gave him a kiss on the forehead "I tried."

"Listen, since it's not a guy trip any more, why don't you come with me? Can you schedule being away from the gallery next week?"

"Sure, there's really nothing special going on right now. I'd like that a lot." She put both arms around him and kissed him on the mouth.

Conner was wide-awake at 2:00 a.m. He had fallen asleep after they'd made love, but now his thoughts were relentless. He gave up after an hour and made his way to the living room with a cup of decaf. He stared into the darkness, thoughts of

Sean tearing at him.

"Unbelievable, un-fucking-believable. How could things be this fucked up? How could the system become this broken?"

It was still early when they arrived at the crepe house. Conner's teeth were hurting and he worked his jaw as Jan watched him out of the corner of her eye. She reached over and took his hand. He returned her smile, wanting the day to be right for her.

Conner complimented Jan on her restaurant choice, but she knew the Kona coffee was a bigger hit than the crepes. They had planned a long hike on one of Jan's favorite trails in West Yellowstone but at breakfast they decided since Jan was going to Colorado they would return Conner's rental car first.

Conner struggled with his anger as he exited the Hertz office at Jackson Hole Airport. The excessive drop fee for not taking the car on to Denver had poured gasoline on the embers. Anger was close to the surface as he walked toward Jan's car, involuntarily shaking his head, muttering. "Forget about it, damn it, enjoy the day".

Jan was behind the wheel, "You want to drive, hon?"

"No, I'm good if you are. You know where we're going. I'll be the tourist."

"Sounds fine to me. Sit back and relax."

The back of the SUV was filled with empty cardboard boxes for use at the gallery. Impossible to see directly behind her, Jan used her side mirrors as she slowly backed up.

Bam! A loud bang on the back window caused them both to jump. As Jan leaned her head back and placed her hand over her heart a big man surfaced at her door and yelled at them through the window. Jan looked toward Conner as the tirade continued. The repeated 'motherfuckers' and 'fuck yous' were easily heard over the CD. Conner's eye twitched slightly. The man's face became red and contorted with malice as Jan looked back at him and began to roll down her window. Conner put his hand on her arm to stop her. He opened his door and got out of the car.

The big man had a large head and a round face covered with a three-day beard. He had the appearance of a bouncer from big city nightclub. The obscenities continued as Conner came around the front of the car.

"Fuckin' bitch drivers, what the…" he stopped when he noticed Conner. The bouncer had a friend who was approaching from behind him. Both men eyed Conner as they tried to assess what he was capable of.

Conner had realized that at first the guy had a legitimate complaint, but he had taken it too far. He had become unreasonable and abusive. A familiar calm overtook Conner as he rounded the front of the car. He looked in to the big man's eyes as he walked forward, waiting for, hoping for one more 'fuck you'.

Conner was not conscious of how he appeared; the fire in his eyes, the hard, half smile on his face, the purpose in his step. The man was quiet and had taken two steps backward as Conner approached. Conner quickly glanced at the man's friend, now standing beside and a little behind the big man. His lip curled into a sneer as he looked at the smaller man. Then the half smile returned to his face when he looked back at the bouncer. His mind was moving quickly, enjoying immensely the vision of kneeling on the big guy's chest and punching his face repeatedly, not caring what his friend might try to do. He was going to beat this big, fat, noisy, rude son-of-a-bitch in to a pulp. He'd worry about the friend after that.

Conner looked straight into the eyes of the bigger man as he started talking; still hoping for one more surly remark.

"You were standing directly behind the car when the lady backed up. She couldn't see you in her mirrors. She backed up very slowly."

The big man's mouth opened slowly as he looked in to Conner's eyes. He had no doubt of Conner's intent and everything about his presence spoke to the fact that he could do it.

"Sorry, man. I was wrong. Shouldn't have lost my shit. Tell the lady I'm sorry."

"You tell her." Conner looked toward Jan and motioned to roll down her window. "Hey listen, sorry about all the cussin' and such. You look like a nice lady."

Jan still felt bad for scaring the big man. "I'm sorry, too. I couldn't see you."

"No harm, lady, no harm. You both have a nice day." The man looked back at Conner, contritely, as if to say, 'OK, that works for you?'

Conner's expression didn't change, "Yea, that's fine." Disappointed, he turned and walked back to his side of the car. The two strangers talked in whispers as they continued toward the rental car office.

"You alright?" Jan asked as he shut his door and reached for his seat belt.

"I'm good. Just couldn't tolerate that rude bastard; not today." Conner was trying to give Jan a broad smile. "Be careful backin' up."

"Got it. Let's go for a hike, baby". Jan said, returning the smile.

DENVER, COLORADO
October

Thomas Little wasn't a physically impressive individual, something which ran contrary to the tenor of his voice; its deep timber conjured the vision of a big, rugged man. No one listening to the radio assumed he was a slightly built, five feet seven inches tall. The medium suited him well; his deep voice and strong projection gave the perception of authority with no threat of his almost nerdy appearance undermining the image.

Little entered the Denver talk radio market two years earlier and had recently signed a contract for national syndication. His programming style resonated with the public and his message was well received. Prior to hosting a talk radio show he had been on the fringes of journalism, mostly of the Internet variety, the 'new' media. Then came a news story that brought him into the national limelight; the sting operation of the community organization network, ASPON.

The mainstream press had done their best to ignore the story when it first broke. When finally addressing it, the original spin was to be critical of the young people that had exposed so much corruption within ASPON. However, talk radio and several conservative blog sites beat the drum until it became well publicized. Finally, even NBC and CNN were forced to report the deep-seated corruption within the organization or look very foolish ignoring it. Thomas Little had been at the forefront of the bloggers on this issue; his relentlessness and clever writing was pivotal in bringing it to a national consciousness. The public furor finally escalated to the point that conservative members of congress had enough momentum to dismantle federal funding for ASPON. His involvement in such a tremendous story was the tipping point for Little's career.

He next surfaced on the national scene the following year, as part of a group of Internet journalists who exposed Tyrell Dant, the Alternative Energy Czar. Mr. Dant and several cronies had created a company to build wind turbines. In fact they had no real physical address and created nothing. As Energy Czar, Mr. Dant funneled millions of dollars of federal funds through the phony corporation and into the hands of himself and his conspirators. Thomas Little exposed their scheme resulting in several indictments.

These events created considerable notoriety for Little as he ventured in to Denver talk radio. He loved the bully pulpit radio provided and committed to taking it as far as possible. However, he didn't abandon the investigative work he'd done previously, and was presently immersed in an investigation to expose the corruption permeating Citizens First; the dream child of the same powerful people that had been instrumental in the inception and orchestration of ASPON.

The powers behind ASPON realized soon after the 2008 election that the days of that organization were numbered. Too many voter fraud allegations brought against them by too many states to withstand the public scrutiny and pressure from congress. The prostitution sting had been the final blow. The power brokers were fully cognizant of the incredible advantage the organization had afforded them in 'winning' elections and in rallying public support from the constituencies they targeted. The ability to wield this much power and siphon this much money had reached well beyond any of their expectations. It was a dream come true and now a reality they weren't willing to abandon. Months before ASPON's scandals became a threat to its existence; the people behind it were busy laying the groundwork for other, similar organizations. ASPON never dismantled, it merely splintered and took on a new name in each chapter or region. These renamed offices of the old organization became separate 'community organizations' thus avoiding the scrutiny as well as the indictments that besieged ASPON. Citizens First was the umbrella that these splinters affiliated under, guarantying central control.

Just as ASPON had involved itself heavily in voter registration and brought voters to the polls in 2008, the affiliates under Citizens First picked up the torch in future elections. The organization was instrumental in many states in registering new, first time voters. In many congressional districts there was a high correlation between the new voter registration and unexpected election results.

Thomas Little was one of many who were deeply suspicious of the link between these community organizations and Citizens First. In spite of his efforts he was refused any cooperation from the attorney generals in many of the states in which voting irregularities occurred; being told there was 'little indication to warrant investigation of the community organizations'. The fact that Citizens First was a layer further back provided adequate cover, adequate because both the justice department and the press were too lazy, or too complicit, to dig any deeper than the surface.

It became incumbent upon private citizens, and reporters of integrity, to investigate these claims. Little and his associates were one such determined group. However, Citizens First had been able to accomplish things that ASPON had not. It had a much more sophisticated structure and enacted more thoughtful strategies, which weren't as likely to expose intent. It removed from its ranks the blatantly foolish 'volunteers' and low level workers that had become such easy targets during the investigation of ASPON. The government funding that flowed in to the treasure chest of Citizens First took more circuitous and ambivalent pathways, making identification of funding conduits very difficult to unwind.

Those that controlled Citizens First had learned valuable lessons. They had consolidated their power. They knew to be vigilant against threats. They knew to protect their organization they must be proactive, aggressively proactive.

Two and half hours from Chicago the Southwest flight arrived on time. The Hertz shuttle waited at the rental car shuttle island on the west side of DIA.

"Fontaine, gold member" he said as he threw his bag on a shelf and took a seat. The air was crisp and cool, made more so by the wind blowing off the Rockies. The big man hardly noticed; being a Chicago native the cold never bothered him. He'd only brought a light jacket and it was still in his bag.

Not about to leave any evidence in his rental car of where he'd been Nick used the GPS in his phone. He entered the street address that Stuart had given him in Cherry Creek on the south side of down town. Nick left the terminal and drove on to Pena Blvd, merging on to I-70, headed toward Denver.

As he headed west toward the mountains he realized he'd been looking at a cloudbank, not the mountains as he had thought. It struck him that he didn't give a shit about seeing the mountains; nature was over rated as far as Nick was concerned. 'Leave me in a big city the rest of my life and I'll be just fine. Cities got liquor, food, pussy, the occasional snort of coke, and a ball game every now and then. What the fuck do you need with a forest, or a mountain or any of that shit?' He couldn't see it.

It was mid-afternoon with minimal traffic around the city. He would drive to this Little guy's address, get a feel for the house and the neighborhood, and then go get something to eat. "I don't know how that goddamn Southwest plans to keep any customers if they starve 'em all to death," he muttered. Turning south on I-25 he headed toward downtown and exited on to 6th Ave west toward Cherry Creek.

It was a weekday and the neighborhoods were quiet. The occasional school bus made its slow trek through the suburbs and Nick impatiently turned to avoid getting behind one. His turn led to a cul-de-sac and he had to return to the same street; which at least allowed his GPS to end its repetitious 'recalculating'. The school bus was gone. Three girls walked down the street together, talking as they carried their obligatory backpacks, oblivious to Nick's car. After passing them he slowed the car, checking street numbers on mailboxes as his phone told him his destination was two hundred feet on the right. Nick knew to verify what he heard, it'd been wrong before. The black numbers were evident on the white pillar. He examined the house for less than a minute before he drove away and took the first left.

Nick stopped his car in front of a vacant house. He pulled on his jacket and gloves as he walked over to the 'for sale' sign and pretended to write down the information. Stuffing his hands in to his jacket pockets he continued to look at the house, walking to the driveway on the far side. Then, promptly, he turned away from the house, walked down the driveway to the street and kept walking past his car, back toward Westwood Avenue, purposefully but not hurriedly. No one was on the sidewalks or in their yards.

On the front porch of the Little house he pretended to ring the bell. He waited, quietly, not wanting to draw the attention of someone that may be in the house. After a minute, he walked around the side of the house toward the back. There was no fence, 'good, probably no dog.' There were neither window stickers nor lawn signs warning of a security system. At the back of the house there was a door to the garage. Nick turned the knob. Unlocked. He peered inside, no cars. He returned to the front door and pretended to ring the bell again. Nick used this opportunity to turn and look out at the neighborhood, assessing the surroundings while he casually waited for someone to come to the door.

Confident he had learned what he came for, he crossed the lawn to the mailbox. Taking some paper out of his pocket, he opened the box and put the paper in, but withdrew it along with a letter and stuffed both in his jacket pocket as he turned back up the street. Nick had learned long ago that the best way to be inconspicuous was to act purposeful; don't hesitate, don't look around.

Once in the car, he sat back in the seat, closed his eyes and thought about what he had learned. After a minute he pulled the envelope from his pocket and read the front; Mr. and Mrs. Thomas Little. "Shit, married, a little more complicated but expected. Hopefully, no kids. Fuck it; like Costello said, I'm making more money than I've ever dreamed of, I'll handle what comes".

He pulled from the curb and drove down the street, opening the letter as he went. It was an invitation to a wedding two months from now. There was a separate notice explaining where the reception would be and stating regrets only. Nick laughed out loud as he threw the invitation out the window.

"Oh, I better call with their regrets. After all, I'm the only one that knows."

Back on I-70, Nick exited on to Sheridan. The rental car map showed a lake at Berkley Park that was worth investigating. The park and rec center was on his left as he turned on to 46th Street and parked between the playground and the lake. A young mother sat on a bench watching two toddlers play on the swings as a jogger ran on the path that hugged the shoreline. A number of cars were parked in front of the rec center but Nick saw no other people. He got out of his car and walked down the sidewalk toward the edge of the lake. Having removed his coat and gloves the late afternoon air braced him as he rubbed his open hands together. The water was only a short distance from the jogging path and he crossed it to get to the bank. As he picked up a rock and threw it out in to the lake he unconsciously nodded his head, pleased that he had taken the detour. Everything was ready; it was time to go get something to eat, a room, and a nap.

Nick drove three blocks to a nearby McDonalds and it was nearly five o'clock when he got back on the road. He was about to have his first experience with Denver rush hour. Most times he'd be furious with himself to have gotten mired in stop and go traffic but Nick was on a job and when he worked he was always calm, almost patient.

Finally exiting the snarl on the east side of Denver, he left I-70 at Airport Blvd. He had selected a hotel near the airport, convenient for his early morning flight and it should provide a parking lot full of rental cars. Nick knew that people were less likely to notice someone driving off in their rental as opposed to their own vehicle.

No one was behind the counter in the lobby. Nick leaned over the desk to peer toward the back as he rang the bell. A young Asian woman sprang up from behind the desk nearly hitting Nick in the head with hers. An involuntary gasp escaped her lips, startled and frightened by his size and features. Her face flushed as she apologized and her voice trembled slightly as she asked to help him.

As Nick handed her his ID and credit card she hardly looked at him, still embarrassed and a little afraid. It wasn't the first time a woman had behaved in such a manner around the big man from Chicago, but he didn't like it any more this time. His teeth were clenched as he scribbled an illegible signature.

"That's room 308, Mr. Fontaine. The elevators are behind you and to the left. Will you need a shuttle to the airport or directions for the morning?" There was no eye contact as she slid the small envelope containing the keys across the counter.

Nick said nothing. He took the keys, reached down for his bag and walked to the elevator.

"Gook bitch. Don't worry; you won't have to look at me, slope head. I'll be giving it to you from behind so I can pound your slant eyed face in to the wall at the same time, you fuckin' bitch."

Thinking about doing to the clerk what she so deserved made Nick feel better. It also made him horny. He thought about calling an escort service to get the edge off but decided against it. Such activity could draw attention, especially since he had a tendency to get carried away. More than once a pimp had shown up at Nick's room to settle up for damages done to his product. Invariably, it was a regretful decision for the pimp.

Once in his room, Nick threw his bag on the floor and walked over to the TV. He hit the movie menu to see if there were any good ones to bide his time. 'Vin Diesel's latest sci-fi action thriller; that'll work.' Before starting the movie he decided on a hot shower and pondered jerking off. He decided not to, enjoying his pent up energy right now and thought he might need it for later. Besides he wasn't sure what lay ahead at the Little house, maybe that's where he'd find relief; the thought made him smile. After drying off, he wrapped the towel around his waist and stretched out on the bed to watch his movie. That fuckin' Vin Diesel, Nick thought to himself, now he can make a movie.

He had dozed off after the movie and it was 10:30 p.m. when he woke. It was too early for his job, but he was hungry again. He'd go to the bar and grill down the street where he could kill some time and get something to eat.

The restaurant was dark with a long bar at the far end past the dining room. It was a room full of rectangular wooden tables, each adorned with a napkin dispenser, salt and pepper shakers and a bottle of Louisiana Hot Sauce. No one was at the tables. He watched himself in the mirror as he approached the bar and grabbed a stool at the end. The bartender, a tall, skinny kid, barely twenty-one himself, brought him a bar menu and explained that the main kitchen was closed.

"What can I get you to drink", the young man asked.

"Just give me a coke." Nick's expression revealed disgust as he pointed to the bar menu and asked, "Is any of this shit any good."

"The hot dogs are good, they're those big all beef park franks, and actually the nachos aren't bad either; but I'm not sure I'd recommend anything else, really."

"All right I'll tell you what, get me that coke and bring me two hot dogs and the nachos."

"They're big ole hot dogs, Mr. You want one at a time to be sure?"

"Do I look like I'd fill up that easy, kid? Where's the shitter?" Nick slid off of his stool, as the bartender pointed toward the front door.

"Go past the door and around to the left."

A Coke waited for him when he returned. As he took a drink from his glass he surveyed the bar for the first time. A bald headed man wearing a suit and tie sat at the other end; his tie was pulled loose around his neck and he was mostly interested in stirring his drink. He had all the appearance of weary business traveler; likely had walked over from one of the hotels on that street, like Nick had. Two women had come in while Nick was in the restroom and were seated at the bar midway between him and the bald man. Both were wearing dark pants suits and also had the look of business travelers. The one with his back to Nick was doing all of the talking; very animated with hands flying and bouncing on her stool, all of which had her friend laughing out loud.

Nick looked them over while he waited for his food. The talker had too big of an ass. 'Why the hell would you wear those pants with that ass? Stupid bitch. Her only hope is if she has some big titties to match that ass, then she might be worth fuckin'.' He was trying to get a look past the fat one at her friend when his food arrived.

"Here you are, sir. Let me fill that Coke up for you."

Nick looked the young bartender up and down as he filled the glass from the fountain dispenser. "What's your name kid?"

"Michael." The young man offered an outstretched hand, "How 'bout you, what's your name."

Nick looked at him for a full two seconds and then looked at the bartender's hand for two seconds more before taking it in his. "Don't worry about my name Michael. I'll never be back here." He kept a firm grip on the young man's hand as he continued. "You ain't a bad lookin' kid. But you got a little piss ass mustache like my grandmother used to have."

Michael was starting to blush; intimidated by the grip the big man had on his hand. "Shave that piece of shit off so you don't look like such a pussy. Try growing it again in a few years; maybe it'll work then. But if it still looks like shit, have enough sense to shave it again, for Christ's sake. There's nothin' looks worse than a half ass moustache." With that he let go of Michael's hand. "That's the best fuckin' tip you'll get tonight."

The young man almost fell over backwards when Nick let go of his hand, not realizing he had been pulling back until the big man let go.

"Uh, yea, thanks," he said as he walked toward the other end of the bar, suddenly interested in helping the other customers as he held his right hand in his left, trying to rub the pain out of it.

While Nick ate his food he decided neither of the two women were worth fucking. 'Unless, of course, I had 'em both at the same time and they were into some kinky lesbo shit. Yea, actually that might work'.At midnight he paid his tab with cash and exited the bar.

It was only two blocks back to his hotel. He was pleased to see that the parking lot had continued to fill up over the past two hours. Using a room key to access a side door, he took the stairwell up to his room. Throwing his carryon bag on to the bed, he slid a large hand under the folded clothes, lifting them out and placing them on the end of the bed. His hard rubber jimmy and thin leather gloves were on the bottom. He set them next to his clothes and then grabbed the small flashlight and empty knife sheath before turning the bag over. Two supports were built in to the bottom of the bag, which ran parallel to its length. Nick took the thumb and index finger of his right hand and firmly gripped part of one of those hard rubber supports. It took all of his considerable strength to pry the end away from the bag while simultaneously pulling before a portion of the support came free.

He held it admiringly in his hand as he muttered, "This is the best set up that Johnny Spano ever gave me".

Nick was holding an eight-inch knife in his hand. Half of the length consisted of the hard rubber handle, which was only about a half-inch in depth and an inch in width. The double-edged blade made up the other four inches. It had been disguised perfectly when residing in its metal lined sheath within the rubber support at the bottom of the bag. Nick rarely carried a gun, and the knife had saved his life more than once. Since that first time, he hadn't gone a on a job without it.

He left the room and exited the building through the same side door. He walked toward a dark corner of the parking lot, looking for a car that met his criteria.

Once inside he leaned under the dash and while shining his small light with one hand, was able to pull the ignition wires loose. With his knife he stripped the insulation from the wires, touched them together and started the engine.

Nick had paid close attention on his return from the Little house and retraced his route to the same vacant lot in Cherry Creek. At this late hour, the neighborhood was very quiet and no interior lights were on in any of the houses. Before getting out of his car he turned his dome light switch to the off position preventing the interior lights from coming on when he opened the door. He exited the car and slowly closed the door until it struck the latch and then pushed it firmly to finish closing it silently.

He walked down the street as if headed home from a neighbor. He surveyed the surroundings as he approached the Little house and then darted around to the back. As before, the back door to the garage was unlocked. He eased it open, listening intently for any sounds coming from the house. The small flashlight was adequate to survey the garage: a BMW coupe, 500 series, and a Lincoln Navigator next to it. 'It's a good bet they're both home,' he thought, still wondering about any kids.

Closing the door behind him, he continued to survey the garage and his gaze stopped on a golf bag standing upright near a closet with bi-fold doors. A cover was over the club heads, coated with thin layer of dust. Unsnapping the cover to reveal a set of men's clubs, Nick noticed the dust.

"Aw Mr. Little, you should have gotten out more while you had the chance".

Nick drew the nine iron from the bag, but his attention was drawn to the putter as his eyes narrowed in contemplation and the corners of his mouth turned up in a smile. He dropped the iron back in to the bag and pulled the putter halfway up to estimate its weight. His smile broadened with appreciation for how heavy the club was and he took morbid delight at the half moon shape of the head.

He turned, still smiling, to shine his light on the door leading to the interior of the house. He went to the door, silently, and put his ear close and listened. Nothing. Not a sound. On his earlier reconnaissance Nick had seen there was no dead bolt, only a locking doorknob. He turned the knob gently and found it locked. With his knife he worked the blade between the latch and the strike plate as he pulled the door open. There was a single stair leading in to a large laundry and storage room. Pulling the door closed behind him he drew a measured breath as he cautioned himself against getting cocky; everything was going too easily.

Nick stood there, waiting for his to eyes adjust. A light came from the kitchen, not bright, but enough that he wouldn't need his flashlight. More good luck; flashlights were dangerous. He silently, slowly walked to the kitchen. The light came from under the stove hood; the type of light left on to prevent someone from stumbling about in the middle of the night. Nick took his time, moving slowly, peering into the darker perimeter as he moved through the kitchen; the last thing he wanted was to trip over a chair leg or step on a cat bowl.

Off the kitchen was a room, which appeared to be a den or office. The dim light carried from the stove hood well enough to make out silhouettes of the furniture. A desk stood against one wall and he ventured that direction, slowly, noiselessly. The desk was mostly clear, just a laptop plugged in to a charger with a neat stack of loose papers next to it. Above the desk hung several pictures, which he inspected with his flashlight. There was a photograph of the Littles dressed in Christmas season attire, her in a low cut red evening gown standing next to her smiling husband dressed in a dark suit and wearing a green tie. The face of the man in the picture confirmed he had the correct Thomas Little, but Nick continued staring at the picture for a different reason. 'Goddamn, how did this wimpy little fuck end up with this babe? Look at those tits, Jesus H. Christ.'

He continued to stare at the picture, thinking about how horny he'd been all night when suddenly he heard the sound of a door being gently closed and noticed the beam of a distant light penetrating his dark corner.

He quickly shut off his flashlight and slid it in to a pant pocket. He crouched down as he firmly gripped the handle of the putter with both hands. The light had come from the stairwell that was just off the end of the den. 'This could be lucky as hell or bad news,' Nick thought. He listened to the fall of footsteps on the carpeted stairs as they made their way down and turned away from the den toward the kitchen. A light came on in the kitchen and he heard a cabinet door open and close. The whirring sound of an ice dispenser and the clink of ice dropping in to a glass. Several long seconds passed as Nick worked at steadying his breathing. Then he heard the refrigerator door open followed by the clink of a ceramic dish on a granite counter top, the sound of a drawer opening, the tingling of silverware, what sounded like a paper towel being torn off a roll.

While Nick interpreted every sound, he was making his way to the wall against the stair well; silently, he positioned himself behind that wall at the end of the stairs. Large hands with thick strong fingers wrapped the handle of the putter as he breathed quietly and regularly through his mouth. His mind raced as he anticipated this person's next move. but was secure in the thought that they hadn't heard him and probably didn't have a gun. But who was in the kitchen and who else was awake? 'Goddamn it I hope it ain't a kid' he thought.

Several more seconds passed.

Come on, Jesus Christ.

"Shit, shit that hurt." A muffled voice came from the kitchen a split second after Nick heard what sounded like a chair bumping a table.

'Ahaa', Nick thought, 'it is the man of the house. Poor bastard stubbed his toe'. Nick stifled a chuckle; God could this be any easier? Thomas Little's footsteps were barely audible on the tile floor, but he seemed to be approaching the den. Nick, behind the wall, gripped the putter in both hands and raised them to shoulder height, ready for a baseball swing, a single death blow.

The footsteps stopped. No one appeared. Nick's mind raced; 'what the fuck!' He realized Little had turned the other way, on to the carpet toward another room. His back against the wall, Nick spun his body to the left 180 degrees as he stepped around the wall at the foot of the stairs. One long step on to his right foot brought him just three feet from Little as the slender man continued toward the living room carrying his plate and glass.

Nick wasted no time in gauging the distance and the putter was already swinging in an upward arc. Massive hands with white knuckles and bulging forearms swung the club with all the speed and ferocity Nick's powerful body could generate. He drove the toe of the heavy metal putter through the bone at the back of Thomas Little's skull. The dead man dropped to his knees instantly and fell forward on to his face; water glass and brownie falling noiselessly out in front of him on to the carpet; a scarlet stream staining the plush beige carpet. The man never uttered a sound. The only noise had been the sound of shattering bone combined with a thud like an ax hitting a tree.

Nick had let the putter handle go as the body fell for fear of it being stuck in the man's head and causing him to crash against the wall if he were to hang on to it. As his victim slumped toward the floor, face first; the putter dislodged from his skull and to Nick's relief fell silently to the carpeted floor.

The big man continued to stand there; beaded sweat on his face, trying to slow his breathing as he listened intently for any commotion from an upstairs bedroom. After several minutes, the assassin started breathing more normally and whispered to himself, "Not bad, one down and no one the wiser yet. You are a fuckin' pro Nicky boy. Maybe I should put in for a raise." This smart-ass comment made him wince involuntarily as it conjured up a vision of Costello leaning across the desk screaming at him.

Nick took a step toward the body with the thought of checking for a pulse but then shook his head muttering, "What the fuck, he's dead as a hammer".

Nick started up the stairs with the putter in hand. The light was on in the stairwell and was enough to light the hallway once he reached the top of the stairs. There were two doors on the left, one on the right. All were slightly ajar. The fourth door at the end of the hallway was shut completely. He reasoned that this was the master bedroom because Little would have shut this door behind him to keep from disturbing his sleeping wife. Gripping the putter in his right hand he slowly made his way down the hall toward the closed door; steadily, quietly, listening for any sound.

He turned the door handle slowly, pushed the door open two inches and soundlessly released the knob. The bedroom was dark. He pushed the door slowly until it was wide open. It was a crapshoot; he needed to let enough light in to the room to determine the layout, but certainly didn't want to disturb 'the sweet widow Little'. The words made him smile a wicked smile as he stood at the doorway; standing against the doorjamb in a weak attempt to minimize his silhouette. He stood motionless for over a minute, as he listened and let his eyes adjust to the dimmer light of the room.

The form of a person was under the covers on the opposite side of the bed. No obstacles in his path at the foot of the bed. An armoire was against the wall between two windows; chairs on either side of the armoire. Only sheers covered the windows but barely any light came through.

Nick stepped into the room and started around the foot of the bed, the blood stained putter gripped firmly in both hands. Just as he reached the far side of the bed the covers suddenly moved as Sandra Little stirred.

"Tom, did you knock over a book case or what? I told you to turn the lights on when you get up." She spoke loudly enough to be heard in the hallway. "It doesn't bother me and I don't want you to break your neck."

Nick was motionless and holding his breath. He could make out enough of the woman to see she was on her side, facing away from him toward the door. He took two steps closer toward the head of the bed.

"Tom, did you hear me? Tommy? Tommy?" Sandra Little rolled on to her back and pulled the covers partially down her body as she contemplated getting up. Her head was still turned, looking in to the hallway. She was naked and both breasts were exposed in the dim light. This was enough to make Nick pause for just a moment, but only for a moment, before swinging the club in an upward arc over his head and bringing it down with inconceivable force; the flat putting surface of the club smashing the sternum and ribs just over her heart. Nick's frightening face was the last thing Sandra Little saw as she turned her head in the direction of the whistle made by the propelling club handle. The sound of the impact made the same sickening thud, but the shattering of bone was louder than before. The only other sound was the burst of air driven from Sandra's lungs by the impact.

Nick stood there for a moment, looking at his victim and listening.

"Not sure she's dead, but I do know she ain't goin' anywhere" he muttered as he headed for the bedroom door. "Never killed any kids before; this might be a little weird."

He walked down the hallway to check the other bedrooms. At the room on the right he first repeated his earlier routine of pushing the door wide open, slowly and quietly, while combining his silhouette with the doorjamb. The bed was made and unoccupied. He went across the hall to find another bed fully made with an assortment of throw pillows against the headboard.

'What is it with these broads and their throw pillows? Don't they have any idea what a pain in the ass they are to throw off the bed every night?' He thought about Audra, that bitch he'd lived with for over a year. 'She must have had ten fuckin' throw pillows on that bed every night. What a pain in the ass.' He stuck his tongue between his teeth and smiled as he thought about the last time he saw her. She was givin' him shit about fuckin' her friend Beth. At first he just ignored her, but she wouldn't shut her mouth. He had shoved her hard in the chest, knocking her over the end of the bed. But the stupid bitch got back up. Nick had grabbed the smallest, firmest pillow off the bed and proceeded to punch her in the face with it. Holding her up by her hair as he punched her over and over until she was unconscious. Now that was good use of a throw pillow. Nick bit his lip now to keep from laughing out loud.

He checked the last door on the hallway, not changing how he opened it or where he stood, but quickly realized it was a bathroom and turned to head back down the stairs.

Moving more quickly and not being concerned about being so quiet, Nick descended the stairs to check out the rest of the house. As he did, he realized there were no pictures of any kids anywhere. Nick finally returned to his first victim and noticed the blood flow had stopped. As he looked over the body of the dead man, it struck him again how this puny little puke could get that gorgeous bitch for a wife. He decided to go check on his handy work up stairs and finish the job right.

Nick turned on the overhead light in the master bedroom. It would take an awfully nosey neighbor to peer in through the window sheers at two in the morning. He walked over to the side of the bed to inspect the body of Sandra Little. Her eyes were open and there was a trickle of blood from the corners of her mouth and both nostrils. Nick confirmed she was dead by touching a cornea with the tip of his index finger.

Nick gazed down at her chest. At the site of impact there was a dent where her sternum and been fractured and a slight split in the skin with some minimal bleeding. A deep purple discoloration made a perfect imprint of the putter's clubface.

"Hell of a heart shot", Nick said out loud, "and the tits are still perfect." He marveled at what he considered to be perfect breasts and nipples and after a few seconds took a gloved hand and rubbed both her breasts, "Real to boot", he muttered. He then grabbed the top of the sheet and blanket that covered her abdomen and in one sweeping motion sent the covers flying off the foot of the bed.

"God damn, Jesus H. Christ. This bitch is gorgeous. Shaved and perfect", he said out loud as he put his hands between her thighs and pulled her legs apart, exposing her genitalia. "Fuck I'll bet this was a fun spot to be."

After almost a full minute he finally turned away to start looking in the armoire that stood against the opposite wall. Opening the doors at the top, he looked for anything of value and found a man's wallet, a watch and a large wad of folded money. He pulled the cotton sack that hung from his back pocket and dropped the three items in it.

Opening the top drawer he found a large jewelry box. Lifting the lid, he found some rings that looked like school rings or fraternity rings, stuff of no fence value. There was a nice diamond studded Rolex watch that he added to his bag. Under some of the papers was a leather passport and ticket holder containing two passports. He put both of them in his bag before pulling all the drawers out on to the floor, spilling their contents over the carpet.

Next, Nick headed for the walk-in closets in search of more

valuables. The first was lined with men's clothes on hangers. The end of the closet was solid shelving containing men's shoes and folded clothes. There was no obvious place to hide anything and he was supposed to be a crack head, not a professional cat burglar.

Sandra Little's closet was larger and instead of accessing it from the end, the door was in the side, allowing a person to walk to the right or the left after entering. Against one end was shelving, completely filled with women's shoes. Against the other end was more shelving extending from the ceiling about half way down. These shelves contained more shoes as well as some folded sweaters. The bottom half was made up of drawers, and one of them had a lock. He tried this drawer and found it to be in keeping with the Little's casual approach to security, unlocked. It was deceivingly deep as Nick pulled it out fully. Bingo; her jewelry drawer, filled with earrings, bracelets, bangles, necklaces, several watches and several large velvet bags with more jewelry inside. He really didn't give a shit to look at any of it, it had to go and no one was going to ever get it anyway. He scooped out the contents and dumped it all in to his cotton bag.

Nick kept opening drawers until he found the one containing her bras. He pulled several out and inspected them. "36 D, gotta like that." He was talking out loud. "She was a game bitch, too; push-ups, see-throughs, lots of lacey ones; God damn." He then opened another drawer and found her panties. "Lots of sexy shit here," he said out loud again, "oooh, man, lots of thongs. I mighta fucked up killing this bitch."

Hanging on to the pull cords of his cotton bag, he patted his jacket pockets to ensure he hadn't dropped any of his things. He took one last glance at the late Sandra Little and shook his head as he turned off the light and left the bedroom. There was no reason to return to the other body, he left through the kitchen and out through the garage.

Once back to his car, he slid in to the driver's seat and reached under the dash to touch the wires together. He drove away neither fast nor slowly, reveling in how easy everything had been; smugly acknowledging that it wasn't just luck, either. Soon the stolen dark blue Ford was back on I-70 headed west toward Berkley Park and the lake. After parking in the same spot as earlier in the day, the big man from Chicago put the car in park but instead of getting out he sat, waiting patiently. As he so often repeated, to himself or to anyone for that matter, Nick was 'no rookie'; he knew just what to expect from his targets and from the police.

If there was a cruiser that was hidden from view they would be waiting too, giving the people in the parked car time to initiate their intended activity. Nick didn't want to be on his way to the lake with his bag of stolen articles if Denver's finest decided to make an appearance. Once comfortable that enough time had elapsed, he moved quickly, jumping from the car and heading to the lake. It wasn't hard to find two softball sized stones along that rocky shoreline and add them to his bag of loot. After pulling the draw strings tight and tying them in repeated square knots, Nick held them in his hands as he spun his whole body in a circle. Once, twice, spinning like a discus thrower, letting go of the bag on the second revolution to watch it fly out over the lake, further than he had imagined he could.

The trip back to the hotel was uneventful with very little traffic at this time of the morning. There were even more cars in the lot than when he had left, leaving no empty spaces where the Ford had been parked.

"Oh well, fuck 'em." Nick laughed out loud as he thought about the poor schmuck looking for his car in the morning and then purposely parked it on the opposite side of the lot. After killing the motor, Nick again patted his pockets to take inventory and started to reach over to the passenger seat for the tools used for breaking into the car. But a vision of

Sandra Little lying naked in her bed stopped him and he sat there motionless, staring straight ahead. Exploding with rage, he slammed the steering wheel with both fists to the sound of breaking plastic.

"Goddamn it I should have fucked her first!"

TAMPA, FLORIDA
January

"Hey, Connie, how's it going? Sean Murphy dropped his briefcase on the kitchen table. "How's my girl today."

"Hi, Mr. Murphy. She was up when I left to get the kids from school, but she's laying down now." Connie was getting a snack of milk and Oreo cookies for the kids. "The kids went upstairs to put their backpacks away. They should be down in a second for snack. You're home early today."

"Actually, I have to go back out for a meeting at 5:00. How's your schedule today? Can you stay a little late if Mo decides to sleep?"

"No problem, what time are you thinking?"

"I should be back by 7:00."

"I'll do whatever. If Mrs. Murphy gets up and wants me to go, I will. If she stays sleeping I'll get dinner ready and have it for you and the kids when you get home."

"You're a star. Thanks. I'm going to peek in on Mo."

Karen and Jeremy came in to the kitchen followed by Rosie, their yellow lab. Karen twirled in her attempt at a pirouette.

"Daddy!" Karen spotted her Dad in mid-twirl and ran across the kitchen to wrap her arms around her Daddy's leg.

"Hey, pumpkin. How's the best first grader in the world today?" Sean picked her up and kissed her on the lips. He held her up to his chest with one arm and leaned over to tussle his son's hair.

"What's up, little man? How was school today?"

Jeremy shrugged his shoulders, "School."

"Here's your snack, guys." Connie put glasses, plates and napkins on the bar counter.

Sean set Karen in her stool. "Wow, pumpkin, Connie's got Oreos for you today. You must be living right."

"I live with you and Mommy. That's right isn't it?"

"You bet it is, baby. It's really right." He turned to Jeremy as the boy climbed up on to his stool. "You back drinking milk again, bud?"

"Yea, it's good again. But I never did stop drinking it with Oreos, though."

"Well, that's good. Somehow, son, that just wouldn't be right."

"Dad, how much longer do I have to go to school?"

"No talking with your mouth full. I think forty-two more years. Yea. That's right. Forty-two."

"Dad, I'm serious."

"I know son, that's what's so sad." He gave Jeremy a wink and a big smile. "I'm going to check on Mom, I'll see you guys in a bit."

Sean quietly eased the bedroom door open and peeked toward the bed. Mo sat on the edge of the bed holding her head between her hands. The lights were off and the curtains were drawn, the cracked door provided most of the light.

"Hey, honey, how are you doing?" Sean left the door cracked. He sat next to her and put his arm around her, drawing her in to him.

"Hey, baby. I'm just waking up. Can't quite get my bearings." She turned to smile at her husband.

Sean smiled back and kissed her on the forehead. "Did the kids wake you up?"

"No. One good thing about losing hearing in my right ear is that

I can lie on that side and not hear a thing." She forced a broader smile as Sean squeezed her hand.

"Oh, for silver linings." Sean kissed her again. "I asked Connie if she could stay while I'm at my meeting if you want to sleep longer."

"Oh, that's right. Today is Thursday. I think I will lie down for a while more. I was going to take another pill."

"Head pounding pretty hard today?"

"Yea, pretty hard." Mo's eyes filled with tears as she leaned against her husband. Her voice trembled, "I'm so glad we have you. Me and the kids. I know they'll be fine forever because of you."

"Because of us." Sean's eyes filled with tears. He steadied his voice, wanting to sound stronger than he felt. "We're going to come out of this, you know."

"I know. You go throw those kids around like you like to do. I'm going to take a pill and lie down for just a while more. I want to get up and have dinner with y'all when you get back. OK?"

"OK. I love you."

"Thank you. I love you, too. I'll be good as new when you get back."

The kids were already playing a video game when Sean returned to that end of the house. He loved rough housing with the kids, but right now he was glad they were preoccupied.

"Connie, Mo is going to rest till I get back. If you can make supper, that would be great. For 7:00, I guess will work fine."

"How about ravioli, salad, and garlic bread? Sound OK?"

"Perfect. I'm going to go to my office and finish preparing for the meeting. Thanks for everything." He smiled at her and glanced back in to the den. The kids were focused on their game and didn't notice him.

Sean dropped his brief case next to his desk and sat heavily in his chair. He placed his folded hands palm down on the desk and leaned forward to put his forehead against the back of his hand, and closed his eyes. He tried to think about his meeting but couldn't. It didn't matter right now; he couldn't stop thinking about Mo. He thought of how she tried so hard to smile, but the pain was so evident on her face. It had taken the spark from her eyes. Sean hated how frightened and frustrated she is. He knew how she worried for her children and how miserable it made her to think about not watching them grow up. Sean let out a low groan, almost a growl, which lasted until he ran out of breath. Then Sean Murphy began to cry, his shoulders shaking, tears flowing over his hands.

Finally, he decided he just needed to hold her, to be next to her. Nothing else mattered. He kicked off his loafers and got up from his chair. Half way across the room he stopped to reconsider, thinking he was being selfish by waking her up. As he started back to his chair, he changed his mind again, wanting so much to hold her. Slowly, he crept in to his bedroom and lay down next to his wife. She was on her left side and he laid on his left, spooning her in the cradle of his body. As he put his right arm over her she moaned quietly and pleasantly. Soon after lying there, feeling her familiar warmth and filling his nostrils with her scent, tears began to flow down his cheeks again.

Sean wasn't sure but he felt he must have nodded off several times while he lay there. His left shoulder hurt and his left hand was asleep as he turned his body to look at the clock on his night stand; 4:35. Rolling off of the bed he made his way to the door while massaging his left hand with his right. Sean was almost thankful of the distraction of his pending meeting now as he retrieved his shoes and brief case from the office.

Sean stopped in the den, "Jeremy, do you have any homework?"

"Yes, sir. Some vocabulary words," Jeremy never lost focus on the video screen.

"When this game is done, I want you to get that done. What about you young lady?"

"No, Daddy. But I can draw pictures while Bubby does his vobulary stuff."

"Great idea. We'll eat when I get back. I think your Mom is

going to join us for dinner, too. She was just going to lay down a little while longer."

The meeting was almost a waste of time for Sean, not much of what was discussed was pertinent to his work. He had been invited to attend the semimonthly meetings by the chief editor of the magazine, presumptively because he was one of their top columnists. The true reason was that Sean had an abundance of common sense and a sixth sense about what the readership wanted. He was never sucked in by the latest 'hot story' that often resulted in lost subscribers and apologizing editorials. It was this abundance of innate good sense that Mr. Denny-Jones took advantage of.

The editorial board for the The Constitution required videoconference to include the New York, Tampa and Denver offices. Today's meeting was untraditionally short because most of the New York contingency was headed to a charity function. When business had concluded and Mr. Denny-Jones asked for any questions, Sean spoke up.

"Sheila, do we know any more about the Thomas Little murder? Any inside scoop from out there?"

Sheila was the regional editor for the Denver office. "No, Sean. It is incredibly quiet. They are still calling it a home invasion. But I know the chief investigator thinks the whole thing doesn't smell right. He's not convinced that Little wasn't singled out. But, even he admits he has nothing to base that on, just his gut and thirty years of investigating."

"I'm with him. But I don't know shit, either. But I agree, it just doesn't smell right." Sean shook his head as he spoke. "Thanks, Sheila. Hey, how's the grandbaby?"

"Beautiful. Fun. Wonderful. Thanks for asking."

"Good night everyone, we need to get on our way, up here." Mr. Denny-Jones was anxious to get his group to the dinner on time. "Sean, call me tomorrow about that Citizens First info you referred to."

A chorus of goodnights and goodbyes were followed by black screens. Shirley, the marketing director, said goodnight and left the office. Mike Dooley, Sean's editor asked Sean if he had time for a drink.

"Yeah, it's early, and I could probably use one. Down stairs at Mitch's?"

"That was my thought." Mike and Sean had worked together for nearly eight years and had forged a tremendous respect for one another during that time. But although they were good friends, they rarely did things together socially. Both with young families and working long hours, there wasn't much time for social lives in general. What time Sean did have to himself he mostly spent doing outdoor activities and working out, both of which were low on Mike's list of 'fun stuff to do'. It was nights like tonight or occasional dinners and hockey games that they spent time together.

Mitch's was a pub on the street level of their downtown office building. Mostly business people that worked downtown patronized it, but it was also close enough to the Ice Palace Arena to garnish some trade from games and other events held there.

Mitch was behind the bar himself when the two walked through the front door. Neither man frequented the bar, but Mitch was an old fashioned proprietor that took pride in learning the names of his patrons, no matter how infrequently they came.

"Mike, Sean, great to see you. Single malts, I presume."

They both walked up to the bar to shake Mitch's extended hand. Mike said, "That'd be great for me. A Balvenie over the rocks."

"Ditto. How you doing, Mitch?"

"I'm doing fine, if I lie just a little bit." Mitch smiled at the two men. "Whatever table you land at I'll find you, gents." Minutes later Mitch arrived at their table with drinks and a bowl of large cashews. "Enjoy, fellas."

After a sip of his scotch to wash down the cashews, Mike asked

Sean, "You feel like updating me on Mo, buddy? I understand if you don't."

"No, I'm glad to. Thanks for asking. You know I don't mind talking about it with you. Really, you're one of the few people that I do talk to about it." Sean took a swallow of his drink. "Things suck, basically. She varies from low-grade headaches to monsters; so bad that she can't function. As you know, it's been going on since late August and its now mid-January and we just now saw a neurologist this week."

"Un-fucking-believable. Was he worth a shit, at least?"

"Yea, I think so, I hope so. Nice guy, compassionate, seemed thorough and to know what he was talking about. Of course, what do I know about evaluating a neurologist? He was able to rule out some things and he's scheduled her for an MRI and a CAT scan. Guess how long?"

"Shit, don't tell me. Even after all of this?"

"Oh yea! Welcome to the PHA, mister! Another six weeks."

Mike shook his head and then asked, "Has he got any ideas?"

Sean took another pull off his scotch and pushed against his bottom lip with his tongue as he tried to rein in his emotions. "His suspicions are cancer, a brain tumor. She's lost the hearing in her right ear now, so he feels he knows what area of the brain it's in. A temporal lobe, he thinks. I'm learning more about the brain than I ever wanted to know. The good news is that the odds say it is not metastatic and the location should be operable. Most of these are treated with a combination of surgery and radiation. And I guess there is a chance that it's not a tumor, but all indications are that it is."

"God damn it, man. I am sorry. How are you and the kids holding up?"

"I have good days and bad, like Mo I guess. The kids are OK, but there're times that they just miss their Mom. She was a huge part of their day, every day. Now she might have several days in a row that she's hardly around them, just unable to cope. But she really tries. I am hopeful that this new medication the neurologist gave her will be better. It's supposed to provide her more relief and not make her so groggy. We'll see."

"I don't know how, but Trish and I would do anything to help y'all, you know that."

"I do know that, buddy, and I am grateful. Right now we've got it handled."

They finished their drinks and Sean stood reaching in his pocket. "I've gotta run, Mike."

"Me too. But I've got the drinks; you go on. Give Mo a hug for me, will ya?"

"You bet. Thanks for the drink and the conversation. I appreciate your concern very much. Say hey to Trish."

When Sean got home it was seven o'clock on the dot. Connie was still there, but Mo was up. She had showered and dressed and put on her make-up. She felt better and always wanted to look good for Sean the times she felt up to it.

"Hey guys, how's everybody?" Sean was looking at Mo as he addressed everyone. He gave her a wink and a big smile. "Feel a little better, hon?"

"Daddy!" Karen was holding a piece of her crayon art as she ran across the kitchen.

Connie spoke up, "Karen, show that one to your Daddy real quick, but you promised to color with me before dinner."

"Looks like another horse; you must like horses a lot." Sean held Karen in one arm and held the artwork in front of them with the other hand.

"It's a dog, silly. It's Rosie. Horses have hairy tails."

Connie walked over to them and grabbed Karen in her arms, "Come on, lets add a cat to that picture, OK?" Looking at Mo she added, "Dinner is ready but can sit for as long as it needs to."

"You're sweet, Connie, thanks."

Sean and Mo took the opportunity to go into the living room and be alone.

"Where's Jeremy, hon? Still doing home work?"

"Yea, I heard him repeating his words and definitions out loud just a minute ago."

"You look terrific, sweetie. Are you feeling better after your nap?"

"I do, I feel better than I have in a while. I think it was that snuggle you gave me earlier."

They sat close to each other on the couch; kissing, talking, whispering, even laughing. Sean couldn't believe it. He couldn't believe how good it felt to have his wife back. Mo finally said they should go eat and Sean reluctantly agreed.

At Mo's request, Connie stayed for dinner. The kids were giggly, for reasons only they knew, and Mo was enjoying it. They all talked and laughed and Sean noticed that for the first time in weeks, his wife had a sparkle to her eyes. He wondered if this could be the beginning of a change for the better. Oh my God would that be wonderful, he thought.

That night Sean and Mo made love in a way they hadn't for a long time. In fact, for the last two months, Sean had almost felt guilty the few times they'd had sex. He had felt that Mo was only doing it for him, and it was more discomfort than pleasure for her. Not tonight, tonight she was aggressive and desirous. She was lovely and sexy and Sean was in heaven, eager to please her over and over. They eventually fell asleep, but Mo woke up in the middle of the night and started kissing Sean on the neck and chest. He gratefully responded and they made love again before finally sleeping through the night.

MIAMI, FLORIDA

March

Stanley was filled with the warmth that true contentment creates. He was pleased with himself; feeling smug. It occurred to him how it was considered a bad thing to be smug. Well isn't that just tough shit!

He was looking around his 'bunker' thinking about how he loved being there and how much his life had improved in the past several years. The proof had really come when they moved from the dump on Palmetto Avenue to a custom home in Kendall. Sheri still clerked at a Dollar Store but she didn't really give a shit. Besides, Stanley wasn't about to let her quit, why should he, she'd only watch TV all day and drink beer. As a matter of fact, as far as Stanley knew, Sheri didn't give a shit about anything but her beer.

The Meshes hadn't been intimate for nearly two years. Sheri had lost interest and he was unable to achieve an erection. The medications he took for his blood pressure and diabetes prevented him from taking anything for erectile dysfunction. When the problem first occurred he had been extremely discouraged. He was eager to have sex and his impotence embarrassed and frustrated him. Sheri hadn't helped the situation, not caring one way or the other about having sex with him, eager to tell him that the only orgasms she'd ever experienced she'd given herself. She taunted and ridiculed him on both occasions he failed to become erect and he never tried again after the second time.

Tonight none of this was on his mind. He sat in his recliner and looked around his room and smiled. For the first time in his life he was in a position of power; and he gave himself the credit for making it happen. Years ago he'd realized the importance of pleasing the right people. He knew that would make everything fall in to place. All of this was proof of how smart he is, how crafty he is; and how stupid most everyone else is.

Now he had power over so many people - no matter how educated or how much money they had. Many times it didn't even matter how well connected they were. Stanley held their destiny in his hands...and he loved it. It was intoxicating to decide the fate of other people. Sure, Leach's office usually made the call, but it was up to him to 'handle it'. He mostly rejected applications and he found it amusing how easy it was to validate those rejections within the system.

The reason for his contentment tonight was such a rejection. An old, rich, sniveling, Jew had come to his office begging on behalf of her husband that needed open heart surgery. Stanley had such easy grounds for denial. The man was seventy-two years old; too old, end of story. Indeed, he could have easily made a special allowance based on the man's excellent physical health, which was exactly the case the old kike was pleading. But what delight there was in looking across at her, dressed in her fine clothes and wearing her gold and diamonds and saying 'Mrs. Goldman, I can't do anything for you'. After which he gleefully witnessed her course through the range of predictable behaviors; remaining calm to present her argument at first, and then turning to a frustrated rage, followed by hysterical crying

112

and begging. With a disdainful air he had Yolanda escort her from his office.

God, how he enjoyed feeling smug. It occurred to him he had never experienced that emotion until a few years ago. It was his turn. God damn it, it was his turn to feel smug.

Smiling outwardly, Stanley yelled out loud, "How's it feel you rich Jew bastard. Stanley Mesh has got you by the balls. How's it feel?" He threw his head back with his arms outstretched and fists clenched and let out a long, air filled 'yes'!

He shoved a fat hand into the side pocket of his chair and felt for a familiar cardboard folder. Panic shot through him when he couldn't find it. He turned in his chair, squirming onto his large belly and leaning over the arm to look in to the pouch. When he saw it he felt relaxed again and pulled it from the side pocket..

Sweating and breathing heavily from the panic and the effort he leaned back in his chair. He smiled at himself for his bout of panic. Stanley knew no one ever came in to the bunker, not even Sheri; it couldn't have disappeared for Christ's sake. He leaned back in his chair and held the folder above his face, tilting it slightly to take full advantage of the light from his lamp.

Contained in the folder were two pictures facing each other. One was smaller than the other and had obviously been cut from a book or magazine. The other was a five by seven photograph of a woman holding a little girl. They were pictures of the same woman taken years apart.

"Ah, Lisa Ray, how sweet it is." Stanley didn't remember much of his literature, but he did remember that revenge is a meal best served cold. Lisa had been a high school classmate; pretty and outgoing. Someone had left a note in Stanley's locker, supposedly from her that said she wanted him to meet her after cheerleading practice. He couldn't believe it; it was preposterous. But in the back of his mind he kept thinking, what if it's true? Better judgment warned against going, but hope overwhelmed him. He convinced himself he'd be able to catch her alone. Reality wasn't as kind. The rest of the squad spilled out of the locker room as Stanley approached Lisa. It was predictably awkward and embarrassing. The other girls laughed and teased him. Lisa Ray was embarrassed for herself and did nothing to salvage Stanley's dignity.

Nearly twenty years had passed and Lisa's four-year-old daughter was diagnosed with leukemia. It was not a case that normally reached Stanley's desk for assessment, but he had stumbled on her file quite by accident while doing Leach's bidding on another case. Lisa Ray was married and had changed her name. But Dan Compton and had been her high school sweetheart and the name Lisa Compton was enough to make the bells go off.

Stanley could hardly believe his luck. He had the authority to pull her file from the system and take personal control of it. It was a rare form of leukemia that required very expensive treatment.

"My God Lisa, if only I could." Stanley thought back on that day. "But when the cost of treatment is so high and the prognosis is so poor, the rules of the agency don't permit it."

Lisa brought the picture that day. She cried and begged, pleading with him to make an exception for her Marie. Stanley remembered how she sat at the edge of her chair grasping the picture in her fingers, rocking back and forth as she trembled and tears streamed down her face. Sobbing and breathless she finally stood and placed the picture of her and Marie on the desk in front of Stanley. She turned and slowly walked to the door. With her hand on the knob, she stopped. Lisa looked at the floor and tried to regain her composure. She spun around and walked back to his desk. Lisa Compton offered herself to Stanley as she unbuttoned her blouse; not just for that day, but as many times as he wanted if he would just allow her baby the treatment she needed. After all, he had wanted her once, now she was his for the taking. He feigned disgust and pity while denying her but inside Stanley was experiencing a rush of pleasure that almost overwhelmed him.

It was two days later that Dan Compton came to his office. He showed up without an appointment and barged through the door.

Stanley was frightened as he thought back on Lisa's sexual overture, but Compton wasn't there to accuse Stanley; he had come to bribe him. He held out a large manila envelope and spilled $50,000 cash on the desk. Again, Stanley feigned shock and disgust and called for security to have the man thrown out.

Marie Compton was dead in six months.

Stanley had his revenge; he had made them crawl. He showed them that neither her beautiful body nor his bank account had the power Stanley Mesh had. Reliving those days in his mind brought back the rush. It was euphoric. It was erotic.

TAMPA, FLORIDA

April

"Thanks, Connie. We shouldn't be later than 5:00, probably sooner. You're a doll."

Mo pulled on her sweater as she spoke to Connie. It was April, but unseasonably cool and Mo's thin body didn't handle the cold. Sean helped her with her sweater.

"Sorry I'm a little late, but I think we'll be alright on time." Sean had been delayed by a phone call from New York as he was leaving the office.

"Honey, we haven't been to a clinic yet that we haven't waited for at least an hour. I'm sure we'll be fine." Mo smiled at his apology.

"Well I was hoping that since this was a consult it might be different. They might actually run on schedule."

They drove to the Moffitt Center on Fowler Ave. The Neurologist, Dr. Johnson, had arranged for the radiologist and oncologist to join the meeting. .

Mo's condition had deteriorated more rapidly over the past six weeks. There wasn't a day that she could function more than a few hours without stopping for a nap or just lying down in the dark.

She was tired all the time. Nausea overcame her as soon as the medication wore off. The relentless headaches were getting worse as the efficacy of the medication diminished.

The Murphy's didn't know what to expect at this meeting, but they felt any information that may result in a plan, a strategy to beat this thing would be welcome news. Mo was tough and very willing to fight on and Sean had confidence that she would and could beat it, whatever it was. They wanted a diagnosis. A plan. Something.

They were right on time as they entered Dr. Johnson's outer offices. The receptionist recognized them and called the nurse right away. The nurse's smile and manner were reassuring as she escorted them back to a small conference room several doors from the waiting room. Mo and Sean entered the room to find the doctors already assembled. After the introductions Dr. Johnson took charge of the meeting.

"Dr.'s Keating and Styles and I have obviously discussed your case fully. We are all in agreement, which frankly isn't always the case, as to what the probabilities of the diagnosis are, what the next step to confirm that diagnosis is and what the treatment options are."

The other doctors nodded in agreement as the Murphy's glanced in their direction. Dr. Johnson continued.

"I'm afraid that the images have led us to believe that we may have a worse situation than I thought we had based on the statistical occurrence of these tumors. As you know, I had thought the most likely type of tumor that you may have was a glioblastoma. As we discussed I was basing this on the statistical occurrence of certain brain tumors, as well as the clinical signs that you have presented. I'll cut to the chase."

Sean and Mo were breathless. He sat by her side holding her hand and now reached in to her lap with his other hand to hold both of hers as Dr. Johnson continued.

"By the character of the images we have seen, it is our opinion that you likely have a gliosarcoma. We base this on the structure of the tumor as revealed by the MRI imaging. Unfortunately these tumors bear a more severe prognosis and are more likely to metastasize than glioblasotmas. These tumors rarely occur in women, rarely in people your age, and rarely in this area of the brain. So we don't arrive at this presumption, nor share it with you, lightly."

"So, uh. So. I mean...go on, I'm sorry." Sean tried to wrap his mind around what he was hearing. Mo squeezed his hands reassuringly and smiled when he looked at her. He tried to return the smile but couldn't.

"The potential for good news is that the position of the tumor is where I had felt it would be based on your clinical signs and the plain rads we had taken. This is good from a treatment standpoint, because it is operable. The bad news about these tumors is that they do not respond to treatment as well as the glioblastomas and as I've said, they have a greater tendency for metastasis. Mrs. Murphy, do you have any questions yet?"

"No, don't worry about me, doctor, I won't hesitate to ask when I do."

"Well the next step is to do a biopsy. It will give us confirmation, or refutation, of our diagnosis based on what we have so far. The biopsy will involve a hospital stay and general anesthesia."

The consultation lasted for another half an hour with Dr. Johnson first explaining the details of the biopsy procedure and then the potential surgical treatment. The radiologist and oncologist both spoke to treatment and prognosis.

When they were finished, Sean spoke up. "It seems all we've talked about is the bad tumor, the worse one, but we don't even know if that's the case, right? I mean, that's the reason for the biopsy, right?"

"That is right, Mr. Murphy." answered Dr. Keating, the radiologist. She leaned toward him from across the table as she continued, "It is imperative that we perform a biopsy for absolute confirmation, but we will all be very surprised if it comes back other than a gliosarcoma. We feel we would be doing you an injustice if we did not tell you that at this point, even without the confirmation of the biopsy."

"What about metastasis?" Mo asked. "How do we know about that since there is more potential of that happening with this tumor?"

"We will biopsy several lymph nodes in your head and neck area looking for any cancer cells that may have spread through the lymphatic drainage. We will also do some more imaging of your chest and abdomen looking for any tumors in these areas, concentrating on the lungs and liver."

"And the prognosis with metastasis is worse yet, I'm guessing," Sean's voice little more than a whisper.

Dr. Styles spoke for the first time, "now that would be a premature discussion. Let's follow through with the diagnostics that we've laid out and let the results dictate further discussion. Let's hope for the best concerning metastasis."

"Well, doctors, you've all been great. I appreciate your time and knowledge and wisdom. I think you'll be gratified to know that I am going to be a statistic that will help you discuss the upside with your next gliosarcoma patient. I will win. I will beat this thing." Mo smiled as she spoke.

All three doctors nodded in affirmation and smiled. Dr. Styles said, "That is exactly the attitude that can beat these things, Mrs. Murphy."

Sean was stunned. He was trying to absorb what he didn't even want to hear. He got up from the table and cleared his throat. He nodded to the three physicians and said a throaty thank you as he and his wife left the office.

OCALA, FLORIDA

June

"Well, Sean, my man, I can't tell you how good it is to see you. I'm sure glad you saw your way clear to make time for some fishing." Bubba Striker opened the lid to his grill and checked the steaks as he spoke.

"Well, I'll tell you, Mo practically kicked me out. She was right too; I needed a break. I've been working my ass off lately. And frankly when I'm not working I'm spending most of my time with the kids. Haven't taken any time for myself, I guess. And, you know, really, most of the time I feel like I don't do anything but worry about Mo."

"Well I'm sure the stress has been awful. Hell, I can see it on your face, buddy." Bubba flipped the steaks. "You're pretty rare, like your old man, right?"

"I like more than a grill mark, but yeah, pretty rare."

The scene from the patio looked across miles of open cattle pasture strewn with massive live oaks. A huge thunderhead stood on the horizon at the edge of the setting sun. Thinner clouds radiating to both sides of it reflected pink while the thunderhead formed a huge dark silhouette in a halo of bright white light.

Sean stood at the edge of the patio looking at the western sky. Conner approached with a bottle of wine. "It's hard to beat a Striker sunset. Bubba, you've done it again."

"What can I say, buddy? God just likes me more than most people." Conner grinned at the old joke between them.

Beth Striker walked on to the patio carrying a tray. "I didn't know if you boys were done with these snacks or not so I brought them out. There're some olives and nuts left, and a little cheese."

"No thanks, Beth. I need to save room for that side of beef Bubba's cooking," Sean declined as Beth held out the tray.

Conner grabbed two olives from a small bowl, "I won't let it go to waste, Beth."

"I can't believe we have the Murphy men here for dinner. What a treat this is. It's been too long, I know that." Beth raised her wine glass and nodded at Conner and Sean. "You're right it has been too long," Bubba agreed and raised his glass of diet coke in response. Bubba didn't drink alcohol and never had. His father had been a mean drunk and Bubba had sworn he'd never become like him. At age sixty-five, he probably never would.

He turned to his wife as he closed the lid to the grill, "Honey, these steaks will be ready in just a minute. How's the rest of the fixins; ready to put out?"

"I've just been waiting on you, I'll bring everything out."

"Let me help, ma'am."

"Conner, you certainly raised a polite one," Beth smiled over her shoulder.

The conversation and laughter never paused throughout dinner. Sean relaxed for the first time in months. Conner watched him, discreetly he hoped, and felt relieved that his son was enjoying himself so much. The wine played its part, but to be away from the stresses of work and home and in this setting, so familiar and comfortable, allowed him to shed some of the weight that had burdened him so heavily. Conner knew it was to be a brief respite, but he also knew that it was healthy for him and would give him the strength to rejoin the battle. It was important for his family, and for him, that Sean stay strong.

They became more raucous as they began talking about the Wiggs brothers and exchanged tales of their escapades. They had all known the Wiggs family, which only added to the fun, but Bubba had known them the best and related most of the stories.

"You know, growing up those boys hardly ever wore shoes. I mean even to school, Sean. And we're not talking about the thirty's or something, this was in the 1950's and sixties. Hell they all worked on cattle farms and later, horse farms and even then they hardly ever wore shoes. Can you imagine getting your bare foot stepped on by some two-year-old wearing toe grabs? Or just mucking a stall in your bare feet in all that manure and urine? Those boys were nuts.

"One of the great stories about those kids that just typifies what redneck crackers they were, and how damn tough they were I might add, were their hog hunting escapades."

Beth chimed in, "I thought I'd heard all the stories about those boys, but I don't remember this."

"It's unbelievable, Beth. Go on, Bubba", Conner threw in.

"Well, Sean, you probably know this, but the family was dirt poor. It was just old man and the four boys, I think the mother had run off, God bless her. None of them ever worked longer than it took to buy some new vehicle or boat or gun and then they'd quit. Most of what they ate, they either grew or killed themselves. I'm rambling; let me get back to the hog hunting."

"Bubba, rambling? Why I declare!" Beth winked at Sean.

Bubba tilted his head forward and looked at Beth over the top of his glasses. "As I was saying. Old man had an airboat that was his pride and joy. And as I recall, they never owned dogs. As much as they hunted dear and hogs and poached the occasional bear, they never used dogs."

Conner added through his laughing, "Well, hell, there's an easy answer to that. They poached so much they couldn't afford to have the baying hounds alert the warden."

Bubba continued with the hog hunt. "So old man would pilot the boat. He rarely drew a sober breathe now Sean; I don't know if you knew that."

"And the remarkable thing is that I never knew any of those boys to drink a lick," Conner added.

"You're right about that." Bubba responded. "Well, he drove that boat like a mad man; total abandon. When they'd hunt, there'd be two boys and old man in the boat."

"What was that old man's name?" Sean interrupted.

Bubba hesitated, "Well...shit I don't know. Everyone just called him 'old man'. The boys called him old man. And Sean, I don't mean 'the old man' or 'my old man', just 'old man'. They called him that to his face. Even all 'old man's' cronies just called him 'old man'."

Sean was laughing, "At what age do you suppose you get the name, 'old man'?"

Beth slapped the table as Conner poured more wine.

"Anyway, there'd be two boys and old man on the boat. He'd be piloting and one boy would be up on a seat next to him, helping him look for hogs. The other boy would be standing up in front hanging on to a nylon strap that was bolted to the deck of the boat. It was about a four-foot strap that the boy would grab on to and lean his weight against for balance. Well you can imagine flying along in an airboat, down the slews, or across a marsh, or across the tidal flats standing in front of the boat with that crazy drunk coot driving. And I'm telling you Beth, he had no clue how to throttle back; balls to the wall 90% of the time.

"They may go down the Withlacoochee or the Oklawaha or that marshy side of Hernando Lake, or maybe down the Waccasassa out to the flats, it didn't matter. Same set up;

old man'd be driving, the two boys watching, until someone saw a hog."

"They'd shoot it?" Beth asked.

"Darling, these are the Wiggses we're talking about. Shoot it? My God woman that would be sane! What a foolish notion. No the boy on the front of the...well first, let me back up. Someone spots the hog and hollers and waves and creates a commotion big enough so the others see it too. Remember, this is an airboat so no one can really hear shit. Once old man sets his sights, it's Katie bar the door. If there's any throttle left he shoves her full forward and the chase is on. And I mean I don't give a shit over what, through what, in to what, he's an obsessed man.

"Now imagine, the one boy is standing up in the front; standing! And at some point we've left the water and we're flying across open ground. I mean it was a sight to see. There were many times old man would hit something, a steep bank, or oyster bar or whatever and off the front that boy would sail. Amazing none of them ever died."

"Well, now damn it Bubba what are they doing?"

"Well, Beth, as soon as the chase starts in earnest, the boy standing pulls his hunting knife from its sheath and sticks it in his mouth, never letting go of his nylon strap. Old man is running the boat closer and closer and the hog is running its guts out, and not in a straight line mind you. So if the hog doesn't beat him to the trees, he eventually gets the boat alongside that hog until he gets close enough for the boy in front to jump out on to the hog's back and slit its throat."

"My God, I don't believe it! Slit its throat?" Beth threw herself back in her chair.

"And remember some of these hogs would be big and with big tusks. It would be a noisy, bloody battle."

"I suppose someone that uses a gun is a puss?" Sean was almost as shocked as Beth.

Conner said, "Isn't that amazing. Great story. And a true story."

"What an amazing bunch, tougher than nails." Sean commented.

Beth stood up from the table and grabbed two remaining glasses as she headed toward the kitchen. "I made that fruit compote that you like so much, Conner. Everyone want coffee?"

A chorus of 'yes, thank you' followed her in to the kitchen.

Conner said, "I've got just one more Wiggs story and we'll quit picking on them, at least for tonight. Davey is out in the National Forest in a deer stand hunting with his muzzleloader. I think in season, even, imagine that. He climbs up in to the stand, loads his gun and as he is trying to stick his tamp rod back in to its holder on the underside of the gun he drops it. It falls to the ground below him and sticks in the dirt straight up, like a spear, or lance or something. Shit, he says, but really no big deal; you only get one shot with a muzzleloader anyway, it's not like he's going to reload for a second shot.

"So it's getting dark and he hasn't seen any deer and it's time to give it up. He starts out of his stand, maybe twenty feet in the air, and boom, he falls; from the top. Now he thinks he's hunting alone, but the devil's with him, I'm telling you. He falls to the ground on his side and lands right on his ramrod. It goes completely through one thigh, in an upward direction, comes out the other side and goes in to his opposite butt cheek sticking in to his pelvis; into the damn bone! Now he's lying there, wind is knocked out of him, hurting like hell from the fall alone, plus he's been skewered through both legs! He starts to get his wits about him, and tries to get up, but can't. This damn ram rod has got his thighs pinned together."

Conner looks over at Bubba to see the tears running down his face. "You remember this story, Bubba?"

"Oh, God yea. I damn near pissed in my pants when three days later Davey is telling me this story. With his golly-gee,

125

Gomer Pyle expression on his face."

"Well, Sean, he finally struggles to his feet and commences to jerking on the ram rod, trying to pull it out of his leg. But the end of it is firmly lodged in his pelvis and he can't budge it."

"Jesus, think how much that hurt pulling on that thing, trying to get it out and it's stuck there. Damn." Sean grimaced as he spoke.

"So he can't get the rod out, it's dark, he's alone and a mile from his truck. He gathers up his pack and his gun and off he goes, walking the whole way with his thighs stuck together."

Bubba was laughing and he slapped the table. "Sean, that was so damn funny, him telling me that story several days later. He's got that goofy expression on his face, and he's walking back and forth with his knees together to mimic how he walked out of the woods that night; and he keeps saying to me 'can you believe it Bubba, can you believe it'. Damn I thought I'd die laughing."

Bubba got up from the table and was walking like a penguin, imitating Davey Wiggs when Beth came out with a tray of coffee and dessert.

"Now what are you up to?" Beth laughed as she spoke, setting the tray down hard on the table.

"Just more stories, hon, just more stories." Bubba wiped his eyes with the back of his hand.

"Are those boys, men I guess now obviously, still alive?" Sean asked. "It sounds like they should all be dead."

His father answered as he added cream to his coffee. "As a matter of fact, every one of them is dead. One died in a boating accident, one in a car crash, one on his Harley, and Davey had some off the wall lung disease where the lungs became fibrotic or something. I'm not sure really."

Bubba added, "Yea, but how's this for some sad irony. Davey is on a list for a lung transplant. Shortly after that his brother gets killed on his motorcycle and is listed as an organ donor. They don't make the connection to Davey, his lungs go to someone else and Davey dies without ever getting a transplant. And that was even before this bull shit health care system we have now."

Beth glared at her husband.

"Sorry, Sean, bad topic."

"No problem, Bubba. You're right, what a sad deal."

After dessert, they moved to the rattan couches under the fan. A breeze helped make the humid night pleasant.

"So, the plan for tomorrow is to get out of here about 8:30 or 9:00 which will put us on the water about 10:30." Bubba was lining out the next day's activities. "There's a minus tide in the afternoon, so I'm optimistic we might do some good. Obviously, Sean, this isn't the best time of the year for reds, now that it's getting hot. But actually we've had such an incredibly cool spring that I think we might do just fine. The tide is definitely in our favor. We can get way back in there with the air boat to those pools and if the fish are in there, we'll get 'em."

Beth asked, "Why wouldn't the fish be back in those pools, honey?"

"If the waters too warm. Those reds won't come in to the shallows it seems once the water warms up. But like I say, I can't remember when we've had this cool of a spring, so maybe we'll be OK."

"We'll have fun regardless."

"You thinking about any spots in particular, Bubba?" Conner asked.

"Oh, the usual, I guess. But I think we ought to try to go way back in on Muddy Creek, to the trees if we can. Again, if we're to do any good the fish gotta be there, but if they are, this tide ought to be perfect."

Sean said, "Now I brought my bag and my cot tent, is the plan still to stay out there on the hammock tomorrow night?"

"I think that's the plan. It should be pretty out there on the water tomorrow night."

"Sounds great to me," Sean said. "That might be my ultimate decompression for the week end. Being out on that hammock, sitting around a campfire sounds perfect."

"You boys just be sure to call me and let me know what you decide so I don't worry, OK?" Beth looked directly at Bubba.

Bubba grinned, knowing that she had every right to give him that hard look. "I promise. Conner here will remind me, I hope."

"You see, Sean," Bubba continued, "I've got a good dose of the coyote in me and it makes me a little scattered sometimes."

"He's also in love with drama," Beth chimed in, "so pushing the envelope is a constant. I might head to bed boys, is there anything I can get you before I go?"

Everyone was good so Beth leaned toward her husband and kissed him good night. She stood and kissed each of the Murphy men on the cheek.

"I'm so glad you're here, Sean. It's wonderful to see you. Should you call Mo?" Beth couldn't resist.

"Actually, I don't call her; I've been letting her call me. I don't know when she may be laying down and I don't want to disturb her. She calls me anytime she feels like it and it's been working out best that way. But thanks for thinking about it."

"She just thinks everyone is as forgetful as me," said Bubba.

"Well good night boys." Beth went on to bed.

The men sat under the breeze of the fan to finish their coffee and talk fishing. Bubba was optimistic that the cool weather would pay dividends.

"What do you know, the global warming seems to have taken another powder this spring." Conner said. "Or I should say, the last couple of years."

"Sean, I kept all those articles you wrote when that bullshit was getting exposed for what it was. That's when I first realized how damn funny you are." Bubba winked at his young friend as he coaxed his big orange cat on to his lap.

"When the exposed e-mails started to unravel the whole global warming scam it provided me with a lot of material. I didn't have to be very imaginative, it just kept coming and people like Al Gore made it easy. That bloated buffoon was..."

"Ah, yes. The 'King of the Canard' I believe you called him." Conner and Bubba laughed out loud.

"You know that really was a pivotal time in my career. My writing on that topic got me more exposure than I'd ever had. It allowed me to break through." Sean took a sip of wine and leaned back in the rocker. "It's also when I first realized how much hate some people can have for those that disagree with them."

WACCASASSA RIVER, FLORIDA

June

The day was clear and already getting hot when they arrived at the public dock on the Waccasassa River. Once on the water, Conner insisted that his son take the seat on the control platform, next to Bubba, where he could see better and be more comfortable.

"I get out here a lot more than you, Sean. You take the seat." Conner sat on the cooler in front of the control platform.

There was no shortage of osprey in the trees lining the river's edge that day. An occasional anhinga was seen perched on a protruding stump to dry outstretched wings. The shoreline was dotted with large white egrets standing in the shallows, motionless as they hunted small fish and crustaceans. As they approached a large blue heron left his spot on the bank to fly down river, as if to lead the way.

Bubba nudged Sean with his right elbow, pointing to a bald eagle perched on the limb of a snag off to their left. Sean reached forward and tapped his father's shoulder, pointing to the eagle as Conner turned back to look at him. Conner spotted it and then looked back at the two men behind him mouthing the word 'wow' as he held his hands one above the other. Bubba nodded in agreement.

A school of mullet boiled the water's surface in front of them, several jumping completely out of the water, as they fled some predator. When they left the river and hit open water Bubba ruddered to the right and accelerated, taking them west toward Cedar Key. Several dolphins joined in the adventure, swimming thirty yards from the boat, keeping pace and heading the same direction. Conner pointed at their escort and smiled back at Sean.

They hadn't gone much further west when Bubba left the open water and headed north again into Dry Creek. The first order of business was to run to the hammock and drop their camping gear. It was heavy and taking up too much room in the boat for them to fish comfortably. It was a mission quickly accomplished and in several minutes the men were back on the boat heading out Dry Creek toward the gulf.

Once around Compass Point and past East Pass the boat was in open water again and headed toward West Pass. Sean was watching an osprey flying about two hundred yards out in front of them. The majestic predator slowly descended closer to the water as she flew up stream. Suddenly she took several rapid beats of her wings and made a sudden, steep glide toward the water. Adjusting her wings just prior to colliding with the water she stretched out her talons to pluck a fish from just below the surface. The weight of the big fish made it difficult to get altitude and it looked as if she'd have to drop the fish. Finally the raptor gained enough elevation to get help from an air current and she banked off toward the trees to the right. Sean was so engrossed in nature's display that he didn't realize the boat had stopped.

Bubba had gone to the front and Conner had taken his place at the helm. "We're going to meander up these little runs and try to get some bait fish."

Bubba with a casting net was a man on a mission. His skill and strength made it look easy but the Murphy's knew better and were glad to let their friend take charge. Bubba stood braced with knees bent in the front of the boat as he held the net out away from his body until the right time to throw it, only to haul it back through the water and up on to the deck where he'd shake any fish loose and repeat it all again.

As the boat made its way up the narrow inlet, there were rises on the surface of the water just ahead and to the right of the boat. Conner had seen them at the same time as Bubba and steered the boat in that direction.

Bubba waited until he was close to the spot where he had last seen the ripples and cast his net. He hauled it back and in to the boat. Two six inch mullet and a pin fish were in the net. He grabbed a spot on the weighted bottom of the net and pulled it up as he shook the fish on to the deck. Sean jumped from his seat and grabbed the slippery, flopping fish one at a time, tossing the mullet in to the bait cooler and the pin fish in to the live bucket.

Bubba's next cast found a rock, snagging his net and resulting in a chain of his favorite profanities. Dressed in Wrangler jeans and white rubber boots, he jumped overboard, into what was about two feet of water to walk the short distance to the net. It took nearly a minute and several more expletives before he managed to free the net and wade back to the boat. Once back in the boat he sat on the deck and elevated his feet to let the water run from his boots. The hunt for more bait fish continued for another half an hour until Bubba was satisfied they had enough and stowed his net.

"We all set, girls? Let's head to the Muddy." Bubba pushed the throttle forward and spun the boat around in a tight circle to head back out to the open water.

They couldn't have asked for a prettier day, warming up

considerably as the sun marched higher in the sky, but the breeze was constant, not only keeping the fishermen cool but also lessening the threat from mosquitoes or no-see-ums. On the drive to the river the topic of the unusually cool spring had come up again, and Bubba repeated that it was the only thing that gave him any optimism about getting in to the reds today.

Conner was feeling so content that it gave him a tinge of guilt when he thought about Mo. He was with two people that he loved dearly, doing what he loved to do on a day that was unbeatable for its serenity and beauty. He didn't want to feel guilty and he hoped that Sean wasn't. They all deserved this day, all for different reasons or, hell, maybe for no reason at all. He knew Mo was happy for all of them.

Bubba steered the boat in to Muddy Creek and headed north toward the trees. The water was shallow and Bubba throttled back slightly as he slalomed around the oyster bars. Finally, he slowed up even more and headed straight for the bank, trying to hit it at 90°. Conner saw it coming and gripped the front of the ice chest. Bubba turned to Sean and winked as the bow of the boat bumped the bank. He hit the gas and up they flew on to dry land. A large grassy expanse lay in front of them that was encircled by the meandering Muddy Creek. This was Bubba's short cut, which saved time and the bottom of his boat in the shallows of Muddy Creek.

Sean had fished this area of the gulf his whole life. When he was old enough to go by himself or with kids his age, he remembered how shocked he'd been that everything looked so different. There were few landmarks on those tidal flats; a recognizable point of land here and there or the occasional clump of trees, but very little that the uninitiated would appreciate. Not only are there very few landmarks, but the real challenge was in the fact that the visual landscape is always shifting with the tides. Eventually, Sean had developed the same feel for that area that the older men had and he could find all of the creeks, runs, and most of the fishing holes.Bubba clipped across the grassy flat about twenty miles per hour not afraid of any surprises on this stretch. After a few minutes he began to throttle down and slow the boat as the creek came back in to view. He steered a little to the right as he approached the water to bring the bow perpendicular to the bank. It was about three feet down to the water as Bubba gently throttled forward to let the hull ease over the side and gently set itself in to the shallow water below. The men stood and pulled off their headgear.

"This is the edge of a long deep hole, we call Brian's Hole." Bubba was explaining, mostly for Sean's benefit. "This baby has produced a lot of fish over the years, but who knows, today it may not. It's big enough that we will fish this end and then move up to the other end and fish it before we give up."

The day consisted of moving from hole to hole, some producing fish and some not. But the day evolved in to everything they had hoped for; perfect weather, a limit of reds and one trout for good measure. It was evening and the light was waning when they returned to the hammock.

In the remaining light, they set about getting their camp organized; throwing up cot tents and getting the kitchen and lanterns in order. Bubba opened his requisite diet coke and the Murphy's each cracked open a bottle of Corona. They all pitched in to make a dinner of fresh fish and vegetables. With bellies full and bodies tired from a long day in the sun, the three men sat back with their coffee and Bubba asked about Jan.

Conner responded, "Things are great. We're going back and forth a lot; me there and her here. But right now she's taking care of her mom. Her mother lives with Jan's sister in Seattle, but her and her husband have gone to Italy for vacation so Jan's pulling the duty."

"Her mom go to Jackson?"

"Yea, Jan's taking care of her at her house."

"Is she an invalid?"

"No, but she doesn't need to be alone, that's for sure."

"So there's a little hiatus in the love affair, I guess," commented Bubba.

Bubba switched his attention to Sean to ask him about his work.

"Dad and I have had this conversation before, Bubba," Sean was saying, "But I never thought I'd be writing for a news or opinion magazine. I'd always pictured myself writing screenplays or being a playwright. Frankly, politics always drove me crazy; pissed me off actually."

"Well, you've become well known in that arena now, Sean." Bubba answered and then laughed as he added, "Those liberal pussies in Hollywood would have no part of you now!"

"Oh, I'm sure that's true. I'm also sure I never had a shot there anyway. The movie business is the most nepotistic business in the world."

"Well now that there's a lot of water under that bridge, are you glad you're doing what you're doing? You happy with the choice?"

"Without a doubt, Bubba. I made the right choice for me. I'm good at what I do and I've become passionate about it. I'll tell you though there is a part of it that...what should I say, bothers me about the world I live in. It's the degree of animosity that exists; it can be a little unnerving."

"Hell, son. Politics can be passionate with a lot of people. On both sides of the fence."

"Believe me Dad, I get that. But passion is one thing. Hate is another. I've learned that some people have contempt for me that... well, it's shocking, and a little scary. I believe there are people that would kill me if they thought they could get away with it. And, hey, I thought we were just arguing ideas back and forth in a democracy." Sean laughed and raised his coffee mug in a toast, but Conner saw the seriousness in his son's eyes.

The next morning, Bubba had the fire going and the coffee on when the other two rolled out of their bags. The sun wasn't up yet but daylight was making its way in through the leafy canopy of the hammock. Conner had already walked over to the stove and poured himself a cup of coffee. He was bent over the grub box trying to locate the cream when Sean arrived at the fire.

"You didn't have to dress for breakfast, it's supposed to be casual," Bubba said to Sean who had walked up dressed only in boxer shorts and flip-flops.

"It's no trouble, I just feel you guys are worth it, that's all," Sean quipped in reply.

"Conner," Bubba was saying as he made his way to the cook table, "I know you've always fancied yourself as kind of a stud, but you never looked like that boy. Never."

Sean was standing at the fire as his dad brought him a cup of coffee. Sean was just under six feet and had similar facial features to his father, but instead of being bald, Sean had a full head of curly hair. Like his father, he was broad at the shoulders but was bigger through the chest and his arms were considerably larger. At thirty-four years of age, Sean had an enviable physique; very muscular with little body fat.

"You still doing your martial arts stuff, Sean?" Bubba asked.

"No, I haven't done Tai Kwon Do in a couple of years. You know it's funny. There were a few years there that I was really in to it. Then once I got my black belt I kind of lost interest. It was weird really; I didn't anticipate that.

"Hey, but I am boxing again. I don't go much now, since Mo's been sick. But I do enjoy it; as much as anything, it's the guys at my gym. They're a good bunch and we have a good time. Good work outs, great camaraderie, you know."

"They might not let you come back if you don't back off a bit though," Conner chided his son.

"What's that about," Bubba asked.

"Oh, I was telling Dad that it's been a great stress release when I do go. But lately, with Mo's deal, I guess I've been getting a little carried away, getting a little too aggressive, but not really realizing it. The other day a couple of the guys weren't too happy about it.

But they're good guys and I just need to watch it. And they're right; nobody goes there to get hurt and we're all friends."

Conner asked his old friend, "Well, amigo, what's the plan for today?"

"Right now my plan is breakfast. Then I thought we'd try and slay a few more reds this morning, come back for lunch and break camp. Sean, where'd you go, I thought you...."

"I'm over here taking a leak. But I can hear you, press on with the plan."

"Well I thought you were trying to make it back to Tampa before it got too late, right?"

"Yea," Sean said as he came back around the tree. "But I figure if we start back to the dock by 2:00 or so that should be good. That work for y'all?"

"Doesn't make a shit to me. I'm great with any plan y'all come up with," Conner said, bent over the ice chest again, digging out the breakfast sausage.

"I think that gives us time for a good amount of fishing this morning just like your Uncle Bubba planned. Conner, you're looking in the wrong ice chest, sweet heart. It's that one by the table."

After breakfast they shared the cleanup duty and then returned to their cots to get dressed for another morning of fishing. Once dressed, Sean returned to the table to grab another coffee. As he filled his cup he glanced over to the clearing just south of the hammock and saw Bubba conducting his morning prayers.

Bubba had both hands held out from his sides and was facing into the east. Sean could hear the sound of his voice but the words were unclear. Sean watched him bring his right hand toward his body and remove something from a leather pouch that hung around his neck and toss it gently into the air toward the east. He then turned toward the south, again with arms outstretched and began speaking again. He went back to the pouch and offered some tobacco to the southern direction.

Sean watched Bubba pray to all four directions and then to the sky above, each time repeating the ritual of praying followed by the offering of tobacco. Then he knelt on his right knee and put his open hand on the soil as he bowed his head to the ground. The morning breeze shifted toward Sean, carrying Bubba's words toward him but the only words Sean understood were the words 'abundant Mother earth'. After a minute, Bubba stood and returned to the camp. Bubba smiled at Sean as he approached the table.

"It always makes me feel better to thank our Creator for another day, Sean."

"I've never known you not to be spiritual, Bubba. Have you been that way your whole life?"

"Only since I've been awake, Sean. Before that I was a scared, angry prick. I woke up about thirty years ago, I guess. Had to, I'd be dead or in prison by now if I hadn't."

"You've been a good man all my life, Bubba, so I guess it's working."

The four hours they spent fishing that morning wasn't as successful as the afternoon before, something they were prepared for, knowing the tide wasn't as favorable. The sky was a pale, cloudless blue and the June air remained fresh with a slight breeze out of the east. There was such a strong connection between these men. Just being together in that wild, boundless environment was what they really enjoyed, catching fish was only the rationale for being there; so three additional reds were simply icing on the cake of a great morning.

Returning to the hammock at noon, Conner made them all sandwiches while the others started gathering their things. Conner, in typical fashion, used wheat tortillas instead of bread, which generated an eye roll from his son. They ate as they broke camp and within an hour were back at the boat landing of the Waccasassa; in another hour they were at the Striker farm, unhooking the boat and sorting their gear in front of Bubba's barn.

The goodbyes were short but each Murphy got the usual strong, heartfelt hug from Bubba as he sent them off. They made their way over to County Road 326 in north Marion County and followed it to I-75 south. The next stop would be Sean's house in Carrollwood, just north of Tampa.

"You know Dad, I haven't heard you talk politics in a long time until this trip. I hadn't really realized that until this morning. You always used to be pretty engaged in thinking and talking about it. I realized today that it's been a while since I've heard you bring it up."

"It's funny you should say that, because I was thinking the same thing. You know, I just got away from being so immersed in thinking about politics and keeping up with it like I always had. Certainly, as you were growing up, you heard me pontificate, or maybe rant is the better word, about all different things political."

"Believe me I remember, but why the change?" Sean asked.

"It was at a time when I became overwhelmed with frustration and sadness about the direction our country was going, and unfortunately is still going. That time really corresponded with the loss of your Mom. I guess I struggled so much trying to recover emotionally from your Mom's death that I couldn't cope with any other extraneous frustration and disappointment. So I just disengaged myself from politics. Following your Mom's death, when I sold the farm in Ocala, I changed my life a lot. I was just seeking a way to be happy.

"But I've felt bad, you know, over the past several years, because I've been so proud of you. You've forged yourself a name and a great career based on your political insight; you've developed a great writing style, which incorporates your sense of humor so well. I feel that I haven't been as much a part of that as I could be. I don't know what I mean by 'a part of it', that's stupid...."

Sean interrupted, "I know what you mean. Just sharing it and tossing some things around like we used to."

"Yea, that is what I mean. But also letting you know more often how right I think you are about so many things you write about, your insight, all of that. This weekend, especially listening to you and Bubba talk, I realized that I would like to, I don't know, re-engage and be more involved in that part of your world again. Am I making sense, because I feel like I'm rambling?"

"Sure you make sense, and I'd like that. Your opinions and intuitiveness have always been something I enjoy and admire, Dad."

"Well, I'll tell you. Bubba thinks I've just shriveled up and died," Conner was grinning as he said it. "He's missed my animated rants that filled the air with blue and fireworks."

"Dad there's something else. Something else I need to talk about with you. I wanted to come on this trip for several reasons. First off, Mo wanted me to come. She's seen how the stress has been eating at me and knew a break would help. And I knew the same thing; I needed a break. But I also wanted the chance to talk to you, to let you know what's going on with Mo right now. As much as we talk on the phone, I don't know why I felt compelled to talk face to face, but I did. This process of weaving through this Public Health Agency has been a nightmare."

Conner interrupted, "I know it has. It's been very evident with everything you've told me. It knots me up listening to you talk about it."

"Well, I haven't even told you everything, not nearly. I haven't wanted you to be as frustrated and angry as we've been, and sometimes I just can't even face talking about it."

Sean took an involuntary, short breath and his bottom lip started trembling slightly as he tried to speak. No words came; he turned his head to look out the side window trying to compose himself enough to continue. Observing his son in this much pain shook Conner; his heart felt like it was sinking through his body like a stone. Sean turned his head to look forward at the road ahead. Tears streamed down his cheeks.

Conner had both hands on the steering wheel but took his right hand and put it on his son's, which was gripping the center console. Conner squeezed his son's hand.

"It's just so fucking hard, so fucking hard," Sean's voice was rising. "I'm watching my wife die and no fucking body will help us." He lowered his voice again, "Oh, shit. I'm sorry, Dad. I'm blubbering like a baby."

Conner continued to squeeze his son's hand, "Can I suggest something to you?"

"Of course."

"Scream right now. Yell out at the top of your lungs, from your gut as loud as you can. Scream!"

Sean hesitated; he did nothing.

"Yell out son, scream!"

"Aaaaaaarrgh. Aaaaaarrgh." Sean screamed as loudly as he could. It sounded animal like, primordial.

"Again, damn it. Scream. Get that shit out of you. Let God know how fuckin' mad you are."

Sean roared out in long, protracted yells, several times in a row, only taking time for another breath in between. When he finished, he stopped and hung his head and cried for a minute. Then he raised his head and screamed again, two more times. He leaned back and wiped his face with the back of his hands. In the mean time his father had dug a Kleenex box out of the console and handed him a wad of tissues.

Conner had not pulled the car over but had kept heading south on the interstate, driving in the right lane a little slower than the flow of traffic. He was quiet now, concentrating on driving and was holding on to his son's hand again.

"Thanks, Dad. I do feel better. At least I'm not blubbering anymore," he forced a smile as he said it.

"If what you're going through didn't make you cry, you'd be a... shit, I don't know. A calloused piece of shit I guess."

Sean was quiet and fairly composed as he reflected on

141

something, "You know, I'd forgotten about this; but it's in my head now, a really clear vision of it actually. I guess it was about a month after Mom died and we were at Bubba and Beth's. Actually, you were staying there at the time and Mo, the kids, and I came up to see you. I remember sitting on their back patio and you and Bubba were out underneath one of those big oak trees below their house. You were both sitting on something I remember. Stumps, or something; it doesn't matter. I could tell Bubba was talking to you but I couldn't hear him. Then I heard you yell. You screamed out time after time. Shit you sounded like a lion standing over his kill. I remember the goose bumps it gave me. You know, the hair stood up on my neck. I went back in to the house, a little shook up actually, and y'all came up a while later. I'd forgotten that till now, but I always thought it was some cathartic...something."

"Well, as our man Bubba tells it, it's a way of getting the poisonous shit out of us. I don't know what it does. But I can tell you this, there have been times in my life that it brought me back from some pretty dark places."

Sean smiled at the road ahead, "Well, I feel better."

"Do you want to tell me the status of things, Sean, or drop it for now?"

"No, I do want to tell you. We finally got an OR scheduled and have the biopsy surgery a full six weeks after Dr. Johnson had put in his request. We got those results back and, you remember, it was a good news bad news deal. The tumor came back as a gliosarcoma, the bad one, but there wasn't metastasis to the lymph nodes."

"Yea, I'm with you. I remember that."

"Well we had a meeting with Dr. Johnson just a few days ago and he is putting in a request for treatment. It will be surgery and radiation for sure and he's still consulting with the oncologist about chemo as well. It's been a long nightmare but at least we're finally getting somewhere now."

"That's fantastic. So now you're waiting for a surgery date?"

"Waiting being the operative word." Sean was looking out the side window as he said it.

Conner and Sean could hear the Murphy kids playing in the pool in the back yard when they got out of the Toyota in Sean's driveway.

"That's a racket. I hope Mo isn't trying to sleep." Sean said as he gathered up his cot tent and sleeping bag. "Can you grab that duffel for me Dad?"

Once in the house, Conner said he would go out to the pool and check what the kids were up to. He didn't want to intrude on Sean and Mo.

"Hey, Connie, don't you look relaxed and enjoying life?"

"Well, hi there, Mr. Murphy." Connie was dressed in her bathing suit, lying on a chaise lounge. She put her magazine down on the table next to her to give Conner her full attention.

"You've got to call me Conner. Or even Murph. But you have to stop the Mr. Murphy stuff."

"Oh, I'm just old fashioned, I guess. My Mama raised me that way. You know 'yes ma'am' and 'no sir'."

"Well, actually, good for you."

"Grandpa!" Karen had just seen her grandfather.

"Grandpa!" Jeremy saw him next. They were both wearing their swimming goggles and apparently playing a game which involved diving to the bottom of the pool to retrieve plastic toys.

"Watch me, Grandpa, watch me!" Karen was out of the pool and running toward the diving board.

"I'm not watching anybody until I get two big hugs. Get over here pumpkin head. You too, Mr. Brown."

Jeremy had to make one more dive to the bottom of the pool but Karen stopped her forward progress in an exaggerated, dramatic way and turned to run toward her grandfather. She ran around the end of the pool as fast as her little legs would carry her and threw her arms out wide as she collided with

Conner's thigh. Conner put his hand on her back and pressed her in to his leg. When she let go of his leg she smiled up at her grandfather, about to give him his instructions.

"Kisses, pumpkin head, kisses first," Conner said as he bent at the knees.

His granddaughter leaned in and gave him a kiss on each cheek before running toward the diving board yelling, "Watch me, watch me, Grandpa."

By now Jeremy was hugging his grandpa's waist. Conner tussled his hair as he watched Karen run and jump off the end of the board. Her antics consisted of running off the end with arms and legs going in every direction as she flew down to the water. She then swam under water toward the swim out at the other end of the pool, surfacing twice for air on her way.

"Were you watching, Grandpa, did you see me?"

Conner looked up from Jeremy's bionic soldier that he had rescued from the bottom of the pool.

"I sure did see you, honey. That was great."

"I can dive now Grandpa. A real dive. You want to see?"

"Of course I do, Mr. Brown. How 'bout doing it for me?"

"You bet!"

Jeremy had his goggles around his neck as he ran to the diving board. He walked out to the end as he raised his outstretched arms above his head with hands folded together. He hesitated for just a second at the end of the board and then bent his body forward and propelled himself off of the board. He went mostly straight down, not getting much distance with his new-learned technique. When he surfaced he treaded water as he looked over at his Grandpa.

"That was the real deal there, Mr. Great job. A real dive."

The praise seemed to release Jeremy from his spot and he swam a quasi breaststroke to the side of the pool; all smiles.

Karen never took off her goggles but kept running to the diving board to do her chaotic leap while imploring her grandfather to watch her. Jeremy was back at task, throwing his figurines out into the depths and valiantly retrieving them, apparently before any of the bad guys could get them.

Connie said to Conner as he took a chair next to her lounge, "They sure love their Grandpa."

"They're wonderful, aren't they?" The old yellow lab didn't waste the opportunity to get some attention from a new visitor and propped her head on Conner's lap while she stood wagging her tail.

"They certainly are, Mr. Murphy. They're great kids and they are very easy, very polite, and compliant. 'Pumpkin head' is pretty easy to figure out with Karen's beautiful red hair, but Mr. Brown? Where did that come from? I've heard you call Jeremy that but never knew why."

"Gosh, I think he was just a baby when I came up with that." Conner was scratching Rosie behind both ears as he searched his memory. "And I'm not sure exactly what I meant anymore, or why at least it's Mr. Brown and not Mr. something else. One day when he was still not walking yet I was messing with him and he was so serious. He seemed so purposeful and focused as he studied my face and observed my every movement. It was comical; his face looked like that of a very attentive old man and it was really odd how long he held that intensely inquisitive look. I called him Mr. Brown that day, and, I don't know, it just stuck with me. I think I'm the only one that calls him that, but I guess I'm not sure."

Sean walked out to where Connie and Conner were sitting and took a chair next to them.

"Hi Connie, everything good?" Sean said, smiling at the nanny as he said it.

"No problems at all. Can you tell by the harsh working conditions I'm contending with this afternoon?"

"Well, thanks, as usual. You're a life saver."

"How's Mo?" Conner asked.

"She was lying down but awake when I went in. She's getting up now; she seems OK." Sean gave his shoulders a little shrug as he spoke. "She won't want to come outside in this bright sunshine though."

"Well let me pop in and give her a hug before I get on the road." Conner stood and looked toward the pool. "Hey, ragamuffins, come kiss Grandpa goodbye, he needs to go."

Both kids clambered out of the pool yelling hi to their daddy as they headed for Conner. They reached him as he squatted down to wrap his arms around both of them. He kissed them and told them how much he loved them before letting them go. Conner stood to say goodbye to Connie as Sean was now hugging his kids and telling them how much he missed them over the weekend.

"Did you catch a big fish, Dad?" Jeremy asked.

"I sure did, buddy. And we'll have some for dinner tonight."

"I don't like fish, Daddy." Karen spoke up.

"I'll bet there's some macaroni and cheese in there with your name on it. We'll see, baby."

"Bye, Connie. I'm sure I'll see you soon," Conner said as he bent over to give her ankle a shake.

"I won't stay long, Sean. I need to go and I don't want to be a bother to Mo."

"She always loves to see you, Dad. But today looks like it's a tough one for her. That might be best."

As Conner approached the kitchen, Mo was coming in from the other side. He was startled to see her. She was thin, maybe not any thinner than the last time he'd seen her, but he couldn't get used to how drawn her face looked. Her hair was pulled back with a clip, and she had no makeup on. It was out of character for her to look unkempt, but it only bothered him because he knew it bothered her not to have the energy to deal with it. Her head was cocked slightly as she walked toward the counter. She put her hand out to lean on the counter but

146

misjudged it slightly and had to lean further than she thought, causing her to do an awkward little shuffle to the side to catch her balance.

"I'm quite entertaining, really," she smiled at Conner as she said it. "A little like watching a land lubber walk on a boat for the first time."

Conner continued toward her and took her in his arms. "I love you, sweetie," he said after almost a minute of holding her close to him.

"I love you too, Conner. Thank you. Sean says you guys had a great time."

Conner backed away but was holding her left arm with his right hand, not willing to let her go. "We did have fun. It was great actually. And just as great to see the two ragamuffins out at the pool."

"Yea, they are just about perfect, I think. They love their Grandpa."

"Well, I'll let you guys go, I need to try and get a few groceries in the house." He hugged his daughter-in-law again briefly. "I love you Mo."

He kissed her on the cheek and she smiled up at him. Conner turned toward his son and gave him a hug as well.

"Thanks for taking the time to come with us for a couple days, buddy. It was a lot of fun."

"I enjoyed it, Dad. I'm glad I went."

Conner's thoughts were full of worry about Mo as he made his way back to I-75 South. His eyes filled with tears as he thought about how she looked and how she must feel. He hated that his family was dealing with something so dreadful. He loathed the fact that a young woman as beautiful and caring as Mo was so sick; the idea that his son could lose his wife, as he had, but at even a more horrible time in their lives. 'The kids, oh God damn it, the kids.' He couldn't bear the thought of them losing their mother. He was overwhelmed by the thought of his precious daughter-in-law not being able to raise her children and see them grow and live their lives.

Conner took his own advice and screamed at the top of his lungs. It was almost a roar that started deep in his belly and was released through his wide-open mouth. He was gripping the steering wheel tightly and shook it as he screamed, looking straight down the road, through tear filled eyes.

TAMPA, FLORIDA

June

"Hello, Sean, this is Dr. Frank Johnson. How are you today?" "I'm good Frank. Have we got some news?" Sean sat down as he took the call.

"Well, I do have news, but I'm afraid it's not the news we wanted. Can you come to my office today and we can talk about it."

Sean didn't answer. His mind was reeling and he felt like his body was in a free fall. "Sean. Are you there?"

"Yea, hey, Frank, uh, hang on just a second." He put the receiver on his lap as he took measured breaths. He closed his eyes as he tried to clear his head. He opened his eyes and looked at his watch; 3:30. "What time Frank? What time do you want to meet?"

"Well I'll be wrapped up at 5:00 and can simply wait till you get here. This isn't much notice, I know, but I didn't want you to be stewing all day thinking about it. Will that work for you? Five-ish?"

"Yea, I guess. Yea, that's fine. I'll leave here in a few minutes and pick up Mo and head to your office. We can be..."

"Sean, I thought we might want to discuss this between us, without Mrs. Murphy. It might give us a chance to discuss the alternatives without adding to her stress or frustration with this process."

"Jesus Christ, Frank."

"Sean, this isn't good news, but there are avenues we need to be exploring to get this on track. I want to tell you what the strategy needs to be. At least what I think it needs to be if you agree. Then we can involve your wife in the discussion. Does that seem fair?"

"OK, OK. Yea, that's fine. Thanks, Frank. I'll see you at 5:00."

Sean buzzed his secretary on the intercom, "Inez, can you come here a second."

Inez, a plump, forty something, came quickly with pen and pad in hand. In three years she had taught Sean the value of a highly proficient secretary. Sean finished typing notes on to his laptop before he looked up.

"Sorry. I need you to call Gil Stevens and tell him that I'll speak with him tomorrow concerning the speech on the 23rd."

"Yes, sir."

"I'm going to e-mail you my notes for today's meeting. I'd like you to clean them up and print three sets of hard copies then take them over to Bill's office when you're done. OK?"

"Of course, Mr. Murphy," Inez was well aware of his wife's condition and the awful stress her boss was under.

"Thanks, I'm going to be heading out in just a minute," Sean said as he returned to his computer.

Inez was almost to the door when she stopped and turned back toward her boss. "Is there anything else I can do to help you, Mr. Murphy? "

Sean looked up, grateful for the compassion in her voice.

"Inez, you're very sweet, and thank you very much. I'll be fine. I'll be in bright and early in the morning."

Sean made one more call to explain to the chief editor his reason for missing this afternoon's meeting and to let him know Inez would be bringing copies of his notes. Bill Simon understood and wished him well with the consultation. Bill, like all of Sean's colleagues, knew about Mo's condition and was very sympathetic. Sean, in general, was well liked and was recognized as a top performer and a leader at 'The Constitution'. Sean thanked Bill for his comments and headed out the door.

The small flurry of office activity had provided a brief distraction but now alone in the car his thoughts returned to Dr. Johnson. He knew what the thrust of the news would be, but what did Johnson have in mind to be back on track as he put it? Sean began to formulate different scenarios in his mind. He decided it was a foolish exercise and concentrated on taking solace in the fact that the neurologist was an extremely competent physician and had shown the utmost compassion through this ordeal. If he said he had a strategy, Sean would wait to hear it. He arrived at the Moffitt Center at 4:30 and parked in outpatient parking.

Sean decided to take a walk to kill the thirty minutes, knowing he couldn't sit still in a waiting room. His thoughts returned to different scenarios of what Johnson might say and after several minutes realized that he was walking very fast and almost hyperventilating. His mouth was dry and the back of his shirt was stuck to his sweaty back.

"Jesus Christ, Sean, get a grip," he said to himself out loud. "Stop with the bull shit scenarios."

Sean walked slowly toward the office hoping he wouldn't have to wait long once he got there.

"Hi, Mr. Murphy. Dr. Johnson said to watch for you and bring you right back to his office when you arrived. It certainly has warmed up out there, hasn't it?" Sean thought he returned the smile, but he wasn't sure.

Sean followed the woman down the hallway past several exam rooms. The door to Dr. Johnson's office was open and he heard them approach. He came around his desk to greet Sean as he entered the office.

"Thanks for coming in on such short notice, Sean."

"That's fine. I'm a little early I think."

"It's perfect. Have a seat." Dr. Johnson gestured toward a chair in front of his desk and then shut the door to his office. Rather than walking around to the back of his desk, he took a chair next to Sean.

"Well, let me cut to the chase. I've left you hanging with my phone call which was not my intent, but I'd much rather have this discussion face to face."

"That's fine. I understand."

"And I hope you don't mind that I have asked to speak with you alone, but that was really a decision based on a 'best interest of the patient' consideration. Our options are limited so it's not like we are excluding Mrs. Murphy from a treatment decision or anything like that."

"I trust you, Frank. I'm sure your reason for meeting with me alone is fine."

"OK, so here's the deal, Sean. The PHA has denied me, or anyone for that matter, to proceed with Mo's treatment. They have the authority to call the shots and they have done so. I was shocked at this decision based on...."

"What the hell is that about? I mean we...I'm sorry, go ahead."

"Don't apologize, I understand your frustration. I was floored by their decision based on the fact that there has been no metastasis. That being said, I wouldn't have expected them to deny treatment even if there had been metastasis, but the fact that there hasn't been... well, I couldn't believe it when I got the treatment request back.

"What they are telling me is that the reason for denial is that it is a tumor that has a poor prognosis and, shit, this is hard for me to even say to you. And it has been going on for too long, making the prognosis even worse."

"Going on too long! Are you kidding me Frank? Are you fucking kidding me?"

Sean jumped from his chair and started to pace as he looked up at the ceiling. He stopped and covered his face with his hands as he stood there. He began to rub his head from front to back as he resumed pacing the floor. Every word was coated in frustration when he finally spoke.

"Don't those God damned morons know that it's been going on

152

so long because of them? Because of their fucking incompetence. Their God damned bureaucratic red tape bull shit!?"

Dr. Johnson didn't respond. He waited for Sean to vent. He only spoke when it was apparent Sean was finished.

"Let me tell you where I've been with this Sean."

"I'm sorry, Frank. But God damn it! God damn it!" Sean fell back down in to his chair. He looked across at the neurologist and said, "Frank, when I said I trust you, I was serious. I know you're on our side. I know it. Tell me what the hell we do now?"

"Let me catch you up to where I've been so far. Immediately upon getting notice of the denial I was in touch with their office at the PHA. I informed them that I was going above that office, over their heads to the next level of review. That's pretty much standard procedure with many denials and they more or less expect that. I have put my argument together and I've scheduled a presentation."

Sean was doing his best to focus on what he was hearing.

"Five people sit on this panel, only two are MD's, the other three are bureaucrats; pencil pushers or bean counters of some type. Actually one of the MD's is a woman; and she is a complete bitch. On my first appearance in front of this panel I discovered what an idiot she is. I was so astonished by what came out of her mouth that when I left there that day I immediately researched who the hell she is.

"It turns out that she was basically a failed physician. She was in family practice, started about ten years ago, well before the government took over. She couldn't make a go of it. She was so incompetent and from what I here, such an abrasive bitch, that she couldn't develop a practice. After only a couple of years of floundering around she had also generated several malpractice claims against her. I found out that by the time the PHA was established she couldn't even get malpractice coverage any more. Now, Sean, this is in a field of medicine that has had a tremendous shortage of doctors virtually forever. To fail in that arena, she must have been pathetic. Now she sits on this panel, makes a better living than she ever has, basically can't be fired and has power over peoples' lives. You can tell she relishes it. You can imagine the chip she has on her shoulder and the disdain she has for successful docs. I can't even begin to describe to you the ignorant shit she spews while sitting on that panel. I swear I could go out on the street and grab any person walking down the sidewalk and they'd know more about medicine than her.

"Anyway, sorry I digressed, but I start thinking about that bitch and I about lose my mind. The other MD is a good guy, reasonable. Was a good physician before this job; an older guy that basically quit his practice rather than deal with the new government system. He's looking for a few years of income before retiring, is what he's told me. Then out of the three bureaucrats, there's one, another woman, that seems to be very reasonable and to be a good person. The other two are just quintessential bureaucrats; everything is by the book. These two guys have their little actuary charts and they don't detour off of them. Everything has to fit in to a row and column; oh, for God's sake we could never stray off of that.

"So, to boil it down, with your wife's situation we fit in to a row and column that treatment is not an option. The combination of cost versus prognosis puts us in the category of denial of treatment and as far as these people are concerned that is the end of the story; no room for discussion. It will be my job when I meet with them to push her case out of that spot on their chart, make them see that she doesn't fit in to that row and column as their underlings had thought she had."

Sean listened intently, stuffing his emotional reaction for now, and analyzed what he heard to see if he could see a crack in their wall of denial.

"Do all of these people have the same clout on the panel, the same vote? Or does one of them chair the panel that may have more influence?"

"There is a chairman," Frank answered. "He is one of the staunch bureaucrats. His vote is equal and, truthfully, I don't feel he has much clout with the others on the panel."

"OK."

"What I have done so far is to put together the case that I think has potential to sway this panel. I am basing my argument on the fact that there is no metastasis, the location of the tumor makes it operable and Mo is a young, strong woman with a will and a reason to fight for her life."

"What about the fact that this has gone on for so long because of their system. That they are part of the problem that caused the very reason that she's been denied," Sean was almost shouting.

"Frankly, Sean, I'm not...."

"Well, listen Frank, I don't mean that you should say it like I just said it."

"I hope you think I'm more diplomatic than that." Dr. Johnson smiled. "I am going to very briefly touch on that subject early on in my presentation. But I can tell you that they don't care. That won't matter to them a bit. All they know is that based on when the clinical signs began and the tumor size, their 'charts' tell them the cancer is at 'this stage' and that the prognosis and treatment cost is based on that fact. End of story.

"In addition, I don't want to give Dr. Futch, she's the bitch, any excuse to retaliate against what she construes as an accusation of wrong doing by her beloved PHA."

"When is this meeting?"

"Three weeks from today." Dr. Johnson looked at Sean's expression, "I know, I know. Believe it or not I pushed very hard for any opening they had and pulled every string I knew how to pull. Three weeks is very fast for this process. I can't tell you the number of people that die before this part of the process can even take place."

"Thanks for everything you do. It's just so unbelievable," Sean leaned forward with his elbows on his knees and looked from the doctor to the floor. He put his head in his hands as Dr. Johnson continued.

"I've even taken it a step further. Honestly, I've taken a chance by doing this but I think it will pay off. It is absolutely forbidden for anyone that is an advocate for the patient during this appeal process to contact any members of the review panel. I broke that rule and contacted both John Hirschel and Lois Stark. He's the MD and she's the one bureaucrat that I have any faith in. I've made my case to them one on one. Actually both of them were understanding and I think that we have them on our side. The question is, can they be influential enough with their other panel members to make a difference."

Sean looked up, "Sounds like it was worth a try. How fast will they make a decision after you meet with them?"

"Usually within a few days, or less even. That's the only part of the process that seems to move quickly."

Dr. Johnson stood up and walked to the window. "Sean, there's one more thing that I wanted to ask you about that may act as our fail safe measure in this process. It is most of my reason for meeting with you alone today. I really didn't want to...I don't know, put you on the spot I guess in front of your wife. I just didn't know if you thought this crossed the line somehow with your work."

"I don't get it. What are you talking about?"

Frank Johnson sat back down across from Sean. "If I fail at the panel, which I hate to say, I very well could, there may be another route to pursue. By you, actually, not me."

"Go on."

"Apparently there is a guy at the top of this entire food chain; within the application for treatment and appeal process. It is my understanding that he has the final say if he wants to involve himself, in any of these cases. My source told me that he has intervened both positively and negatively in several cases that my friend knew about. And they were at different stages of the appeal process. The guy presumably has a lot of clout; the final word for patients in Florida at least."

Sean sat back in the chair, "I assume you have a plan?"

"That's just it. I don't have a plan. I didn't know if you could use your political connections to influence this guy, or if that was something you were even comfortable doing. If that was a line you crossed or not. Sean I simply don't know enough about your world, being on the fringe of politics as you are, to know what is kosher or not."

Sean was amused by this, thinking how everyone does have their own niches in life that seem to intimidate or confuse those on the outside. Sean certainly didn't understand Dr. Johnson's world.

"Frank, I can tell you this. There isn't a line that exists that I wouldn't cross for Mo. But really, to use any influence I may have to affect this outcome isn't crossing any line; certainly none that I recognize or care about."

"That's great. I was hoping that was the case but I just didn't know and I thought you should have the chance to think about it without your wife present. I see now that it was unnecessary."

"Do you have a name for this person?"

"I do. His name is Mesh. He has an office in the main regional offices of the PHA in Miami."

"Do you know anything about the guy?"

"I know he's been with the Public Health Agency since its inception. That's all I know."

Sean bit his lower lip as he thought about how best to approach this Mr. Mesh. "The problem may be this. If he's been part of that agency since the beginning there is a good chance he's on the opposite side of the political fence than me. Many of them were political appointees, if not officially, they certainly got their jobs as a result of political favors. I doubt if I'll have much rapport, no less any clout. I just need to look in to it. At least it's another avenue."

Dr. Johnson leaned back in his chair. "Do you want to schedule a time to bring Mo in and let me tell her about where we are?"

"No, that's fine. I'll talk with her. Thanks though. Thanks for everything."

It had been two days since Sean had met with the doctor and he still hadn't told Mo about their conversation. He was waiting for a time that she felt better, a little stronger. She seemed to vacillate between horrible and slightly better. He wanted to pick a time when he felt she'd cope with the news somewhat better. But as he drove home from work he knew he had to tell her tonight, for his sake as much as hers.

When he arrived home he found a note Connie had left explaining she had gone to the store and the kids were with her. He found Mo sitting in the living room with the curtains drawn. She leaned against the armrest with her knees bent and her feet on the couch in front of her.

"Hi honey, how was your day?"

"It was fine actually. How are you doing?"

"Not bad, really. Just waiting for the kids to get back. I was lying down when they left."

Mo swung her feet on to the floor and patted the couch next to her. Sean sat and put his arm around her, kissing her on the cheek. She turned her face to his and kissed him on the lips.

"I've got news from Dr. Johnson finally." Sean wanted to disguise the apprehension he felt and sound as strong as he could. He held nothing back, even explaining what Dr. Johnson had related about the different panel members. Mo always wanted to have all of the information, about anything. Sean respected that and tried to be thorough, expecially in this circumstance. They had turned their bodies slightly toward each other, holding hands and looking at each other as he spoke.

When Sean was finished, Mo smiled at him, "I know that Dr. Johnson will do everything he can and I know you're going to do everything you can do. We will prevail, we will win and I'll fight hard for both of us, for all of us."

Sean smiled back at her and put his arms around her to hug her tightly. He held her, wanting to feel her body, wanting her to be part of him. His face was pressed against hers. Tears were flowing from her eyes against his face. His heart was breaking, his entire being felt so heavy, so unable to cope, so inept to help this woman he loved so dearly. He didn't know anything to do but hold her, squeeze her tight to him in the hope that it somehow did something, anything.

They both heard the sound of the kitchen door followed by little footsteps across the tile floor. Mo leaned back and smiled at him.

"I'm going to clean up. Go have your wrestling match. I'll come join you in just a minute."

LONGBOAT KEY, FLORIDA

July

It was nearly 7 p.m. when Conner returned from his evening walk on the beach. He had planned to skip dinner but the walk had changed his mind. Dressed in shorts and sandals, he grabbed a bottle of water and hopped in the Toyota, unsure of his destination when he pulled out on to the road. He settled on a grouper sandwich at Jessie's Café and kept heading north on Gulf of Mexico Drive. The parking lot was nearly full when he arrived, which almost changed his mind, but Jessie's blackened grouper would be worth the wait.

When he walked in, Jessie was at the hostess stand, "Well hello there handsome. Have you come for dinner or to take me away from all of this?"

Conner kissed her on the cheek, "I'd take you away if it wasn't for that pesky husband of yours."

"You've always been too focused on details, Conner."

"How's the wait? Should I eat at the bar? That way I can talk to your pesky husband, anyway."

"Don't tell him that you're mad about me, he might poison your drink."

Conner gave Jessie a wink and headed for an empty stool at

the end of the bar. Jessie's husband, Tanner, walked down the bar to greet his friend. They shook hands as Conner took his seat on a stool.

Conner motioned to the television that was turned off, "No game tonight, Tanner?"

"Live music tonight, brother. Jessie wants it off for these guys; they're supposed to be good. I know we're paying them like they're good. You know me; I hate all of 'em. Fuckin' arteeests. What a joke. But hey, I draw beers and mix drinks. She's the brains of this outfit."

Conner looked over at the two musicians as they tightened guitar strings and turned knobs on amplifiers.

"You going to eat, Conner, you want a menu?"

"I am going to eat, but I know what I want. Bring me a blackened grouper sandwich, no fries but give me a little salad with it instead. And a Dos Eques dark, OK?"

"Not a problem, coming up."

Conner turned to look at the musicians as they talked back and forth and made a production of tuning their instruments and testing their equipment. Both men were in their forties and the one with long hair repeatedly flipped it out of his face by throwing his head to the side. Conner was shaking his head as Tanner brought his beer and glass.

"Quite a sight, huh?" Tanner said as he followed Conner's stare toward the musicians. "I'll tell you what. If Jessie doesn't like them, I'll call you at eleven and you can come back over and we'll beat them up and throw them in the dumpster for fun."

"They're a pair, all right."

"Testing, testing," came over the microphones. The two performers appeared very serious as they repeated their mantra. They stopped and picked up their guitars again, but now the sound was coming through the amplifiers. This seemed to cause some consternation, as they jabbered between themselves and adjusted more knobs.

Tanner stood in front of Conner, leaning forward with his hands on the bar. "You know Conner it absolutely fascinates me to watch all of these arteeests when they come in here. There is no other profession on earth that takes such pride in the fact that they have to spend time to prepare in front of their audience before they can perform anything. It's like they think this little ritual is entertaining, or that we think that it's proof of their talent. And listen, it doesn't matter if they play in here ten consecutive nights, they will still go through this bull shit routine every night. I mean, what happened to their equipment since last night? Is there some ogre, some dark spirit that fucks with their stuff between every performance? I mean every one of them, every time, every piece of equipment. Give me a God damn break."

Tanner wasn't letting up, "What if your secretary walked in each morning and had to fuck with her equipment for thirty minutes before she could answer the phone or type a letter. What about the waitresses, you want them to walk up to your table and rearrange the silverware and glasses five times while you watch them. "Testing, testing" she'd say and another one would have to walk over and look at the table and they'd talk and act important, like it's such a big fuckin' deal."

Conner chuckled at his friend's tirade.

"I mean, this is Mutt and Jeff, not the fuckin' Beatles. I hate 'em. I haven't even heard 'em or met 'em, and I hate 'em. Fuckin, arteeests." Tanner turned and started to walk away when he turned back toward Conner. "I'm calling you at eleven."

The sandwich was great, as always, and actually the music was pretty good, too. Conner thought about calling Jan as he drove back to the house. He was anxious to hear her voice and talk for a while. He was to see her in three days and the expectation made him miss her even more.

"Hello."

"Wow, it's great to hear your voice, baby. How are you?"

"Conner, I'm so glad you called! I've missed you a lot today. I've been working on schemes to rid myself of one 'old lady' today and not coming up with anything fool proof."

"Your Mom been a handful today?"

Jan laughed, "No, not really. I'm teasing. We're actually doing pretty well. I think your visit may even work out OK this time. You know, she's just got her ways and it can be a little trying at times. But things are good."

They talked about the showing that had just concluded at Jan's gallery. She was excited because it had generated more revenue than any showing had in several years. The two lovers caught up on small things as they laughed and teased each other. Then Jan asked about Mo, wondering if there'd been any news from the appeal hearing.

"Honey, that's Sean calling me on my cell right now, let me call you back in a bit."

"Sure."

"Hey, Sean, how's it going?"

"We've been denied by the appeals panel."

There was silence. Neither man had anything to say. Finally Conner asked, "Are you going to Miami?"

"On Monday. I don't know what else to do. Maybe this Stanley Mesh will be reasonable. Shit someone has to be, don't they?"

"I hope so. You want company for the trip?"

"Dad, I appreciate that, but I don't know. You're supposed to go to Wyoming on Saturday, aren't you?"

"I can postpone that trip, no big deal."

"We'll talk about it."

"OK buddy. Good night. I love you."

"Love you too."

"Tell Mo I love her." Conner's voice cracked as he said it. He wasn't even sure Sean was still on the line.

Conner walked out to the beach and sat at the water's edge. The full moon was behind him lighting the white foam of the surf as it gently rolled in. His sadness made it hard to breathe. His mouth became dry and bitter tasting. He wanted a drink; to go back to the house and get a drink. But he couldn't move, he felt paralyzed as he stared in to the surf. He thought of nothing in particular, he just felt sadness, complete and utter sadness. It overwhelmed him; it was so oppressive. Conner didn't know how long he sat there on the sand, but the moon had tipped in to the western sky.

The phone woke him in the morning. It was daylight, later than he usually slept.

"Hello."

"I woke you, I'm sorry."

"I'm sorry I didn't call you back last night. Mo got denied treatment...and I was...I just sat on the beach. Sorry, honey."

"Please don't apologize to me. I'm very sorry for the news and I completely understand. As a matter of fact I figured that's what happened, which is why I didn't call you back last night. But I guess I did want to check on you this morning."

"Thanks, baby, but I'm fine. Need to wake up though. I'm still a little groggy. It's early out there, huh?"

"I haven't been up too long either. Why don't you call me back later this morning? I'm not going anywhere today."

Two hours later Conner called Jan from his cell phone as he drove north on the interstate toward Bubba Striker's. He explained that Connie was taking the kids to Busch Gardens so that Sean and Mo could have the day alone. That he needed a 'Bubba fix' and would spend the night in Ocala. Jan knew Bubba was good for Conner's spirit and was pleased he was going there.

"Do you want to cancel coming here on Saturday, honey, I'll sure understand. Maybe you want to be there in case Sean needs you after Monday."

"I've thought the same thing. I think I'll play it by ear, right up to the last minute if you don't mind. I offered to go with him to Miami, but he's not sure yet. I wish you could come here."

There was a long pause.

Conner said, "Sorry, that wasn't fair to say. I know it's impossible."

"Actually I was just thinking how I may be able to do it," Jan replied. "I'll let you know by tonight. I sent Mo a card today and sent some flowers to the house."

"Thanks, Jan. I love you and I'll talk with you later. I don't know what you have up your sleeve but I'm not going to talk you out of it. Just let me know."

"Love you, too. Drive safe."

MIAMI, FLORIDA

July

"I'm glad you came with me Dad. It's great to have your company. Hopefully Jan isn't upset with you."

"Not a bit. She's a good one, that girl. She was able to get her sister in Phoenix to help out with her Mom for a few days and she's actually coming out here. It'll be great."

"That's terrific, when?"

"Tomorrow, actually."

"Wow, that's short notice. Good for her."

"Well, I called her the same day you told me about today's appointment and it all just worked out."

"Well that's great. Good for you."

It was 10:45 when they pulled in to the client parking lot of the Regional Offices of the Public Health Agency of America. Sean stopped at the guardhouse at the gate and gave his name and who he was there to see before proceeding under the barrier to find a parking place.

"You want to wait in the lobby, or here in the car? I'll leave the keys with you if you want."

"Let me have the keys. I'm going to walk across the street there to that Coffee Bean and get a coffee."

"That's my Dad. 95° and going after hot coffee." Sean paused to gather himself and added, "Wish me luck."

Conner cocked his head, "You kiddin' me. Break both your legs."

Sean entered through the front doors only to be greeted by more guards and a metal scanner. He muttered under his breath as he emptied his pockets in to a plastic tray. This is perfect. A public health agency and they're worried about guns. Maybe if they didn't piss so many people off with their policies and incompetence they wouldn't worry about getting their heads blown off.

While he returned his belongings to his pockets the guard instructed him to turn off his cell phone, explaining there was no cell phone use in the building. Sean shook his head; it was like a maximum-security prison, for Christ's sake. He asked the same guard where he might find a building directory. The guard silently pointed to an information booth well down the hallway.

"Yolanda, come in here now." Stanley was not happy about this next appointment. He looked up from his computer monitor as she entered the office, pen and pad in hand. "Who the hell is this Sean Murphy?"

"Well sir, he is the husband of a Maureen Murphy, the patient, and he has been scheduled since the middle of last week."

"Well somehow I missed that until this morning."

"I personally entered it in your planner, sir, I know it was there."

"I don't need your God damned insolence, Yolanda."

The young lady started to defend herself but Stanley raised a finger into the air and gave her a hard look. Yolanda said nothing, but couldn't disguise the sneer on her face.

Stanley ignored the impudent look and continued, "I don't know how I missed it, and I'm not saying it wasn't on my planner. I overlooked it. OK? Got it now?"

Yolanda stood silently, not changing her demeanor.

"My question is; who is this guy? Or maybe who is his wife? For the last hour I've been trying to track his progress through the system and all I see is that this Mrs. Murphy had an initial application for treatment denied, then her doctor went to an appeal hearing and he was denied the first of last week. You with me so far?

"The point is; how the hell does he end up in my office this quickly? Thousands of appeal denials never make it up to this office. And those that do; number one, I know about them; and number two, they never happen this fast. You with me now Yolanda? So again, who is this guy, or this woman?"

Yolanda finally spoke, "I'm quite sure I don't know, sir. I have given you the file and what you have just gone over is as much as I know as well."

"You can be absolutely worthless, Yolanda. Go on, get out of here."

Stanley decided to call Sid Leach. Certainly he should know; but if he did, why hadn't he called? He was probably just busy, an oversight.

"Hello, Mr. Leach's office."

"Hello, this is Stanley Mesh in Miami, is Mr. Leach available?"

"Good morning. Mr. Mesh. I'm afraid he is out of the office all this week. He has accompanied several congressmen on a fact finding trip to Paris and on to Bonn."

"Has he got his cell with him? Does the same number work there?"

"He is carrying his phone, Mr. Mesh. And yes, that same phone works all over the world. However, they are in the air right now, so you won't be able to reach him."

"I thought flights to Europe were at night?"

"When he flies with congressional delegates they always charter the planes and they seem to fly at any time. Can I give him a message when he calls back in? I'm sure he will as soon as they land."

"No. Thanks. It will be too late."

"I'm sorry Mr. Mesh, is there anything else I can do for you?"

"No, uh-uh. Thanks."

"Good bye, Mr. Mesh."

Stanley was very unhappy. He didn't like surprises. Who else might know who this guy is?

There was a knock at his office door. Yolanda opened it carrying some papers. "Here sir, I hope this helps. It's a Google search on Mr. Murphy. The address listed corresponds to the one on his wife's application."

At first this only served to make Stanley mad. He didn't mean 'who is this guy' he meant 'who does this guy know'; didn't Yolanda understand a God damned thing? But before he launched into her, it struck him that this would be better than nothing and held his hand out for the papers.

"Mr. Murphy is here. It's 10:55, sir."

"Well he'll just have to wait, won't he?"

"I'll let him know, sir."

Stanley looked at the papers as he dismissed her with a backward wave of his hand. She had turned to leave and didn't see it, now completely resolved to start looking for another job.

The Google search was lengthy in that it listed titles and dates of articles and editorials published on both Sean's blog site and in "The Constitution" magazine. It also listed speaking engagements and articles written in other magazines. Stanley didn't need to read the detail, he had what he needed, this Murphy was politically connected, and that's how he got here so fast.

One thing didn't add up, this guy's politics sure as hell aren't Sid Leach's politics. And Stanley was under no misconceptions; he held this position because of Sid Leach and for Sid Leach. Today's circumstance was very peculiar, in all the years that Stanley had been in this position no one had catapulted up the ladder like this Murphy guy without a directive from Sid. Could this guy have such clout that he can get around Leach? Maybe he should just cancel this meeting until he can talk to Sid?

"Yolanda, come in here," Stanley barked over the intercom.

As his secretary opened the office door he changed his mind.

"Never mind, forget it," he told her.

No, if this was a Sid Leach deal and he had merely forgotten to call, he'd be pissed if I cancel it now, Stanley thought. I'll just be pleasant and non-committal until I can get a hold of him. He stuck the Google report in his desk drawer and opened the Murphy folder, having scanned through it before he only took a few seconds to refresh his memory. Really, Stanley never read these things in any detail. It was a lot of work to go through the medical records and panel hearing transcriptions. Anyway, what was in these folders was pretty well pointless; either Sid or himself had made the decisions well before these people ever showed up to his office.

"Yolanda, please send Mr. Murphy in."

Conner was sitting on a bench in the shade of a tree where he could see the front door of the office building. It was 11:30 when Sean walked through those doors in to the hot Miami sunshine. Conner was conflicted, as he tried to determine if a short meeting was good or bad. They met half way between the building and the car.

"Well, that didn't take long. What's the deal?"

They walked toward the car as he spoke. "Shit, I'm not sure. That was a little strange. He wouldn't give me an answer today, saying that he never does it that way. He had a little more fact finding to do and would call me in a few days."

The two men stopped speaking as they approached the car and got in. Once inside and their seat belts fastened, Conner resumed his questions as Sean backed out of the parking space.

"How was the tone? Did he seem receptive?"

"Yes and no. He was very noncommittal. I presented our argument, pretty much like Frank Johnson and I discussed it. He didn't ask any medical questions at all. As a matter of fact he didn't ask one question about Mo."

"I don't know," Conner put in, "maybe this guy doesn't look at the medical stuff. Maybe there is a whole different set of criteria that he looks at."

"Maybe. But wouldn't that be bizarre? I mean it is a medical issue. A woman is sick and needs treatment. What the fuck else do these people need to concern themselves with. Five years ago that was all that needed to be considered.

"I'll tell you one thing, Dad, I feel like I need a shower after just being in that guy's presence. He was the sleaziest guy I've been around in a while, especially to have that position of authority. His tie had a stain on it, his teeth were crooked and his hair was greasy. He looked like an ugly, fat toad sitting behind that desk. He smiled a lot I guess, but it seemed forced or strained somehow. The whole experience was weird; almost surreal."

"He sounds like a...a little bureaucrat," said Conner.

"Yea, I guess. Just a little bureaucrat."

"Well, do you have any gut feeling about it at all?" Conner asked.

"I'm not sure, I wish I did, but I don't. I thought at first it seemed like it was going in the right direction but then he started asking me about my work. That made me uncomfortable; hell I'm sure this guy and I are polar opposites politically. But, I don't know; maybe it doesn't matter. At least if I was naïve enough I'd say it doesn't matter, but I'm not. I also don't know if it was just an attempt on his part to be pleasant by asking about my work. Maybe I was reading too much in to it, but his goofy little smile seemed even more forced and phony as we were talking about my work at the magazine."

"So, buddy, it sounds like wait and see for now. Trying to read something in to such an ambiguous meeting will probably just drive you crazy."

"I think you're spot on, I'll just drive myself crazy. Let's go get some lunch at the Cuban by the turnpike, sound OK?"

"Sounds good. You need to call Mo?"

"I'll call her from Papi's."

Stanley had called back to Mr. Leach's office and got an ETA for his Paris arrival, and this time left a message. He knew it would look better to take Sid's call on his office phone instead of his cell so he returned to the office after lunch. He checked his watch again; it was 4:00, later than he'd been in that office in weeks. Stanley was restless; Sid should have landed two hours ago, maybe he's not going to call. Just then the light on the desk phone started blinking and a few seconds later Yolanda's voice came over the intercom.

"It's Mr. Leach on line one, Mr. Mesh."

Stanley picked up the phone. "Hi, Sid, how's Paris?"

"Just sitting down to a late dinner at Pierre Gagnaire. What's this all about?"

"Do you know a Sean Murphy, Sid?"

"Of course I know who he is. Why, what's this about?"

Stanley related the day's events and the reason for his confusion about Murphy's appointment. He made certain to clarify that he was very noncommittal about giving Murphy any sort of answer or even any indication of what his answer would be.

"Well, Stanley, I think you've done well. However, I do take exception to the fact that you thought there was a possibility that I may have dropped the ball by not calling you. Stanley, I never drop the fucking ball."

"You're right, sir. I'm sorry."

"Remember it, Stanley. I don't know about this Murphy situation either. I need to make a few phone calls in the morning and call you back on my decision. My gut tells me, fuck him. I hate the cocksucker and a denial would be exactly what he deserves. Good night Stanley."

Stanley heard the phone click off before he could say good-bye.

LONGBOAT KEY, FLORIDA
July

"I can't believe you're here, but I'm sure glad you managed it. Your sister gets an 'A' in my book."

Conner and Jan were lying in his bed as the first rays of morning light pierced the sky. She had arrived at the Tampa airport the night before, on the 9:55 p.m. flight through Denver.

"Well, I didn't tell you last night, but I wasn't sure I'd get out of there. Jody's flight didn't arrive to Jackson until noon; it was an hour late. By the time I got her squared away with the house and Mom, I almost missed my plane. Four days isn't much but it sure beats not being here at all."

"I know, me coming there would...."

"Shhhh," Jan interrupted, "We've been through that already. I was thinking this morning when I first woke up, what you told me about my Mom. You said I was doing exactly what I needed to do. Well, you are doing exactly what you need to do, staying close to Sean and Mo like you are."

"I appreciate that, honey, very much."

"I'm just glad that it worked for Jody to take a few days and fly up from Phoenix to pitch in with Mom."

Conner leaned over and kissed Jan. "Maybe she knew how horny I was."

Jan punched him on the shoulder, "At least I'm good for something."

After a light breakfast they took a long walk on the beach. Jan had never lived by the ocean and on each visit she was becoming more of an enthusiast. It was warming up quickly as the sun made its march across the sky but the breeze off the water kept it pleasant. They were barefoot as they walked on the surf's edge. A bigger wave occasionally washed over their ankles as Jan kept her constant vigil for any unbroken shells along the shore.

Three brown pelicans flying over the water in a line suddenly and simultaneously folded their wings and dove in to the gulf.

"Pelicans fascinate me. They fly so gracefully and effortlessly yet they dive like they've been shot out of the sky. The just seem to fall in a heap. Yet they seldom miss."

As if to prove Conner right, all three birds surfaced and threw their heads back to swallow their catch.

A little further down the beach was a flock of terns standing on the beach, well out of the surf. They were all facing the same direction, into the wind and toward the ocean. They mimicked well-trained soldiers, disciplined sentries, waiting for orders, not to be distracted by the likes of beachcombers, or anything else for that matter. He nudged Jan, pointing to the flock of avian soldiers.

"I love it when they do that. Have you ever figured out why they do it, or what they're doing?" Jan asked.

They stopped walking to watch the birds, "No, I have to admit, I still don't know. Now I think I've wondered about it for so long that maybe I don't want to know. Somehow it may spoil it for me."

"As inquisitive as you are and how enamored you are with nature, I don't believe that."

Conner smiled broadly, "Yea, that's bull shit, I'd love to know. I've just never encountered anyone that did. Maybe it's time I worked harder at finding out."

"Oh look Conner there's a crime scene. I guess it's the season, huh?" Jan pointed toward four posts with yellow caution tape strung between them; the same tape police use to protect a crime scene.

"Yea, it's the season. I think this is probably the third nest now on this stretch of beach."

They held hands as they continued down the beach.

"What kind of turtles are they? I don't think you ever told me."

"They're Logger Head turtles, and they get very large, upward of two hundred pounds. The females will bury over a hundred eggs in a single nest."

"And it's only now, in the summer that they nest?"

"Actually the nesting season starts in May and goes through the summer and in to the fall. The volunteers that are part of this conservation effort walk the beach early in the mornings and look for signs that a turtle has came on to the beach. It's usually pretty evident because of the flipper marks and the furrow made by the body of the turtle dragging itself across the sand. Then they look for the area where the sand has been disturbed, the nest, and fence it off to hopefully keep anyone from inadvertently disrupting it."

"How long before they hatch?"

"I think its fifty-five days. Not all of the eggs hatch and the survival rate of these little guys making it very far is pretty lousy, so all though they lay a lot of eggs, there is a significant attrition rate."

Conner stooped to pick up a sand dollar that had made it to shore unscathed and handed to Jan.

"An amazing thing is the journey they make after they leave these sands. The ocean currents will take them south from here around the southern tip of Florida and up the eastern coastline, and then across the Atlantic to the waters of Western Europe. Eventually they will end up off the coast of West Africa, where they live out most of their adult lives. The females return here after about about twenty years, laying their eggs on the same beach they were born."

"Incredible. I'd love to witness the little guys heading for the water at some...look at our friend here"

They were approaching their usual turnaround point as Jan pointed to a young blue heron standing in the sparse sea oats only twenty feet away. The bird was focused on a stone crab making a sideways scamper across the sand. Jan had no sooner pointed to the heron when it took several long, rapid strides that quickly overtook the crab. With her beak, she seized the crab by a claw and shook it violently, tearing the claw from it's body. The crab attempted another escape only to find its other claw in the beak's grasp and several violent shakes dispensed of it as well.

Having rendered her prey defenseless, the big bird's next aim was to render it immobile as the same process continued with the crab's legs, one at a time.

"What the heck is that bird doing? Is it a young bird that doesn't know how to hunt yet?" Jan was incredulous as she watched nature's display.

"Oh, contraire, mon ami. Keep watching" responded Conner.

By this time the crab had already made another failed attempt to escape and was in the air a fifth time, only to have one more appendage shaken from its body. It landed back in the sand but this time unable to muster much of an escape before the heron had one more leg in her beak and the shaking had begun yet again. The process continued until all six legs had been removed; the crab was reduced to only a body, no appendages, no ability to move. The bird stood there for several seconds, maybe savoring her victory, or perhaps, delightfully anticipating her meal. Then with startling force she drove her beak with a loud crack through the shell of the crab. Once, twice, three times in rapid succession she whipped her head into the crab's body. With the shell well ventilated to allow for digestion, the heron picked up what remained of the crab and raised her head vertically until her neck was straight out from her body. Opening her mouth as wide as possible, she swallowed the crab. Jan and Conner could see the large bulge make its slow peristaltic journey toward the gullet.

"Oh...my...God," was all Jan could say as she witnessed the crab shell that was three times the diameter of the heron's neck make its way from head to body, where it's outline disappeared from view. "That was absolutely incredible. I guess the woman on the beach is the dummy, not the bird, huh?"

"Isn't it amazing what all creatures' figure out or just instinctively know to do? I love it when we have a chance to witness things like that."

The heron simply meandered off, undaunted by her audience.

"The brutal part of the whole process though is when the heron screams in agony," Conner continued as they began walking back in the direction of the house.

"The bird screams, what are you talking about? I didn't hear a sound."

"Yea, but she hasn't passed that shell yet."

"Oh Jesus, you're a mess, Conner."

They made it back to the spot where they had left their towels, a small ice chest and two surf chairs. Conner opened the ice chest and pulled out a bottle of water, opened it and handed it to Jan. She drank several gulps before handing it back to Conner, who finished it in one long draw.

"Come on." He took her hand and they walked out in to the water. Once waist deep in the water he handed Jan his cap and sunglasses and dove in. When he surfaced, it was her turn and she did the same. They walked to deeper water and Conner turned his back to her and squatted down, reaching behind him to wrap his forearms behind her knees as she wrapped her arms around his neck and let him pick her up. Conner kept walking in to the deeper water until it was up to his shoulders before turning and looking back toward the shore.

"I am always surprised by the shallowness of the gulf," Jan remarked. "We must be a hundred yards form shore."

"It really is amazing," Conner said as he turned back toward the ocean, "see that sand bar out there about a hundred feet?"

"Not really."

"Where the water is light colored again, more tan, I guess."

"Yea, now I do."

"I'll bet if we swam out there we could stand up again, maybe only waist deep."

"Hey, maybe we could walk to Mexico!"

"Everything's a damn joke to you isn't it Jan. You're going to have to be more serious to hang with me."

She pretended to choke him with her arms followed by a kiss on his cheek. They eventually made their way back to the beach where Jan donned her large straw hat. She grabbed fresh orange wedges from the ice chest and they positioned themselves side by side in their chairs in the surf. After a time Jan broke the silence.

"Honey, have you given more thought to getting married?"

"Sure, I think about it a lot. I don't see a reason not to. That doesn't sound right; I'd love to. I guess there are financial issues that need to be discussed, but frankly, I think if we get married I would want to be fifty-fifty going forward."

"In principle, I agree that it makes it easy, but I don't think that's fair to you."

"None of that matters to me, Jan. Let's just move forward."

"Well in typical Conner fashion; problem solved." Jan laughed as she said it and Conner raised his beer and winked.

Jan wore a floral print sundress and sandals to dinner. As they walked from the car toward the restaurant Conner told her how gorgeous she looked.

"Well, thanks, honey, I appreciate that."

"I mean it," Conner said as he stopped and turned to face her. He put his hands on her hips and pulled her closer. "You are gorgeous and sexy, and I'm going to devour you when I get you home."

"Let's eat fast then," Jan gave him a kiss.

"How dare you bring another woman in here, Conner Murphy!" Jessie had her fists on her hips as Jan and Conner approached the hostess stand.

"Jessie, this is Jan. I actually thought you two had met before. Jan's been in here with me."

"Jan, it's a pleasure," Jessie said, shaking her hand. "I suppose Conner hasn't told you that we're engaged, has he?"

"You know he did forget to mention that," Jan's eyes were wide with mock surprise.

"It should be about a ten minute wait, unless you want your table outside, Conner, then it might be a little more."

"We'll wait for that table. It will give us a chance to go to the bar and talk your no good husband in to setting you free."

"Good luck, but I don't think he's that smart. It really is a pleasure to meet you Jan. I'll come get y'all as soon as that table clears."

"You know I ought to charge you one hundred dollars for that anthropology lesson, Tina." Tanner was pointing his finger at the woman sitting on the stool across from him. Over her shoulder he saw Conner and Jan approaching the bar. "Conner, my man, what a pleasure. Especially since you've brought this lovely lady back again."

Tanner held his hand out to Jan, "Tanner Oakley, chief bottle washer at this dive, a pleasure to see you again."

Jan shook the bartender's hand as Conner said, "Jan Thomas."

"I remember you, Tanner. But I don't think I met your wife when I was here. She's very funny."

Tanner was shaking Conner's hand when he looked back at Jan with a quirky smile. "She is that. But don't let that fool you into thinking she doesn't have a mean streak. That woman has tormented me for over thirty years."

Jan smiled, "Thirty years. Boy, it must be rough for you to hang in there like that."

"I'm paving my way to heaven, Jan. That's the way I look at it."

"How about getting us a drink before I start crying, you old fool," Conner took a stool next to Jan.

"What will you have, Miss Jan?" Tanner winked at Conner.

"How about an amaretto sour?"

"And you, Mr. Congeniality?"

"Bring me a Grey Goose on the rocks, please, sir."

While they waited for their drinks the young woman that Tanner had been talking to finished hers and left. Jan leaned across the bar as Tanner returned with the amaretto sour and vodka.

"So, Tanner, what was the anthropology lesson that you so generously gave away tonight?"

Conner groaned, "My God Jan, couldn't you have left well enough alone? You've just given this ape a license to bore you the rest of the evening."

Tanner looked directly at Conner letting his jaw drop and raising his eyebrows in offended surprise.

"Ape? Ape?" he repeated. He then turned to face Jan. "A wise ape with some incredible insight, I'll have you know. I'll tell you what, Jan, why don't we take this opportunity to ignore the pedestrian oaf that followed you in here and we'll elevate the conversation to a more cerebral level."

Jan cocked her head to the side and said with a demure, idolizing tone, "What a wonderful opportunity for me. Please share your wisdom and insights with me." She took her cocktail napkin and fanned her face with rapid, little feminine movements.

Tanner looked back at Conner, "Now I see why you two get along so well. You know, sarcasm is the lowest form of humor, according to my mother anyway." Tanner walked to the end of the bar to fill an order for a waiter.

Conner raised his glass in a toast. As Jan touched her glass to his he said "To a woman that can hold her own." He leaned in and kissed her.

After helping another couple with their drinks Tanner returned and Jan tried again. "Tanner, I really do want to know what your anthropology lesson was, you know."

"Don't mock me woman. Inside this rugged, manly exterior, you'll find a fragile little boy."

"I'm serious, Tanner."

"Well, there was a brief little blurb on the news," Tanner motioned to the television above his head, "where they were doing a deal on women in the work place; lamenting over the fact that these women deal with such horrible treatment from their male colleagues all the time. They had a woman on there that's in sales and she was talking about the fact that if she is not pleasant to her male customers, obviously it won't generate her many sales, but when she is pleasant and maybe smiles or touches them on the arm or some such thing that the men all think she's coming on to them. And Tina, the woman at the bar, started going on about how right that was and how all men are such pigs, bastards, sex fiends, etc."

"And obviously you came to the rescue of the male gender and defended their intentions," Jan said.

"Not really." Tanner got more serious as he leaned in to the bar. "It fascinates me though how people can take their opinions of social conduct and attribute another's reaction to that code of conduct while totally ignoring millions of years of our specie evolving. For millions of years men spent all their time hunting, gathering, protecting their family unit and procreating. When a woman was ready to submit to the act of procreation she would do things like smile, touch, be tender, etc. That sparked some neurons in the man that signaled 'O boy, I'm gonna get laid'. Now feminism rolls in to our culture forty years ago and those unconscious, instinctive physiological functions are all supposed to go away, just because Gloria Steinhem said so. And listen, I obviously understand about social mores and striving for civilized behavior but it is simply stupid to ignore behaviors that have been ingrained in our species for a couple million years just because it doesn't fit your mold of proper social behavior at this point in time."

Jan smiled at Tanner. "So you're not saying men aren't pigs; they're just pigs for a good reason."

Tanner smiled back, "I told you I'm fragile, Jan. Don't toy with me."

"Well if it makes you feel better. It's all that instinctive male behavior that I love the most about Conner here. I'm not out to change a thing about him."

Jessie walked up to the bar with menus and a wine list in hand. "Your table is all set. You ready."

Conner drained his glass and set it back on the bar as Jan gathered her drink and napkin to take to the table.

"Please, Jessie, I've absorbed all the knowledge that my little brain can handle tonight," said Conner.

"I very much enjoyed seeing you tonight, Tanner," said Jan. "Take care."

Jessie winked at her husband and he blew her a kiss.

MIAMI, FLORIDA

July

Stanley Mesh was driving to work when his cell phone rang. By the ring tone he knew it was Sid Leach. He smiled to himself. Leach hardly ever called his cell but at least this time Stanley was going in to work on time.

"Yes, Mr. Leach how are you?"

"Good, Stanley, good. Listen, I've only got a minute till we board this plane. Hold it, hold it just a second." Stanley heard muffled scratching noises over the receiver. "Can you hear me?"

"Yes, sir, no problem."

"I wanted to get away from that silly little kike bitch before I said anything. I think the honorable representative from California may be the stupidest fucking thing I've had the displeasure of being around in a while. She can also be led around by a nose ring though so she has value; will vote anyway that Samms and I tell her to. Anyway; shit they're telling us to get on." Stanley heard him shout, "I'll be wrapped up here in two seconds,"

"All right Stanley, listen. I couldn't get much information on how our boy Sean Murphy was able to work the system. That's probably a good news, bad news deal. Good because no one with any real clout

183

backed him or I'd be able to find that out; but bad because I wish I knew where the leak in the system was. My best guess is that spic representative from the Tampa district somehow got him a meeting with you. If I'm right, it's no big deal. That Cuban prick's got no sway. Bottom line Stanley, deny the son-of-a-bitch. I have to go."

The phone line was dead.

Inez's voice came over the intercom, "There's a Mr. Mesh on the line for you, Mr. Murphy."

Sean hurriedly grabbed the telephone, "Hello, Sean Murphy."

"Stanley Mesh, Mr. Murphy. I'll cut to the chase. I have to deny your appeal. I'm sorry. Even after doing a lot of bending of both the dollars and the prognostic indicators, I just couldn't make it work."

Sean couldn't breathe. A few seconds transpired, "Where do I go from here, Mr. Mesh?"

Stanley heard Sean's voice crack. He paused before he answered. "I'm not sure I know what you mean, Mr. Murphy."

"I mean who do I talk to in order to save my wife's life, for Christ's sake?" Sean was unable to keep from shouting.

"Well, Mr. Murphy, I thought you knew. I am the final authority on a decision such as this. That is precisely why I look at these requests, appeals, so deliberately. It's a painstaking decision that I don't make lightly. Will that be all, Mr. Murphy?"

"I don't know what to say. Yes, for now, I guess. Jesus."

"Goodbye, Mr. Murphy."

Stanley leaned back in his chair and lifted his stubby legs to rest his unpolished shoes on the desk. His computer was on and Sean Murphy's web site was on the screen. Stanley scrolled through the titles in the 'articles archive' portion of the site.

"My, my, my. All of those opinions. All of those inspirational thoughts and yet ol' Stanley has the control, doesn't he, Sean old boy." Stanley talked out loud. He felt smug and powerful. "I think I'll call it a day."

TAMPA, FLORIDA

July

Sean couldn't even think. He started to hyperventilate; it made him lightheaded, dizzy. He put his hand over his heart; it pounded so hard he thought his chest would burst. He knew he had to get control. His head was swimming; the office around him appeared surreal. He leaned back and closed his eyes, concentrating on taking deep, measured breaths.

Minutes passed before he could open his eyes. When he did they immediately focused on the photograph of Mo and the kids, sitting on a tea cup at Busch Gardens, all of them laughing. His family, the family he was supposed to protect. Love and protect. Tears ran down his face. His mouth was dry. His whole being felt so heavy that he couldn't move.

Finally, Sean stood and started to leave. As he walked around his desk his thigh hit the corner of the desk with enough force to knock the picture over, face down. He stared at the back of the frame. He didn't right it; he couldn't bear looking at it again. He walked in to the outer office, past Inez's desk. She didn't speak as she watched him go. He muttered something, unable to form the words and kept walking out in to the hallway.

The drive home was unbearable. He didn't really know what to do. He needed to tell Mo, but how, when? Would he tell the kids anything? Connie? All he wanted to do was hold Mo, gather her up in his arms and hold her. He didn't want to use words like denial and no treatment. He didn't want to say anything; he just wanted to hold her.

God damn it! Tell her what? Tell her that the government of the United States has said that she needs to die. The government doesn't think she's worth saving. The government doesn't care if she wants to fight for her life. The government has precious programs it would rather fund than give Maureen Murphy, the young mother of two beautiful children, the right to fight for her own life!

Sean leaned forward in his seat as he gripped the steering wheel hard with both hands. There was little traffic on Dale Mabry Avenue and he was unaware how fast he was going. His eyes filled with tears as he started shouting obscenities, then he screamed that primordial scream that started deep in his gut.

Once parked in his driveway he sat in the car. He was calmer now, but wanted to be sure he could stay that way before going in to the house. Connie's car wasn't there. He looked at his watch; she'd be picking the kids up at swimming lessons. Sean entered through the garage. The house was dark with curtains drawn and no lights on. By process of elimination he found Mo in the bedroom. She was lying on her side on the bed as he opened the door.

"Hey, honey. I heard you come in. Come lay down with me for a while, would you?"

Sean kicked his shoes off and lay behind her. He spooned her body into his with his chest pressed to her back and his arm over her, trying to touch as much of her as he could.

Sean didn't know what else to do but to tell her. There wouldn't be a better moment and she would want to know as soon as possible. Mo said nothing while he talked and remained quiet when he was finished. She took her hands and held his as she silently wept. They lay there, holding each other tightly, tenderly, as tears streamed from their eyes.

Conner took the news as Sean expected he would, with a mixture of sadness and rage. Sean had been conflicted whether to wait one more day before telling his father since Jan was still visiting. He didn't want to ruin their last day together, but he also knew that Jan would be consolation to him. It was the better choice. Jan helped him get through the initial shock and heartache; it helped to have her there.

TAMPA, FLORIDA

August

"Hi honey."

"Hey, baby, how are you feeling?"

"Well actually, I feel pretty good, believe it or not."

Mo had called Sean's private line at his office in the Sykes building. He couldn't help but notice that she sounded better this morning than she had in a while; there was more strength and energy to her voice. The last several weeks had been very dispiriting to Sean, as her condition had continued to deteriorate.

"Listen, Sean, honey, I'm not sure what your day is like but I have a plan."

"Really. What is it?"

"Well, I was thinking about sending Connie for the kids, they have their little crafts camp on Tuesday morning."

"Yea, right."

"And I thought if you could get away from work, the four of us could go to Busch Gardens together."

Sean was incredulous. He couldn't speak.

"I guess it doesn't work, huh?"

Now Sean was quick to reply, "Are you kidding, it works perfectly.

I'll beat the kids there! But...are you sure you're up to it, honey?"

"I'm very sure. I don't know where this energy came from but I would love to do this if you can."

"I'll be less than thirty minutes. I love you, honey."

"Oh, Sean, I love you, too."

Sean was wrong about beating Connie and the kids to the house. Mo must have already told Connie to go for them before she called. That realization made him smile. When he entered the house he found Jeremy and Karen so excited that they were bouncing up and down. He went in toward the bedroom to look for Mo. He found his wife coming down the hallway, dressed in shorts and a sleeveless blouse, carrying her big straw hat and sunglasses. She was very thin and pale but Sean thought she looked beautiful.

"Let's do this, I'm really excited," Mo reached out for her husband's hand.

It was a typical hot and humid August day in Tampa but two things were in the Murphy's favor; there was a pleasant breeze that blew all day and the standard afternoon thunderstorm never came. The morning consisted of walking through the animal exhibits with Jeremy lingering in the reptile exhibit for what seemed an eternity to his sister; made more unbearable since she had her hands over her eyes through most of it. After lunch the kids begged for the amusement rides and their parents happily agreed. It had been a tradition for Mo to join the kids on most of the rides whenever they came to the park, but she couldn't muster it today, and it took a stern word from Sean to keep the kids from pressing the issue. It was the only time all day that he noticed an expression of sadness on Mo's face.

"I'm sorry, honey, did I seem mad. I just wanted them to stop bugging you about it and pulling on you," Sean explained.

"No, honey. Believe me, I know they don't take 'no' very easily. I just wish I could do it, that's all." Mo's eye's filled with tears but she quickly turned her head toward the carousel not wanting to be sad and waved and smiled at her giggling little girl as she went by on her spotted pony.

Sean had some moments of melancholia, but was mostly very happy. He couldn't believe how good Mo looked and how much energy she had. Her head had its usual tilt and she was very thin, but her eyes were bright and her smile was radiant. In spite of a few struggles with her balance and frequent visits to the restroom, Sean was elated how well she was doing.

When evening came they stopped at a stand for churros and drinks and then headed to the animal park. They rode the tram over the outdoor zoo as Karen sat on her mother's lap and pointed to every animal she saw, making certain her mother looked at each one. Mo's plan was a huge success. The best family day they had had in a very long time.

They stopped at a Pizza Hut after leaving the park, which was Jeremy's choice. The kids ate so many breadsticks that they hardly touched their pizza when it finally arrived. Jeremy jabbered away on the drive home about the snakes and all the cool stuff he had learned about them. Karen fell asleep and didn't wake up to be carried to bed by her father. Mo sat on Karen's bed and stroked the hair of her sleeping little girl for a few minutes before kissing her gently on the cheek. Her tired little boy was in his pajamas and under the covers when she came in the room.

Mo sat on the edge of his bed. "Boy, I sure had fun today, Mr. Brown."

"Me too, Mommy. We have to do it again real soon!"

Mo felt her eyes fill with tears as she leaned forward and kissed her son's forehead. "I love you."

"I love you, too Mommy. Good night." With that, Jeremy rolled over on his side and Sean took Mo's hand to leave.

"Hey, that's Grandpa's name for me! You're silly, Mommy."

Mo turned and blew him a kiss as Sean closed the door.

Sean and Mo made love that night for the first time in

weeks. They kissed and hugged in silence for a long time afterwards before they fell asleep. Sean woke up once during the night to find that Mo had gotten up. He thought that she was probably in the bathroom again and fell back to sleep so fast he didn't notice that she didn't return. Mo had gone to sit on her children's beds, one at a time, just to look at them. She marveled at them and silently wept. She was back in bed, asleep when Sean woke in the morning.

Sean was up and in his morning routine when he came back to the bedroom, cup of coffee in hand. Mo was awake now with her head propped on a pillow.

"Can I get you anything before I leave, honey?" Sean asked.

"Let's see. Yup, you can. A kiss, a hug and an 'I love you'."

Mo had been planning this for about two weeks, after she had really started to decline, more so than Sean had realized. Her discussions with Dr Johnson had frightened her horribly. She was terrified of what was going to happen to her; terrified for her family more than for herself. She was feeling worse every day. She wasn't afraid to die anymore, she was afraid of the living hell it would bring her family by dying the way she was dying. Early yesterday morning Mo had taken a massive dose of dexamethasone, which worked better than her expectations; it had done as Dr. Johnson had predicted, relieving her pain and giving her a euphoric feeling. The day at the park with her family had been marvelous, but this morning she could feel the toll it had taken on her body.

Sean had left for work, and the kids had gone to Long Boat Key with Connie for a day at the beach with their grandfather where they would spend the night. Today was Sean's day to leave the office early and go to the gym mid-afternoon. That always put him home between 4:30 and 5:00 p.m.

The bed was made and she opened the drapes for the first

191

time in months. Mo took the note from her nightstand that she had written last night and laid it on Sean's pillow next to her. It was addressed to Sean. She then took her full bottle of hydrocodone and one by one swallowed them with water before lying down on the bed. She was dressed in the silk pajamas that Sean had given her on her last birthday.

Mo's plan was that Sean would find her body when he was alone; it worked as she'd hoped. Sean came home, still excited from yesterday's events, but worried about the toll it had taken on Mo. He hadn't spoken to her all day, which was unusual; she called him at least once every day. He reasoned that she was wiped out from their outing and had slept most of the day.

When Sean walked in to the bedroom he was stunned to see the drapes pulled back. At first he was elated to see the sunlit room but it turned to dread almost immediately. He walked quickly toward the bed but stopped when he saw the note. He knew instantly. He put his hand on his wife's face; it felt cool. He looked at the envelope but didn't pick it up; instead he lay down next to Mo, facing her, so that his entire body was touching hers. He put his arm over her and held her while he cried. He didn't know how long he'd laid there, but finally he got up and walked to the other side of the bed. He bent over and kissed his wife on the forehead and then sat in a chair and opened the envelope.

My dearest Sean,

Tell our precious children I will always be with them in their hearts and watching over them. I wanted a longer life, but I couldn't have had a better life, all of it because of you. I love you and will be with you forever.

Your wife, your lover, your friend,

Mo

"Hey, buddy, how you doin'? Just about to put the hotdogs on the grill for these munchkins."

"Dad, I have something to tell you."

TAMPA, FLORIDA

August

Sean waited a week after his wife's death to have the service to allow for travel of friends and family. Mo's brother spoke and was able to illustrate very well who she had been and the positive way she had touched so many lives. There were old stories of their childhood that provided some smiles and quiet laughter as Bill made an effort to be more uplifting than maudlin. In spite of this, the tragic death of a young wife and mother deeply saddened all that attended and few mourners had dry eyes. They gathered at the Murphy home in Carrollwood after the service. Cars lined the streets for blocks and people crowded shoulder to shoulder throughout the house and spilled in to the yard and out to the street.

Sean was coping, having found some peace in the end of Mo's suffering and consumed with his children's needs. He was faring better than his father whose sadness was overshadowed by his anger.

The Strikers and the Ingleses had escaped the main throng of people and stood under the shade of a magnolia on the side patio as Jan approached.

"Have any of you seen Conner lately, I can't seem to find him."

"No, hon, I haven't," answered Maggie, looking to the others as she spoke. They all shook their heads in unison.

"Bubba, could I talk to you for just a minute," asked Jan.

"Of course you can," Bubba stepped forward and took her arm, escorting her several feet from the others.

"Bubba, I am so worried about Conner. I knew this would be hard on him, but I didn't expect him to be so angry."

Bubba licked his bottom lip with the tip of his tongue before he spoke, "What are you worried about, exactly?"

"Hell, maybe that's a good question. I guess I really don't know. But you saw him last night after dinner, when the six of us were sitting out here on the patio. He's like a powder keg, or...maybe that's not the right description. I don't know; he just seems capable of doing anything right now. I pity the person that puts himself in Conner's way right now."

"I know. I see it as well. Bud and I were talking about the same thing. I'll keep an eye on him. For a long while if I have to. He's a tough son-of-a-bitch and he's capable of doing someone a lot of harm if they spark him. I haven't seen him like this in a long time; and you're right it could get ugly. I think what he needs to do is blow off some steam, but I also know that it could turn into something he might regret."

Jan looked at her friend, not relieved by what she heard.

"I'm not saying anything to help, am I?" Bubba gave her a toothy grin. "I guess what I'm trying to say is you're right. But I won't let anything happen to him. OK. I'll stick with him for as long as I need to."

"Thanks. I'm leaving late tomorrow on a red eye. I wish I could stay, but I just can't."

"We know that. And he knows that. This will all diffuse with time, honey."

A man was moving toward them as they were talking. Bubba knew him and took Jan by the arm to put himself between her and the man. He sneered as he spoke.

"Well, Cooter Williams. I'll be goddamned. You must have sobered up long enough for an appearance."

The man was tall, standing six foot four with thinning gray hair and a pale complexion accentuated by spider webs of blood vessels covering his nose and chin. The eyes seemed covered with a yellowish film, serving to dull the blue and emphasize the red. He ignored the insult.

"Bubba." He nodded at Striker before turning to Jan and extending his hand. "Joey Williams, ma'am. Pleased to meet you."

"Jan Thomas," she responded.

Turning his attention back to Bubba, he asked. "Do you know where I might find Conner?"

"No, I don't."

"I was just looking for him myself, Joey," said Jan. "Oh, wait, here he comes."

Conner approached from behind Joey as the big man turned to greet him. He stretched out his hand to Conner.

"I wanted to offer my condolences, Conner. I'm very sorry for your loss, for Sean, for their children."

Conner hesitated, looking hard in to the bigger man's eyes. Finally he took his hand and shook it. "Thanks. I'll let Sean know you came by."

After an awkward moment of silence, Joey said, "OK, I'll be going then."

"OK."

As Joey Williams walked away Bubba said under his breath, "Snake."

Conner gave Jan a squeeze on her arm to acknowledge her as he walked by to talk with the Ingleses and Beth.

"Who was that, Bubba?" Jan asked.

"A swamp rat. He epitomizes everything wrong with this country, at least what this country has become. He made a fortune as a trial lawyer, suing people and destroying lives and livelihoods. After he amassed a fortune he went to DC for a stint and became one of the chief lobbyists for the trial lawyers. He was probably more instrumental than anyone in killing any type of tort reform while he spent years entrenched in crooked politics.

"Years ago, he and Conner and I were pretty good friends. We all lived in Ocala as young men, but old Cooter there just became more and more unscrupulous over time. Conner and I didn't cotton to his ethics or his politics. He's a mal hombre. I'll tell you, when I think about situations like Mo's, I think about the greed of people like him; they're the ones that created all this shit."

LONGBOAT KEY, FLORIDA

August

Conner Murphy's house sat back further from the water than most on the gulf side of Longboat Key. It was also an odd shaped piece of property, almost a triangle, all of which had made it affordable twenty years earlier. The shape of the lot, as well as its location, had created a challenge in designing the house. But Molly had been up to the task and created a lovely home; functional and perfect for their needs. The second story offered a view of the water and the apex of the triangular lot provided private access to the beach. Because it had been Molly's design, the home provided Conner with many memories and he loved thinking back to how she had incorporated so many small details that added so much.

But now wasn't one of those times. It was 1:00 a.m. and Conner was wide-awake. He was sitting on the upstairs veranda staring out at the water, not even cognizant of the gentle breeze or the beauty of the moonlight reflecting off of the gentle surf. Conner was lost in his thoughts; thoughts mired in anger.

The Strikers had stayed with Conner for two days after Jan left. Bubba had kept his word and stayed until Conner was less edgy, as he put it. He had called Jan on their way home to reassure her that Conner was getting back to his old self.

In truth, Conner wasn't less angry he was just less volatile. An incident at a gas station had made him realize how close he was to being out of control. He hadn't hurt either of those young men but the incident served as a wakeup call to rein in his emotions.

The Striker's had left after dinner and not long after that Conner made his usual evening phone call to Sean. It was obvious that Sean was distracted with work issues so Conner didn't keep him long. He tried Jan, who was just as preoccupied with her mother. Again, Conner didn't want to pester with small talk and promised to call tomorrow. Unsuccessful with his phone calls, he decided he was tired enough to go off to bed. Unlike the past several nights, there was little tossing and turning and Conner quickly fell in to a deep sleep.

Two hours passed and Conner was startled from his slumber. He lay there, keenly alert, listening for what had woken him. His heart rate was accelerated and he felt anxious as he lay there listening. There was no sound except the noise of the rolling surf. He realized it was his thoughts that had jarred him back to consciousness, thoughts that had no intention of loosening their grip. Out of frustration, Conner violently snatched his covers to the side. He swung his legs over the side of the bed to put his feet on the floor. He sat there, naked, his elbows on his knees and his head in his hands. With his open palms he rubbed his head as he slowly nodded it up and down. He wondered if he would stay mad forever.

"God damn them all." He continued to rub his head as he muttered the words. "God damn them all that made this happen."

He stood and stared out the window and shouted, "God damn me for doing nothing."

Conner walked across the room and grabbed a pair of thin cotton pants from the back of a chair. He decided to make some coffee and sit outside on the veranda. As he made his way to the kitchen, the big grey cat meowed loudly and made his way from the den in search of company.

Conner's mood softened slightly at the sight of his cat. "Hey, there, Mr. Biggs, how's my insomniac buddy."

While the coffee perked, Conner occupied himself by feeding the cat and filling his water bowl. Once the pot had filled enough for a cup, Conner poured it in to a mug and ventured on to the veranda.

Conner stared in to the darkness. The cool breeze carried the sound of the surf up to the veranda and the full moon was overhead. Conner's senses were oblivious; as he looked straight ahead, trance like, teeth unconsciously clenched, shoulders rigid.

His mind began to wander to childhood memories of growing up in rural Nevada; memories of being raised by simple, hard working people in a community where everyone cared about each other and their country. Where self-reliance was taught and revered but was never void of compassion. His mind brought in to focus the heroes he had as a boy. Some were people he knew, like his father and other veterans of WWII. Most had been quiet, unassuming men that had fought and risked their lives in the deadliest war in history yet never sought acknowledgment; instead they rarely talked about it. In his mind's eye he could see those men and remembered admiring them for what they did. They were a generation that led by example, not by words.

Conner had other boy hood heroes. Some were historical figures like George Washington or Daniel Boone; men whose lives championed the human spirit. And those that capitalized on their freedoms to accomplish great things such as the early explorers Clark, Freemont and Powell.

He had grown up learning about and believing in the constitution of the United States; that it was the greatest document ever created. He marveled at the intellect and selflessness of those uncommon men, joined by a common goal to create a structure of governance that would preserve freedoms for future generations.

But as a young man he had also learned of the enemies of freedom and the human spirit. He was only a generation removed from the horrors of Nazi Germany but even more vivid were the current events of his own youth that documented the atrocities committed by the Soviet Union, communist China, and the Khmer Rouge. Conner had become fascinated and horrified by the terror that could be inflicted on a race of people by such regimes; by the absolute control these governments could exert over any and every individual. The story of all modern totalitarian regimes was rooted in the same false premise of being 'for the good of the nation and its people'. The self-anointed elite identified the villains, usually straw men, and used them as targets to rally the masses against. The propagandists would perpetuate the furor by expanding the list of villains while calling upon the elite to vanquish them too; all the time exalting the elite as selfless leaders that protected the people. The story was always the same; the power of the state increased as they eliminated their dissenters and usurped the freedoms of the citizens.

The books he read as a youth that described this misery in human terms had fascinated Conner. "One Day In The Life Of Ivan Denisovich" by Alexander Solzhenitsyn had impacted Conner greatly in its portrayal of the severe cruelty experienced by political dissidents in the gulags of the Soviet Union. Conner's mood had been affected for weeks after reading of the Jews' experiences in the Nazi camps as depicted by holocaust survivor Viktor Frankl in "Man's Search for Meaning". But the book that had the greatest impact on young Conner Murphy was George Orwell's "1984". In spite of it being fiction Conner felt witness to the destruction of another human being's spirit and dignity by a tyrannical government and saw it as a warning of what could be.

Conner hadn't touched his coffee. He continued to stare out at the ocean as he wondered how far down the abyss his country had fallen. How a young woman in the prime of her life could be denied that life by a bureaucrat. Conner's anger was intensified by the knowledge that his family's experience was not isolated; he knew many people with similar stories.

Conner stood and walked to the railing. He gripped it firmly with both hands as he spoke out loud, "It isn't just the PHA, it's everything."

After a minute he walked back to his chair and fell heavily in to it. The PHA had become what so many feared it would be: a vehicle to destroy freedom. Conner had always known that once the government had the power to make decisions about people's health it could control all facets of people's lives.

All during Mo's ordeal, he had been deeply saddened by the fact that such a beautiful, promising young life was losing a battle to a wicked disease. His sorrow was for her, his son and his grandchildren. All the while she was sick, Conner kept shoving his anger down deep; he didn't want it exposed to Sean and Mo knowing that doing so would only add to their frustration; a frustration that was already overwhelming for them. So he stuffed his anger; stuffed it down deep in to his soul where it has been smoldering.

Conner had absolutely no illusions about 'righting a wrong'. Mo was dead, that would never change. That wrong could never be righted. But what he could do was deal with those that were responsible. He also knew that Mo might have died with the best of care, but that didn't matter to him. The point was that she had wanted the opportunity to fight for her life. A right taken from her by some incompetent, uncaring bureaucrat; taken by a government, which didn't care about the human spirit or about the dignity of the individual.

Just before daylight Conner took his morning walk on the beach. His usual interests didn't concern him this morning;

in fact, he hardly noticed anything around him. As his feet splashed through the surf he found himself smiling. A sinister smile created by a conscious realization that he had nothing to lose; and he loved the freedom it afforded him. He thought of times during his life in which he had been in encounters with bad people. The type of human debris that he worried may harass his family or destroy his property if he were to take action. During those times, Conner chose discretion and walked away even though it galled him to do so. He knew that his position as a business owner, a property owner and a family man put him at a distinct disadvantage because his adversaries had nothing to lose. But now it was his turn. No one could really hurt him anymore. No one could do anything to him that he feared enough to prevent him from exacting revenge. He was enjoying that position; it made him smile.

When he reached his usual turnaround point on the beach he didn't linger as he usually did to take in the surroundings, he simply started back. His mind was buzzing as he recounted the conversation with Representative Dominguez, the congressman that had arranged the meeting between Sean and Mr. Mesh. Conner had called him two days ago to ask some questions about what he knew regarding the PHA process; specifically the final appeal. He was able to speak directly to the congressman because of Sean's connection but chose to present himself as a grieving father who was simply looking for answers to help provide closure. Jose Dominguez turned out to be very communicative and very compassionate. After explaining what he knew about the appeal process, he volunteered to Conner that he also knew a little bit about Mr. Mesh as well. Certainly that was serendipitous; it was exactly the information that Conner sought and was now receiving unsolicited.

Dominguez said the bureaucrat had been described to him as being lazy and inept. He was in a position for which he was totally unqualified but had apparently been put there as a political payoff of some sort. That certainly wasn't unique to government bureaucracies, Conner had commented, to which the congressman agreed. Mr. Dominguez went on to explain that currently his staff was working behind the scenes in an attempt to provide enough evidence to have Mr. Mesh and another PHA employee in Jacksonville investigated. The best hope for the consequence of such an investigation, he explained to Conner, would be to have them removed and replaced by someone competent for such vital positions but he also admitted it was an uphill battle to get any traction for such investigations within federal bureaucracies.

Apparently the other person, a woman in the Jacksonville office, had been linked to the misallocation of large sums of money, and more than once. But the Mesh character, as Dominguez referred to him, just seemed to be monumentally ill qualified. It would be unfortunate if it were true, the congressman told Conner, but there were also accusations that Mesh has a sadistic streak; accusations that Dominguez said were a little difficult for him to believe at first, but with what his people had uncovered, there actually seems to be some justification. At the very least, he concluded that Mr. Mesh was far too interested in his own power.

Conner ended the conversation by saying he was disappointed with the system but didn't really blame any one person. He also said that his daughter-in-law's disease was such that maybe there was no helping her. He thanked the congressman for his time and understanding.

When Conner returned from his walk he drank a bottle of water and mounted his stationary bike. His mind continued to race as he developed his plan. He even realized the perfect night; a night Sean was giving a speech at the River Walk Marriot in downtown Tampa.

Conner wasn't yet certain what he'd do to Mr. Stanley Mesh. He knew that would sort itself out when he confronted him. All he did know was that Mr. Mesh was about to regret the day he ever took a job at the PHA. He also knew that he wanted to find out who controlled this little bureaucrat. Conner was certain this clown was a pawn and the real problem resided higher up the food chain. How high did this run, he wondered? Hell, if he got lucky, he would take them all down.

After an hour on the bike Conner did two hundred crunches, fifty pushups, and ten pull-ups. He left the exercise room as he wiped the sweat from his face and head with a towel. Entering his small study, he went to the gun safe, tumbled the combination lock and opened it. From the top shelf he removed a pistol. It was a .41 caliber Remington model 95 derringer; manufactured in 1888. During that era they were referred to as whore guns, used by prostitutes that concealed them in their undergarments to be used at close range in self-defense.

The derringer was small enough to be completely concealed in the palm of Conner's hand. It had two barrels, over and under, and only fired two rounds. The bullets were heavy and in the world of ballistics, traveled slowly. When they hit a man it was like hitting him with a sledgehammer. The gun wasn't accurate at a distance, but was perfect when you were up close and personal. The beauty for Conner was that he had bought a pair of them many years ago from a cowboy gun collector in Winnemucca, Nevada. There was never a record of the transaction and there was no way to trace this gun to him.

He closed and locked the gun safe and walked in to the bedroom where he set the powerful little gun and a handful of shells on his dresser. He closed his eyes and put his head back as he inhaled deeply through his nostrils, holding his breath for a moment as he thought through his plan again. He knew Mesh was a bad person; but was he a dangerous man? That he didn't know, but he did know that Mr. Mesh had killed all of the Murphys he was going to kill; Conner was taking no chances.

On Monday morning of the following week, Conner drove to a Wal-Mart in Sarasota and paid cash for a cell phone with prepaid minutes. After dropping his Toyota at the body shop, he took a taxi to the Sarasota airport where he rented a small sedan. He left for Miami very early the next morning. Conner planned to drive to the PHA building where Mesh worked and follow him. He wanted Mesh to be alone when he confronted him. Conner wanted two things from his encounter with Mesh: a reckoning and information about who pulled his strings. He also knew that whatever happened, he didn't want it to end up at Sean's door.

MIAMI, FLORIDA

August

Conner was tempted to go to the Coffee Bean across the street from the PHA building but decided against it. He parked out on the street, not wanting to have any record of going past the guard shack to enter the parking lot. It was 11:00 a.m. when Conner used his new cell phone to call the Regional Office of the PHA and asked for Mr. Mesh's office. After listening to an inefficient automated system, so typical of government agencies, Conner finally had the option to push zero for the receptionist. The woman transferred him to Mr. Mesh's office.

"This is Yolanda in Mr. Mesh's office, may I help you?"

"Hi, Yolanda, this is Barry Green. I work with maintenance and we have a problem down here in the parking lot that I need to contact Mr. Mesh about."

"He's on the other line at the moment, can this wait or is it an emergency?"

"Oh, it's not really a big emergency. You see, one of my guys ran in to Mr. Mesh's car with a riding mower. Buggered it up pretty good."

"Oh, my. He just bought that car. I better tell him right away."

"We'll be waiting down here, then. Hey, Yolanda, what's your direct number for that office, please?"

Conner had parked in good position to see the front door and the entire parking lot. He didn't have to wait very long before he saw a man burst through the front doors hurriedly heading for the parking lot.

"I do believe that's my boy." Conner said as he picked up his binoculars and focused them on the agitated little man.

Stanley ran up to his brand new yellow Volvo and then realized that no one was standing there waiting. He flapped his arms up and down like a bird unable to get off the ground and then spun himself in a complete circle.

"Wow, that little prick really must love that car," chuckled Conner.

Stanley then decided to run to the front of the car, deducing that was the obvious place for a lawnmower collision since there was lawn on that side of the parking lot. He looked at the car carefully, running his hand along the front of the hood and then walked to each side to inspect the fenders. He returned to the front and stood there, staring at the car, when suddenly he dropped to his knees to look at the undercarriage. After a minute, Stanley struggled back to his feet, using the hood to push himself upright. He flapped his arms again, twice.

"Jesus, this would make a good you-tube video. This guys an idiot." Conner was quite amused as he continued looking through his field glasses. "There you go, big guy. Get some help figuring this out."

Stanley left his car and walked to the guardhouse at the gate. He stood at the window of the shack with his fists stuck in his sides as he railed at the confused guard inside. Finally, Mesh walked away, with his shirttail hanging out and repeatedly wiping sweat from his forehead with an open palm.

"This is Yolanda in Mr. Mesh's office. May I help you?"

"Yolanda, this is Barry Green with maintenance again. Listen it turns out that it isn't Mr. Mesh's car so don't worry about telling him anything."

"Oh...well...I already did. As a matter of fact he already went down to check it out. Well, I'll tell him you called back when he returns. Thank you."

"Oh, you're welcome."

Conner wasn't sure what this 'government man' would do for lunch or how long his workday was. For all I know, he thought, this guy will leave at noon and take the rest of the day off. He decided the prudent thing to do would be to follow Mesh if he left for lunch. Conner was fully cognizant that he didn't know much about how to follow someone without being noticed so he just used common sense; not allowing Mesh to get too far ahead, but he also avoided being so close as to be obvious.

The yellow Volvo went west two blocks and turned on to 12th Avenue. It crossed over the Miami River and continued south for several more blocks. Stanley took a right in to a strip mall and virtually flew across the parking lot toward the far corner where he parked in front of a small restaurant named Beppo's. The lot was full, which caused Conner to marvel at Mesh's luck for finding a space at the front. Conner watched Stanley enter the restaurant under the sign boasting of authentic Tuscan cuisine before he parked his car. A minute passed before Conner started toward the restaurant for a better look at the man he was following. As he passed in front of Mesh's car he realized that it was parked in a handicap space.

"This bastard probably cheats at every step," Conner muttered to himself.

Dean Martin's 'Amore' greeted Conner as he entered the small foyer of the restaurant. The air inside was saturated with the aromas of garlic and oregano; the pungent odors didn't square with his memories of Tuscany. A sign just inside the door asked patrons to please wait to be seated. There were two dining rooms and Conner peered in to both. He saw Mesh sitting at a corner table, back against the wall, facing the room. He was at a four top but sitting alone and the other place settings had been removed. Conner mused that Mesh was probably wise not to sit with his back to the door.

"Just one for lunch?" the young hostess smiled brightly as she looked at Conner.

"Just me, thanks. Can I have a seat at that table toward the back?" Conner asked, motioning at a table next to Mesh.

"Certainly, follow me please."

The young lady set the menu down in front of a chair facing away from Mesh toward the dining room. Conner ignored her gesture and sat in the opposite chair and reached across the table for his menu.

"Linda will be your server and she'll be right with you. What would you like to drink?"

Conner smiled up at her, "I'd just like water with a lemon, please. Thanks."

Mesh had taken the magazine he was reading and held it in front of him while he waited for his food. This didn't allow Conner to see his face so he concentrated on his own menu. In the mean time Linda brought a basket of bread and his water and placed them on the red and white-checkered tablecloth.

"Do you need a few minutes?" she asked Conner.

"No, hon, I'm good. I'll have your Caprese. Thanks"

"Nothing else to drink, water's OK?"

"Yea, thanks. Water's fine."

"I'll get that right out for you."

Linda was back with a large plate of spaghetti and meatballs and another basket of bread for Mesh's table.

"Excuse me sir," the waitress said, needing Mesh to move his arms and magazine in order to put his plate in front of him.

Mesh looked at her and said nothing. He hesitated before moving his arms and placing his magazine to the side. He then took a large paper napkin, unfolded it and stuck an end of it behind his buttoned shirt collar.

Conner looked Mesh over; totally indifferent to how obvious

he may appear. But Mesh was oblivious as he dove in to the plate of food in front of him.

As Conner assessed the man across from him he muttered under his breath, "This son-of-a-bitch is quite a vision." Sean nailed it, he thought, he's a fat little toad - a fat grotesque little toad. This ugly little shit isn't just fat, he's doughy and soft looking. The thought of touching him makes my skin crawl, no wonder Sean said he felt like he needed a shower.

Conner couldn't get over Mesh's appearance and demeanor. He was awed by the fact that this miserable looking little man had the power to determine the fate of a person like Mo, and it only stood to reason that she was not the only bright, happy, productive person that this troll had passed a death sentence on. He wondered, how many other lives had this vile little creature destroyed?

By the time the waitress had returned with his Caprese Conner had worked himself in to such an emotional lather that it was all he could do to not jump from his chair and knock Mesh from his. He looked down at his plate, knowing that he needed to calm down and relax.

"Is everything all right, sir?"

It was a full second before Conner looked up at the waitress, "Yea, yea, I'm good. Thanks."

"You're fine with water still or can I get you something else?"

He forced a smile and said, "I'm fine, thanks."

"I'll leave this check with you, then, but there's no hurry."

Conner turned his focus on his food to purposely stop looking in Mesh's direction. The thick slices of mozzarella and tomato were good and Conner relaxed a little bit. Half way through his meal he looked over at Mesh again, now leaning over his plate, noisily sucking strands of spaghetti through his lips. The fat man was busy twirling a large forkful of noodles while chewing the last one, not wasting an instant between swallowing one and stuffing his cavernous mouth with another. Conner pushed his own plate away; appetite ruined by the display in front of him and leaned to one side to grab some cash from his opposite pocket. He left a tip for Linda and picked the check up from the table before taking the few short steps to Mesh's table.

"Excuse me. I'm not from around here and I was hoping you could help me with some directions," Conner said in what he hoped was a pleasant sounding tone.

Mesh looked up at him, cheeks bloated as he chewed another enormous bite of food. When he finished, he wiped his mouth with his sauce-spattered napkin and smiled a phony, condescending smile filled with yellow teeth.

"I'm not from around here either. Can't help ya. Go ask the waitress why don't ya?" He then flashed another quick, yellow smile before taking his fork and pushing an entire meatball in to his wide-open mouth.

Conner's immediate instinct was to shove the man's fork through the back of his head, but he simply smiled at him and turned to leave. Conner paid his bill and returned to his car to wait.

He had known this little bureaucrat was going to be a detestable sort before he ever saw him or talked to him; what he didn't know was that this bastard would surpass his imagination. After leaving Beppo's, the Volvo returned north on 12th Avenue and pulled in to a Wendy's parking lot only two blocks from the restaurant. Conner was incredulous. Stanley managed to finish his large frosty before reaching the office.

It was 3:30 p.m. when Mesh walked out through the doors of the PHA building and headed to his car. Conner saw him easily from his vantage point across the street and left his spot in the shade of the oak to return to his own car. Mesh headed west again on 12th Avenue until he accessed the Dolphin Expressway, took it east to I-95 and then south to US-1 toward Kendall.

Conner hoped that Mesh was headed home as he thought about his inexperience at tailing someone and worried he'd be discovered if Mesh went on a series of errands. Conner's luck held as the pursuit continued down 87th Avenue and finally to Kings Creek Drive, where the yellow Volvo pulled in to a driveway. Conner continued past the house and turned right at the next intersection. A block down that street there was a vacant house with a for sale sign. Conner turned around in the driveway and returned the way he'd come. Mesh's car was still in the driveway.

Conner continued past the house to retrace his route back to I-95. On the way he pulled off the road and parked at the outer fringe of a Publix parking lot. He walked to the back of his car and with his pocketknife removed the screws holding the license plate. He stood on one end of the plate and pulled the other end toward him, bending it in half. He flattened the plate out again and refastened it using only the screws on the left side.

There was nothing to do now but kill time. He drove to South Beach, parked his car at Collins Park and strolled the boardwalk. Going over his plan wouldn't hurt anything. At 9:00 o'clock he returned to his car and drove north to the Fontainebleau. He parked his car in the guest parking area of the large hotel and leaned his seat back all the way, making him barely visible to someone walking by and comfortable enough to get some sleep. Conner set the alarm on his watch for 2:00 a.m. He woke just before the alarm and got out of the car to stretch. He went to the back of the car and bent his license plate at the crease to about a 60° angle. The bend made it difficult to read but hopefully easier to justify to a police officer than no plate.

The drive to the vacant house near Mesh's took thirty minutes. When he drove past the house he noticed the Volvo wasn't in the driveway, but he thought nothing of it, presuming it was in the garage. He smiled as he thought that Stanley wouldn't want to take a chance of someone hitting it with a lawnmower.

As he approached the house on foot and the house came

into view he scolded himself for his little joke. He'd done nothing to confirm this was Mesh's house. What if it was the home of a friend or a mistress? Certainly that would fit; he could be leaving work early every day to see a woman. Conner's plan had been fairly precise; check the house out tonight and confront this bastard tomorrow night when Sean had an alibi; he hadn't left room for error.

Conner kept walking, anxious that he may have already screwed things up. He found a door around the side of the garage and started to turn the knob. He stopped. What about an alarm? Certainly someone that ruined lives on a regular basis had reason to be paranoid. Conner stood motionless, unsure what to do. He thought how most homes with security systems were eager to advertise the fact with window stickers or yard signs.

The house was dark and there were no streetlights but the moon was full and directly overhead. He searched windows for stickers as he began to circle the house. The paint was faded and peeling in places. Several sections of the aluminum soffit hung askew and in the back of the house the rain gutter spout had fallen to the ground.

It made Conner feel strange and anxious to sneak around someone's house. As he continued his inspection through the backyard, a small separate building became evident. It wasn't of a size or structure that revealed its purpose. There were windows, which seemed to eliminate it as a storage shed yet it seemed far too small to be an apartment or mother-in-law cottage. A detached office, Conner thought, but why? Why would a government bureaucrat that couldn't put a proper day in at his regular job want an office at home? His intuition told him there was some significance to this building.

He reminded himself that he had yet to confirm it was Mesh's house and focused on finishing his reconnaissance and finally came full circle to the side door of the garage.

Conner hesitated before trying the door. His right eye stung from a droplet of sweat and he rubbed it with the back of his hand. He took a deep breath and turned the knob slightly. Unlocked. Slowly he started pushing the door open. It squeaked loudly. He stopped pushing and cursed under his breath. He listened. No sounds. He pushed the door even more slowly but the creaking was just as loud. Again Conner cussed and waited. He could just fit his head through the door but the interior of the garage was too dark to see. Sweat ran from under his cap and he wiped it away with his palm. He decided to give the door one more quick, hard shove to let more light in; that time it made no noise. Conner shook his head, thinking he'd have made a terrible burglar.

There was just enough light to make out the yellow Volvo. Next to it was a small sedan, the make and model of which he didn't recognize. A nervous tingle ran up his neck when he saw the interior door leading in to the house. He stood motionless, pondering his next move. Unconsciously he felt his pocket for his gun. Not now. He needed to stick to the plan.

He was silently chiding himself for his nervous state as he pulled the door shut with a firm yank to minimize the noise. There was a loud shriek. Conner jumped backwards nearly falling over. There was a longer, deeper yowl and Conner realized he'd wedged a big yellow cat in the doorway. He shoved the door back open and watched his victim bolt in to the garage and under the sedan.

"Shit! Fuckin' cat! About gave me a heart attack!"

Conner knew the mystery building behind the house needed further exploration. The detached building had a single door facing the house. There were two windows on the side facing the backyard and a single window in the wall opposite the door. The wall bordering the neighbor was solid. Blinds were drawn over all of the windows and there were no screens in any of them. Even on closer inspection there was nothing to clarify the purpose of the building. After circling the structure Conner walked back to the single window on the back wall. He took the small flashlight from his back pocket and shined it through the window to ascertain how it opened and how it locked. It was a sliding window with the bottom half being movable and a single twist lock at the center, which seemed to be in the unlocked position.

"I might be an amateur, but I seem to be a lucky one," Conner whispered to himself. He took his fingertips and grasped the small lip at the bottom of the window, trying to heave it upward. Nothing. He adjusted his grip and tried again, pulling upward as hard as he could. Nothing.

"Don't tell me it's corroded or painted shut or some such. Hell this asshole doesn't paint his house enough to paint the windows shut." As Conner muttered under his breath he shined his light all along the edges of the window frame, looking for a reason it wouldn't open. He readdressed the lock and decided it may not be in the full open position.

He decided to push against the top of the bottom window, pushing it in as he pulled upward with his other hand. Nothing, the window didn't budge. He thought about breaking the window, and started thinking about what he might use to do so when he decided to try one more time to open it. He positioned his hands in the same way as before but shifted his body so that his shoulder and hip were fully behind the push of his upper hand. He shoved hard against the top of the window until he feared he might break the glass. It was enough this time. The window came up several inches. Placing both hands at the bottom, he raised the window the rest of the way. Conner stood quietly and listened; not aware of how much noise he might have made; his breathing was the only sound.

He took his light to examine the shade covering the window. Reaching in, he grasped it from the bottom and gave it a tug, it responded by rolling upward. Conner held on to the shade to controll the speed at which it rewound.. Behind the shade was a drawn curtain. A sudden realization caused a small jolt of fear to shoot through him; maybe someone was in there! He stood motionless and listened again, this time for several minutes. Silence. Finally he decided to part the curtains just enough to look in. It was too dark to see. He thought to hell with it and shined his flashlight into the room.

No one was there.

To his surprise, it did appear to be an office more than anything else. There was a small desk against one wall with a laptop on it and a large easy chair in the center of the room facing a wall-mounted television. A bookshelf stood against the opposite wall, which housed only a few books, mostly magazines and random papers littered the shelves. Conner shined his light at the other two windows noting that they too had curtains drawn over the shades. Shining his light at the door nearly straight across from his observation point he determined two dead bolts securing it. Conner wondered what might be in this room that Mesh was so anxious to protect.

He took a rag from his pocket and wiped the window frame and glass. He then pulled two gloves from his right rear pocket. They were simple white cotton gloves, most often used by ropers to prevent rope burn. They were the only gloves Conner had in Florida and the thought of them being white hadn't struck him until now. He smiled and shook his head, reminded of what a poor spy he was as he looked at his bright white gloves in the moonlight. The light thoughts allowed him to relax for the first time since he had started his prowling.

"Ahh, I look like the sorcerer's apprentice," Conner whispered to himself. "Oh, no. Mr. Cellophane from "Chicago". The song from the musical started going through his head when he realized that the character in the play was lamenting the fact that he was invisible to everyone around him. Conner was anything but invisible wearing his gloves. Swinging one leg up and through the window he grabbed each side of the frame and pulled himself inside.

Directly to his left, in the corner of the room were several pieces of furniture stacked in haphazard fashion. To his right was a large black chest that he quickly realized was an old gun safe with its door standing wide open. Using his light to look inside, it was evident that there were neither guns nor ammunition housed in the safe. On the bottom were two cardboard boxes that had seen better days, both with torn corners and one with a fist sized hole in the side. The boxes were overflowing with magazines; in fact several had slid off the top and were lying on the floor of the safe. It was evident at a glance they were pornographic magazines and Conner reached down to pick one up. "Sadistic Delight" was the title of the first and had a naked woman with her hands and feet bound and a ball shoved in to her mouth, in the background of the picture stood a masked man with a small whip in his hand. The entire box was apparently filled with different issues of the same magazine, at least as deep as Conner had the desire to dig through it.

He picked a magazine from the top of the other box. "Pain Is Pleasure" was the title of this magazine. There was a picture of a large breasted naked woman with what appeared to be tourniquets around each breast and clamps on her nipples. The look on her face revealed anything but pleasure. Conner grimaced as he looked at the picture and continued to dig down through the stack. All of them were different issues of the same magazine. He couldn't help but see another cover that depicted a woman's backside literally covered with whip marks, most of which were bleeding.

"This is fuckin' unbelievable," Conner said out loud. He dropped the magazine back on the stack and examined the top shelf where normally ammunition would be stored. The shelf contained old videotapes, stuffed toward the back in chaotic fashion. To the right of the tapes and more toward the front were several stacks of DVD's, all in plastic cases. Upon close inspection Conner realized that none of these seemed to be produced for typical commercial purveyance. "All black market shit," Conner muttered to himself.

Using his flashlight, he looked at several individually, discovering that they were all labeled, some on the case but most on the disc itself. All the labels were hand written with different handwriting. A quick sample was all Conner needed; "Sarah Gets Hers", "Thirteen and Thirsty", "Make Her Beg for Mercy". As Conner set the DVD's back on the stack he shuddered involuntarily causing him to knock the stack over. They remained on the shelf and he did nothing to straighten them.

He walked over to the desk that was void of anything but a laptop. It was closed so Conner opened it and hit the space bar several times, the screen stayed blank, Conner pushed the on off button briefly and the monitor began the startup procedure. When the desktop finally materialized a window appeared asking for a password. Conner closed the computer and went to the bookcase.

On one shelf were several bound manuals; official publications of the Public Health Agency of the United States. One seemed to be an employee manual, another a directory of offices and personnel, another labeled "Procedures for Case Review". As Conner set the small stack of books back on the shelf he couldn't help but notice the layer of dust that covered them. There was little else on the shelves that seemed to be of any importance at all; random papers that consisted of advertisements and flyers, bank notices and billing statements. There was no order to any of it.

Conner stepped toward the sliding closet doors located next to the only exterior door of the office. It was then he discovered the wooden sign mounted above the exterior door. 'Stanley's Bunker' read the sign. Conner couldn't help but think what a peculiar word 'bunker' was for someone's office. Pondering it further though it seemed more relevant: 'this isn't an office, it's a hole where a miserable little creature hides out from the world. Where a nasty little man protects his ugly little treasures and escapes any threats posed by normal human beings.'

The contents of the closet were not revealing. Several light jackets and a raincoat on hangers and a blanket wadded up and stuck on the single shelf. Conner slid the door shut and used his light to survey the room. There were two photographs hanging on the wall above the desk that he hadn't noticed.

The picture on the left was of a younger Stanley Mesh standing next to a nicely dressed black woman, a little heavy but still attractive. The woman was smiling at the camera, as was Stanley, but his expression looked forced; almost like the smile he'd given Conner at the restaurant. He continued looking at the picture, thinking about Mesh's expression today. In this picture he looks like he doesn't want to smile but knows he has to. Today was different; it was all about condescension and arrogance.

The other photograph was of Stanley standing with a well-dressed man. By the weight Stanley had gained, it was obviously a more recent picture. The other man was taller and slighter than Mesh and probably twenty-five years his senior. Conner gave a little grunt of realization as he noticed a striking contrast between the two pictures. In the first, Stanley was forcing a smile, while the woman seemed genuine in hers. In the second, it was the other man that looked to be forcing a smile and Stanley appeared to be beaming. Conner couldn't help but think that the man was subtly, maybe unconsciously, leaning away from Mesh.

Conner shined his light around the room, curious now to find other pictures. There were none. 'How odd,' Conner thought, 'there are no pictures of any family, of any friends of Mesh doing something fun or memorable. After all wasn't this his 'bunker', his 'man cave'; the place he goes to revel in who he is and what he likes to do.' The only pictures Mesh had were perfunctory acknowledgements of some sort of milestones in his sorry ass life. Conner shined his light back toward the gun safe, knowing he was right; this was the place where Mesh went to revel in who he truly is.

Conner decided to sit in the recliner; he was tired and pretty overwhelmed with all that he'd done today and all he was discovering. He placed his flashlight in his lap and put the palms of both hands on the arms and pushed back to make the foot rest open and the chair back recline. Conner shut off the light and closed his eyes. He was tired enough that he almost dozed off, and then sniffed several times, scrunching his features slightly as he realized the chair seemed to have an odor. It was subtle but very unpleasant.

He opened his eyes and after a moment they adjusted to the moonlight coming in the open window. He leaned the chair forward and forced the footrest down, wanting to escape the odor of the chair by leaning forward. It didn't help. He started to stand to escape the odor completely when the thought struck him to look in the side pockets of the chair. The left pocket contained trash, candy wrappers and food wrappers that were wadded up, some stuck together with an old piece of melted chocolate. The wrappers stuck to his cotton glove and Conner shook his left hand rapidly to free him of the debris.

He almost disregarded the right side pocket, fearing more of the same disgusting refuse but decided to look. He reached between his legs to recover his flashlight and while leaning over the arm, pulled the pocket open to look inside. This pouch was empty except for a small cardboard folder. He retrieved it and used his light to see the contents as he opened the folder. There were two photographs, one was a portrait of a girl and the other was of a woman holding a child. The woman was very attractive and the little girl in her lap looked very much like her. Further examination led Conner to believe that the other photo was likely the same woman at a much younger age. Could this be his wife? Conner couldn't believe that a stylish, attractive woman like her would marry a creature like Mesh. And if it was, why was the photograph here, hidden away instead of on the wall, or on his desk. Hell, Mesh would have a shrine to this woman if she consented to marry him! No, this is a woman that Stanley probably lusts for, someone he doesn't want the real Mrs. Mesh to see.

Conner returned the pictures to their hiding place and got up from the chair. He stood a minute, contemplating what to do next when he focused on the desk again. There were only drawers on the left side of the small desk. The top drawer was a mess, papers and pens strewn throughout with several tootsie rolls scattered in. The middle one had several small extension cords and what looked to be another plug in for the laptop.

The bottom drawer contained only a single spiral notebook. Conner pulled it out and opened it to find writing on the first page. Without reading it, he turned several of the following pages but found them to be blank. He set the light on the desk in front of him so that it shined across the desk, towards him, and picked up the notebook to flip through the pages as if fanning a deck of cards. No other pages were written on. Laying the book flat on the desk he opened it to the first page while again holding the light in his right hand. There were three quotes written at the top of the page.

"Death is the solution to all problems. No man—no problem." JS

"Humanitarianism is the expression of stupidity and cowardice." AH

"Possessing power over the lives of others is to hold the key to immeasurable pleasure" SM

As Conner read the quotes his heart began to race. He clenched his teeth as loathing filled his being. He had heard the first quote before, several times. He instantly knew who JS was; it was Joseph Stalin, the mastermind behind the destruction of millions of lives and the oppression of millions of others. Conner read the second quote again. His breathing was quick and shallow. The words churned his stomach as if they were a physical threat. Who was AH? The realization struck him like a slap. Adolf Hitler.

He leaned back in the chair, staring at the note pad. Why would anyone write this vile crap...and then keep it...to what, refer to it? Conner leaned forward again, almost trembling as he did so. He read the third quote again. *"Possessing power over the lives of others is to hold the key to immeasurable pleasure."* SM

Stanley Mesh.

There were several blank lines below the quotations before a heading appeared.

THE VANQUISHED

Below the heading was a list of surnames.

Peterson

Roosevelt

Henderson

Samson

Mathews

Fernandez

Johnson

The list continued, line after line and row after row of names. The Vanquished? How did Mesh 'vanquish' anyone?

Were these the people that he denied? People sentenced to death by not allowing them treatment; is that what this is? Conner was in a cold sweat and felt light headed as he continued to scan the names.

Goldman

Han

Murphy

Conner stopped breathing. He swallowed rapidly several times as he fought the urge to vomit. He dropped his light to the desk and closed his eyes tightly, feeling as if he was going to pass out. He took a deep, long breath in and let it out slowly. He picked his light up from the desk and read the name again.

Murphy

He now knew what he didn't know before, or at least didn't acknowledge before. He would kill Stanley Mesh.

Conner stood and paced the room. Should he do it now? He went to the door and turned both dead bolts, but as he turned the second knob he hesitated. He thought of Sean. He put both hands against the door as he leaned into it.

He spoke out loud to himself, "No, Murph old boy, not yet."

Conner was in a hurry to leave now. He returned to the desk, closed the notebook and placed it back in the bottom drawer. He left through the window, reaching in to close the curtains and pull the shade before closing it. He walked directly to the garage door and wiped the knob before returning to his car.

He spent the rest of the night driving. He was angry, as angry as he had ever been in his life; but his emotions vacillated between rage and sorrow, at times with tears running down his cheeks as he drove aimlessly around Miami.

It was ten minutes after 7:00 a.m. when Conner parked his car on the opposite side of the street from the Mesh house, three doors down, between two houses in hopes of not drawing attention from the occupants of either one. He opened the newspaper and began to read it, intermittently glancing up to monitor any activity from the Mesh's garage. At 8:20 the Volvo pulled out of the garage and drove past him. Stanley never looked his way. Fifteen minutes later the sedan backed out of the garage and Mrs. Mesh drove by, as oblivious as her husband to Conner's presence. Conner took a good look at her as she drove past; her appearance gave him some sense of joy.

"Maybe old Stanley's getting a taste of hell while he's still on this earth," Conner muttered aloud.

A cigarette dangled from Sheri Mesh's lips and a large cloud of smoke emanated from her nostrils as she passed his car. She leaned forward in her seat with hunched shoulders and both hands gripping the steering wheel as she looked straight ahead. Her stringy black hair fell close to her face and neck. Conner felt she made a perfect caricature of some 'sad sack' going off to work on a Monday morning, hung over and dreading the coming day.

He followed the sedan to a lower-end strip mall about four miles away. A Dollar Store anchored the strip. Sheri parked her car and got out with another cigarette between her lips, eyes in a partial squint to escape the smoke and purse in hand. She walked to the entrance of the Dollar Store, took one last drag on her cigarette and flicked it out to the parking lot before walking inside.

As Conner pulled away he couldn't help but think it odd that the wife of a man in Mesh's position, however undeserved, worked for minimum wage as a dime store clerk. Conner went for coffee at the Coffee Bean he'd passed two blocks before the strip mall. While he sat drinking his grande Café Americano he dialed information for the number of the Dollar Store on Cardinal Ave.

"Connect me," Conner wondered why he talked in a mechanical tone just because the recording did.

"Dollar Store."

"Hello, is Mrs. Mesh there?"

"Sheri? She's working the register. She'll have to call you back."

"No big deal. This is Ted, a friend of hers from Melbourne. I was going to stop in and say hi if she's still gonna be there this afternoon."

"She's here till 5:00, honey."

"Great, I'll be there before that. Bye." Conner hung up the phone hoping the rest of the day would fall in to place.

"This is Yolanda in Mr. Mesh's office how may I help you?"

"Ted Mathews, Yolanda, from the Jacksonville office. How are you today?"

"Doing well, Mr. Mathews, how may I help you?"

"I'm headed to Miami today and was trying to see what Mr. Mesh's appointment schedule was like today. I'd like to pop in for a quick second."

"He has no appointments this morning on his calendar. This afternoon he has a two o'clock and then from 3:00 to 4:30 is his monthly videoconference with the district officers. Those conferences usually run over though."

"Well, heck, I won't be in Miami till this afternoon and he'll be pretty wrapped up, won't he? I'll make it another time."

"Can I leave Mr. Mesh a message or tell him what this is regarding?"

"No," Conner said, "just a personal call. No big deal at all.

Thanks anyway."

"You're welcome Mr. Mathews." After she hung up, Yolanda said under her breath, "the fat jerk has a friend, I'll be damned!"

Conner was not only pleased that he knew how much time he had but also gratified that he would have time to get some rest. He headed back toward the beach and the Fontainebleau Hotel. It was big enough that he wouldn't be noticed nor identified as not being a guest. He'd be able to shower at the pool changing room and clean himself up. Then maybe get some sleep in a lounge by the pool.

It was three hours before he woke, groggy and famished. It was noon. He went to the tiki bar and got water and a grouper salad. He spent what was left of the rest of the afternoon walking and sitting on the beach.

As he sat looking out over the water he thought how he had first come to Miami with Molly many years before. They loved the pastel appearance of the waters and the sky there, always amplified when the sun was low on either horizon. He smiled a melancholy smile envisioning Molly sitting on a towel on that very beach; legs crossed, beer in her hand, laughing out loud as she teased him about his farmer tan. Conner continued to stare at nothing, retaining the image of his lovely Molly as long as he could. When it faded he stood and went for another walk.

As he walked on the beach, he became cognizant of how much he had calmed down. He was becoming resigned to what had to be done and it brought him a sense of peace. He found it odd to feel such calmness when he knew precisely the lethality of his plan.

He called Jan using his own cell phone and they chatted briefly. He hadn't called her the day before and he knew another day not hearing from him would seem strange. He told her only that he was walking on the beach but neglected to tell her which beach. After saying goodbye, he called Sean. His son didn't pick up so Conner left a message on the voice mail, telling him he loved him and wished him luck with his speech tonight.

Conner glanced at his watch: 3:00 p.m.. He left the beach and headed for his car. Within an hour he was sitting at Stanley's desk with the spiral notebook open before him. Conner read the quotations again and scanned through the names again, his gaze unwavering for minutes as he saw Murphy. He read Stanley's quote a final time:

"Possessing power over the lives of others is to hold the key to immeasurable pleasure." Conner took his gloved hand and replaced the notebook to its drawer. He had no idea when Mesh might enter 'his bunker', or even if he would. He had a very strong hunch, though, that this where Stanley spent most of his time. Conner fully intended to kill him tonight; this was the night that Sean would have a patent alibi. He didn't want to do it in the house and he had no intention of killing Sheri Mesh. But if Stanley didn't visit the bunker tonight, he would take care of him in the house and Mrs. Mesh would hopefully...not be an issue. Conner stopped thinking about that scenario and decided to focus on Stanley coming here, as he knew he would.

Conner laid on the carpeted floor, flat on his back with his knees bent. He took several long, slow breathes as he let his back and shoulders relax and sink to the floor. He continued to take deep, measured breaths, pleased that he felt so calm. Conner fell asleep.

A noise jerked him awake. He lay there trying to identify what it was, heart racing, holding his breath. It was the sound of a key in the lock.

He rolled to his stomach and jumped to his feet, fully alert. He walked quickly but silently toward the door, pulling his gun from his pocket as he went.

"Whaaat? What the fuck you want, now?" The sound of a man's voice was loud through the door.

Conner continued toward the door. He thought it was Mesh, but he wasn't sure. One of the dead bolts had already been turned to the unlocked position.

"Shit," The same voice from the other side of the door.

227

Conner never stopped moving and quietly slid the closet door open and walked in. He pulled the door closed and listened. Nothing, not a sound. Conner concentrated on his breathing. He realized he wasn't frightened. He was experiencing the same emotional buzz he felt when stalking game: excited but apprehensive about losing his quarry. Minutes passed. Then the sound of a bolt turning and the door being pushed open.

"Fuckin' whore. She needs to figure out I ain't her nigger before I..." Conner couldn't hear the end of Stanley's muttered threat due to the sound made by the closing door. Then came the sound of both bolts being turned, locking them in. Conner was motionless, listening, trying to assess what Mesh might be doing, or what part of the room he was in. He heard the TV come on and heard the blathering of an announcer claiming the best deals ever offered at the local Chevrolet dealership. Conner then heard the sound of the fat man plopping heavily into his chair.

Conner slid the closet door open and walked to within a few steps of the chair.

"Hello, Stanley."

"Haaa! What the fu..." Stanley blurted. He spun his chair to face Conner, panic obvious on his reddened face. He'd been holding a Coke in his hand and had spilled some of it on his crotch when he involuntarily bounced forward.

"Can I call you, Stanley?"

Mesh only looked at him, unable to speak. His eyes were wide open and they looked bizarre being magnified behind his thick glasses. Conner nodded toward his crotch.

"Piss yourself or just spill your coke? Conner was speaking slowly. "You never did say if I could call you Stanley?"

Conner stood three feet in front of Mesh who had to lean his head back in the chair to see Conner's face. Conner's tall and muscular frame created an intimidating presence only amplified by his calm attitude and sardonic smile. His hands were at his sides and the derringer was completely concealed in his right. He continued staring into Mesh's face, curious if the fat, little shit had any response.

"What do you...who are...how'd you get in here?"

"Let me see, fat boy. How 'bout this? I'll tell you who I am and then you'll realize that nothing else matters. My name is Murphy."

Mesh cocked his head very slightly as he squinted his eyes and frowned. The name meant nothing at first. As the realization hit him, Stanley's mouth turned to a grin, showing his stained teeth. Conner felt the rage well up inside him as he watched Stanley's countenance change.

"That name holds the key for immeasurable pleasure, you miserable piece of shit?"

The look on Stanley Mesh's face turned to a mixture of bewilderment and fear. He opened his mouth to say something but Conner didn't want to hear it. He took a quick step forward while positioning the gun in his hand. He pushed the derringer firmly in to Mesh's chest, over his heart, and pulled the trigger. The sound of the report was muffled partially by the end of the barrel being stuffed in to the man's flabby chest, but was loud enough in that small room to make Conner's ears ring. The impact of the bullet propelled Mesh's body backwards so that he was reclining fully in the chair. His feet had flown upward as his body was flung backwards but now they rested on the footrest. His mouth twitched slightly and his eyes were even wider than they'd been. His glasses were crooked on his head so only his left eye was magnified. His mouth jerked open as he took an agonal breath, then another. Then Stanley Mesh was dead.

Conner stood there looking at the remains of this little bureaucrat. How could a being such as this have been the perpetrator of so much pain? He shook his head with the realization that this creature was only a willing pawn. Others had orchestrated the things that happened to his family. Mesh's eyes were still open as Conner leaned forward and swept his glasses from his face. With a gloved index finger he touched the cornea of Mesh's left eye confirming through lack of any reflex that the man was dead.

"It's not bad served up lukewarm either," Conner said as he looked in to the dead man's face one last time.

Conner dropped the gun back in to his pocket and laid back down on the floor where he had slept earlier. He wondered who might have heard the shot and was in no hurry to walk outside before dark. Conner had been certain that Stanley would come to the bunker that night; he was just as certain that his wife wouldn't.

Just as he had marveled at his calmness earlier, he now took notice of the fact he felt no remorse. He really felt nothing. It made him think about some of the good horses he had raised and raced over the years and how it had made him sad when he'd had to put some of them down. Tonight triggered none of the same emotion. This was more akin to shooting a rabid raccoon. He lay there thinking of some of those good horses, waiting for darkness.

CHICAGO, ILLINOIS

August

"What do ya mean, 'no'. Who the fuck you think you're talkin' to, bitch."

"I appreciate the drinks, Nick, but I'm not goin' home with you. I got my little girl to think about and my Mom has to go to work. She works the midnight shift."

"Fuck your mother, and fuck you, too. You think I spent all night buyin' you drinks and talkin' to you so I could go home and jerk off?"

"Sorry, Nick. I gotta go. I didn't promise you nuthin'". Lauren quickly pulled away before he could wrap his thick fingers around her wrist.

"Hey, big guy; let the little lady be. With a mug like yours you oughta be used to jerkin'off." The words came from a large round man standing behind Nick, ten feet down the bar. His moniker was appropriately Big Mike, a self-professed 'wise guy'. His size and loud mouth intimidated most people, but Nick Kowalski knew him for what he was, a wannabe and a loser. The fat man had known Nick a long time and thought that provided him license to make a joke at his expense.

Two men stood next to Big Mike. They were chuckling at his joke, thinking they were now part of something.

Although Nick had been facing Lauren, he knew who made the comment and his short fuse lit instantly. By the time he grabbed his beer bottle from the bar, and turned toward the fat man, his face was already red. The large vein in the center of his forehead protruded and pulsed. Lauren took her opportunity and bolted out the door.

Nick attempted to disguise his rage by smiling an exaggerated smile. "That's funny, Mike, very funny."

Big Mike gave his head a quick nod as he looked at his two lackeys with a grin that said, 'see boys, I know Nick Kowalski.' Nick was closing the gap between himself and Mike as he passed the beer bottle from his left hand to his right, grabbing it around the neck. In the blink of an eye, he swung the bottle hard in a downward arc, broke it on the edge of the bar and continued the circle with his arm. The crash startled everyone as glass and beer went flying. He took his final step toward Mike as his right hand passed in front of him in the continuation of the arc. He pushed off with his right hip and threw his weight forward and drove the jagged edge in to Big Mike's left ear.

The fat man's scream pierced the air as he fell sideways in to the bar, his head bent well over his body. A severed artery sprayed blood into the air while a heavy stream ran down his neck creating a puddle on the bar. Nick twisted his hand, driving it in to the side of the round head; cutting the ear and jaw of the fat man as he screamed in agony. When Nick took his hand away and threw the bottle to the floor there was blood on the mirror and bottles behind the bar and on the faces and shirts of the two men standing beside Big Mike.

Nick's face was almost purple, his upper lip and forehead shiny with sweat. The muscles in his neck bulged to freakish proportions, straining the tendons until they were as taut as bowstrings. His eyes appeared to quiver in their sockets as he started to speak.

"Don't you ever think you can talk to me like that, you fuckin' tub of shit. You fuckin' limp dicked, lard-assed piece of shit." Nick then turned to the two stunned onlookers, throwing his head and chest forward he growled "Aaarrrgh"; the two men took a startled jump backwards as he knew they would.

Nick wasn't done, "Any of you say a word about this to anyone, and I'll cut your balls off with a broken bottle. Got it!" He turned to the bartender, "That goes for you too, Mickey. Throw me a towel."

As Nick walked out wiping the blood from his hand he could hear the fat man making sobbing noises. His two friends were still motionless. Mickey had seen Nick in a rage before, but this might be his worst. Goddamn he wished that son-of-a-bitch would quit coming in to his bar.

The next morning the phone rang before Nick's alarm had gone off but he had incorporated the ringing in to his dream. Finally, Nick shook his sleep off sufficiently to realize it was his phone and groped the nightstand for his cell.

"Yea, what is it?" Nick's answer was barely audible.

"It's me slugger. Your best pal. Got a message for you."

"Stuart, you little sweet heart..." Nick suddenly flushed and his heart started pounding as last night's incident shot through his mind.

"Nicky, boy, you there?" Stuart was laying on the sugary sarcasm.

Nick cleared his throat as he swung his legs over the bed. "Yea, I'm here. What you need?" He decided to back off his usual antagonism with Stuart; this wasn't the time to be a smart ass.

"We need to meet, chum. Got a delivery for you."

"You mean a job?"

"What the fuck were you thinking, a bouquet of roses?"

"Yea, whatever." He wanted to tell this pencil neck to kiss his ass, but he wasn't sure he was in the clear and wasn't going to push his luck.

"I hope your schedule isn't too tight today, I know the demands on someone of your social prominence, but we need to meet at noon."

"Always the comic, Stu baby. Where?" Nick was starting to relax, realizing there was no way this is how it would go down if Costello had found out about last night.

"Meet me at Humboldt Park. You know it?"

Shit. Nick didn't like the sound of this; he was worried again. They always met in the city, in a busy public place. "What the fuck we goin' there for Stu?"

"Because that's the area I'll be in. I've got another appointment. The world doesn't revolve around you. Matter of fact, Nicky boy, I can't think of a Polack it does revolve around."

"Take West Division Street to Humboldt Drive and head north into the park. I'll be sitting on one of the benches on the left side of the street, under the trees."

Nick disregarded the insult. He knew the park well enough to know the area Stuart referred to but he couldn't get past such a change in their normal routine. "What kinda appointment you got up there?"

"Hey, Nick, fuck you. You want to know my schedule; you call Mr. Costello. You have his number. Call him. Otherwise, fuck you. Be there at noon, asshole."

Nick set his phone down and walked to the kitchen, trying to control his rage. He wasn't nervous now, just pissed off. He was going to figure out how to kill that mu-tha-fucker, that skinny, little arrogant piece of shit. He grabbed a carton of orange juice from the refrigerator and swilled half of it in several big noisy gulps. He turned around to face the bedroom, staring in the direction of his phone, as if it might turn in to Stuart or somehow start talking again. He stood there in his briefs as he conjured a vision of him stabbing Stuart in the neck, pulling the blade out and watching his life pump out in scarlet gushes. He raised the carton back to his mouth and drained it in three more gulps before lowering it from his face and crushing it slowly in his hand as he glared at the telephone.

Nick pulled his BMW over to the side of the road. During the forty-minute drive to the park his nerves had been on a roller coaster. He hadn't heard from Stu or Mr. Costello in over a month, and then he gets a phone call the morning after he cuts that fat fucker's ear off in a public bar. Coincidence? A big fuckin' coincidence if it was. But Stu's a pencil pusher, a pussy; Mr. Costello wouldn't send him up to handle me, would he? That's crazy. Nick sat behind the wheel, surveying the park and the few cars parked along the road.

Stuart was sitting on a bench in plain view. Nick didn't budge, just sat in his car and studied the other man's movements. Stuart was reading a newspaper with what looked like a large envelope on the bench next to him. He hadn't noticed Nick's car; in fact, he hadn't looked up from his paper once in the five minutes Nick had been there.

"Oh what the hell, this is bull shit." Nick muttered to himself as he climbed out of the coup. He closed the door and hit the button on his keyless entry as he walked away from it, listening for the door locks to click.

Stuart looked up at him as if he sensed his approach. He glanced over at a dark sedan parked at the curb thirty feet to his left. An old minivan was parked between Nick's BMW and the sedan and he hadn't seen it. But he saw it now and stopped. He looked back at Stuart who was looking at him. Nick looked back at the sedan and tried to see through the tinted windows. His heart pounded as he turned his body to be at an angle between Stuart and the car. His head swiveled back and forth as he shoved his hand in to his jacket pocket and grabbed his .25 caliber semi-automatic. His body was in a slight crouch with his knees bent, ready to move in any direction.

Stuart looked from the car back to Nick. "What the hell are you doing?" The annoyance was evident in his tone.

"Who're your fuckin' friends in the car?" Nick responded, not turning his head nor changing his stance. "Who're you lookin' at?"

"I'm looking at a thick skulled idiot, I guess. Get your stupid ass over here before you draw attention to yourself, you clown."

Nick was puzzled, but started to relax. He stared directly at the sedan but still not able to see inside, but felt by now he'd have seen some movement. He straightened his body and brought an empty hand out of this jacket pocket as he looked back at Stuart. The expression on the man's face was a mixture of annoyance and bewilderment. Nick walked the final twenty feet to the bench.

"I know Mr. Costello thinks you have some modicum of value, but I'm still trying to figure it out."

Nick's emotion was turning from fear to anger as he sat on the bench, on the other side of the envelope from Stuart. His face was tight and he was biting his bottom lip as the image of plunging his knife in to the man's neck floated through his consciousness.

"What's the deal, delivery boy?" Nick finally asked.

"Everything's in the envelope; your itinerary, tickets, car confirmation, the target, all the details. It's all self-explanatory. The only thing you need to hear from me is that this hit is to send a message. It's to be brutal and obvious that someone wanted this asshole dead. Got it?"

"Loud and clear."

Stuart was standing to go as he said in a sardonic tone, "I think Mr. Costello will be interested to hear about your behavior this morning. Looked pretty guilty to me, Nicky boy."

Nick bolted from the bench in such a sudden movement that Stuart made a small, audible gasp. The bigger man was standing so close to him that Stuart could feel his breath as he attempted to meet his stare as calmly as he could.

"You tell Mr. Costello any fuckin' thing you want. But when you totally change the way of doin' things and there's a black Lincoln parked thirty feet away that you're starin' at as I walk up, I get nervous. I ain't stupid, asshole. And I guaran-fuckin-ty I'm gonna out live your worthless ass."

The vein in the middle of Nick's forehead became engorged as his neck muscles began to bulge. Stuart blinked several times as his face flushed. He turned abruptly and walked off without saying another word.

Nick smiled and talked out loud as he walked back to the BMW. "That was perfect," he told himself. "He damn near pissed himself. He won't say shit to Costello."

OCALA, FLORIDA

August

"Thanks for letting me borrow the boat, amigo. I barely beat the rain getting off the water." Conner was talking to Bubba Striker who'd just turned off his Kubota mule, having returned to the barn from feeding his horses.

"Almost get nailed by a bad one did ya'?" responded Bubba as he walked to the feed room with a broken feed bucket and dropped it in a trashcan. "Damn thing only lasted twenty years and then the handle snaps off just like that."

Conner returned the smile. "Shame. Yea, the sky opened up as I was pulling away from the dock. I sat there on the shoulder of 326 for fifteen minutes waiting for it to slow down enough to see. Summer in Florida."

"It went right around us this afternoon. Got black as hell and the wind blew and then it went around. Get your business done?"

The men were leaning on opposite sides of the bed of the mule, facing each other. Conner had asked to borrow the flats boat and Bubba had no hesitation in saying yes, as was customary. Conner hadn't given a reason why, which Bubba thought strange but didn't ask. It wouldn't have mattered why; he would give his friend anything he owned for any reason. But Bubba had seen Conner get the small bag out of the Toyota and toss it in the bed of the truck before he pulled from the yard for the Waccasassa River.

Conner ducked his head for a second and looked back at his friend. Bubba was smiling at him.

"I ain't prying, no big deal, let's go sit under a fan and have a cold drink." Bubba's orange cat had jumped on to the feed bin between the two men and he scratched him behind the ears as he spoke to Conner.

"Sounds great. Where's Beth?"

"She's running a few errands," Bubba responded as he led the way toward the house. He stopped at the door to kick off his muckers before walking inside. Conner stepped out of his Merrils before going in and shut the door behind him.

"I'm havin" a Pepsi. What can I get you?"

"You know I think I'll have a cold beer if you have one."

"I do. I think. Beth always keeps a few around." Bubba was barely audible with his head stuck in the refrigerator. "Yes sir. Sierra Pale Ale, is that worth a shit?"

Bubba was placing the drinks on the counter as he asked his friends opinion.

"Perfect actually. Hand me that church key."

Bubba handed the opener across the counter to his friend and led the way to the patio. Although the rain had gone around, the storm had dropped the heat of the August afternoon.

Conner took another swallow of his beer before saying, "I sank that bag in a deep channel in the gulf."

"You know I love you like a brother Conner. Hell I love you more than I ever loved my brother," Bubba was smiling a gentle, knowing smile. "That piece of shit needed killing, amigo, and I can't tell you how glad it makes me that you did it."

Conner felt his face flush. How the hell does this mystic son-of-a-bitch know the things he knows? "Well, I guess I'm glad you're not a cop, brother."

"Shit." Striker through his head back and laughed. When he stopped he smiled at his friend and then started laughing again, hard, till tears wet his eyes. Conner couldn't help but laugh with his friend as he watched him.

"What the heck are y'all carrying on about?" Beth had walked out on to the patio from the house, several bags of groceries still in her arms.

"Our man here says he's glad I'm not a cop. Hell, I don't know, it just struck me funny."

Beth shook her head and headed back in to the kitchen. "It's hard to be a cop when you've been an outlaw your whole life."

Beth walked back out to the patio with another beer for Conner and one for herself. As she sat down in a third rocker the doorbell rang. She looked at Bubba with a pleading smile, "Would you get that, honey?"

"My pleasure, baby. You rest up and let Conner tell you some lies. Who is it anyway?"

Beth looked at him with an expression of exasperation. Then she spoke to Conner, "Honey, you see what I live with. Sorry, baby, my x-ray vision is on the blink."

Bubba was already in the house when she said it. He walked to the door and threw it open to find Joey Williams standing there.

"Hey, Bubba. How are you?"

"I gotta tell you Cooter, you're the last person I thought I'd see standing here."

"I haven't been here in a hundred years. I came to see Conner, his son said he was up here with you."

"He's right. Come on in." Bubba shut the door behind him and led the big man to the patio. "We shoulda taken bets, y'all, we'd still be guessing who it might have been."

Both Conner and Beth looked at Joey with surprise, frozen in their chairs.

"How y'all doing? Beth, Conner."

"Hello, Cooter. Fine thanks," responded Beth.

Conner stood to come over to the taller man and shake his hand, "Cooter."

"Sorry to barge in like this, but I really wanted to catch up with you about something important. In person."

"OK, yea, I guess. Sit down," Conner responded.

Beth spoke up, "Can I get you something to drink?"

Joey tipped his head in Beth's direction, "No ma'am, I'm fine, thanks. I'd like to talk in private, Conner, if you don't mind."

"Well don't that beat all," Bubba said in disgust.

Conner looked at the sullen expression on Joey Williams face and put his hand on his arm, turning the bigger man toward the kitchen. "Let's go inside."

Bubba wasn't pleased but said no more, knowing it was none of his business. He sat back in his chair and decided he needed to relax. Whatever he thought of Cooter Williams, this wasn't his purview.

Conner pulled the sliding door closed behind them to give Williams the privacy he sought. "How'd you know I was here?"

"I went by your house. I didn't have a number for you and I couldn't track down your cell. So I called Sean and he told me you were here."

"Must be important."

"Can we sit down, it's a fairly long story."

"Sure," Conner motioned at a chair as he sat on the couch next to it.

"You may not know any of this I'm about to tell you. I wasn't in this loop myself. Knew nothing about any of it, but last night I had a conversation with...an acquaintance, that filled me in. It was a bit of an end around really, the purpose of ...this person telling me anything had a whole different, oh, what, consequence than my reason for telling you."

"So far it's clear as mud, Cooter."

"Yea, I know. Bear with me. This fella and I...shit, I don't know how to really explain any of that. Listen, we worked together for a few years. We became pretty friendly. It was when I was in D.C.

We worked at a very high level then. Our contacts were only with members of Congress that were at the top of the heap. Most of our interaction really, Conner, was behind the scenes with the people that pulled their strings." Joey stopped and looked at the ceiling for a moment. "They got anything to drink in here stronger than a beer? Some scotch maybe?"

Conner's head jerked back involuntarily and he looked hard at the man sitting across from him. He was tempted to tell him no and to get to the point. But it was obvious that he was on the edge. He was a serious alcoholic and wasn't going to get through his message if he didn't have a drink to calm himself and focus.

Conner stood and walked to the armoire where Beth kept a small bar. He opened the top doors and looked inside.

"Johnny Walker black?"

"That works. Neat, huh?"

Conner shrugged as if to say 'yea, why not'. He took a bourbon glass from the cabinet shelf below and poured several ounces in it. Returning to his place on the couch he held the glass out for the other man as he sat down. Joey nodded his thanks and took a large swallow of the scotch. He grimaced a little and then gave an audible sigh.

"Thanks."

"Yea."

"I'll cut to the chase. Your son Sean had taken his wife's medical case to the top rung of the PHA, a guy in Miami. He pleaded his case to this guy and still got denied. I think he even had a Tampa district congressman in his corner but it didn't matter. Maybe you know all that."

Williams took another drink from his glass as Conner told him to go on; not affirming what he knew.

"Well it turns out this guy's been murdered. Had a hole blown through his heart the size of your fist."

Conner looked at him, never changing his expression.

"It seems he was murdered not too long after your son buried

242

his wife."

"Yea, so? Are you implying he's a suspect?"

"No, not in the sense that you're thinking. The police aren't looking at it, at least not any more. It seems Sean was giving a speech the night this guy was killed. He couldn't have done it."

Conner couldn't help but feel a little elation; he hoped that it didn't show on his face.

"But listen, Conner." Joey drained the rest of his glass. "There are people that don't care about his alibi."

Conner slid to the edge of the couch and straightened his back in one motion. "What the fuck are you talking about?"

"There are people that hate Sean, viscerally, completely. They think he had something to do with it. That he did it. They also know how smart he is and think he's fully capable of arranging it. They look at the fact that he had an alibi as proof he was involved, not proof that he wasn't."

"That's insane!" Conner shouted.

Hearing the shouting, Beth and Bubba looked in to the house and then at each other, concerned and confused but not wishing to interfere. Conner was still sitting, staring hard at Williams; becoming angrier by the second.

"The cops have any proof of any of that bullshit theory?"

Joey stood up. "Conner, I'm not talking about the cops. I'm talking about people who have their own set of rules."

"Start making some fuckin' sense here you booze soaked son-of-a-bitch!"

"The kind of people I'm talking about will take all of this in to their own hands. They will kill him, Conner. They don't care about the cops...or the law. They hate Sean, they're afraid of Sean and they will kill him."

Conner jumped to his feet and hit Cooter in the chest with his open hand, knocking him back in his chair. The blow was loud and so was the grunt that came from big man's throat. Conner stood over him, fists clenched, screaming.

"Who, Cooter, who is going to kill him? Who the fuck are you talking about?"

Bubba was up from his chair and was pushing the sliding glass door open. Conner heard it and looked in his direction. He tilted his head slightly and gazed hard into Bubba's eyes while he held his index finger in the air. Bubba understood and backed away. Conner looked back down at Cooter.

"People that can get it done, Conner." Joey's voice was quiet and resigned. "I'm telling you to warn you...and him. I have nothing to do with this kind of shit anymore. It's made me...in to a...booze soaked son-of-a-bitch. The only reason I even knew about this deal was because my...friend...wanted to vent about something else and Sean's name came into the conversation. May I?"

Williams had his hands on the arms of the chair, pushing himself to his feet. Conner moved to the side, allowing him up.

"I don't know who, Conner. I don't even know when. But these guys don't fuck around. I'm sorry."

Joey was heading for the door when Conner said, "That's it? Someone is going to kill Sean, anytime now, so look out." His tone dripped with sarcasm.

"I'm sorry Conner, that's all I know. And yea, you've summed it up."

Joey Williams walked out the door.

"What the hell was that about?" Bubba asked as Conner reentered the covered patio. "He's a slippery, no count..."

"We know all that, honey, let Conner talk," Beth interrupted.

Conner walked over and sat where he'd been sitting earlier and took another pull from his beer.

"I've got to get my head around this, give me a second."

Conner was staring out across the long expanse of pasture to the west of the house. Neither of the Strikers said a word, respecting their friend's feelings and concerned about how obviously distraught he was. Conner's mind was whirring faster than he could control it, flipping from one thought to another before he could grasp the last.

His mind was a jumble of fear for his son, rage and disgust for the people that threatened him and guilt that he may be the cause of the danger his son faced. He knew that he needed to get a hold of Sean immediately and convince him of the gravity of this threat. Sean had to leave, Conner thought, he needs to get the hell out of Florida until...until this sorts itself out. They can go to Jan's. No. No, that doesn't make sense. Colorado, the cabin. That's it.

"Amigo, you OK?" Bubba couldn't just keep looking at his friend's twisted expression and say nothing.

"Yea, yea. Sorry. Cooter says that someone, some people, are going to kill Sean."

"What!" Beth's voice was louder and more shriek than she had intended and it had startled even her. "Sorry, but that's the most preposterous thing I've ever heard. That damn old drunk hasn't a...hell he doesn't know....he doesn't know shit Conner! I don't believe it."

Bubba was looking at Conner's face, he knew it was true and he knew why it was true. Sean had a lot of political enemies and this reckoning provided by Conner was the last straw. Bubba Striker was under no illusions about the fact there are very bad people on this earth, people that would destroy the lives of others or kill them if necessary to satisfy their ambitions.

"Honey, Cooter Williams didn't spend all this time tracking down Conner and then driving here to spin some tale. He knows the kinds of people that do such things and obviously he thinks it's true." Bubba looked from his wife to Conner. "And obviously you think it is, too."

"It wouldn't matter if I doubted it. I wouldn't take the chance on not heeding the warning. But, you're right buddy, I do think it's true."

"Well you need to call the police, and right away," Beth said as she stood up. She really didn't know where she was going. She was filled with nervous energy and thought she had to do something, but she sat back down not knowing what to do. Her husband raised his eyebrows at her suggestion; he didn't agree but he didn't want to influence Conner, at least until he heard his opinion.

"No, I'm not going to do that. At least not yet. I'm going to get on the road and head to Sean's. I'll call him on the way and...I don't know, warn him I guess."

"What can we do, you want me to go with you?" Bubba asked.

"No. Thanks. I may need you to do something but I'm not sure what yet. I better go." Conner stood from his chair and bent to kiss Beth on the cheek. She stood up instead and threw her arms around him, hugging him hard. He returned the hug and kissed her cheek.

"You be careful, you hear me Conner Murphy?"

"I will hon, thanks. Thanks for everything."

He turned to Bubba and they hugged each other as well. As they separated Bubba said, "Don't leave me hanging. Let me know what you decide and what you're up to."

The two men walked through the house and out the front door. As Conner sat in the front seat of his Toyota, his friend walked up within inches of the open door. "I will do anything you need done, brother, I hope you know that."

"Bubba, I know that as well as I know anything."

It was 5:30 p.m. when Conner pulled out through the front gate of the Striker's farm. He reached his son on his cell and told him part of the story. He told Sean that Cooter had tracked him down at Bubba's and gave him the message about the pending threat. Conner didn't tell Sean about Stanley Mesh, he wanted to do that face to face. He had a two-hour drive in front of him.

TAMPA, FLORIDA

August

S team rose off the tarmac now that the obligatory afternoon thunderstorm had moved to the east and left the sun unchecked to bake the Florida landscape. The shuttle swayed gently on its single rail as it coursed its way from the gates to the terminal. The glare of the sun through the high windows of the shuttle caused many in the crowded cars to squint as they searched pockets and purses for sunglasses. Nick Kowalski stood with his back against the car for balance, holding his carry-on in front of him. The doors slid apart and Nick filed out with the others, heading toward baggage claim as he looked for signs directing him to the rental car counters. As he approached the Hertz desk he saw a sign directing Gold Members to proceed to level three of the garage.

As he stood waiting for the elevator, Nick's size and muscular physique drew the attention of people walking by. One of them, a well endowed young woman, intimidated by his looks, made a point of looking straight ahead as she walked around him. But Nick had no such desire to be discreet and stared directly at her chest as she passed and spoke loud enough for her to hear, "Well hello, doll."

The woman quickened her step as a jolt of fear and revulsion shot through her.

Nick drove his blue Chevy Impala out of the terminal as he opened the manila envelope. First stop was to pick up a little merchandise that Mr. Costello had arranged. His instructions were to use a gun on this Murphy guy and, if at all possible, one shot in the back of the head; execution style. The boss was pretty adamant about making this look like a hit, he really wanted to scare the shit out of somebody, Nick thought. Hell, it was all the same to him. For all he knew this Florida redneck might have his own rifle or something, a gun might be a little insurance for old Nicky boy.

The directions and contact information had been provided in his envelope. There were only a few turns between the airport and the strip joint, and Nick had easily memorized all of it on the plane.

The Bay Club North was a square, windowless structure of cinder block construction resembling a military bunker more than a nightclub. It was three blocks from the interstate and only fifteen minutes from the airport. Nick was a little surprised at how many cars were in the parking lot this early in the evening. He chose a space between a van and a limo, which provided him with a little cover as he got out of the car. Nick stood next to his car for a long minute, surveying the parking area, getting a feel for things and checking to see if there was anyone just 'hanging around'; Nick wouldn't like that. The only other person was a man in a coat and tie, in a hurry to get from his car to the front door of the club. Nick also wanted to determine if there was any police presence, not keen on the idea of walking out of the club with a gun if this was the type of joint the cops liked to hassle. There were no patrol cars in sight as he started walking toward the door.

"Ten dollar cover charge, mister." The bouncer was sitting on a bar stool just inside the door. He was wearing a black tee shirt with 'SECURITY' written across the front in white lettering. The bearded young man was about Nick's size but carried more body fat and less muscle and certainly wasn't as intimidating. The younger man was conscious of this and his face flushed when Nick raised his index finger toward his face.

"I'm not a customer. I'm here to see Whitey Allard."

"Just a minute then." The bouncer started off his stool when he noticed a fortyish, scantily clad woman coming toward him. He returned his weight to the stool and motioned toward Nick with a short sweep of his arm.

"Hey there, big man, how can I help you? You look like a VIP room kinda guy to me."

"You look a little old to be dancing, honey. No offense, you still got great tits and all."

"My, aren't you a charmer."

"Stella, he says he's here to do business with Mr. Allard," interrupted the bouncer.

Stella took a step back and put her hands on her hips, "Are you the man from Chicago?"

"That'd be me."

"OK. Whitey said to bring you back when you got here. Follow me."

The club was dark, lit by purple neon lights over the bar area with spotlights focused on the girl performing center stage. There were tables scattered around the three sides of the stage that weren't occupied by the bar. In one far corner, where the light was even dimmer, several couches were arranged in a circle surrounding an elevated floor. Three men sat on two of the couches, leaning back, taking in the performance of the two naked women on the small stage between them. Nick took a minute to look at the dancer on the center stage; the tall, lithe performer was hanging upside down from a pole using only her legs while she tugged at each nipple with her finger tips and pouted her lips, staring directly at a patron sitting only a few feet away. Nick was wondering if the thong was coming off next when he looked back toward Stella, impatiently waiting for him at the end of the bar. Once Nick caught up with her, she knocked twice on a mirrored door and walked in.

"Your man from Chicago is here, Whitey."

As the blonde stepped to the side, Nick walked past and proceeded toward the big desk near the opposite wall. Whitey Allard was a moderately sized man, with blonde hair that was almost white. His complexion was so fair to be almost translucent, like some tropical fish seen in small aquariums. His eyes were the palest shade of blue Nick had ever seen. Whitey stood and extended his hand as Stella left, closing the door behind her.

"You're Nick, I presume?"

"That's right."

When they released each other's hands, Whitey motioned to one of two chairs across the desk from him. Nick took a seat and began inspecting the wall behind Whitey, which was covered with glossy pictures of naked women. Nick approved as he looked from picture to picture.

"I can see why you'd wanna spend a lot of time in here, Whitey, but you oughta get out in the sun more."

"I don't appreciate rudeness, Mr. Kowalski."

Nick raised both hands, showing his palms in a peace offering. "Hey, sorry. Forget it." He shrugged his shoulders in a mock gesture of contrition.

"Mr. Costello requested a .25 caliber semiautomatic." Whitey chose to ignore the other man's insolent behavior as he pulled a large manila envelope from a drawer on the right side of his desk. He placed it in front of him. "Baretta Jetfire 950, 9 round capacity, clean, no history and no numbers, unloaded but has two full clips."

Whitey pushed the envelope toward Nick and turned his hands upward in a gesture of giving him a gift. Nick leaned forward and grabbed the envelope. As he did he turned to look behind him, almost an involuntary action to cover his back and, for the first time, he saw the Asian man standing at the back of the room. The man must have been behind the open door when Nick had entered the office. He was very unhappy with himself for not noticing this bastard and he was even less happy that the man was still standing behind him.

Nick turned back to face Whitey, "What's with the chink?"

"If you're referring to Mr. Jo, he's Korean. He is with me at all times. Mr. Jo has a black belt in five different martial art disciplines. Let's say he's around to put my mind at ease." Whitey had a smug tone to his voice, leaning back in his chair as he spoke.

Nick looked across the desk and said nothing for several long seconds. Then he put on a big smile, "I don't give a fuck if he's Bruce Lee himself, if he doesn't stand where I can see him I'm gonna tear his fuckin' head off and shit down his neck. We clear?"

Whitey's complexion turned from pale to red. Nick didn't know if it was embarrassment or rage, and he didn't care. Whitey motioned to his bodyguard to come around to the side.

"Satisfied? Open the envelope and inspect the gun."

"Don't need to. I know you don't know me from Adam, but I also know there's not a man alive that would fuck with Mr. Costello." Nick stood to leave. "Hey, I don't suppose you could send a couple of these babes over to the Embassy Suites tonight, huh?"

"My girls are for my friends. That wouldn't work out."

"Oooh. That's pretty good."

Nick turned to Mr. Jo and leaned back slightly to better reveal his waist. As he did, he tugged on his belt. "Hey, look, slope, I've got a black belt in 'streets of Chicago'. Maybe you'd like a lesson some time."

Nick was laughing as he walked out of Whitey Allard's office and was still shaking his head when he went past Stella and the bouncer at the front door.

He typed 2706 Azalea Ave in to his phone as destination and entered current location as the departure point. Now that he had his gun, his plan would be the usual; he'd go by the mark's house and check things out before going to the hotel and getting some supper. By 8:30 p.m. he was checking in to the Embassy Suites on West Shore Boulevard.

"Fontaine. I got a reservation for tonight."

"Certainly. I'll need a form of ID and your credit card, please." Nick studied the lobby as his paper work was being prepared.

"Mr. Fontaine, if you'll initial the rate here, the date of departure here, and sign at the bottom that's all I will need from you. We have you in room 476. Have you stayed with us before?" The young clerk was pushing the envelope containing the room key across the counter.

"Yea." answered Nick.

"Then you know about our complimentary breakfast down here on the first floor from...."

"Yea." Nick reached down to grab his bag and headed toward the glass elevators down the hallway that skirted the large atrium.

Upon entering his room Nick threw his bag on the couch in the sitting room. He walked to the coffee table and grabbed the TV remote before falling back in to the easy chair next to the couch. He scanned the TV menu for 'adult features' and selected "Naughty Housewives IV", watched it for several minutes and then turned the volume up on the way to the shower.

When Conner arrived at his son's home, Sean's car was in the driveway. He knocked on the kitchen door and walked in. Connie was in the kitchen doing the dishes from dinner.

"Hi Mr. Murphy. I kept a plate for you in case you hadn't eaten."

"You're a jewel, Connie. I think I'll do that in just a second. Where is everybody?"

"I think Sean went to take a shower and change and the kids are in their rooms. Jeremy had a little homework and I think Karen is coloring. Or something." She shrugged her shoulders and gave Conner her bright smile.

"I'll check in with Sean real quick and be right back."

Conner walked to the master bedroom and found the door wide open but the bathroom door closed and he could hear the shower running. He returned to the kitchen to take Connie up on her offer.

"Great, sit right here and keep me company and I'll get it right out. Is ice water fine?" Connie was digging silverware out of the drawer to set a place on the high dining counter opposite the kitchen sink.

"That's great. So what's for dinner, anyway?"

Connie had opened the oven door and was bending down to pull a foil-covered plate out with her mitted hand.

"Pork chops, green beans, and, of course, macaroni and cheese." She put the plate in front of him and pulled the foil from the top. "If I don't include macaroni and cheese the kids will starve to death."

"I'm sure that's right."

"Actually Jeremy's getting better about eating other things now, more grown up things, but it's a battle with Karen still."

"Have any Cholula sauce, hon?"

"It's a Murphy house, ain't it?" Connie teased.

Conner doused his macaroni and cheese with the spicy hot sauce, "I'm glad to see I raised Sean right."

"That apple fell pretty close to the tree, as far as I can tell," Connie replied.

As Conner ate his dinner he recalled that he hadn't eaten since leaving Long Boat Key at dawn that morning. He was glad Connie had thought of him.

"Hey, Dad. You getting recharged there?" Sean walked into the kitchen wearing Wranglers and a tee shirt that said Steamboat Springs across the front.

"I think Connie here may have saved my life. I was starving to death." He stood and grabbed his plate and glass to bring it to the sink. "It was absolutely perfect, young lady. Thank you very much."

"Anything else? There's ice cream or some cookies."

"No, no dessert. But I would like a cup of coffee if I can do that."

"You can do anything you want Mr. Murphy. Just give me a couple minutes."

"Well I think I'm going to have a little scotch, Dad, while you have your coffee. Come with me and we'll sit in the cigar room. Connie, you don't mind bringing Dad's coffee when it's ready do you?"

"Of course not. Just cream, right Mr. Murphy."

"Exactly. Thanks again for dinner."

The two men crossed the formal living area through double doors to a bar and cigar room. Conner took a seat in one of the four red leather chairs while his son pulled a bottle of McCallans from the shelf and poured it over ice. He took a chair across from his father.

"I guess after giving it more thought I'm falling back in to the incredulous column again, Dad. I understand that Williams must think it's true, but it seems a little farfetched to me."

"Well, that may be because you don't know the whole story, buddy. But that's one of the reasons I'm here; to fill you in."

"OK, but hell, kill me? I know shit like that happens and I am also fully aware of what a lightning rod I am to some of my opposition, but Jesus Christ, that's over the top."

Connie came in to the room with Conner's coffee.

"Here you are, sir." She turned her attention to Sean. "I'm going to get those kids in the bath, if that's alright with you."

"Sounds spot on to me. Dad and I have some things that we need to go over, then we'll both be up to put them to bed, OK? If you don't mind Connie, shut those doors behind you. Thanks."

Sean turned back to his father; "I'd be a lost ball in the tall grass without her these last few weeks."

"I can only imagine. Listen, do you remember...hell of course you remember. The guy you went to see in Miami at the PHA office."

"That weasel. Of course. I can still see that fat bastard looking across his desk at me with his gnarly toothed smile, asking me about my work; and never asking me one damn thing about Mo. Oh yea, I remember."

"Well, he's dead. Murdered."

"Good."

Conner just looked at Sean, waiting for it to sink in.

"Well, I mean it. I think the...What's that look about? You think I did it, for Christ's sake. I almost wish I had, but...."

"I know you didn't do it. He was murdered the night you were giving your speech last week. But believe it or not, that's exactly why some people think you were involved; precisely because it did happen on a night that you had a perfect alibi."

"What do you mean, like I contracted it or something like that? Jesus, what world do they think I live in?"

"Whoever these guys are that Cooter is talking about, they apparently hate you for a lot of reasons. This is icing on the cake for them. A justification for what they want to do anyway. Apparently these are some powerful and obviously dangerous people."

"Damn, this is unbelievable. Did Williams tell you all of this?"

"Some; and some I read between the lines. Not hard to do. But Sean, listen to me. I killed the little bureaucrat, I killed Stanley Mesh."

Neither man spoke for a long minute. Sean was stunned. Conner looked back at him, giving him a chance to digest what he had said before continuing.

"I was incensed at what had happened to Mo. To you and Mo. The kids. I knew that I had to deal with that bastard in some fashion. I didn't even know what I was going to do, really. But then when I met him and saw what he was, it became obvious to me that I was going to kill him. To eliminate his venomous existence from this earth. I had no intention of telling you about it. I didn't want to burden you with the knowledge of it."

Conner slid forward in his chair and leaned forward with his elbows on his knees. "And I sure as hell didn't want any of this coming back on you. I thought I had timed it perfectly to prevent that."

"Hey, let me tell you something. First off, when you said that little prick had been murdered, I said 'good'. I meant it. Good. You should get a medal as far as I'm concerned. And something else, if these guys, whoever the hell 'these guys' are, are using this as an excuse to come after me, it was probably only a matter of time until I gave them that excuse. The reality of it is; my recent opinion pieces in the magazine and on my blog may be the real reason. I haven't let up on the PHA since the funeral. I don't intend to and they probably know that. I don't want you to feel one shred of guilt over this. As a matter of fact, thank you. Thank you very much for what you did. Now, tell me how all of this took place."

Conner proceeded with the details of the story including what he found in Mesh's 'bunker'. When Conner finished, Sean was leaning back in his chair, staring straight ahead. His eyes had moistened as the memory of his wife's suffering became very vivid in his mind but his overall countenance was one of anger; anger filled with loathing and repulsion for the dead bureaucrat.

Connie knocked gently on the door. "The kids are ready for bed, gentlemen."

"Dad, you go up, I'll be there in a minute."

Once the kids were tucked in and Connie had gone off to her room the two men reconvened in the cigar room. They lit a couple of Macanudos and talked about what Sean should do. Conner was adamant that he should leave the state; that the entire family should go. Reasoning that if this is a vendetta, God only knows what their revenge may consist of. Sean mentioned the kids' school but Conner rebutted that their father staying alive and keeping them out of danger was a hell of lot more important right now. Sean agreed and also admitted that working from some other location was very doable, at least for the short term. They kicked around going to the cabin in Colorado but changed their minds. It was probably too obvious and it was too remote, which might not be in their favor. They discussed Jan's place in Wyoming, but that idea didn't taste right to either one of them.

Finally, Conner suggested the Ingles Ranch in Elko. The more he verbalized the idea the more it made sense to him. Bud and Maggie not only had the home ranch, but they had several ranches scattered about northern Nevada as well as the old cabin in Lamoille, at the foot of the Ruby Mountains. Conner would call Bud and discuss it with him but he knew it would be fine; he knew Bud wouldn't hesitate to throw in on the idea.

Father and son spent the next two hours planning details. It was decided that they would drive out to Nevada in Conner's old diesel Ford Excursion, which was big enough to hold a lot of luggage and extra things that the kids may want to bring to make them more comfortable. Conner spoke to the fact that they should load up on cash before leaving and not use any credit cards as they made their trek. He had no idea how sophisticated the 'bad guys' were but wanted to eliminate all possibilities of revealing their location.

They decided the first order of business was to get Sean and his family out of harm's way. Once that was accomplished they could focus on who could be trusted in getting the lawful protection they would need.

"You're thinking of leaving tomorrow, then?"

"I think so, buddy. We have no idea what these guys are thinking, for all we know they're already on their way. I guess you'll want to go in to the office in the morning and at least try to tie some things up, huh?"

"Oh, I'll need to do that for sure. Right now I can't even process what I need to do, but..."

"Sorry to interrupt you, son, but don't tell anyone where you're going or how you're going, right."

"No, no. Don't worry; I get it. If we're taking this seriously we need to go all the way. I understand. What I was going to say is that I'm not going to try to figure this out right now. I'm tired and, like I said, I can't quite get my head around everything. My plan will be to get up about 4:30 and start sorting things out."

"Sounds like a good plan. We've covered enough ground tonight. But listen, one more thing. I'll have to go down to Longboat and get my stuff. How 'bout if I do that while you're at the office and I take the kids with me. I'd feel better about them if they're with one of us if you don't mind."

"No, of course not. That's a great idea. Well, goodnight. I'll see you bright and early in the morning."

"Yea, what is it, 11:00 o'clock. I'm gonna call Bud and then head off to bed. It's only 8:00 their time. Hopefully I can get him. Goodnight, buddy."

"Goodnight."

"Listen. One more thing. You still keep that Glok in the locked drawer of your nightstand?"

"Yea, I do"

"Load it and unlock your drawer."

Conner had been so certain that the Ingleses would have no problem with the idea when he and Sean were discussing it earlier. But now, as he was about to call Bud, the reality of what he was asking struck him hard. Jesus, he thought, Bud might think I'm crazy; not just the whole premise of someone actually trying to kill Sean, but then asking to put himself and Maggie at risk by providing his family with sanctuary. After several minutes, Conner decided there was nothing to do but relay the story and ask the favor; he had to for his son's sake. Whatever decision Bud made was understandable, he'd figure something out.

"Hello."

"Maggie, how are you, this is Conner."

"Murph, you old dog, is everything good with you? Is Sean faring all right, and the kids?"

"Actually, I think things are going along OK. You know it's like what you and I had talked about at my place that night before y'all left. The only glimpse of a silver lining around a protracted illness such as what Mo dealt with is the fact that when the end comes there is some sense of relief. The suffering is over, and a fair amount of the grieving has already occurred."

"Well, I know that Sean was also dealing with the frustration and misery that the damn PHA had caused them, is he getting past that a little now?"

That question gave Conner pause. "Yea, I would say he's working through that too."

"Well, I was just about to tell you that the outlaw isn't home, but he just walked in through the mud porch. It's Murph, honey. I'll give you to Bud, come see us soon, sweetie."

"Bye Mag. Thanks."

"Murph, how are you, man?"

"Good. How're things with you?"

"Things are fine. Had to go down to Midas today and argue with the mining guys. They needed to punch a new road in and the yahoo they've got building it is an idiot. He's got a drainage culvert where he doesn't need one and doesn't have one where he does need one. Dumb bastard. I wanted to build the thing for them with my guys but they didn't like the price I gave them. They'll regret it before it's all done; I'm looking pretty cheap about now. So what's up, anything new?"

"Yea as a matter of fact there is, and actually it's a pretty big deal. You got some time for me to tell you about it, or do you want to call me back?"

"No, I'm good. Maggie's making me up a little snack and I'll eat while we talk. What's up?"

It took Conner nearly thirty minutes to reveal the whole story. He didn't go in to great detail about the killing of Stanley Mesh, but he did tell him that he did it. On the one hand he hated burdening his friend with that information but on the other hand he knew Bud deserved to know everything if he was going to put himself at risk providing safe harbor for Sean. Bud never interrupted him, listening intently to the words and the emotion in his friend's voice.

"Well, I guess that sums it up. It's an awful lot to dump on you, I'm sorry for that."

"Don't be. When will you be here?"

Conner's eyes welled up and his voice cracked a little as he said. "About five days I'm guessing."

They talked for another ten minutes about the logistics of getting the family packed up and on the road and possible routes across the country. It was nearly midnight when Conner went off to the extra bedroom, feeling pretty good about their plan and gratified that he had the friends he did.

Conner was exhausted from a long day that had started on Longboat Key at four that morning. Hundreds of miles of driving and a boat ride to the gulf. That was enough in itself, but the emotions of the day had worn on him the most. He made his way to the spare bedroom and fell into bed.

Unfortunately, sleep was short lived. In two hours Conner was wide-awake and staring at the ceiling. His back hurt and his mind was buzzing with all the planning for the trip. He felt if he could beat one or the other he might be able to get back to sleep. He left his bed and went to cigar room to lay back in one of the leather recliners hoping it would relax his back. It worked and after twenty minutes Conner fell back to sleep

As Nick approached the Murphy house, he congratulated himself on his wisdom of always practicing his preliminary reconnaissance. It had helped him be prepared for a small obstacle that needed to be dealt with

If the dog was in the house it would be more of a problem, but he wouldn't know that until he got there. Nick circled around to the back of the house and peered through the gate in to the pool area and back patio for the dog. He stepped through the gate and gently closed it behind him. He moved two steps toward the back door and saw the big yellow lab.

Rosie was sound asleep by the back door to the kitchen. She was old and her senses had dulled with time. Nick undid a button, reached inside his shirt and pulled out a package of meat. He squatted down as he tore the package open and whistled softly. Nick kept repeating the whistle. The dog finally picked her head up and barked. The bark was low and not menacing. She did it again. Nick whispered to the big lab, calling to her as he pushed the meat a few inches toward her.

The lab rose up slowly and gave one more bark, louder this time.

"Shhhh. Girl. Shhhh. Come here, now, come here."

Nick had won her over. Rosie's tail started a slow wag and she started to come toward him with her head low to the ground, submissively. She sniffed the hamburger and her tail kept wagging as she took her first bite. Nick waddled closer to her, still on his haunches, and scratched her behind the ears with both hands as the dog kept eating. Still moving his thick fingers in a soothing rhythm, he reached around both sides of her neck.

In one sudden motion, he squeezed with his powerful hands threw his weight over his arms. The snapping vertebrae made a loud, sickening crack and the dog's body went limp underneath him. He left her lying with her face in the half eaten package of meat and headed for the door.

Nick always appreciated a good moon because it allowed him to work without a flashlight. Flashlights drew attention. The kitchen door had no dead bolt and the door lock was no challenge for Nick.

Conner woke. He listened for the sound that he thought had woke him. A bark? He wasn't sure. There was only the faint sound of the air conditioner. Sleep had a strong enough grip that he began to doze again. Somewhere between sleep and consciousness Conner heard another noise.

A creak? Sean? Connie? Wouldn't they turn a light on if they were up? He sat there motionless, trying to listen over the sound of his own breathing. He felt a tingle at the back of his neck and his palms started to sweat. He wished he'd grabbed a gun from Sean's safe. Another creak, someone was walking in the house, in the dark.

If it's an intruder, he will surely have a gun. If I shout for Sean, this guy will do one of two things, run or shoot me and whomever else he can kill. Conner couldn't take that chance. He wasn't even certain where the sound came from. Where is he? The only thing that made sense was to try and grab him, hopefully get the drop on him and then start shouting for Sean to come with a gun. Where is this bastard? Christ, is there more than one?

Conner got to his feet as quietly as he could, sliding out of the chair sideways so the chair back and footrest wouldn't move. His eyes were adjusted to the dark but the light was very dim in the interior of the house. Conner peered from the cigar room in to the living room, wearing only boxer shorts and a tee shirt. He stood motionless looking for any movement. Nothing. He heard another creak. God damn it, he's going up the stairs! His bare feet stuck to the tile floor making a faint snapping sound as he took each step. He ignored it; there was no way he was going to let them get up those stairs to his grandchildren.

Conner came around the corner from the living room where it opened in to the foyer at the bottom of the stairs. He stopped. In front of him was a silhouette barely visible in the dark. The man was on the third step with his back to Conner. He was stopped, listening. The two men were only ten feet apart.

Neither man moved. Then the silhouette cocked its head as if to hear better and was motionless again. Conner held his breath. A few seconds went by and the silhouette looked down at his feet again and started to climb another step. Conner broke in to a sprint.

The noise of Conner's running feet alerted Nick and he started to spin toward the sound. Conner knew he was discovered so he screamed his son's name at the top of his lungs as he plowed forward as fast as he could; head and shoulders down like a football safety making an open field tackle. Nick's position on the steps impeded him from spinning as quickly as he needed to in order to face Conner head on. He had only brought his gun partially around and the outside of his right knee was vulnerable to Conner's shoulder.

Conner's yell for his son was loud, but the impact of the collision was just as loud. Conner drove his right shoulder in to the side of Nick's right knee with all of his force. Nick slammed hard against the stairs and the back of his head smashed in to the sheetrock of the wall behind him. He lost his grip on the Beretta and it fell to the floor but Nick was not only powerful, he also had the quickness of a cat. In spite of both cruciate ligaments being destroyed in his right knee, Nick spun out from under Conner and grabbed his right arm. He leaned his weight on to his left leg and hurled Conner across the foyer in to the wall eight feet away. Conner flew like a rag doll. His shoulder collided first but his head whip lashed into the wall and nearly knocked him unconscious. He fought to keep his wits as he got back on his feet.

Nick was on him again, wielding a knife in his right hand. Conner brought his hand up just in time to grab Nick's right wrist and stopped the blade inches from his neck. Conner was no match for the bigger man's strength as Nick turned his hand with such force that Conner lost his grip on the wrist and the knife continued in an arc that slashed in to Conner's chest. He yelled out as the knife sliced deep into the right pectoral muscles. The wild thrust of the knife caused Nick to shift his weight on to his injured knee and he lost his balance. Conner saw his chance as Nick's head came past him and downward and he threw his left fist catching him right behind the ear. The blow drove the big man to the floor, but he managed to catch himself with both hands.

Nick rebounded instantly, turning and swinging the knife at Conner's right thigh. The knife slashed through the muscle just above Conner's right knee as he tried to jump backwards. The leap backwards and the pain from the gash sent Conner to the floor. Nick was on his feet again, standing over Conner, ready to finish him. He hesitated for a moment, when he changed his mind from slitting Conner's throat to opening his belly. It was his last hesitation.

The sound of the Glok was deafening in the foyer, but Nick never heard it. Sean pulled the trigger as he pushed the barrel of the gun under the base of the big man's skull. Most of the blood and tissue was carried upward and away from Conner but some of it spattered his face. He was unaware of it, thinking only that he had never heard a sweeter sound.

"Jesus, Dad, you look like shit."

"Son, you've always had such a way with words. And a keen eye for the obvious." Conner lay on his back with his left leg bent at the knee and his left hand on his bleeding chest.

"Connie, go check on the kids," Sean was looking up the stairs, holding his open hand out toward Connie who had come half way down. "Don't let them come down the stairs."

Connie's expression was one of horror. Conner on the floor with blood all over him, a huge strange man lying face down in a pool of blood. It was more than she could take and she burst in to tears. Sean softened his words.

"Connie, go on up. Make sure they're OK. I'll be a few minutes, hon. Dad's fine. Everything is going to be fine."

Connie couldn't speak; she turned and hurried back up the stairs.

Sean turned his attention back to his father, "You are going to be fine, right? Can you get up?"

Conner reached out with his left hand and his son grabbed it firmly. Conner started leaning up as Sean pulled and the effort made the older man groan with pain. His butt was just off the ground when his left foot slipped out in front of him on the bloody floor and he slammed back on to the tile.

"Damn!" Conner blurted.

"Sorry, Dad. Here, sit there a second." Sean walked behind his father and put both hands under his father's arms and lifted him up from behind. Conner stood unsteadily at first, then turned slowly toward his son and put one hand on the young man's shoulder for support.

"That big son-of-a-bitch kicked my ass," Conner forced a grin that his son returned. They both laughed briefly and softly, feeling the elation that they were both still alive.

"The first thing we've got to do is get this bleeding stopped. Let's get you to the den and on a couch with some clean compresses. The way you're bleeding you're going to need a doctor Dad. You'll need stitching up."

The two men started a slow walk toward the den; Conner with his left hand on his son's right shoulder for support as they made their way. By the time Conner sat back on the couch he had time to consider a doctor.

"Listen, Sean, I don't think..."

"Hang on, let me get some towels. Try not to make a mess while I'm gone." Sean turned to wink at his dad before he ran off toward his bedroom. His light hearted comments belied the worry he felt for his father.

"Smart ass." But Sean hadn't heard him.

Conner was a little alarmed by the amount of blood he was losing and decided to examine his wounds. He pulled his boxer shorts up on his right leg to expose the wound. The gash was about four inches long, making a straight line across the front of his thigh. As he parted the edges of the wound to gauge its depth, he didn't think it looked as though any large vessels had been cut. The pain of doing so made him wince but he was grateful that it didn't appear to be as deep as he'd feared.

Leaning forward he pulled his tee shirt over his head. The effort tugged against the wound in the right side of his chest and he let out a long, low moan as he slowly removed the shirt over extended arms. Still leaning forward he looked at his chest with a grimace on his face as he realized it was bleeding worse than the wound on his leg.

"Damn, that's a little deep," Conner whispered to himself. With the fingers of each hand he pulled the wound edges apart to estimate the damage. The gash was also about four inches across, starting at his sternum and extending over the right nipple. When he pulled the wound edges apart, it caused a small artery to spray him directly in the left eye. It stung and he cussed out loud.

"Shit."

"You're a hell of a nurse," Sean was standing over his father with an armload of towels. "I think you're supposed to stop the bleeding, but hey, what do I know."

"I thought I already pointed out that you're a smart ass, I don't need further proof. Listen there's no doubt I need some stitches or these wounds will take forever to heal. They also need to be cleaned up properly. But a doctor will complicate the shit out of our ordeal. Unless you think we need to call the cops. What do you think?"

Sean pushed a folded towel on to the wound in his father's right thigh.

"Keep some pressure on this. Lean back." Sean sat next to him and gently pressed another folded towel against the chest wound. "I'm not sure about the cops. Obviously this was self-defense, an intruder in my home. The gun is legally owned, etc. I guess I'm just worried how deep does this corruption run, who are the bad guys? I'm a little concerned about having to stay put while the cops do their investigating. We'll be sitting ducks."

"I think you're right about all of that. But what I've been thinking about is how far will they...the bad guys, go to cover their trail if we start to expose them by calling the cops in on this? On one hand I think it's the smart thing to do and on the other I think we're setting ourselves up, as you said, like sitting ducks. Shit, I don't know. I just think we need to be more certain before we call the cops, because there is no turning back after that."

"I need to check on Connie and the kids. I can't believe they didn't wake up, but it is amazing what they can sleep through. I think Connie might be a wreck though. I'll be quick and we'll figure out how to get you fixed up."

Sean returned to the den in a few minutes to find his father hanging up the phone.

"I thought we weren't calling the cops," Sean said, a little alarmed and agitated as well.

"I didn't. Don't worry about that. I think that's the right choice for now. How're the kids and Connie?"

"Sorry. Well, Karen never did wake up. Apparently Jeremy did but Connie told him how she had stubbed her toe, which explained what he'd heard and the reason she was crying. Pretty smart, that Connie. I think she's calming down finally, too. . But she has no intention of coming down stairs until we get that gorilla out of the foyer. Which brings up another small detail, old man." Sean shook his head and smiled at his father, "How's the saying go, 'this is a fine mess you got me in to'."

"I've got an idea about that, too. When you walked in I was calling Brian Mead. He's on his way to sew me back together."

Sean couldn't help but laugh out loud. "I would expect nothing less from you, Dad." He continued laughing.

"You're mother always thought I was very predictable, too," Conner said with a little laugh that stopped immediately due to the pain it generated in his chest. "I also called Bubba Striker. He's on his way, too."

Sean looked at his father inquisitively, waiting for an explanation, which wasn't immediately forthcoming.

Dr. Brian Mead was a man Conner's age that had been his veterinarian for over twenty years on the horse farm in Ocala. They had enjoyed a good professional relationship and had become close personal friends. Conner had called him, getting him out of bed, and Mead responded by telling his friend it was one thing to wake him up for a foaling emergency, but Conner didn't even own any horses any more for Christ's sake. Doc Mead tickled himself with that barb and it made Conner smile at his old friend. Conner explained he needed help and his friend told him he was on his way. He asked Conner how he'd managed to get so cut up, but Conner said it was a long story and he'd explain it all when he got there. Murphy had already decided to tell his friend there had been an intruder in the house, but nothing more. He knew he could ask for his discretion and get it.

Bubba Striker drove like a bat out of hell and his pickup was in Sean's driveway by 6:00 a.m. He backed his truck to the garage door and he and Sean wrestled the big chest freezer out of the back. It wasn't long before Sean and Bubba had it plugged in to the wall and the corpse of Nick Kowalski stuffed inside.

"I hope you didn't have to throw out much of your elk and venison to make room for this bastard, Bubba," Sean said to him.

Sean cleaned the blood off the tile floor at the foot of the stairs using some old bath towels. He stuffed the soiled towels in to a trash bag and then in to the freezer with the cooling Nick Kowalski. The last thing to do before the kids woke up was to get Conner out of the den and on to the bed in the spare bedroom. This was accomplished just as Doc Mead showed up.

"Bubba, Sean, hell this is like old home week. How y'all doin'?" Brian was his cheerful self as he came through the kitchen. "Is my patient around or has he commenced to bleed out?"

"He doesn't have a big enough heart to pump all his blood out that fast," Bubba shook hands with his veterinarian. "Come on, I'll take you back to the surgery suite. You won't know what to do without bedding on the floor and no flies buzzing around your head, will you?"

"The only reason I will is because of suturing up the likes of you and Conner over the years. You know, honest to God, I think this is the fifth time I've put stitches in this stubborn old bastard. I was thinking about it on the way down here. It may be more, but I know it's been at least five."

Brian Mead wasn't convinced that he was getting the full story this time. But he was also too good of a friend to press it. He cleaned, sutured and dressed the wounds and left antibiotics with instructions for his patient. It had taken nearly two hours.

"Conner that leg wound isn't too bad. It's not too deep in to the muscle. The one in your chest is a different story. I did what I could to pull that muscle belly together. But I hate that for two reasons. I hate leaving buried sutures in these traumatic wounds because of the possibility of infection and unfortunately, it won't take much to pull them apart. I left that drain in because I feel it's going to be a pretty productive wound. Just snip that suture and pull that drain in forty-eight hours. Meantime, keep it very clean.

"You need to put this arm in a sling for at least two weeks, to limit your motion and activity on that side. And by the way, it's not going to be fun pulling that drain out."

"You got it. I'll do it. Thanks, doc, you're a star. Always have been."

"You know you can always call on me Conner." Mead tipped his head toward Bubba, "I would appreciate a better looking nurse though."

Conner grinned back at him, "I'll see what I can do. Thanks again."

Conner's wounds fouled their plans to leave that day. But they remained worried about reprisals and were determined to get on the road as quickly as practical. The kids were a little confused about going on a trip so soon after starting back at school, but it all sounded like a great adventure to go on a road trip around the country with Dad and Granddad.

Sean was unsure about asking Connie, not certain if the whole dynamic would work with them traveling together and then staying at the Ingles ranch. She solved his dilemma by telling Sean she didn't want to go. Her family was in Tampa and on top of that she was frightened. Connie cried when she told Sean and apologized for leaving him and the kids in a bad position. Sean assured her that he understood completely and told her she was making the right choice. "Connie, my work is here and we will be back here at some point. We aren't disappearing forever. When we return from...wherever, whenever that is, we will be sure to call you, OK." Sean had made certain not to tell Connie where they were going; a burden she didn't deserve.

Conner spent most of that next day in bed. His wounds hurt and he was weak from exhaustion as well as blood loss. Bubba stayed to help Sean with the packing and to shuttle the Excursion up from Longboat Key along with a list of Conner's things. On that list was the mate to the Remington derringer and the box of .41 caliber shells.

Connie had promised to help until they left and her assistance was invaluable in getting the kids packed for the trip. She made dinner that night and Bubba stayed over, insisting on spending the night to provide an additional armed guard in case the 'ugly son-of-a-bitch in the freezer' had a friend come calling. With Conner hurt and Sean exhausted, they were both grateful for their friend's insistence. Conner had gotten up for dinner, prompting a lot of questions from the kids, who were told that a big window had broken at the beach house and Granddad had been cut pretty badly, but he was going to be fine.

After dinner the three men sat on the patio and discussed their plan for the next day. Conner told Sean he wasn't going with them, not just yet.

"You don't think you feel up to it, or what? Maybe we don't have to leave tomorrow." Sean was surprised.

"It's not that, buddy. I'm going to find Joey Williams and get more information on exactly who's involved in this. I think we've got to know who is behind this to get some sense of whom we can trust. But we've all agreed, you need to get out of here."

"Do you really think he'll tell you anything? He seems like he'd be more interested in saving his own skin," Sean responded.

Conner shot Bubba a glance. "I think with Mr. Striker's persuasive help Cooter will be a fountain of information."

"Does he still live in the same place in Inverness?" Bubba asked.

"I'm ninety-nine per cent sure he does," answered Conner. "That old place has been in his family for five generations and he always loved it. I can't imagine him leaving there."

"So you're thinking about catching up with me in Elko, or what?" Sean asked his dad.

"Oh I'm hoping it's before that; somewhere on the way."

Bubba sat his coffee down and tipped his cap back on his head. "You know, fellas, I've listened to a lot of your plans and they all seem pretty smart to me. I think you'll be damned hard to follow. Right up until you buy a plane ticket, Conner, with your name and destination on it."

"I've thought of that, you wise old codger. When we finish our business with Williams I'm going to go to the Ocala airport and have Daryl Wright fly me in one of his charter King Airs. He won't need to put my name on any dossier. I'll pay cash and no one will be the wiser."

"Man, speaking of wise old codgers," said Bubba. "I like it. There'll be no issue with you carrying a gun that way either."

The plan was final; everyone was leaving in the morning: Connie for her sister's. Sean was headed west with the kids. Conner and Bubba would pay a visit to Joey Williams.

INVERNESS, FLORIDA

August

Conner had not spoken to Jan since being hurt; he missed hearing her voice. It was mid-morning when he called from his cell phone as Bubba drove north on I-75. He didn't mention anything about the attack, instead he asked about her and her mother. He was pleased to hear that her situation was about to resolve itself; she was flying with her mother back to Seattle in three days.

"I'll be free! I'll be free!" she exclaimed in a mocking voice. "I'm kidding. Kind of. It's like you always said, Conner. I did what I needed to do, and I'm glad I did it. But I'm so glad it's almost over. I can't wait to have you back again. I miss you so much."

"I miss you too, baby. It won't be long now."

"I miss you too, baby," Bubba yelled loud enough for Jan to hear.

"I love you Conner, and tell that mad man I love him, too."

"I'll tell him. Love you, bye."

They exited I-75 at the Wildwood exit to head west on SR-44 to Inverness. It had been many years since either of them had been to the Williams' Plantation House, but their memories hadn't failed them in finding it. Several miles west of Rutland, on the right side of the high way, was the large private entrance to the Williams estate.

Bubba drove past the elaborately landscaped entrance, through the large iron gates and down the long, oak lined lane in to the historic old plantation. It had been in the Williams family since 1899, but the original farm and house dated back to the Civil War. The newer mansion, built just prior to World War II, was now the main house and was occupied by Joey Williams.

He lived alone. His first wife left him after finally losing her capacity to deal with his constant philandering. Through the divorce she maintained full custody of their three children and, by his choice, he never had contact with them again. Williams married several more times, always to much younger women and never for more than two years.

Bubba parked under the porte cochere at the front of the house. Conner was slow to get out of the truck, not eager to bear full weight on his right leg and hampered by his right arm being in a sling. The two men climbed the few steps on to the wide front porch and approached the enormous double doors of the old antebellum style mansion. Bubba rang the bell and then impatiently rang it a second time when no one came to the door.

"It's big house, Bubba. It takes a while just to walk across the foyer," Conner smiled at his friend.

"Fuck 'em."

The door opened and a black maid with a floral print dress and a full white apron answered the door.

"May I help you gentlemen?"

"Good morning, we're looking for Mr. Williams, please," Conner spoke up first.

"Business or personal, gentlemen."

"Well, it would be personal, little lady. We are very old friends of Mr. Williams. We go way back to the days when everyone called him Cooter." Bubba winked when he said it.

The maid's eyes grew wide at his remark. "Well Mr. Williams is out of town, in Dallas, Texas, until late tomorrow. He informed Ms. Liola, that when he returns to Florida he'll be going directly to his home in Yankeetown, on the Withlacoochee. You'll have to reach him there, I 'spect."

"And who is Ms. Liola?" Bubba asked.

"Why she be the head of the staff here at the mansion, suh."

"You've been very kind. Thank you." Bubba tipped his cap and turned to go.

Conner stopped his friend by grabbing his arm, "Wait, we need to find out where his place is in Yankeetown."

"I know the place. I know where it is."

"OK. Thanks ma'am." Conner smiled and nodded to the maid.

They were weaving their way down the long lane toward Hwy 44 when Conner turned to his friend. "Does it strike you that he has black house servants. Maybe I'm being too hard on the man, but it's like he still thinks it's still a civil war mansion; or some crap."

Bubba shook his head slightly, "That old bigoted prick. It doesn't surprise me in the least. He'd have black slaves if he could get away with it. And listen, he ran with all those liberal pricks in Washington that tell the rest of us what Neanderthals and homophobes and bigots we are. The hypocrisy is never ending, amigo, never ending. Let's head to my place and see if Beth has any elk stew left over from yesterday. It looks like we're on hold for two days."

"Sounds great, laying a little low for two days would probably be a good idea for me anyway. Are you positive you know where his place is in Yankeetown?"

"Yea, I'm positive. It's the old house that Johnny King used to own. He sold it to Cooter when he moved back to Texas. It's really not much more than a fishing cabin; not much house."

"Drive on, Jeeves, I'm gonna take a little nap." Conner said as he laid his seat back in the crew cab pickup and closed his eyes.

YANKEETOWN, FLORIDA

September

Two days of rest at the Striker's had served Conner well. He was in a lot less pain already and had regained some strength. Sean had called early that morning. They were in Beaumont, Texas, not as far as he'd hoped but he didn't want to be too hard on the kids. Each day he stopped by mid-afternoon to let them go swimming in the hotel pool. All and all, everything was going along fine, no worries.

It was 9:00 a.m. when Bubba and Conner crossed Hwy 19 toward Yankeetown. They worried at first that they might miss Williams, especially if he went out fishing early, forcing them to wait the rest of the day for his return. After further consideration they decided that the way Joey sucked up the booze he probably didn't see many early mornings anymore. And wasn't he to arrive late; just more reason for Joey not to roll out early for a full day on the water.

Bubba turned off of Hwy 40 on to Riverside Drive.

"There she be. It looks the same as the day Johnny sold it to him. I'd guess that's his Caddy out front."

"Let's go," said Conner as the truck pulled to a stop behind the black Cadillac.

The drive way was a simple loop in front of the house, unpaved and covered instead by a thick layer of oak leaves. The small house was under a thick canopy of trees; it's mildewed exterior was testament to how shady and damp the dense foliage kept it. There was a small screened in porch that both men accessed to reach the front door. As the screen door slapped shut behind Conner, Bubba knocked on the front door. They waited more than a minute and Bubba knocked again, louder. No one came to the door and no sounds could be heard from within. Bubba tried the knob and it turned, he looked at Conner and shrugged his shoulders as he pushed the door open. He stepped partially through the doorway and stuck his head in to look inside. There were no lights on and little sunlight made it through the trees to penetrate the small windows of the cabin.

Bubba pushed the door wide open and both men walked through the door as Conner yelled out for Cooter, calling him by his nickname. They were standing in the living room looking at each other, silently questioning their decision to have come this late when Williams walked out from a bedroom dressed in sweat pants and a sweat shirt.

"This looks rather ominous. To what do I owe the pleasure of this little visit?"

"You headed out for a jog, Cooter?" Bubba asked, not really knowing if he was joking or not.

"Hardly. The Goddamn air in here is all screwed up. It's either too hot or I'm freezing my ass off. I picked the 'freezing my ass off' setting last night so I could sleep."

The tall man was disheveled. His long silver hair resembled an abandoned bird's nest and his blood shot eyes burned against a waxy, grey complexion. But his deep voice and smooth southern drawl, for which he was famous, was still intact. A reporter had once likened his courtroom oratory to sounding like dark molasses. Joey Williams walked past his guests toward the little kitchen as he continued to speak.

"I know you boys are far too upstanding to indulge in my vices, but I plan to have a little hair of the dog. I need to break through this fog somehow. How about some coffee, gentlemen?"

"I think we're good," responded Conner for both of them. "Is anyone else here, Cooter?"

The old attorney was retrieving a half empty bottle of Makers Mark when he turned to Conner. "You've been hanging around the likes of Striker here too long, Conner. A debonair gentleman such as I does not bring a lady to a fuckin' fish camp on the Withlacoochee. Yes, gentlemen, we are alone."

Williams pulled a quart of half and half out of the refrigerator, still in the plastic bag from the grocery store. He opened the carton and poured several ounces in to a tall glass, added an equal amount of bourbon and plopped two ice cubes in to the mix.

"God damn ulcers seem to be worse when I first get up." Noticing Conner's arm was in a sling he added, "looks like you could use a little of my medicine, Conner."

Williams walked back in to the small living room and gestured to two chairs as he sat in the middle of the couch. He lifted his glass in a toasting gesture and took a swallow of his 'medicinal' concoction. Bubba involuntarily screwed his own face into a look of disgust as he could only imagine the taste of heavy milk and bourbon at nine o'clock in the morning. Williams leaned back and looked at each of his guests individually, silently inviting them to speak.

"Someone tried to kill my boy three nights ago. In his home." Conner's tone was cool and his voice was low.

Williams took another drink.

"I'm guessing your arm has something to do with that incident. Well, then, I'm glad I warned you. Hopefully it helped."

"It helped this time, but what about the next time. This guy was no fuckin' rummy off the street, he was..."

"I told you I'm not in it anymore, God damn it!" Williams face reddened as he shouted the words.

"You're in it enough to know who the players are. They haven't changed since you quit..."

"If you have quit, you sorry fuck!" Bubba interrupted Conner, not able to control himself.

"Go to hell Striker!" retorted Williams.

"Hold it both of you. Damn." Conner was holding his left hand up, looking first at Bubba and then back at Williams. "Cooter, this guy that came after Sean was not some druggy someone hired off the street for a few hundred bucks. This was a professional. The real deal. The people that sent this guy are obviously the real deal, too. I want to know who they are. I want to protect my family."

"I told you the other day how I heard about this...this shit. It was virtually by accident. A friend of a friend kinda deal. A guy running his mouth. I'm out of the shit, I tell you. I'm not in the loop anymore." Williams took another swallow of his drink and looked straight at the ceiling.

"Maybe you're out, but you know who's in. You were close to the top of that manure pile. Hell, you broke bread and made strategies with these bastards and you know it." Conner's voice got louder with each word.

Williams looked straight at Conner but not into his eyes, he couldn't do that. After almost a minute he looked back at his glass and took another swallow.

"You don't understand. You don't understand the power these kind of people have. All of the things that they can control; all of the resources and money...they have access to so much fuckin' money."

"I don't need to understand, I just want to know who they are. Who's calling the shots on this deal? This deal, damn it!" Conner had scooted to the edge of his chair, becoming even more agitated with Williams' evasions.

"I can tell you this. The people I know didn't send the thug that showed up at your son's house. They don't payroll those types, they hire all that out. So I promise you I don't know who did that."

Conner tried to stay calm; he wanted answers. "But you do know who placed the call, the ones that ordered someone be sent to...shit, to kill my son. You sure as hell know that, don't you, Joey?"

The old lawyer swallowed hard. He looked at Bubba sitting motionless in the chair across from him. Bubba stared back in to the man's eyes. Joey drew a long breath and bit his bottom lip as he turned his head to look over at Conner. He was feeling old and used up. He was looking at two men that loathed him, hated him for what he had become; two men that had been true friends in another lifetime. Joey knew it wasn't them that had changed; it was he who had changed. He wondered right then who hated him more, these two men or himself?

"Sidney Leach. A man named Sid Leach is at that top of that shit pile. He has Bernie Samms in his pocket at all times and I guess I'm not sure which one of them called this in."

"Congressman Bernie Samms. Conneticut?" Conner asked, a little incredulous.

"The one and only."

Both men were quiet for most of the drive back to Ocala from Yankeetown. Bubba was consumed with his thoughts about Joey Williams and how much he had changed; how people course through life on different journeys and get swept up by different circumstances and different choices. As young men, all three of them had been close. The Williams family was wealthy and powerful but Joey had never been pretentious or ostentatious; he was simply their friend. At that time they were all trying to make their way as young men, taking on the challenges of building careers and starting families.

Everything changed soon after Joey became a partner in the law firm. At the time, he was the first to admit his quick ascendance to partner status had been due to his family name. It was less than a year later that the firm was awarded a judgment in a class action suit against the tobacco companies. It was life changing for Williams. He not only shared in the financial bonanza, but more than that. Doors were opened to him that provided opportunities he had never dreamed of. It was only two years later that he won a twenty million dollar malpractice suit and two years after that, a forty million dollar product liability suit.

Williams became drawn by the allure of politics, but remained too wise to run for political office and risk the vagaries of the electorate. He had been mentored early on by men behind the scenes who were very cognizant of what this brilliant, connected, young plaintiff attorney could bring to the table. It had been an easy choice to stay in the background and work the strings of the politicians that favored his ambitions. Soon, he had wealth and power beyond any expectations, all of which seemed to amplify his susceptibility to temptation. He was not only tempted by women, but enjoyed surrounding himself by the sycophants that targeted people such as him for their own parasitic existence.

As Bubba piloted his truck home that day he contemplated whether he hated Joey Williams or pitied him. The hollow look in the old lawyer's eyes had communicated a fear, or a dread, that made Bubba feel uneasy.

Conner was consumed with his own thoughts. He held the note that Williams had given him and read it several times. Referring to it periodically between random thoughts about his family and the deep sadness he felt for how much everything had changed. Not just the changes in his family, with the loss of Molly and then Mo, but also the changes he was witnessing in his country. Changes he had always feared in a nightmarish way, but cognitively had thought were impossible. It depressed him so to think how government had become so controlling in all aspects of their lives. He loathed the power that some people had; people that seemingly answered to no one.

Ever since the intruder had come in to Sean's house, Conner had become more obsessed with the idea of revenge. He learned he was mistaken when he thought he'd satisfied that revenge when he killed Stanley Mesh. There was more to do; he had to do more to protect his family. There were other vile, dangerous people that... had to be dealt with.

He read the note one more time before finally folding it and putting it in his shirt pocket.

THE LITTLE BUREAUCRAT

Sidney Leach
11333 Chestnut Street, Bethesda, MD
301-652-4666

Joey 'Cooter' Williams finished his second glass of Makers Mark and cream before walking out to his Cadillac and retrieving his pistol from the glove compartment. It was a Colt .45 revolver, loaded except for the chamber under the hammer. As he walked back toward the house he straightened his back and quickened his pace almost as if he had more purpose. He pulled the hammer back with his thumb and squeezed the trigger, revolving the chamber. The screen door to the porch slammed behind him and he didn't bother closing the front door to the house. He walked out through the back door of the little dining room on to the covered porch that overlooked the Withlacoochee River. He sat in the yellow rocking chair and leaned back, brought the muzzle of the .45 to his right eye and squeezed the trigger. The impact took off most of the base of his skull and flipped him and the chair over backwards on to the porch.

A blue heron hunting on the marshy bank of the river slowly took flight, heading downstream and away from the report of the pistol.

ELKO, NEVADA

September

It was a gorgeous late summer afternoon, in northeastern Nevada, with an intensely blue sky and not a hint of a cloud. It was Sunday and they were gathered on the back deck for lunch. Bud, Conner, and Sean sat in chairs around the grill while Maggie and Jan were busy in the kitchen finishing with the baked beans and potato salad.

"Bud, thanks again for taking my sutures out. You make a hell of a nurse."

"I've pulled my share of sutures out of my critters over the years." Bud smiled at his old friend, "But I don't remember any of them whining quite as much as you did. I thought I was going to have to put a twitch on you to get you to hold still."

"You can't help but to be a prick, can you?" Conner laughed.

"I'll tell you what though; your vet did one hell of a job. Both those wounds healed great. Not one suture dehisced."

"You don't even seem that sore anymore either. Are you?" Sean asked.

"I'm really not. My leg isn't sore at all. I can feel it in my chest if I do too much, but not as bad as I'd have thought."

Conner pointed to the right side of his chest, "I've got a hell of a dimple right here, where I guess the muscle didn't pull back together, but overall I feel okay."

"Well your male modeling days are pretty well over anyway." Bud couldn't resist another jab.

"I told you that you couldn't help yourself. But you know what that dimple looks like? Like the dimple you see on a horses neck where they've torn the muscle at some point and it leaves a depression. We used to call them a prophets thumb...or thumbprint, or something. Anyway, now I've got one."

Just then Jan called out from the kitchen door for Conner to help carry some things outside. As he walked across the deck toward the kitchen he glanced to his left and stopped. Coming across the side yard, between the horse barn and the house, was a sight that put a broad smile on his face.

"Here comes some ornery looking vaqueros, fellas," Conner pointed to the three riders approaching the tie rail at the edge of the yard.

"Looks like the Western life might suit 'em, Sean," Bud smiled at the sight of the Murphy kids riding up on the ponies. Arturo was riding behind them on a blaze-faced mare, acting as their escort. The men on the deck watched the two children ride up to the rail and pull back on their reins. Their voices didn't carry all the way to the deck but both their mouths formed an unmistakable 'whoa'. Karen's was more exaggerated, as was her pull back on the reins, causing her pony to open his mouth and lift his head.

As both children went to dismount, Arturo said something to Karen that caused her to shift her weight from her right to her left and dismount the correct side of her horse. He stayed in the saddle and the children handed him the reins of their horses and then turned and ran toward the deck. Arturo nodded at the men before turning his pretty sorrel mare away, leading both ponies back to the barn.

"That Arturo is a nugget, I tell ya'," Bud said looking at Sean.

"I'm not sure he hired on thinking my kids were part of the deal. I certainly appreciate what he does for them."

"I'm telling you, he loves it. He's as amiable as anyone you'll ever meet. And you can trust him as well; he's a great horseman and wouldn't put those kids in harm's way for a second."

Karen couldn't contain herself; half way to the deck she threw her arms up and started to yell to her father.

"Daddy, I love him, I just love him."

Sean smiled and waited for his little girl to run up between his legs as he sat in the wrought iron chair next to Bud.

"I assume you mean that pony, Hickory, and not your brother." Sean replied.

Karen was standing between his legs, her red hair glistening in the sun and her beautiful blue eyes looking in to her father's with a quizzical look on her face.

"Of course I mean Hickree, silly." After a few seconds passed she said, "But I do love Jeremy, too."

"That's a relief," her father responded with a big smile followed by a hug.

Jeremy stood next to Bud as he lit the grill.

"Mr. Ingles thanks a lot for letting us ride so much. I think I'm going to make a real good cowboy. I'm pretty sure I'm about ready for some spurs and a real cowboy hat, too." Jeremy took his cap off and wiped his sweaty brow with the back of his forearm, mimicking a gesture he'd learned along the way.

"Well, son, I've got no doubt in my mind that you'll be one heck of a cowboy. And I'd say you're definitely ready for a real hat. A good heavy straw like I wear is perfect for this time of year. The wind is too strong in this country to wear a flimsy little straw; you need one like this." Bud took his hat off to so show it to Jeremy who was now sitting in the chair that Conner had vacated.

"I believe these are made of some sort of palm frond or yucca," he looked over at Sean, "hell I don't know what they're made of really, but they stay on your head and they're cooler than a felt hat, I know that. So Jeremy, we'll get you fixed up right proper in the hat department, ASAP."

"What's an ASAP?" asked the boy.

"It means as soon as possible," Sean answered.

"But, my young friend, we're gonna hold off on the spurs for a while yet. You've got a lot more hours to put in the saddle before we want to complicate things with spurs."

"They don't look complicated, Mr. Ingles."

"No, I suppose they don't. However, when you're learning to ride, they can get you in to trouble. What you need is more experience doing exactly what you're doing before you worry about them."

"Sure. Sounds fine, Mr. Ingles. Thanks."

Sean spun Karen around by the shoulders to face the house, "You two need to go wash those hands before lunch. Go on up to your bathroom and wash up, we're about ready to eat."

The fresh air, the good food and the company of old friends made for a perfect afternoon. After lunch Sean took the kids fishing at the reservoir. Bud had set them up with worms and bobbers, saying the only thing more fool proof would be dynamite and demanded they catch at least one Rainbow each.

After lunch Bud retired to his office and Maggie to her computer to catch up on e-mail. Conner and Jan headed for the couches in the great room to sprawl out and read. Both of them were sound asleep within minutes.

It had been just over a week since Conner arrived at the ranch. Jan came in the next day. The kids were acclimating well. Both of them had periods of sadness thinking about their mother, but found comfort in the loving surroundings of the ranch. Sean, too, had moments of tremendous sadness, always coming when he was alone and usually brought on after watching his children having fun or learning something new. It broke his heart that his beloved Maureen was not able to experience those things.

Conner woke at three the next morning. He wasn't certain what woke him but his mind was whirling with worry about different aspects of his plan. He rose and went downstairs. The past week had been a time to recover both physically and emotionally, but Conner had never forgotten the danger they were in and that time was not in their favor. He knew that a man like Sydney Leach would finish what he started.

His son had his life to live; a career to build and flourish in; children to care for and raise to be healthy, happy adults. Sean would need another woman in his life at some point. Conner wanted nothing more than for their lives to be full and happy. He felt it was his duty, as the patriarch of the family, to make sure they would live and thrive. No one could be allowed to steal that from them, they had stolen enough of it already.

Conner knew he could minimize the risk to his son and family if he handled things himself, alone. He also knew that he couldn't plan for every contingency and at some point he'd have to take action. That time was coming near. Conner had no illusions; what he planned to do was dangerous and might cost him his life.

Conner decided to go for a walk outside. He was wearing jeans and a tee shirt as he made his way to the mud porch where he found a pair of his moccasins. He closed the door quietly behind him and was startled by the sound of someone sobbing. He turned to look across the deck and could barely make out Sean's silhouette in the starlight.

As Conner approached, his son wiped his eyes and did his best to his put a smile on his face. Conner stood next to him and put his hand on his shoulder; his heart ached as he saw his boy sitting there.

"Having a rough night, I guess," Sean said as he put his hand on his father's. "I'm OK, though, I'm OK."

"Something in particular got you tonight, buddy?" Conner sat in the chair facing his son.

"Yeah, it always seems to be...I don't know. Something that

sneaks up on me, I guess." Sean had been looking away as he spoke but now turned his head to look directly at his father. "Dad, you should have seen the kids catching those fish today. Yesterday, I guess. God they were having fun. It was absolutely marvelous."

"I'm sure it was great. They certainly talked about it a lot at dinner. Jeremy was so proud that he had actually provided supper for the table. Very cool."

"You know, Dad. I can't tell you how many times I have thought about something you said a long time ago. I was fourteen and on my first elk hunt. Bubba Striker was there, Bud, and Pat Rodney from Kremling. I had shot that five point that afternoon and we were having dinner at the cabin that night. You were going over the hunt with your friends, explaining every detail and you were as excited as I was. I remember you telling your friends that watching me that day bag my first elk, was the most exciting hunt you'd ever been on. Much more exciting than any time you'd gotten anything. I remember hearing you, and believing you, but not really understanding it."

"Wow, what a great day that was. I'll never forget it." Said Conner, smiling as the memory returned.

"Today, I thought about that again. I've never had so much fun fishing, and I never had a line in the water. Tonight all I can think about is how Mo isn't here to enj..." Sean couldn't finish. He leaned forward and put his face in his hands, sobbing softly.

Conner thought his heart was breaking apart in his chest. He leaned in to his son and put his hand on the young man's shoulder, massaging it with his strong fingers. Sean finally regained his composure and dried his eyes.

"I'm sorry, Dad."

"For what?"

They talked quietly for another hour before Sean said he was ready to go back to bed. Conner told him to go on, that he would sit up for another few minutes. Both men stood and hugged each other hard before Sean walked back in to the house.

Conner didn't feel sleepy the rest of the night. He watched the sun rise from his chair on the deck, determined and confident in his plan.

Several more days were spent at the ranch before Jan had to return to Jackson. The group of friends had spent most of that time all together. Everyone enjoyed themselves, but Jan had noticed a change in Conner. There was moroseness about him that he couldn't disguise as hard as he tried. Jan didn't say anything about this undercurrent of sadness; she simply tried to be loving and caring, knowing that he needed her support.

They made love the night before she left. It was long and tender and sweet. Jan responded to the foreplay with repeated orgasms culminating with them experiencing one simultaneously in each other's arms. Early the next morning, they made love again. After breakfast, Conner took Jan to the airport in Elko.

He explained to her that he was going to go back to Florida for a few days to tie up some loose ends. She looked at him a little funny when he said that and formed a question on her lips, but it remained unspoken. He was glad to not to have to expand the lie and hugged her hard before kissing her on the lips.

"I love you Jan Thomas, thank you for being in my life."

"I love you, Conner. Call me soon." Her eyes were filling with tears as she turned to walk through the door to the jet port.

Bud Ingles had chartered a plane for Conner through a fractional ownership company that he leased from occasionally. Only the two of them knew that the destination was Washington Executive Airport outside of Washington DC instead of Florida. Conner was to leave that afternoon, just after lunch, and his name was not to appear on the flight dossier.

Maggie fixed lunch and Conner spent a lot of time talking to and joking with his grandchildren during the meal. After the dishes were cleared he took both kids to the great room and spoke with them again briefly and gave them each a strong, loving hug when he finished.

"I need to say good bye to your Dad before I go, kids. You be good and I love you both very much."

"Love you, Grandpa," Karen said, giving him a kiss on the cheek.

"Bye, Grandpa, I love you." Said Jeremy as he followed his sister toward the stairs.

"How long will you be gone, Dad?" Sean asked. "You have a plan yet?"

"I think so. I think I know how to make all of this go away. Bear with me, OK?"

Sean's expression evidenced his curiosity but he said nothing more.

"All set, amigo?" Bud was standing half way to the door with Conner's bag in his hand.

"You bet." He turned to Sean and gave him a hug. "I love you buddy."

"Love you, too."

Conner followed Bud to the door to find Maggie standing there. She embraced him and told him to be safe.

"Thanks for everything, Maggie."

"Having your brood here has made me so happy, I should be thanking you."

Bud dropped Conner at the curb of the small Elko airport. They shook hands and Conner thanked his good friend.

"You know I'm happy to do all of this, right? You do know that, right?" Bud said to his friend, not letting go of his hand.

"I do know that. And it makes my heart feel really good, my friend."

"I also want you to know that what Maggie said is very true. Having those kids around has been so good for her. She absolutely loves it. Be safe, amigo."

"I will." Conner grabbed his bag off the seat and shut the door.

WASHINGTON, D.C.

September

It was 9:00 p.m. when the twin engine Cessna Mustang touched down at Washington Executive Airport at Hyde Field, near Clinton, Maryland. Conner had managed a nap on the plane, unplanned really, dozing off while reading a magazine and slept for almost two hours. It had surprised him when he woke and looked at his watch, thinking he hadn't even felt tired. It brought to mind what Molly had always told him when he slept longer than he wanted to; "You must have needed it for you to have slept so long," she would say, mostly chiding him for working too hard and being too hard on himself in those days.

The plane taxied to a stop near the terminal and Conner exited the jet into the warm night air. The copilot followed him down the steps on to the tarmac to retrieve his bag from the compartment at the rear of the fuselage. Conner thanked the young man, who nodded in return and pointed to the glass doors of the terminal just off the nose of the airplane. Conner walked through the terminal building to the frontof the building, only to discover that there were no cabs waiting; reentering the lobby area he approached the young woman behind the counter in hopes she could summon a taxi. The tall brunette was very responsive and polite, making the phone call immediately as well as asking what else she could do for him. Conner smiled and told her a cab was all he needed.

Within ten minutes of her call Conner was in the back seat of the taxi, Joey Williams's note in hand, reading the address aloud to the driver. Surprisingly, at least to Conner, the traffic was light and it was only minutes before they were driving north on I-495 toward Bethesda. At exit 33 the driver left the Beltway and turned on to Connecticut Avenue. Five more minutes, and several more turns, brought them to Chestnut Street. The cabby drove slowly while he and Conner looked for street addresses as they went.

"Here it is sir, that's your number" the man's voice was high pitched with a thick Pakistani accent. "You want me to pull in the drive way?"

By now the cab was stopped directly in front of the house. "No, no, keep going." Conner spoke quickly as he noticed the black SUV parked across the street from Leach's house.

As the driver accelerated, continuing down Chestnut Street, away from the two story brick colonial, Conner looked at the man behind the wheel of the Chevy Suburban. The man returned the stare, curious who might be in a taxi that chose this particular spot to slow down and nearly stop. Conner obviously had no fear of being recognized and was actually pleased with the information gained by his little reconnaissance mission. He was concerned about it back firing, which would depend on how aggressive and astute the guard might be. The cabby looked at Conner in the mirror as he slowed the car again, asking where to drive to next. Conner thought a minute; there was no sense in giving these bastards any opportunity of tracking him down. The prudent thing to do was to have this driver drop him somewhere other than the hotel.

"Just keep going, don't slow down again, please. Listen, is there a 24 hour Wal-Mart anywhere near here?" he asked the driver.

"Not really, not in this neighborhood. Not with these rich people."

"But there is one somewhere, right?"

"Sure, sure, sure, mister. You want to go to the closest one?" The driver was nodding his head affirmatively and smiling at Conner in the mirror.

"Yes, please, let's go."

The driver made his way back on to the Beltway, heading back in the same direction they'd come twenty minutes earlier. On the eastern side of the loop the cab exited on to Hwy 450 toward Bladensburg and then on to Annapolis Road. Conner paid the fare, not wanting the driver to wait. He knew his trail was far from squeaky clean but at the same time he didn't want to make it too easy for anyone that was going to be looking for him. Upon exiting the Wal-Mart with a new cell phone in hand, he located a different cab company through information and called them.

It was midnight when he checked in to the Hotel George on E Street in downtown DC. Immediately upon entering his room, Conner dropped his bag on the floor and headed for the shower. The steamy shower was a bright spot at the end of an arduous day. He hardly dried off when he exited the shower, but instead spread his towel across the bed and laid on it; allowing his damp skin to cool him off as he lay there, looking up at the ceiling, hands clasped behind his head; thinking, planning.

Conner purposefully avoided thinking about his family, not wanting to deal with any sadness or remorse brought on by the possibility of not seeing them again; not wanting anything to cloud what he knew he had to do. Laying in the darkness, reflecting back on Stanley Mesh, Conner remembered being unclear as to what to do until he discovered the evidence in Stanley's 'bunker'; evidence that revealed what wretched scum the man was. That discovery provided Conner with perfect clarity. He knew he was not only exacting revenge for him and his family, but he was protecting people that were strangers to him; strangers, but also fellow citizens that would be the next victims to the sadistic perversions of the little bureaucrat.

Just as it had become evident what needed to be done with Mesh that night in Miami, Conner had gained the same clarity after the gorilla had invaded his son's home and tried to kill his family. Conner had realized that night what he must do to protect his family. That night, when he lay bleeding on Sean's couch, he knew he would kill those responsible. He'd not wavered.

Whether it was due to his earlier nap on the plane or the fact that his mind was busy flipping through different scenarios and strategies, he wasn't drowsy. He lay there on his towel, on top of the bedding, the only light in the room coming through the window from the street below. It was nearly 3:00am, when finally content with his plan, sleep began to creep in and he dug his way under the covers, falling off quickly.

The following morning the concierge was very helpful. She took his letter, indicating she would stamp it and get it out in today's mail, then directed him to what she described as 'a quaint little spot' for breakfast that was only three blocks away. As to his inquiry about a florist, there was a lovely one between the breakfast café and the hotel. Conner had a wry smile on his face as he exited the hotel to the street, wondering if his whole day would go so well; doubtful, he thought.

The diner was pleasant, as the concierge had described, and the poached eggs over corn beef hash couldn't have been better. Oeufs Et Plus served a rich blend of Kona coffee, in which Conner indulged until prudence ruled that he stop drinking it, out of fear he'd be become wired and agitated. Before leaving the restaurant he called Bubba Striker.

"How'd you make out?" Conner asked his old friend.

"Well, I'm just glad at my age that I'm still a tough son-of-a-bitch. I took the truck and my little trailer down to Sean's and picked up the freezer. I was able to get a roller under the end of the freezer and pull that heavy bastard up on to the trailer with the winch on my truck."

"Your winch is in front, how the hell did you do that?"

"Hey, amigo, I might be just a stupid fuckin' horseshoer, buy I'm a smart stupid fuckin' horseshoer. I unhooked the trailer and then stuck one side of the frame of the trailer against the garage door jamb, put the front bumper of my truck against the other side of the front of the trailer to hold it in place and winched it up the ramp. The trailer never moved."

"I'm not positive I follow, but I don't need to."

"Well, I'm gonna tell you, Murphy old boy, that was the easiest part of the day. The dead bastard was frozen stiff and weighed two fifty if he weighed an ounce. I ended up using the winch to unload the freezer and then again to tip the freezer over to get that bastard out of it. Hell, I even needed it just to roll him around. Jesus. I'm telling you, it was a job for three stout men and a monkey, not for one old horseshoer."

Conner was laughing to himself, picturing the dark comedy that took place on the Striker farm that day. "I hate to deprive you of relating all the gory details, but can you put in a nutshell what you ended up doing with the... our friend." Conner was suddenly cautious, realizing several people could hear his conversation.

Bubba laughed at that, "Am I getting a little tedious with this, brother?" He laughed again before continuing. "I cut all his clothes off and burned them in a trash barrel along with the bloody towels Sean had used to clean up that day. Then I spread the ashes in one of my pastures. I wrapped the body up in chicken wire along with several large rocks. Then I put him in the flats boat, covered him with a tarp and hauled his sorry ass out to the gulf where I found an appropriate deep channel and dumped him in. I even used my sonar to be sure I was right over the channel and watched him nestle right in to the bottom. I assume the crabs and catfish have him down to the bare bones by now."

"There's a side of you I'm not sure I ever knew, Mr. Striker."

"Pretty scary, huh? I'm thinking about going in to the body disposal business. Hey, but someday, I'll tell you about getting that great big son-of-a-bitch into the boat and then getting him out of the boat and in to the water; it liked to kill me."

"Weren't you just a little nervous about the warden watching you and wondering what the hell is this guy doing?"

"The thought crossed my mind."

"Thanks for all your help, Bubba."

"I'll always have your back, buddy, you know that."

"You're right, I do."

Conner walked the block to the florist on his way back to the hotel. He found the fragrances a bit overwhelming as he entered through the glass double doors of the shop. A fortyish, effeminate man with short platinum hair and a pleasant smile came to stand in front of Conner.

"May I help you, sir?"

"Yea, you can. Thanks. I want a large bouquet, something a little over the top, ostentatious."

"Sounds marvelous. Flowers?"

Conner was confused. "Flowers, that's right."

"Oh, you silly man. I know 'flowers', but there are a thousand types of flowers." The man put a heavy emphasis on the word thousand and was still smiling pleasantly. "What kinds of flowers are you thinking about?"

"That's a great question. Do you have any pictures or samples to help me?"

The florist laughed an exaggerated little laugh and then pointed at Conner. "I told you you're a silly man. Come with me."

Thirty minutes, and two hundred dollars later, Conner was walking down New Jersey Avenue toward the Hotel George carrying a large bouquet of roses, daisies, irises and much more that Conner had already forgotten the names of. Rather than carry the flowers into the elevator he asked the concierge if he could leave them on a table in the lobby. She helped him by moving some magazines and told him what wonderful taste he had.

"How was your breakfast? Did you enjoy Oeufs Et Plus?"

"I did. It was a great recommendation. The coffee was fabulous. You can feel safe with that one. I'll be down in a bit for these."

Back in his room, Conner sat on the foot of the bed with Cooter's note in one hand and his Wal-Mart cell phone in the other. He was nervous for the first time today, unsure about this part of his plan, as he punched in the numbers. It rang several times. Conner was getting anxious, he could feel the sweat on his palms as he thought the phone was going to click over to voice mail any second now. Shit. He'd have to go to plan B; a plan he wasn't as confident in.

"Heylo." Conner was startled; he'd given up. He hesitated. "Heylo."

"Sidney Leach, is that you? Is that you standing there?"

"Huh? Standing...what?"

"Sid, is that you?"

"Yea, it's me, damn it. Who is this?" Sid Leach held his phone in front of him to read the number of his caller. Not recognizing it only added to his agitation.

"I'm walking toward you. Look to your left. Over here."

"God damn it, who is this?"

"Isn't that you standing right in front of the Washington Monument with that tall blonde? I'm walking right toward you."

"Listen, you fuckin' moron. I'm not in the mall. I'm standing in my fucking living room. I'm not with a blonde, although this bastard likes peckers as much as any blonde, so go fuck yourself."

Leach hung his phone up and tossed it on to the sofa. His face was red from the exchange.

"Who the hell was that, Leach?"

"Fuck. I don't know. Probably one of your stupid ass congressional colleagues. Forget it, let's try and get some work done, Bernie."

Not only had Conner's plan been a success in finding where Leach was located, but his heart raced with elation over the fact that the man was at his home, the perfect scenario. The flowers had a potential dual purpose; for plan B they would have provided the excuse to go to the door of Leach's house and hopefully talk to someone, sniff out his whereabouts. But now they would be his way into the house, to Sid Leach. As Conner hurriedly gathered his things he thought how incredibly lucky he was, how lucky he'd been his entire life.

Conner was wearing jeans and a short-sleeved shirt. He plucked his gray suit coat from the back of the chair and put it on. Reaching in to his bag he removed his gun and the box of ammunition, grabbed a handful of .41 caliber shells from the box and shoved them down in to his right front pants pocket. He then took the Remington derringer, loaded it, checked the safety and dropped it in to his right coat pocket. Conner was moving quickly; fully cognizant of the fact that he had no idea how long Leach would remain at his house. Before leaving the room, he double-checked that he had his Wal-Mart cell phone, his note from Joey Williams and the room key. Conner took the elevator to the ground floor and walked briskly through the lobby and out to the street. He walked the half a block to the corner of New Jersey Avenue where he took his Wal-Mart cell phone from his pocket and tossed it in to the storm drain. Returning up the front steps to the door of the hotel, he asked the doorman to get him a cab while he collected his bouquet from the lobby.

Demarcus Webster had turned twenty-six years old last week. He had found his dream job; it consisted mostly of waiting and watching. That translated to listening to music for Demarcus. At first he'd been disappointed when the Redskins cut him, thinking how unfair it was. His last two years in college he'd been a starting tackle for The Ohio State Buckeyes and they had won the Big Ten conference both of those years. After being drafted in the fifth round all he could think about was the expensive toys he'd be able to afford. Webster knew he wasn't All Pro material but thought he'd be a starter, and on top of that he'd never had a bad injury; it was a was a no-brainer he'd ride that money train for at least four years.

One thing young Demarcus hadn't bet on was how complicated NFL schemes were. He became a constant disappointment to the coaching staff, not only for his incapacity to readily understand the plays, but his lack of commitment to do what was necessary to learn. That combination got him very little playing time and he was released after his first year. The disappointment waned quickly after he fell in to the security gig. This was a much better life; what the hell would he do with that money anyway besides buy music?

Earphones in and seat reclined, Demarcus was totally lost in his new CD. So much so that when the phone in his shirt pocket vibrated it startled him. He snatched the earphone from his right ear and brought his phone up to his head.

"Webster."

"Webster, Lucas here. You were debriefed on last night's events, I presume."

Lucas's formality was always such a joke to Demarcus. "Yes, sir. That's a ten-four."

There was a long pause, which made Webster smile. "So you know about the taxi cab that stopped in front of the Leach residence last night, correct?"

"Yes, sir. There's been no cabs on this street today and the only other car here other than Mr. Leach's, is Congressman Samms, who showed up about thirty minutes ago."

"Well the type of activity that occurred last night makes it imperative for you to keep your senses keen, Webster. Am I understood?"

"Yes, sir." Webster was tiring of this conversation and was anxious to get back to his music.

"That'll be all, Webster." The line went dead.

Conner took the taxi from the Hotel George to the Grand Hyatt on H Street where he paid the fare and went inside. He waited only several minutes in the lobby and then went back outside and took a place in the taxi line. Standing there with his large bouquet of flowers, he felt enormously conspicuous as he smiled back at several people remarking on the gorgeous arrangement. As he waited his turn he reflected on his choice of words in the flower shop, regretting 'ostentatious'..

As his cab pulled from the curb, Conner worried that the perfect scenario of Leach being at home may not exist by the time he got there. But there hadn't been any choice, the few steps he'd taken to cover his trail were the least to be done. Now that the second driver was nearly to Bethesda, Conner was less worried, deciding to have confidence in his old Murphy luck. He changed his focus to mental images of Sid Leach from the pictures he'd found on the Internet. He thought of the incredible reach of this man's power and was intrigued by the paucity of information available on him; a fact, which only served to fortify Conner's opinion of how conniving and manipulative this Leach must be. Obviously he was a man that knew the value of anonymity; deeply aware that the spotlight was for those that craved glory, no matter how brief, not for those that aspired to a life time of genuine power.

The flowers were riding well on the seat next to him with just a hand to steady the vase. As the taxi closed in on Chestnut Street he felt his senses becoming more acute. He acknowledged to himself that he was a bit frightened but it was more a fear of not accomplishing his goal than for his safety. It was a warm day and it was too warm in the cab to be wearing a jacket. Conner considered taking it off but thought better of trying to do that and keep the vase upright at the same time.

Leach paced his living room floor with his cell phone held tight to his ear; pacing while talking on the phone was a hallmark of Sidney Leach.

"Damn it, Leach, listen to me. I didn't call you to discuss how you felt about this. I called to tell you what I'm doing; what I decided to do. End of story. Ya' follow me?"

Sid Leach hated the fact that Mario Costello always called

him by his last name. But because of that, Sid would never call him Mario, always using Costello; consequently his own childish retaliation annoyed him further.

"Costello, I still don't follow why this is any different than any other time you've provided us with a service. They haven't all gone like clockwork, ya' know. We've had other times that your people got jammed up."

The increasing irritation was evident in Costello's voice as he responded, "Listen, I know that there have been fuck ups in the past and we even had a guy get killed in the past. That's precisely why this is a bad deal. We've done a hell of a job cleaning house within our ranks over the past few years. We're down to a core of people that are real damn good at what they do. This fuckin' guy I sent to Tampa was a machine; a God damned killing machine. Did everything just as he was told every time and there was never a mess to clean up.

"Now he's fuckin' dead! The mark obviously killed him and yet...they're not saying anything. The cops don't know shit. You tie that to the fact that...."

Leach interrupted him, "Maybe your boy failed and hauled ass. He might be afraid of the repercussions from you."

"Listen to me. Don't for a fuckin' minute think you know anything about how we do things. You don't know shit. Ya' follow me? The guy's dead. I know it. I don't like the fact that my man's dead and they're not saying shit. On top of that this Murphy prick appears to me to be pretty well connected.

"Listen, Leach, it's like this. I've not survived in my world by being stupid or by taking unnecessary risks. I know when to lay low. This is one of those times. You want someone to go after that mic bastard, than you call someone else. I'm out."

Costello hung up the phone. Leach was livid when he heard the line disconnect.

"That pussy dego bastard! Why can't he just follow through on something he's already been paid for?" Leach was gritting his teeth as he looked down at the congressman sitting at the end of the couch.

"Why has getting rid of Murphy become this important?"

Exasperated by Samms's question, Leach fell heavily in to the chair next to the sofa. He set his phone on the end table between them and leaned forward, moving slowly, deliberately, as he placed his elbows on his knees and looked at the floor for several seconds before looking directly at the man seated next to him. Leach had disdain for this corpulent little man; with an odd voice that sounded like a hoarse, nasal, squeak. The two of them had allied their separate talents many years ago into a symbiotic relationship, but it was times like this that brought Sid's contempt for the man to the surface. He abhorred the congressman's tendency to leave things unfinished and leave loose ends hanging.

"Bernie, I've been at this game a long time. I win at this game. I don't just survive; I win. I prosper. I'm able to do that because I not only plan everything going forward, but I protect everything from behind as well. I keep a constant vigil for those that would destroy me, destroy us, and I deal with them. Murphy has reached a point of considerable prominence in the public arena. Somehow, he has managed to kill two of our people; Mesh in Miami and Costello's man. That means he's a fighter and he's dangerous. I look at that whole package and I see a threat that has to be dealt with in extreme terms. He is the type of person that is capable of tearing down our little fiefdom. You grasp this, Bernie?"

Samms knew the expression on Sid Leach's face well enough to press no further. "OK. I got it. What will you do now? I thought Costello was your man."

"He's my main man, but not my only man. I've got other resources. You and I need to wrap this meeting up so that you can get your ass back to the capital for that press conference. While you're doing that I'll work on getting Murphy taken care of."

The two conspirators walked from the living room to the office where Samms sat at the small computer desk. Leach realized he'd left his cell phone by the couch as he patted his shirt pocket. As he started from the office toward the adjoining living room the sound of the doorbell broke the silence.

"Jesus Christ," Sid Leach turned to throw his yellow note pad back on to his desk, "who the hell could that be?"

Webster saw the cab pull to the curb in front of the Leach residence and watched as the man in the back reached over the front seat to pay the driver. He continued to watch as the man got out of the car and then reached back in to grab the big bouquet of flowers.

"Remember; don't drive off unless you see me go inside, right?" Conner told the cabby before pushing the door shut with his foot.

Webster had taken his left earphone out but it didn't help; he'd left his right one in and the thumping club music didn't allow him to hear anything coming from the direction of Leach's driveway. At first he wasn't able to see what the man had been struggling to remove from the back seat, but once he walked clear of the cab toward the house the large bouquet became evident. Webster grinned and shook his head, realizing what was going on. He replaced his left earpiece as he continued to watch the man with the flowers approach the house.

Conner held the bouquet in his left hand and rang the bell with his right. He had never glanced in the direction of the black Suburban parked across the street. As soon as Conner rang the bell he put his right hand in his coat pocket. The bouquet was large enough to obstruct the security guard's view of the door but Webster did notice the drapes part momentarily on a nearby window.

From the living room window Sid could see the cab in the driveway and the black SUV across the street. He could see enough of his front stoop to realize it was a man delivering a large bouquet.

Samms yelled out from the office, "Who is it, Sid?"

"Hell, I don't know. Twenty to one it has something to do with that red headed broad that made a complete ass of herself last night at Morton's."

Leach walked to the front door and swung it open.

Before Sid Leach could speak Conner stuck his Remington double barrel derringer under the man's chin. He was moving forward in to the house, pushing hard against Leach's jaw to shove him backwards while he continued to use the flowers as a screen, backing Leach well into the foyer. The cab pulled away and Webster gave an audible little chuckle as he wondered what Mr. Leach was going to do while the other two men entertained themselves.

"Keep your rotten fuckin' mouth shut," Conner's voice was low, but clear. The intense look in his eyes and the snarl on his lips intensified the panic that Leach felt as he backed up with his hands held in the air.

"If you make one wrong move I'll blow your head off. This little gun shoots a very big slug; it will make instant pudding out of the inside of your skull. Are we on the same page?" Conner wasn't nervous anymore. As a matter of fact he was feeling elation from the fact that Sid Leach had answered the door himself. "Are we alone, Leach?"

The older man shook his head in short movements as he slowly backed further from the door.

"Whisper, now. So I won't have to kill you. How many?"

"One. He's in the office," Leach gave his head a short nod to his left.

With Leach's back against the far wall of the foyer Conner

took several steps backwards and pushed the door shut with his foot. The gun remained trained on Leach's chest. Conner took two steps back toward Leach.

"This is how it's going to work, you sorry prick. If you make one sound or one move I don't like, I'll kill you. I'm sorry, am I repeating myself?"

Leach stared back at Conner.

"Nod your head that you understand or I'll just kill you now."

Leach nodded.

"Turn around and walk to that first couch."

Leach turned around and walked into the living room and stopped at the middle of the first couch. Conner remained two steps behind him, never lowering his pistol as he laid the vase of flowers on the couch, spilling the water on to the Italian suede.

"Let's go see your compadre," Conner whispered just loud enough for Leach to hear.

When they rounded the corner to the office Conner was standing directly behind Leach with the muzzle of the derringer just inches from the base of his skull. A man working at a small computer desk was facing away from them. The man spoke without turning around.

"Well who the hell was it, Sid? Were you right? Was it the red head?"

Conner's mouth fell open slightly before the corners of his mouth turned upwards in to a smile. He recognized the whiney, raspy voice of Bernie Samms from the countless press conferences and interviews the man had held throughout his career.

"Why don't you turn around and meet him, Bernie?" Sid said in a mocking tone.

Not realizing that anyone had come in to the house, Samms was startled by Leach's comment. He turned quickly in his chair at the same time Conner gave Leach a violent shove toward the large desk in the middle of the room. Samms turned to see a gun pointed directly at his head and let out a little high-pitched yelp. Leach hit the front of the desk hard with his thighs and his forward momentum slammed his upper body onto the desk.

"Well if it isn't Congressman Samms? I'd like to make a suggestion. Keep your mouth shut." Conner smiled and looked directly in to his eyes.

Leach was straightening himself out by pushing himself off of the desk with his hands. He grabbed the gold plated letter opener from the desktop with his left hand and turned to the right as he looked back at Conner. The look on Leach's face now expressed less panic and more anger. Samms expression, conversely, was one of pure horror.

There were two chairs that faced the large desk that Leach had just fallen across. Conner pointed to the one closest to Leach and told him to turn it around and sit in it with his hands on his knees. Leach obeyed; as he turned the small armchair around he stuck the letter opener alongside the seat cushion, hiding it from Conner's view. As Leach sat, Conner looked toward the trembling Bernie Samms and told him to do the same with the other chair.

When both men were seated, Conner backed toward the desk chair that Samms had been using at the computer and drug it across the thick Persian rug to a position where it formed a triangle with the other chairs. He never took his eyes from either man as he pulled his chair in to place and sat down. The contrast in the countenance of all three men was striking. Leach wore an expression of loathing, with hatred emanating from his eyes like heat from an open furnace. Samms face was pallid with fear and glistening with sweat as his lips trembled and the color continued to drain from his face. He leaned forward in his chair, nearly assuming the fetal position. Conner was relaxed, brandishing a confident smile.

The sight of Bernie Samms disgusted Conner as he observed what a weak and pathetic creature the man was. Unconsciously, Conner's face turned from a smile to a snarl, as he feared the fat little man was going to start sobbing or urinate on himself at any minute. He possessed no sympathy for the man, only contempt for all of the heartache he had caused during a lifetime of greed and abuse of power.

Murphy turned his focus back to Leach and observed his defiant posture and the hate filled expression on his face. At least the scoundrel's got some balls, Conner thought to himself. He was about to pass sentence on his two captives when Samms started stammering.

"What do you want...for Christ's sake...who are you....do you know who we are? What the hell is going on here, Sid?"

Conner looked back at the pale and trembling Samms.

"Oh I assure you, Congressman; Sid here is as confused as you are. It seems as though I'm the only one here that's not confused," Conner was smiling again.

"Why are you smiling? What is wrong with you?" Samms voice broke as he finished the question, barely able to make the last word audible.

"Why I'm smiling because I'm thrilled. I never expected to encounter both of you together. And now here y'all are, I'm thrilled."

Leach shouted, "'Y'all', 'y'all'. Why you fuckin' redneck piece of shit. You've got no idea who you're screwing with here Jethro. You're not in some backwater shantytown; you're in Washington DC you ignorant shit. This town is filled with the smartest people in the world. The people that make sure that idiots such as you and the three hundred million other morons just like you can function. And you think you can come in here and threaten us. Fuck you!"

Conner tipped his head to the side slightly as he absorbed the man's arrogance and then slowly shook his head from side to side in a scolding manner as he started to speak.

"Oh I'm not interested in threatening you, Sidney. I've come here to kill you. I'm going to eliminate you, not threaten you."

Leach fell back in his chair and Samms moaned and started sobbing.

"But first I will tell you who I am. I'd hate for you to leave this world in a state of ignorance. It would be an unfair thing to do to an arrogant, elitist bastard like you."

"Who then damn it, who are you?" Samms managed between sobs.

"My name is Murphy. Conner Murphy. Father to Sean Murphy and father-in-law to Maureen Murphy."

Samms turned to look at Leach. "See what you've done, you son-of-a-bitch. You're maniacal obsession with killing Sean Murphy has brought this on."

"Oh, to the contrary, Bernie. You both brought this on. You've both sealed your fate here today with your contempt for the people of this country. With your corruption. With your arrogance and elitism. Your friend Sid only lit the fuse that brings this final explosion to your doorstep."

"Listen to me, listen..." Samms started to stand.

"Sit down!" Conner shouted and leveled the gun at Samms chest.

Samms fell back in to the chair. "I'll show you something. Something you'll want to see. Cut and dry evidence of who Leach hired to kill your son. Let me show you."

"Shut up, you fool. You're not going to buy this bastard off." Leach shouted at the congressman.

"Now, now, Sidney. You don't know that. I may be persuaded," Conner replied.

"It's bullshit, Samms!" Leach was shouting. "It's bullshit."

"Let me show you. It's right here in his desk," Samms was pleading with Murphy.

"Let me inform you of one thing first. I am very accurate with this little gun. I will kill you in an instant if I even think you are doing something I don't like. Comprende, gordo? Show me what you've got."

"He keeps all of the records in the right bottom drawer. Records, phone numbers, everything."

Leach was seething and swore continuously under his breath.

"Very slowly get your fat ass up and walk to the other side of the desk." Conner stood as he spoke.

When the Congressman stood a large wet spot in the crotch of his pants was evident. He walked to the other side of the desk. Conner was suspicious that there may be a gun in the drawer, although he didn't believe this man had the balls to use one. Prudently, he walked to the side of the desk where he could see in to the drawer as it was opened.

"Here's what we're going to do. Sid, sweetheart, you shouldn't move a muscle." Conner paused to give Leach a big smile. "Samms you put one hand on that drawer handle and slowly pull it open."

As the bottom desk drawer opened Conner could see a large, leather bound, binder lying on the bottom. Nothing else was there. He moved back to the other side of the desk, not liking the fact that he was so close to Samms if the little bastard was to throw the book or lunge at him. It wasn't that he was afraid of Samms but he was cognizant that two men did pose a threat if he gave them an opportunity.

Conner had no intention of leaving the house with either of these two bastards still breathing, but he was interested in what information he might learn from Leach's book of secrets; a bonus he hadn't planned on. Conner stood across the desk from Samms as the fat man reached down and lifted the heavy binder from the drawer. Leach stopped muttering. Conner turned his head to see that Leach was looking at Samms. When he did he missed what Leach saw; the expression on Samms' face when he saw the pistol under the binder. By the time Conner looked back at Samms, the doughy little man had regained his composure and was placing the book on the desk.

"So what's in this book of secrets that you think may interest me.... and save you, Samms?"

"His name is Costello, that's all I know. I don't know any more than that. Except I do know he sent someone to kill your son. His information is in here I promise. Can I sit down?"

"Go ahead." Conner remained standing. He glanced at Leach who was staring intently at Samms. Conner looked back at the binder and watched as the man across the desk flipped the cover of the book open. As Samms did so he looked over at Leach and raised his eyebrows slightly. Immediately Leach got up from his chair. Conner looked over and shouted at the man to sit down. He didn't. Conner glanced back at Samms who was still sitting there, looking back at him. Leach didn't move, he continued to stand next to the chair with his left hand visible but his right hand hidden by his leg.

"Sit down!"

Conner took a step in Leach's direction and punched him with an open hand in the chest. Leach fell back hard in to the chair. Samms was bending down, his butt still in the chair but his body hidden by the desk. Conner's first thought was that the coward had hidden himself at the first sign of a physical attack. The thought was short lived.

Leach jumped back to his feet distracting Conner long enough for Samms to swing himself upright with the gun in his hand. He pointed it at Conner's head as Conner swung his gun away from Leach back toward the fat man. Samms pulled the trigger. Nothing. He hadn't released the safety. He yanked the trigger a second time, harder, which made the gun jerk in his hand just before the .41 caliber slug from the Remington derringer shattered his central incisors on the way to his brain stem.

The impact of the bullet hurled Samms' body in to the desk chair, tipping it over and crashing loudly to the floor. Leach had already closed the space between him and Conner before Conner could turn back around. Leach's right arm was swinging swiftly in a large arc as it carried the letter opener toward Conner's back. It found its mark just below the rib cage and the momentum of the thrust carried the four-inch blade to its limit. Conner yelled out in pain as he tried to spin his body to face his assailant. Leach had a firm grip on the handle of the letter opener with his other arm wrapped around Conner's waist. Conner's struggles to break free only served to work the blade of the letter opener back and forth internally. Unable to spin from Leach's grip, Conner took his left arm and swung his elbow with all his strength into the gut of the smaller man. Leach nearly left his feet as he was hurled backwards on to the floor. Leach retained a firm grasp on the letter opener, jerking it free from Conner's back as he fell backwards on to the floor.

Conner let the momentum of his punch spin him around and he lowered the derringer toward his target lying on the Persian rug. The single bullet between Leach's eyes ended it.

Demarcus Webster had taken his earphones out to talk on the phone to his girlfriend. As he started to replace them he thought he heard something.

"What the hell was that?" He muttered to himself.

He was becoming nervous, hoping it wasn't a gunshot that he'd heard. But damn it sure sounded like one. Demarcus stuck his head out of the side window in the hope of hearing better.

"Shit! That was sure as hell a gunshot!"

He grabbed for his phone but dropped it as he pulled it from his shirt pocket. Frantically he groped the floorboard between his considerable highs but couldn't locate the gun. He got out of the car and reached back in to feel under the seat. Finally recovering his phone, he punched the speed dial number for Lucas.

"Lucas"

"This is Webster at the Leach residence. We've got a hell of a deal going on here...I think."

"Calm down Webster. What is the situation?"

"Situation? Gunshots are the goddamned situation!"

"Take it easy. Quickly. Who's at the residence? Are Mr. Samms and Mr. Leach both still there?"

"Yea. And one of Mr. Samms gay buddies. Guy brought him flowers about twenty minutes ago."

"There's a third person there? Now?"

"Yea. That's what I said. Three went in and no one has been out."

"Webster, you need to secure the area immediately. Do not let anyone in or out. I will have a team there pronto,"

Conner was sitting at Leach's desk. He had already looked through the leather binder and found many interesting contacts, several with descriptive notes included. There was only one Costello; a Mario Costello in Chicago with several phone numbers and physical addresses written below the name. Conner pulled his personal phone from his pocket and took pictures of several different contacts he thought were interesting. He viewed them on his screen and expanded the pictures to be certain they could be read. He then e-mailed the pictures to his son's e-mail account at The Constitution. He also e-mailed them to an old acquaintance of his on the editorial board of the Wall Street Journal and a third set to the tip line designated on the FBI website. The message with the pictures was short: 'information given to me by Sidney Leach and Bernie Samms.'

Conner was in severe pain now. The blood that oozed from his abdomen was dark. He finished the e-mails and put his phone back in his pocket. He managed to get up from the chair and step around Samms body, bracing himself on the desk as he circled it to the other side. Once to the other side of the desk Conner straightened his back, it was painful to do so and he drew a deep breath. He kept his eyes focused on the other side of the room and slowly, painfully walked across the office to the living room. He made his way to one of the suede couches and eased himself on to it, gritting his teeth and taking short shallow breaths, as he swung his feet up and laid his head back on the couch. He felt better once he was prone.

Conner knew he was dying and was content. He smiled to himself with the knowledge that his son and his grandchildren were safe. He could see their faces in his mind. Their images faded and were replaced by a beautiful image of Molly. He thought how he had never seen that image of her before; she was beautiful.

JACKSON, WYOMING
September

J an's eyes filled with tears as she opened the letter addressed to her in Conner's handwriting. It was a short note written on hotel stationary.

> *You were the perfect love at a perfect time in my life.*
> *Thank you. I love you,*
> *Conner*

> *P.S. The birds on the beach that stand like sentries at attention are royal terns, they're congregated in a 'highness' and simply resting while they face in to the wind.*

Jan smiled through her sadness. "Oh, damn you, Conner, I love you too."

WACCASASSA RIVER, FLORIDA

January

"If we can't get any redfish today, Sean, it's because they don't exist anymore. There's no more of them. The tide's out, the weather's perfect, we've got the right bait; the stars are aligned my friend."

"I know you're right, Bubba. I just hope I don't catch them all. I don't want you moping all the way back in."

"You come by it honest, I'll give you that. You sound just like your old man."

"Damn, I miss him so much, Bubba."

"I'm sure you do. As much as I miss him, I'm sure you do."

"I would trade having to deal with those bastards if I could have my Dad back."

"Maybe you would, buddy, but he couldn't take that risk. He didn't have a choice."